About the Author

Susan Hughes lives in Midsomer Norton, Near Bath with her husband Simon. She has two strapping sons, Thomas and Samuel.

Her life is full of family and friends, walking her darling dog Sybil, trying to keep fit, her piano lesson with Kim (who she says has the patience of a saint) and trying to have a few alcohol free days a week.

Enjoy
Susan Hughes x

Dedication

I dedicate this book to my husband Simon and sons
Thomas and Samuel who were always available to
support and encourage me.

To my sister Jane Libby and brother Andrew
Gregory a massive thanks for having faith in me.

Susan Hughes

NOT QUITE
CINDERELLA

AUSTIN MACAULEY
PUBLISHERS LTD.

A CIP catalogue record for this title is available from the British Library.

ISBN 9781786938893 (Paperback)
ISBN 9781786938909 (Hardback)
ISBN 9781786938916 (E-Book)
www.austinmacauley.com

First Published (2017)
Austin Macauley Publishers Ltd.
25 Canada Square
Canary Wharf
London
E14 5LQ

Amber hummed happily as she finished making Mr L's tea. Everything in her garden was rosy. At the ripe old age of 26 she had, she thought, the best boyfriend in the world; it would be their one year anniversary on Thursday. She loved her job at Lockyards. The girls she worked with were a real hoot; not only were they colleagues but they were also the best of friends. They were always laughing and joking, more often than not at the expense of someone else, but all in the name of fun, of course!

Francis Lockyard dialled Tom Tranter's office number.

Tom Tranter picked up the phone before it rang twice. "Tom Tranter."

"Morning, Tom, have you been in the office all night?"

Tom laughed. "Morning, Francis, it feels as though I have. I needed to get a few things done here before going out on-site to do some final checks. Some of the boys started as soon as it was light this morning. We're ahead of schedule and I want to keep it that way. We have the inspectors in later today and I want everything to be right first time."

Tom Tranter took no prisoners. He was a hard taskmaster but fair with it and popular with all, especially the ladies. The phrase 'tall, dark and handsome' had been written for him, along with which went the brightest blue eyes that didn't miss a trick and a body that made you go weak at the knees. He headed Lockyard's in Scotland. Whatever job he was doing he put in 150 percent.

"Excellent news. When do you anticipate being able to get down here? The new site has been prepared, we're all ready for you," said Francis.

Tom gave this careful consideration. Even though his project was almost complete, the last inspections were the most important.

"I would say another two weeks, to be on the safe side. I'll be down this Wednesday for the site meeting but I have a few personal loose ends to tie up, one of which is the flat Beth and I have been renting. As we are no longer 'an item', as she puts it, she wants it sorted before I leave, which is fair enough."

Apparently, the beautiful Beth couldn't cope with the thought of living in England so had decided to stay in Scotland. She was a precious little thing, thoroughly spoilt by a very rich daddy who owned an art gallery where she floated around occasionally in an effort to look like she was working. The rest of her time was spent in the hairdressers, at the gym, having her nails done or shopping.

"Is there no chance of you two working things out? I'm sure she would love it here once she settled in," Francis Lockyard said. He had met Beth on various occasions and couldn't stand her. There was no doubting she was a beauty but in his and his wife Sylvia's opinion it was only skin deep; underneath was shear nastiness. She treated everyone as if they were dirt.

"I don't know. We've agreed to a trial separation but between you and me things haven't been going well for some time. Anyway, I won't bore you with that." Tom sighed. "I'll see you Wednesday and by the end of the week I'll be able to give you a full update on the inspections and hopefully a definite date for my arrival."

"Good, good, see you Wednesday. Cheerio." As Francis put down the phone there was a knock on his door. It opened and Amber appeared with his tea on a tray. There was something about Amber that always made him smile. He liked all the girls on reception, they were so full of life, but Amber was his favourite. Every morning she filled him in on the gossip about what was going on with who and why.

It was a pleasure to listen to her. She certainly had the measure of most of the employees, many of whom had worked for him for years. He congratulated himself on that, especially in this day and age. Amber's lighthearted chitchat was like the calm before the storm of each day.

"Ah, Amber, I could do with that cup of tea, I've so much to get through today. Did you have a good weekend?"

"Well." Amber let out a small sigh. "Not the best, I have to say. Phil and I were supposed to go over to one of my old school friends for supper Friday night but he had to do some late viewings on a property he's trying to let, so I had to cancel and, what with it being his Saturday to work and me babysitting for Gloria's daughter Saturday night, we only got to see each other yesterday." She let out a little laugh. "Bet you wish you hadn't asked now."

Mr L laughed. "Never mind, work does tend to get in the way of one's social life sometimes, I can vouch for that."

"Yes, I suppose you're right, but I've warned him no late viewings this Thursday, no matter how much commission he thinks he might miss out on, because we've been going out for a year and I've planned a meal to celebrate." She waggled her finger as she spoke. "What did you do?"

"Nothing. Sylvia and I had a quiet weekend. To be honest, I was glad of the rest. We spent most of our time in the garden enjoying all this lovely weather we're having at the moment," answered Mr L.

"It's great, isn't it?" Amber agreed as she poured his tea. "You know, Tom Tranter called this morning. I had sort of heard, well, to be honest, there's talk going round that he'll be overseeing the new outlet project down here."

Mr L chuckled. "All I'll say is that there will be an announcement shortly to update everybody on the future plans and changes the company is about to make."

"Oh, when is that likely to be?" Amber asked, raising her eyebrows.

"Quite soon." Mr L answered, raising his eyebrows to mimic Amber.

"Ok," laughed Amber. "If you need anything before Dorothy gets in just ring through to reception."

He gave her a nod. "Will do."

Amber went back out to reception. She looked at the clock. It was already 8.30am; Vicky and Melanie would be in at 9am, then peace would be shattered. She mulled over her conversation with Mr L. There was obviously some truth in the rumours going round if they were going to get an announcement.

Her mind drifted on to Phil. One year on Thursday, she still couldn't believe it. The girls said he was a typical estate agent and to a degree they were right. He was smooth, groomed and a sweet talker, not the type of man she usually went for, but, she had fallen for him hook, line and sinker. They had met when she had been on a night out with the girls. She had seen him around but it was Melanie who had got their group and his group chatting.

Mind you, she knew Melanie didn't actually like him that much. She always said men should never have such manicured and clean nails, not that she minded manicured and clean nails if they were on her latest victim. They had been friends since school and now worked together. MMM, Man Mad Melanie. She picked men up and dropped them as though it were sport, her defence being that they bored her in bed after a while.

"What else have you decided to do? Asked Vicky.

"Chicken stuffed with stilton, new potatoes and salad. Just something simple," answered Amber.

"Sound lovely! The cheesecake will really work after that," said Vicky.

"I hope you're going to wear something sexy," chipped in Melanie.

"Well," Amber said thoughtfully. "I do have that black dress you made me buy for Jessica's hen night. I've never had the bottle to wear it since so Phil has never seen it, but it's so low. What do you think?"

"What do I think? I think that's bloody perfect. Have you still got the padded push-me-up we got to go underneath it?" Melanie asked enthusiastically.

"Yes, and the matching knickers. I haven't worn either of them since," Amber made a face.

"What are you like? It's about time it all had an airing then, and, for God's sake, it is not too low, just a bit revealing, sassy, sexy," said Melanie with a wink.

"I'm going the whole hog tomorrow night as well. I've booked myself in for a manicure, pedicure, full leg and bikini wax," beamed Amber.

"Hollywood or Brazilian?" teased Melanie.

"Mind your own business," laughed Amber. "But I will have to leave 10 minutes early tomorrow afternoon to get to the appointment, if that's okay with both of you? It is for a very good cause."

"Of course, it's ok," said Vicky.

"Fine by me – keeping your bush trimmed is important at all times. I always keep mine up together," quipped Melanie.

"I didn't know you had an interest in gardening, Melanie," said Dorothy, standing by the desk with an armful of files.

Melanie swung round. "Oh, Dorothy, I didn't realise you were there."

"I know you didn't, but it makes a change to hear you talk about something a little more interesting than men. As a matter of fact, I have a keen interest in gardening myself," twitched Dorothy.

Amber and Vicky could hardly keep a straight face.

"Oh, I love gardening, but unfortunately the house I share only has a courtyard at the back," said Melanie, so innocently.

"I see." Dorothy looked a little perplexed. "So where is the bush you keep trimmed?"

"Out the front of the house," Melanie replied as if butter wouldn't melt.

"Of course. I do have a lovely book at home with plenty of ideas for things you can grow in pots and containers, which would be ideal for your courtyard. I'll dig it out, if you pardon the pun," said Dorothy.

"Thanks, Dorothy, but I don't want to put you to any trouble," said Melanie sweetly.

"No trouble. I'm more than happy to encourage a worthwhile pastime. I have some very good tips I can share with you. If I say so myself, my pots are always a picture. Dorothy paused for a moment as she pictured her lovingly tended pots overflowing with blooms fit for the Chelsea Flower Show. "They bring such joy to Bernard and myself while we sit in the garden."

"Great," said Melanie, trying to sound enthused.

As she reached the desk Gloria was just arriving. Gloria had started as a cleaner the very same day that Dorothy had started as PA to Mr Lockyard. She was Barbados born – a big warm-hearted family woman who loved life. Her clothes reflected her personality; they were always bright and colourful. She arrived ready to start work wearing an old-fashioned tabard with pockets in the front over her dress. She was always smiling and singing to her Lord. There wasn't one person who had the pleasure of meeting Gloria that didn't walk away from her without a smile on their face.

Personality-wise, Gloria and Dorothy were like chalk and cheese. While Gloria was loud and raucous, Dorothy was prim and proper, but they believed in and upheld the same values. They had realised this on their first day and had been firm friends since. Amber always thought it was funny how two people could be so different but have so much in common, love the same God but display it in such different ways.

"Good afternoon, my honeys." Gloria beamed as she waddled up to the desk.

"Hi, Gloria," the girls replied together.

Gloria reached into her tabard pocket. She pulled out three toffees and put them on the desk.

"Here's a sweetie for each of my sugars, now tell old Gloria what's been happening today before I get that duster of mine working," she boomed.

Amber told Gloria all about the email sent by Mr Lockyard.

"My, my, that certainly is news, that man he works too hard, he deserves to take things a bit easier, all those big decisions he make every day must ware him out," said Gloria.

"What do you think about the idea for the summer party, Gloria?" asked Vicky.

"I love to shake my booty at a party." Gloria did a little dance.

The girls laughed. For someone her size Gloria had great rhythm.

"It's four o'clock; time I wasn't here," said Amber as she went to get her bag.

"Amber, my honey, you are a good girl for babysitting Saturday night. You come for your tea, I cook you something Caribbean to say thank you properly. What evening you free?" asked Gloria.

"Oh lovely, but I can't this week. I'm pretty much tied up every night. I'm doing a special meal on Thursday for Phil, but Monday or Tuesday next week would be good," said Amber.

"Bless me, I would forget my own head if it wasn't fastened on. You did tell me all about this special supper you cooking for your man. Next week will be just fine. You have a good evening," said Gloria.

"Yeah, have a good evening. What are you doing?" asked Vicky.

"I'm going to pop in to see Mum and Dad, then Phil and I are going to the pictures later," answered Amber.

"Have fun. Bye," said Melanie.

"Bye, everyone." Amber waved as she made her way out into the afternoon sunshine.

"That girlie, she is so sweet on that man of hers, he is lucky to have her," said Gloria.

"Yes, he is. I keep telling her he doesn't appreciate just how lovely she is," said Melanie.

"I'm sure he'll tell her in his own way," replied Gloria.

"I'm sure he does as well," agreed Vicky, giving Melanie a look.

"I'm going to pop my head round Dorothy's door to say hello, then get on with the chores. See you two honeys in a minute," said Gloria as she waddled off towards Dorothy's office.

Dorothy was just putting some letters into envelopes when her door opened. She looked up as Gloria's head appeared round it, beaming her usual smile, followed by her huge frame.

"My goodness, Gloria, is it that time already?" said Dorothy with surprise.

"It surely is. You been having a busy day, Dorothy?" asked Gloria.

"It's been non-stop. Time has just flown by and I still have a few things left to do before five o'clock," answered Dorothy as she glanced at the to-do list on her desk. She still had to call Tom Tranter.

"You'd better get on then. I won't be holding you up a minute longer," said Gloria.

"Those few things can wait a moment or two. One of them happens to be a call to your son to book a marquee for the summer party. This year we are having it on our doorstep, literally," said Dorothy.

"Bless you, Dorothy, he will really appreciate it. It's hard for young folk to get businesses going. The girlies told me when I got here that Mr Lockyard is to be easing up his working as well. His dear wife, she will be happy about that," said Gloria, resting one hand on the door handle, the other on her hip.

"Are you talking about me, young Gloria?" Mr Lockyard smiled as he came through his office door.

"I surely am. You been ear-wigging behind that door, Mr Lockyard?" She laughed.

"Not at all. I know you'd give me a good telling off if you thought I'd do a thing like that. I just happened to hear my name," he joked.

Gloria let out a hearty laugh. "I was just saying to Dorothy, your dear wife will be pleased you is going to be taking things a bit easier."

"Yes, Silvia has been saying for some time that I should let someone else take the reins. Tom Tranter is the perfect person for the task. He is more than capable of running the Scottish office and this one. It'll take a while to sort things out, hand things over, then I'll be more than happy to only have to come in a couple of days a week for meetings and updates. You'll like Tom. He's very popular with the ladies, isn't he Dorothy?" said Mr Lockyard with a twinkle in his eye.

"He is, indeed, especially the younger ones," agreed Dorothy.

"My, my, I might be getting on in years but I still like to admire a cutie face. There ain't nothing wrong with these old peepers, thank the Lord. It's just this body that can't keep up, hehehe," laughed Gloria.

Mr Lockyard laughed. Even Dorothy couldn't resist a small chuckle. Gloria was one of the few people who could actually make her laugh.

"Now then, I need to be getting on with my cleaning and let you get on too. Have a good evening," said Gloria as she turned to leave. She was humming Amazing Grace before the door had closed.

"I'm just about finished for the day, is there anything you need me to do for you, Dorothy, before I leave?" asked Mr Lockyard.

"No, I don't think so, I've just got a couple of calls to make and that's me finished for the day as well," replied Dorothy.

Mr Lockyard went back through to his office, only to reappear a moment later with his briefcase.

"Don't go staying late, you'll make me feel guilty," he said.

"I won't be far behind you, no need to feel guilty. Have a good evening," she said.

"And you," he replied, leaving her office. He made his way towards reception. He smiled as he approached the desk.

"How's everything been out here today?" he asked Melanie and Vicky.

"Fine thanks," answered Melanie.

"Good, good. I'm off now, but Dorothy is going to be here a while longer if you need her. See you both tomorrow, and stay out of trouble," he said light-heartedly.

"We'll try our best," laughed Melanie. "Bye."

He laughed, waved and walked through the door, out into the bright afternoon sunshine. 'Glorious,' he thought, 'doesn't everything seem so much better when the sun is shining.'

Tom Tranter sat watching the sun stream through his office window. Work-wise, the day had gone well. He felt mentally exhausted but physically had energy to burn. He would go for a run and maybe do some weights at the gym, depending on how he felt once he'd been running. He stood up and stretched. He looked at his laptop. 'No,' he thought, 'he wouldn't take it with him, there wasn't anything he needed to do that couldn't wait until tomorrow.'

Just as he went to open his office door the phone started to ring. He looked at the clock, it was nearly 5.30pm. He wondered if it could be Beth but dismissed that; she always called on his mobile. He walked back to his desk and picked it up.

"Tom Tranter," he said into the receiver.

"Mr Tranter, it's Dorothy Brown speaking, Mr Lockyard's PA," said Dorothy.

"Hello, Dorothy, what can I do for you?" he asked.

"I've been speaking to some local letting agents regarding short-term lets. I'm afraid the choice isn't huge, but I have found a few for you to look at which are quite close to the office. Without wishing to pry into your personal affairs I thought I'd better check to see if you still had the same requirements now that you and your young lady are no longer, um, how can I put it. ..." Dorothy paused while she tried to think of the politest way to say, 'no longer together'.

Tom Tranter could imagine how awkward Dorothy felt, poor woman. He cut in to help her out.

"My requirements remain the same, but thank you for checking, Dorothy. I'm aiming to be down for good in two weeks, but I'm going to get a flight down Wednesday morning, as I want to attend the site meeting. Do you think you could arrange the viewings for the afternoon?" he asked.

"I'll do my best, Mr Tranter. I'll let you know tomorrow," Dorothy replied.

"Thanks very much, and, Dorothy, call me Tom," he said.

"Oh, um, oh, alright. Goodbye, Mr Tranter, I mean Tom," said Dorothy.

"Goodbye, Dorothy." He put down the phone, smiling to himself. He would bet his last dollar that Dorothy would not call him Tom. He headed for the door.

Dorothy put the phone down. "Oh dear,' she thought, 'she wouldn't be able to call him Tom, it just didn't seem proper to be calling people in his position by their Christian name.' She knew she was old fashioned when it came to things like that, it was just the way she was.

She was done for the day. The call to Tom Tranter had been the last thing on her list. She tidied her desk, picked up her bag, opened the door, had her usual final glance round to see that everything was in its place, which it was, then closed the door behind her.

She walked past the deserted reception. The girls always left on time. In actual fact, there wasn't a soul in sight; no doubt everyone had left on time to enjoy the weather. As she walked out of the doors and the heat hit her, she couldn't blame them for doing so either.

CHAPTER 2

Phil sat at his desk watching Cheryl as she updated the window display. She worked quickly, taking the old sold-subject-to-contract properties that had exchanged out, putting on flashes for the ones that had just sold, and putting in the new properties he'd just taken onto the market. As she bent to straighten up the bottom row she could feel his eyes on her. She smiled to herself. If she had a million pounds in a suitcase she would bet that he had a stiff cock right now. He hadn't been able to keep his hands to himself all day, either playfully slapping her rear or brushing up against her at every opportunity he got. Not that she was complaining, he was a good distraction on the nights her old man was away; it was good for her morale to know she could still pull the younger ones. She purposefully stuck out her backside as she bent to straighten up some details that were already straight. 'May as well get him going a bit more,' she thought.

"There, that will do nicely, does it look okay from where you're sitting?" She straightened up and turned to face him.

"It looks more that okay to me," he replied with a cheesy expression on his face.

"I mean the window display." She laughed.

"No, you didn't, you know you look sexy in that tight skirt," he replied.

"Why, thank you. I'm glad you approve of my office attire," Cheryl said as she gathered together the remnants of the window. She started to sashay past his desk.

"Actually, these need sold-subject-to-contract flashes put on them," he said, pointing to the ones directly behind him.

Cheryl looked to where he was pointing.

"So they do," she said. "You'll have to move over a bit so I can get behind your desk."

"No problem," said Phil as he made his chair roll slightly to one side, giving Cheryl just enough room to squeeze in beside him.

As she stood there fixing the flashes onto the details she felt his hand on the inside of her leg. It slowly started to make its way up towards her thigh. Teasingly, she opened her legs slightly.

"I've been wanting to do this all day," he breathed as his hand massaged the inside of her thigh. "And as much as I love the skirt, it would be better off."

"Have you forgotten where we are?" She smiled seductively down at him.

He looked at the clock.

"It's almost 5.30. Let's close up and get out of here, I've got something incredibly hard to give you in my trousers."

"There's a surprise, you dirty sod. But I thought you were seeing your little girlfriend tonight?" said Cheryl.

"I am, but not till later. We've got time, and it's Amber, not my little girlfriend," corrected Phil.

"Touchy." Cheryl pouted at him as she bent down and grasped him between the legs. "By the feel of this we won't need much time."

Phil let out a throaty sigh. Quickly removing his hand from her thigh he grabbed her wrist, forcing her to leave it where it was. Thoughts of Amber instantly vanished.

"What are you going to do now?" he asked with a glint in his eye.

"Pray that the boss doesn't walk in or that no one is looking in the window," Cheryl replied with a laugh as she wriggled her hand free. "Although you probably need this job more than I do."

Phil let out a laugh too. "Good point. Let's get locked up, then we can go back to my place."

"Sure, I'll meet you there in about half an hour, the old man is away all this week so there's no rush where I'm concerned," she answered.

Phil turned off the lights and set the office alarm. Pulling the door closed behind them he locked it, and with his ear against the door he waited for the alarm to stop beeping. He quickly surveyed the properties in the window. Cheryl had done a good job. All the new properties were displayed; his vendors would be pleased. They made their way along the other shop fronts, around the corner, along the back of the buildings and into the car park which serviced the rank.

As Phil made his way through the traffic he felt the usual pangs of guilt. What was he doing? Amber was everything, and more, that anyone would want in a girlfriend. They were really good together. His parents had practically married them off already and he wasn't averse to the idea himself. He knew Amber wanted to settle down, she had dropped a few hints lately. That was probably his fault with the kind of excuses he was making to justify his lateness and the times he had let her down.

'Him and Cheryl were just a bit of fun with no strings attached, that's all,' he justified to himself. When she had come on to him in the office he hadn't been able to resist the idea of the slightly older woman. Not that he'd said that 45 was what he classed as an older woman to her face, but seeing as he wasn't quite 30 she did have a few years on him. Neither of them wanted anything else from each other. She said she liked to keep herself occupied while her husband was away, and he, well, he had Amber, didn't he?

He pulled up outside his house. As he walked up the path he looked to see if his neighbours were in. Luckily, they weren't. Cheryl always parked her car round the corner anyway, then checked to see that the coast was clear before she came in. She'd told him she was an expert at that due to all the practice she'd had. This didn't surprise him as she was one dirty bitch.

He let himself in, dropped his keys into a pot on the hall table and went through into the kitchen. He checked the home phone, then his mobile – 'no messages on either. 'That was good,' he thought. Loosening his tie, he made his way upstairs. Cheryl wouldn't be far behind him.

Amber reclined the back of her deckchair. She nestled back, enjoying the sun in her parents' back garden. 'If only time could stand still so you could enjoy things for longer when everything seemed to be going your way,' she thought lazily to herself. She closed her eyes against the brightness. She didn't know whether she fancied the cinema tonight, after all. She might suggest to Phil that they change their plans and go for a drink somewhere they could sit outside.

With that idea stored in her mind for a little later, she let herself drift. She listened to the gentle sound of the birds twittering in the hedge next to where she was sitting. She could feel only the slightest of breeze on her face and within minutes she had fallen asleep.

Amber's mum stood looking at Amber asleep in the deckchair. It was a shame to wake her. She looked so peaceful with her eyes closed, a slight smile on her face and the sun making her hair glisten, but an hour had passed and she was making no sign of stirring. She gently laid her hand on Amber's arm.

"Amber," she said softly.

Amber gave a startled jump as she woke.

"Oh, Mum, I must have nodded off," she said.

"Nodded off? You've been asleep for an hour, love. I didn't like to disturb you, but you said when you came in that you were off out later with Phil. I didn't want you to be late." Her mum smiled.

Amber checked her watch. It was just before 6pm. Phil was picking her up at about 7.30pm.

"We were going to the pictures but I've gone off the idea. It's too nice to sit inside, isn't it?" Amber said, looking up at her mum.

"Far too nice. You may need a cardigan later though," replied her mum.

"Oh, Mum, stop fussing, I'm 26, not six," laughed Amber.

"I know, I know, and seeing as I'm always accused of fussing, the cottage pie I've made for tea is ready, so you may as well eat with me and your dad. It'll save you having to make something when you get back to the flat." She ruffled Amber's hair.

"Great, thanks, Mum. You know that I don't mind you fussing when tea's involved." Amber laughed.

"Go find your dad while I go and dish up, I think he's pottering in the greenhouse," said her mum, waving her arm in the direction of the greenhouse as she headed for the kitchen.

Amber clicked her deckchair into the upright position and hoisted herself out of it. She wandered up the garden, past her dad's vegetable plot. She could see him in his greenhouse. He spent hours in there – come winter, spring, summer or autumn – tending to his plants. She knocked on the window as she walked towards the open door. He looked up and gave a wave.

"Woken up then?" he said, as she stepped inside.

"Mum woke me. Good job she did or else I'd have been there all night," Amber answered.

"Too many late nights, I suppose," he kidded her.

"I wish it was, but I actually had quite a quiet weekend. What are you up to in here?" she asked.

"I've just retied some of these tomatoes. Bumper crop this year, real beauties, look at the size of some of them," he said, pointing to a huge red one.

"Wow, you'll have to enter a competition with that one," Amber said, admiring the tomato her dad was pointing at.

"I might just do that," he chuckled.

"Mum said to say she was dishing up. I'm staying for tea as well. I'm having half of yours," she teased him.

"Oh, are you now? Good job your mum always cooks enough for an army then," he said.

"Chop chop, or else we'll get told off for letting it get cold." She wagged her finger at him.

"I'll be right behind you." He saluted.

As Amber walked back towards the house she admired her dad's neatly planted garden – everything in dead-straight rows, flourishing under his tender, loving care. 'Bet there would have been some fresh vegetables pulled that morning to go with the cottage pie,' she thought. As she entered the kitchen she wasn't disappointed. There was her mum heaping broad beans onto the plates.

"That looks yummy, where are we eating?" she asked.

"Outside, I think. Grab the knives and forks. I've made some fresh lemonade, it's in the fridge," replied her mum.

Amber took everything out to the patio table. As she poured the lemonade her mum came out with two steaming plates. Just as she was about to return to get the other one, her dad appeared with his hands full of tomatoes.

"I'll get the other one, I need to put these in a bag and wash my hands. They're for you to take home." He smiled at Amber.

"Thanks, Dad, have I got the prize one?" she asked.

"You have, indeed," he said as he walked towards the kitchen.

He came out a moment later with the tomatoes in a bag, ready for Amber to take home, and the other plate. They chatted as they ate. Amber updated them on the happenings at Lockyard's; in return, her parents updated her on the latest family news.

"Thanks, Mum, that was lovely," said Amber as she placed her knife and fork down on her empty plate.

"You're welcome. Cup of tea?" asked her mum.

"No thanks, I'd better get my skates on, I'll give you a hand clearing up before I go though," said Amber as she stood up and started to clear the table.

"Don't worry about that. It won't take me a minute to load the dishwasher, just stick those plates on the side," said her mum.

"Okay." Amber went into the kitchen with the plates, but instead of leaving them on the side she loaded them into the dishwasher for her mum. She picked up her bag and, sticking her sunglasses on her head, went back out to the garden where she kissed her parents goodbye. Armed with her bag of tomatoes she walked round the side of the house to where her car was parked behind her dad's on the drive.

'God, it's stuffy in here,' she thought as she got in her car. Instead of closing the door she took her mobile out of her bag to give Phil a quick ring while some fresh air blew in.

"Talk dirty to me," gasped Cheryl, throwing her head back as she rocked back and forth on Phil.

"Faster, bitch, fuck me faster," grunted Phil as he dug his fingers harder into her bottom.

Cheryl started to scream out with pleasure, bringing with her Phil's surrender. She felt him shudder violently beneath her with his release, before she collapsed to the side of him. They then lay together, letting their heavy breathing return to normal. Turning her head, she took in the satisfied expression on Phil's face as he stared up at the ceiling. She playfully gave him a poke in the side.

"Hope you haven't bruised my ass the way you dug your fingers into it or I'll have some explaining to do when the old man gets back," she said.

"If I have, you'll think of something," he said, turning on his side to look at her. He flicked at her nipple with his fingers.

Cheryl let out a little sigh. She started to run her hand slowly down his chest. He stopped her before it got too low. She looked lazily at him.

"Not up for round two then?" she asked.

Phil glanced at the clock, then back at Cheryl.

"Better not, I can't afford to be late again, Amber will start to get suspicious. But seeing as you're home alone again this week we may as well make the most of it. Same time, same place tomorrow?" he asked as he bent to lick her nipple.

"I'll check my diary to see if I'm free," said Cheryl as she rolled onto her back.

The phone at the side of the bed started to ring. Phil stretched over Cheryl to answer it.

"Hello," he said.

"Phil, it's me," came Amber's voice. "About tonight, do you fancy going for a drink somewhere we can sit outside instead of the pictures? It's such a lovely evening."

Phil put his finger to his lips to signal for Cheryl to keep quiet.

"Sure, sure, whatever you want," he replied quickly.

"Great, see you later then," said Amber.

"See you later." Phil replaced the receiver and moved back over Cheryl to get out of bed.

"I've got to make tracks," he said, looking at her.

By the time he returned from having a shower Cheryl was dressed back in her office clothes, just slipping her feet into her shoes.

"Didn't you want to take a shower before you go?" he asked as he dressed.

"No, I'm going to have a good soak in the bath as soon as I get home," answered Cheryl.

"Fair enough," Phil said as he glanced out of the window, checking there was nobody about that he knew, that would see Cheryl leave. The street was deserted. No doubt, most people were in their back gardens enjoying the weather.

"Is the coast clear?" asked Cheryl with a touch of sarcasm in her voice.

"Better to be safe than sorry," replied Phil.

They went downstairs. Cheryl picked up her handbag and opened the front door.

"See you in the morning," she said as she left.

Phil went into the front room. Standing at the window he watched her walk down the road. He'd give her a few minutes before he left. It only took him 15 minutes to get to Amber's flat. He would be dead on time to pick her up.

Amber pulled on a pink t-shirt and denim skirt, shoving her feet into jewelled flip-flops. 'No,' she thought, 'her legs were too hairy for a skirt.' She decided on white linen trousers instead. 'That's better,' she thought as she put her flip-flops on for a second time. 'Oh heck, it was 7.20pm and she hadn't dried her hair yet.' She looked in her bathroom mirror. Luckily, she didn't need much make up, being blessed with good skin, and thanks to the weather lately she had a slight tan. 'Just a quick application of mascara and some lip-gloss should do the trick.' Taking her mum's advice, she took a pink cardigan from her chest of drawers and put it next to her handbag. Tipping her head upside down she started to blast her hair with her hair dryer. 'The one good thing about wavy hair was that when you were in a hurry you could go with the shaggy look,' she thought.

She had just about finished when her mobile rang. It was Phil letting her know that he was outside. Was she ready or did she want him to come up? Deciding she was ready she told him she was on her way.

As she stepped out into the evening sunshine she saw Phil sitting in his car on the opposite side of the road. She gave him a wave as she crossed towards him.

He leaned over and opened the passenger door for her. She slipped easily into the seat next to him.

"Hi," she said, looking at him, her blue eyes twinkling a huge smile on her face.

'Christ, he was being a shit,' he thought as he leant over to give her a peck on the cheek. She looked so pretty tonight. He really was starting to feel guilty for cheating on her. Perhaps it was time to tell Cheryl that they'd had their fun but it had to stop.

"Hi, yourself," he replied as he drew his head away and looked at her. "You look really lovely tonight."

"Thanks, you don't look bad yourself." She smiled at him.

"So, which pub do you want to go to?" he asked.

"How about we drive out to The George? We could sit by the canal," Amber suggested.

"Sounds good to me. The George it is. Have you eaten?" he asked.

"Yes. at Mum's. What about you?" she replied.

"Only a quick snack. Didn't have time to get anything properly, had a couple of viewings to do on the way home," Phil lied as they set off. 'He really was a prize shit,' he thought again. "I'll see what's on the menu and order myself something."

As they drove past the pub into the car park it looked as though every man and his dog had the same idea of visiting a quaint country pub on a hot summer's evening. It was packed. Phil managed to squeeze the car on the end of a row of haphazardly parked cars. He wasn't overly bothered where or how he parked it. As it was a company car he wouldn't have to foot the bill if somebody hit it.

The inside of the pub seemed dark, even dreary, in comparison to outside. As they stood by the bar waiting to be served Phil read the specials board. He decided on the lamb shank. 'He'd need something to keep his strength up for later,' he thought as he ran his eyes over Amber. Drinks in hand they wandered back outside to join the masses. Luckily, Phil spotted a couple getting up from a table.

"Are you off?" he asked them.

"Yes," they nodded.

"That was a bit of luck," said Amber as they sat down.

Amber took a sip of her white wine. She felt the cold liquid as it travelled down her throat. 'Lovely.' She glanced around. There were couples deep in conversation, families eating their food, people with dogs, and lots of young people were up on the bank sitting on the grass with their drinks beside them. Everywhere she looked people seemed to be enjoying themselves. She'd definitely made the right decision, giving the pictures a miss and coming here instead.

Tom Tranter turned into Magnolia Avenue. He had been running for a good hour. His clothes were drenched in perspiration and beads of sweat dripped from his forehead. 'That was enough for tonight, he couldn't face the gym as well,' he thought. As he ran down the road he could see his twin sister Yasmin in the front garden of her house watering some plants. His little nephew Luke stood by her side in his pyjamas. He ran in through the gate, stopping just in front of them. Luke looked up at him intently.

"Uncle Tom, you're all wet," he said, pointing at him.

"I am, aren't I? It's because I've been running and it's made me all sweaty," Tom explained, smiling down at him.

"I get all sweaty like you when I do PE at school," said Luke in his most grown-up voice.

"I'm sure you do," answered Tom.

"Do you get all sweaty doing PE, Mummy?" Luke asked, looking up at his mother.

"Well, I don't really do PE now, but when I was little like you, I'm sure I did," she answered.

Tom started to laugh. "I can't remember you doing much PE when we were at school." He made a face at his sister.

"Well, you have a very bad memory. It's probably because I was much better at it than you," she retorted, tongue in cheek. "I've left you some lasagne, it's in the fridge."

"Thanks, better have a shower first," he said, bending down to tickle his nephew.

"Will you read me a story before I go to bed?" Luke asked.

"Uncle Tom probably has lots of work to do," interrupted his mother, placing her hand softly on the top of his head.

"No, I haven't. I didn't bring any work home with me, for a change. So, come on, you can choose some books while I have a shower," said Tom as he put out his hand for his nephew to take.

His nephew took hold of it straight away. Off they went with Tom doing a silly walk and making Luke giggle.

In the bathroom Tom peeled off his clothes and stepped into the shower. He stood, letting the water cascade over his head and down over his toned, muscular body. He was enjoying staying with his sister. They had always been very close, probably because they were twins. She and her husband had readily offered to put him up while he sorted things out with Beth and organised his relocation to Bath. He absolutely idolised his nephew Luke, who had not long turned five. He could hear him shouting outside the door. He turned the shower off and grabbed a towel.

"Hurry up, Uncle Tom, I've got my books ready," came Luke's urgent little voice through the door.

"I won't be long." he shouted back.

"I'll wait for you in my bedroom then," shouted Luke excitedly." He knew he'd get extra stories with Uncle Tom doing the reading.

Tom quickly dried himself and dressed. As he entered Luke's bedroom he started to run towards his bed, pretending to dive on it. Luke screeched with laughter as he landed and began rolling around. They played and read stories until Yasmin appeared in the doorway.

"Time to clean your teeth, young man." She smiled at Luke. "It's way past your bedtime."

"Uncle Tom will clean them," replied Luke.

Yasmin looked at her brother. He grinned back.

"Ok, Uncle Tom can clean them but make sure he does a good job. First, give me a hug and a kiss goodnight," she said as she knelt down and opened her arms.

Luke ran to his mother where she held him tight while smothering him with kisses.

"Night night, mummy loves you," she whispered into his ear.

"Night night, Mummy," he whispered back. "I love you too."

Melanie lay on the sofa wearing her bright pink boxer shorts and vest-top pyjama set, reading OK magazine. Well, you couldn't exactly say reading, it was more flicking through, stopping when a celebrity picture or piece of gossip caught her eye. She stifled a yawn. Feeling a little tired she decided to have an early night.

'Mondays could be quite boring sometimes,' she thought as she closed her magazine and put it on the coffee table. She wandered upstairs into the bathroom. She flossed and cleaned her teeth, then massaged her usual lip cream into her lips. 'Got to keep them kissable,' she thought as she pouted, then smiled to herself in the mirror. In her bedroom, there was a gentle breeze coming in through the window. She pulled back the duvet and was just about to get in when her mobile started to ring. 'Bloody hell, who could that be?' It was nearly 10pm. Gary's name lit up as she opened it. Her heart began to beat a little faster. 'Fuck,' she thought, 'I feel a bit nervous. What's wrong with me?'

"Hello," she answered the phone.

"Hi, Melanie, it's Gary. Remember me? I'm the one you spent all Saturday night and yesterday using as a sex slave. What are you doing?" he asked.

"I was just about to go to bed." She tried to keep her voice as casual as possible. "And I think it was about equal with the sex-slave business."

"That's true. Just tell me, are you going to bed alone or with someone else?" He laughed.

"That would be telling, wouldn't it? What are you doing?" she questioned him back.

"To be quite frank, thinking about shagging you," he answered.

"How nice," Melanie said. "A lot of men think about shagging me."

"I'm sure they do but seeing as you gave me your mobile number I kind of thought you wouldn't mind shagging me again. It just so happens I've knocked off early. So, can I?" asked Gary.

"Can you what?" Melanie asked, enjoying the little game they were playing.

"Can I come round for a shag?" he asked.

"Well now, seeing as you ask so nicely how can I resist?" She giggled down the phone.

"See you in a minute then," said Gary.

'Perhaps Mondays weren't that boring, after all,' she thought as she put her mobile down. Within minutes she heard a car draw up outside. Looking out of the window she recognised Gary's BMW from the weekend. 'Bar managers must be on a good whack if he can afford one of those,' she thought. As he got out of the car she opened the window further and leaned out.

"Christ, that was quick, or are you stalking me?" she shouted down to him.

Gary looked up at the window and started to laugh.

"I'm stalking you," he answered.

"Great, I'll be right down then," said Melanie as she pulled the window back to where it was. She ran down the stairs, opened the door and stood back to let him enter. As she turned to close it he took in what she was wearing. 'Even her pyjamas spelled out fun,' he thought.

"I'm not really stalking you, I was talking to you as I was driving. I have to pass your place to get to mine, that's the reason I'm here so quickly." He felt he should explain. As much as he liked a joke he didn't want her thinking he was some weirdo.

"That's a shame, I did quite like the idea of being stalked," Melanie joked. Suddenly, she didn't feel tired at all. In fact, she felt quite awake. 'He is fucking gorgeous,' she thought as she pushed him towards the stairs.

"I take it you remember the way," she said, referring to where her bedroom was.

"As it happens, I have a very good memory," he retorted as he mounted the stairs, two at a time, with Melanie doing the same behind him.

Melanie closed her bedroom door. She turned, leaning back against it. She looked at him looking at her.

"Come here," he said.

Melanie already felt wet. "You come here," she replied.

Phil watched Amber as she finished her drink. Placing her empty glass down in front of her, she smiled over at him.

"Do you fancy another one?" he asked, smiling back at her.

"No thanks, better not." She shook her head. "I've had two large ones, that's enough for a school night. I'm ready to make a move, if you are."

"I'm ready," he answered, standing up.

It took them no time at all to drive back into town. The roads seemed unusually deserted.

"Coffee?" Amber asked Phil over her shoulder as she filled up the kettle and switched it on.

"That would be nice," he replied as he came up behind her, putting his hands around her waist. He nuzzled into her neck. "You smell delicious." His hands began to work her t-shirt up. "Why don't we leave the coffee?"

Tom Tranter got to his feet. "I think I'll get an early night," he said to his sister and her husband.

"Are we boring you?" Yasmin asked.

"You are; he's not," answered Tom, indicating to her husband who was sat next to her on the settee. He loved winding her up.

"Charming," she said, giving her brother the two-finger salute.

Tom started to laugh. "I thought you'd be glad of some quality time together," he teased them both.

"Good God, don't put ideas into his head." Yasmin laughed as she nudged her husband playfully.

"Night, you two," he said, pulling the door closed behind him.

As he passed his nephew's room he glanced in. Luke was fast asleep, sprawled on the bed with his teddy in his arms. 'Not a care in the world,' thought Tom, wishing he could say that about himself.

In bed, he propped himself up on the pillows. He took his book off the bedside cabinet and opened it to where he'd last been reading, then closed it again. He wasn't in the mood for reading. He switched off the lamp and closed his eyes. As was usual practice for him he mulled over the day's business – what had taken place, who he'd spoken to, whether any areas needed attention, how he could improve anything, any member of his staff he felt needed help. Once happy with that he moved on to what needed to be done the following day; he made a mental agenda. More than satisfied with his working life he moved on to his personal one. Now, that seriously needed sorting out.

It was so unlike him to have let things drift on with Beth, but with so much going on at work it just had. She had constantly moaned at him for making them late for parties and dinner dates. Her one concern in life was which of her latest designer outfits she was going to wear to which function; she probably hadn't really noticed that there was anything wrong with their relationship. As long as everything was focused on her she was happy. When Bath had come into the equation her refusal to live there had brought things to a head. Her asking for a trial separation had given him the space he needed to think things through. Although in his heart of hearts there wasn't much to think through, the truth of it was that he wanted to be with someone he could relax with, someone like himself, with no airs or graces, happy to have fish and chips from the chippie as well as appreciating fine food; someone who would pull on their wellington boots to go walking in the rain without worrying about their hair.

He still had a few clothes at the flat. He would pick them up tomorrow evening, seeing as he had to be there for the flat inspection. He would be glad when that was over, even though he knew they wouldn't find anything to quibble about. Everything had been well looked after.

He smiled to himself in the dark. He had always been the butt of his sister's jokes for making lists. Ever since they were small he had kept a never-ending list that he added to when he thought of something important, whereas she would forget her head if it wasn't screwed on, although since she'd had Luke, even he had to admit she had got a bit better; not a lot, but a bit.

Melanie turned the shower to cool. 'God, that was a far better workout than she would have had if she had gone to the gym,' she thought. 'Could she have actually found someone who loved shagging as much as she did?' As she was pondering that thought the shower curtain was pulled back. Gary peered in at her with a grin on his face.

"Is there room for two in there?" he asked, already stepping over the side of the bath to join her.

"Bloody hell, don't mind me, come on in," she said, already starting to put some shower gel onto her flannel so she could soap him all over. 'Ooh,' she thought as she started to rub the flannel onto his chest, 'this tan is real. I wonder where he's been?' She wouldn't ask. It wasn't her style to seem too interested. She had only known him a few days but, funnily, she felt like she had known him forever.

"You know, once we are all clean we're going to have to get all dirty again," said Gary, breaking into her thoughts.

"We are, aren't we?" she replied as she started to move the flannel down towards his erect penis.

Amber lay with her head on Phil's chest. He had long since fallen asleep but she still felt wide awake. Without disturbing him she gently removed his arm from around her and got out of bed. In the kitchen she filled a glass with water. Phil had been so tender towards her this evening, she felt sure he was building up to asking her to get engaged. She knew exactly what her answer would be, as well.

CHAPTER 3

Amber woke before her alarm clock went off. She pushed the switch to stop it waking Phil who was still sound asleep next to her. She would leave him for another 10 minutes while she had a shower. She took a peep out of the bedroom window they were in for another glorious day by the looks of things.

In the bathroom, she tied up her hair. She massaged in her cream cleanser, ready to wash off in the shower, then pulled her towel off the rail and put it ready to dry herself. While showering she reminded herself that she had her wax appointment after work, and as always she went power-walking with Melanie and Jessica on a Tuesday night.

She dried herself quickly, then let her hair down and gave it a good brush before putting it back up again, pinning it in place and leaving a few bits loose to soften the look. Slipping into her dressing gown she went back into the bedroom. Phil was still sound asleep. She went round to the side of the bed he was lying on and, bending down, she kissed him gently on the lips. He opened his eyes.

"Time to get up, sleepy." She smiled at him.

"I didn't hear the alarm go off," he answered, stretching.

"That's because it didn't. I was awake before it went off," she said.

"How about getting back in to give me a cuddle?" suggested Phil.

"Can't." Amber laughed. "I'll be late for work if I do, and so will you be if you don't get a move on. I'll stick us in some toast while you shower."

Amber was pouring orange juice as Phil entered the kitchen. "What's happening tonight?" he asked.

"I'm having my legs done after work, then walking with the girls," she answered as she handed him a glass.

"No plans involving me then," he teased.

"Not tonight, I'm afraid. Try not to miss me too much," she teased him back.

"I'll try." He gave her a kiss on the cheek before grabbing a piece of toast to eat on the way to the car.

Unlike Amber, Melanie was still asleep when her alarm started to buzz. Groaning, her eyes still tightly shut, she stretched out her arm to her bedside cabinet and felt around until she located it. She tapped her hand up and down until she finally hit the right button and the buzzing stopped. Opening her eyes she was met by Gary's eyes looking back at her.

"Oh God, how can it be time to get up already?" she croaked.

"I take it you're not a morning person?" He grinned.

"I'm never a morning person when I have to get up for work. At the weekend it's never this much of a struggle." She sighed.

"Don't you like your job then?" he asked.

"Yes, but it's work, isn't it? What about you? Do you like your job with all those unsociable hours?" she questioned him back.

"Actually, I love my job and the hours don't bother me at all. I'm at the bar more than I need to be really. Like to keep my eye on things, if you know what I mean." He winked.

"I do admire your drive and enthusiasm," Melanie said, putting on a very conscientious sounding voice.

"Thank you. I'll take that as a compliment. Just one more little question I need to ask you." He grinned.

"You can ask it, but I don't know whether I'll answer it," Melanie said, sitting up.

"Well," Gary said as he pulled her back down, "seeing as though I skived off a bit early last night I've given the guys a few hours off this morning, so I have to be in early for a delivery."

"That's not a question," Melanie butted in.

"I was leading up to it. I was wondering if you make coffee for your conquests?" He asked, tickling her.

"I could take offence at that," Melanie said, laughing as she pushed his hands away and got out of bed. She bent down and picked up his boxers, which had been abandoned there the night before. "In answer to your question my conquests make me coffee. It might be a good idea to put these on." She threw his boxers at him. "Because Henry won't know what to do with himself if he gets a load of your lunch box. By the way, I like mine white, no sugar."

Gary rolled out of bed. He pulled on his boxers as instructed and went downstairs to make the coffee. As he approached the kitchen he could hear a woman singing really badly. 'Perhaps that was Henry's girlfriend,' he thought. He'd better go back upstairs to dress properly. He was just about to turn around when the kitchen door opened to reveal a tall, extremely camp looking man in a silky, floral dressing gown.

"Fuck me," he said, looking Gary up and down. "I've died and gone to heaven."

Gary opened his mouth to say something but nothing came out. He looked over the man's shoulder to see if there was anyone else in the kitchen, but there wasn't. It must have been him singing. Eventually, he found his voice, "Um, um, I've been sent down to make coffee," he said, pointing to the ceiling, referring to Melanie.

"Well, come on then, or else she'll be squawking for it in a minute. I'm Henry, by the way," he said, extending his hand towards Gary.

"I'm Gary, a friend of Melanie's," Gary said, stepping forward and shaking Henry's outstretched hand.

"She likes hers white, no sugar. Mugs are in that cupboard," Henry said, pointing energetically towards a cupboard above the kettle.

"Yes, I've had my instructions." Gary smiled. "Nice dressing gown."

"Isn't it just? I do so love bright colours. They suit me so. It was a birthday present from Mel. She has such good taste, and in more ways than one, I might add," said Henry, momentarily dropping his gaze from Gary's face down towards his nether regions, then back up again, grinning from ear to ear.

"She certainly has." Gary said, turning to fill the kettle and trying not to laugh; at the same time, doubly wishing he had his trousers on.

Henry stood admiring Gary's bottom and was still admiring it when Gary turned from filling the kettle. "Lovely, yes." Henry gave a little cough, raising his eyes. "I mean, lovely to meet you. I'll hurry that girl up. She takes all day in the bathroom," he said as he bolted out of the door, leaving Gary staring after him.

He ran up the stairs and banged on the bathroom door. "Let me in, you lucky bitch. Who's hunk-a-dore?" he shouted excitedly. "Nice ass."

"I hope you kept your hands to yourself," Melanie shouted back. "Hang on a mo."

"Are you borrowing my stuff again?" Henry accused, banging the door once more. "Let me in."

On hearing all this Gary shook his head. 'I'm in a mad house,' he thought as he made the coffee.

"You've met Henry then?" Melanie said as she entered the bedroom.

"Yes, and he wasn't kidding when he said you took your time in the bathroom." He handed her coffee to her.

"Thanks," she said, taking the mug. "He's a fine one to talk, he takes longer than me."

"I can imagine." Gary made a face. "Unusual choice of dressing gown for a man. He said you gave it to him as a present."

She nodded. "He just loves bright and floral. Sums him up really."

"You don't say." Gary grinned. "It might have been nice if you'd warned me your housemate was gay. I would have felt a little more comfortable meeting him with my trousers on."

"I thought it would be a nice treat for him on a Tuesday morning," said Melanie, laughing. "No, I was just joking. It didn't even cross my mind to mention it, honest. Henry's just one of the girls, to me."

"I'd never have guessed," said Gary as he moved towards her. "Look, I've got to get going." He pushed a strand of wet hair back from her face.

"Sure, can you let yourself out? I need to get ready," she said, taking a step back.

"Don't I get a kiss goodbye?" he asked cheekily. "You're not going all shy on me, are you? Because we both know you are definitely not the shy type."

"True." Melanie pouted. "What type am I then?"

He kissed her on the lips. "I'm working on that one."

Gary left Melanie's house with a smile on his face. There was something about her. He wasn't sure what, but he felt like he'd known her forever, which was weird because he had only met her a couple of days ago and didn't know anything about her at all. He only knew that he felt so comfortable with her.

Hearing the front door close Melanie sat on her bed. What did he mean that he was working on that one? He hadn't asked her out on a date. In fact, he had left without even saying he would call her. Maybe Amber was right when she said she was a bit too quick with her sexual favours. For the first time, she wondered if she was a bit too easy, but, then again, bollocks to it, there were plenty more fish in the sea. But a little voice in her head was saying that it would be quite nice if he did call.

Henry came bursting into her bedroom like an excited child. "He's to die for! Where did you meet him? Where did you meet him?" he repeated.

"I met him on Saturday night. He runs the new wine bar in town," she answered him, trying to sound indifferent. "He came back after closing, then came again on Sunday. In more ways than one!"

61

"You dirty bitch." Henry waggled his finger at her. "You wouldn't talk like that in front of your mother, would you?"

"You are not my mother, and if you hadn't stayed out over the weekend being a dirty bitch yourself you would have met him before this morning." Melanie waggled her finger back at Henry. "Chances are you probably won't meet him again though."

"Bet I will. He likes you. I can tell," Henry said.

"Thanks for the vote of confidence but I don't think so. Anyway, you know me, I'm a good-time girl and good-time girls are not into relationships." Melanie lifted her shoulders.

"Come on, melly belly, you like him, admit it. You do, don't you?" he pressed.

"Oh, he's alright. I wouldn't say no to another shag." Melanie hoped that would shut him up, however he was now staring at her intently.

"Oh my God, oh my God." Henry started to shake his hands about wildly. "I don't believe it, you really do like him. I can tell by your face." He started to pace up and down. "Right, we need a plan. I can help you entice him into your web. We'll talk after work. We'll plan your next move." He stopped pacing and looked at Melanie. He then began chanting. "Melanie has got a crush on, Melanie has got a crush on."

Melanie jumped up from her sitting position on the bed. She started to run at Henry. "I have not got a crush on," she shouted at him.

Henry squealed loudly. He turned quickly and flew out of the bedroom door. As he ran down the stairs he continued to chant that Melanie had a crush on. Melanie had already stopped running and stood at the top of the stairs. Giggling, she watched him reach the front door. Whilst opening it he looked up at her.

"Bye, dear heart, see you later," he shouted up at her as he left.

Melanie returned to her bedroom. 'Could he be right? In Henry's words, oh my God, did she have a crush on?'

Amber signed in two visitors who had arrived for the lunchtime conference. She checked reception's list. They were the last two names on it. She showed them the way to where the conference was taking place. Returning to the desk she noticed Melanie was checking her phone for the umpteenth time that morning.

"Mel, why do you keep checking your phone?" she asked her.

"I don't," answered Melanie, putting her mobile back into her handbag.

"You do, you've been in and out of that handbag all morning," said Amber.

"And you've been very quiet, which isn't like you," remarked Vicky.

"Is everything ok?" Amber asked.

"Everything is fine, thank you. I happen to be a bit tired, that's all. If you must know, I had a visitor last night and of course I had to keep him entertained," Melanie answered, gyrating her hips.

"Not the guy from the wine bar again?" Vicky exclaimed.

"Yes." Melanie nodded her head.

"Yes, and you've said nothing all morning," Amber said indignantly. "We want more information than that. That's why you keep checking your phone, to see if you have a missed call or message from him."

"I always check my phone," Melanie replied, a little too defensively.

"You never check it as often as you have this morning. You like him, don't you?" Amber probed.

"Don't you start, you sound like Henry did this morning after he bumped into him in the kitchen," Melanie groaned.

"You mean, he stayed the night again? Tell us then, we want to know everything," Vicky demanded excitedly.

"Not quiet everything. You can leave out anything sordid or perverted." Amber grinned.

"In that case, it's not worth telling." Melanie laughed.

"In that case, you can put in a few of the sordid and perverted bits," Vicky quipped. "We're all ears."

Loving her audience Melanie revealed the happenings of the night before. From Gary's phone call to the moment he left that morning. Amber and Vicky listened intently. By the time she had finished they were just staring at her.

"Stop staring at me like I'm some bloody freak," Melanie said, staring back at them.

"We're just amazed," Amber said.

"Amazed at what?" Melanie asked.

"Amazed that, for once in your life, you're actually bothered about whether a man is going to contact you or not. Even when you've had a so-called steady boyfriend in the past you never checked your phone all the time to see if they'd called or not. Now, be honest, you do like him, don't you?" Amber said, pointing her finger at Melanie.

"Oh, I don't bloody know." She threw her hands in the air. "I've only known him a couple of days and most of that time hasn't been spent in deep, meaningful conversation. In fact, I don't think we've had a proper conversation, but I have to admit something just feels right about him."

Vicky clapped her hands together. "Henry's right, you've got a crush on him."

"I don't do crushes," Melanie said.

"You do now. You now know what the rest of us feel like when we want a bloke to be interested." She put her arm around Melanie, giving her a hug. "Knowing how men fall over themselves for you he'll call, just wait and see."

"I don't think so, he reminds me of me. Anyway, it's nearly lunchtime. Who wants to go first?" she asked, trying to change the subject.

"I'll go seeing as I'm leaving early," offered Amber. "And, Melanie, you could call him, you know."

"I'm not bloody calling him," Melanie said.

"Think about it," Vicky suggested.

Dorothy dialled Tom Tranter's number. He answered straightaway.

"Hello, Mr Tranter, it's Dorothy Brown speaking."

"Hello, Dorothy, I take it you've sorted out some viewings for me," he said.

"I have, indeed. You now have a rather hectic agenda for tomorrow, I'm afraid. I've booked you three properties to view through Hunter's Estate Agents. You need to be at their office for three o'clock. You then have three properties to view through Wick's Estate Agents, meeting in their office at 5.30pm.

"That's great, thanks, Dorothy, I appreciate the trouble you've gone to get everything organised at such short notice. Let's just hope I like one of them." Tom laughed.

"Let's hope so. Is there anything else you'd like me to do for you?" she asked.

"I can't think of anything at the moment. Thanks again, Dorothy. Bye," Tom said, hanging up.

Dorothy put down the telephone. 'Such a nice young man, one didn't mind helping him at all. Now then,' she thought, 'I need to stretch my legs.' Getting up from her desk her knees clicked. "Ooh," she said out loud. Picking up the two gardening books she'd bought in that morning she headed towards reception. As she approached she could see Melanie and Vicky chatting away. Whatever they had to talk about all day was beyond her.

Melanie looked up. She could see Dorothy making her way towards the desk.

"Dorothy Judith alert," she whispered to Vicky, her hand over her mouth.

Dorothy stopped in front of the desk, placing the books down in front of her. "Here you are, Melanie," she said, with a twitch of a smile.

Melanie stood. "Thanks, Dorothy." She started to look through one of them. "It all looks a bit complicated, if you ask me," she said, stopping on a page with a picture of a floral display that wouldn't look out of place in the Chelsea Flower Show.

"Don't be put off by some of the photographs, simple can be just as beautiful." Opening the other book she quickly found a page showing a pot containing what looked like a miniature tree with flowers on it. "You see, one plant in a pot can look just as effective and be far less trouble to look after."

"I see what you mean." Melanie smiled at Dorothy. 'The old stick was quite sweet underneath,' she thought.

"Right then, back to work. You take your time with the books. I'm in no hurry to have them back. If you want to know anything, just ask. Gloria's a keen gardener as well. I'm sure between us we could answer any questions you might have," she said, heading back towards her office.

Melanie sat back down with the books on her lap. "How the fuck am I going to get out of this then?" She looked at Vicky for an answer.

"By buying a pot and planting something in it?" Vicky suggested.

"Very bloody funny," Melanie said.

"Serves you right. That'll teach you to talk about bushes, won't it?" She laughed.

"Oh, shut up," Melanie said, looking down at the books.

Phil sat alone in the office, proofreading a set of details. It had been easy to talk the old couple into signing up for 12 weeks with a two percent fee that morning. "Ker-ching," he said out loud, raising his right arm up in the air and down again. All he'd had to do was walk round the property pointing out what needed attention, which wasn't much. It was a bit tired and dated in places but that was all. He'd played on that, making it sound as though it would be difficult to sell, when in reality he had five applicants who he knew would view it straight away. He felt sure that at least two of them would put forward an offer. 'Poor old dears,' he thought, 'he'd even got them to cancel the other two agents due out later that day.'

He would make a few phone calls to his hot applicants, then as soon as Cheryl got back to the office he would drive over with the details for them to approve, giving them the good news that he already had people interested in viewing. It would be sold before the for-sale board went up. Bringing his best buyers up on screen he picked up the phone and started dialling.

Cheryl swung her car into the car park. As she did she saw Mike Hunter, the owner of the estate agents, getting out of his car. He put up his hand in acknowledgement and, standing back, he waited for her to park. 'No naughty flirting for her and Phil if he was going to be in for the rest of the afternoon,' she thought, smiling politely back. Together they walked round to the office. As they entered Phil looked up.

"Great, you're back. I'm going to run these details over to our new vendors," he said to Cheryl. "Are you in for the rest of the afternoon, Mike?" Phil asked, looking at his boss.

"Yes," he nodded, "got some admin to catch up on."

"I'll update you later then. It's all good," said Phil as he collected his things together. "See you later."

'Bugger,' he thought. He wasn't expecting Mike to be in. He was hoping to be alone with Cheryl later so he would have a chance to tell her that it was time to end their bit of fun. He was going to tell her earlier on but with one thing and another the occasion had never presented itself. There was no way he could say anything when he got back if his boss was going to be in until closing. It was no good, he would have to let her come round after work and tell her then. He had wondered whether to tell her by text, but thought better of it. After all, they did have to continue to work together.

He pulled into his new vendor's drive. 'Nice one,' he thought, working out his commission if he could secure a sale. After his phone calls he had three couples wanting to view and two more going to get back to him. 'A sale was definitely in the bag!'

Beth walked around the flat for the fourth time. Everything looked perfect; nothing was out of place. She paid a cleaner who came in twice a week to see to that, which annoyed Tom. He was always making remarks about the place not looking lived in. She adjusted one of her precious silk cushions. Now she was going back to Daddy's – just a temporary measure until she sorted this little mess out with Tom – everything would have to be packed up. She ran her manicured hand along one of the sofas, feeling the expensive fabric beneath her fingertips and remembering Tom asking her if it was really necessary to spend such an obscene amount of money on a couch.

Her mission to make things right between her and Tom started tonight. She had arranged for a gourmet meal to be delivered from Tom's favourite restaurant. What a palaver that had been; they had only agreed after considerable pressure and the price she'd offered to pay. It was nearly 3.30pm. It was time to start making herself look utterly irresistible. She hoped Tom would be there before the letting agent. She would just double check everything was on track with the restaurant. She picked up the telephone and punched in the number of the restaurant. As it rang she admired herself in the mirror again.

"Hello, Lou Lou's," a voice answered.

"Hello, this is Beth MacDowland, I'm just checking to make sure everything is in order for my seven o'clock delivery this evening," she barked down the phone.

"Hello, Miss MacDowland, everything is absolutely fine. Is everything all right with you? You've not changed your mind regarding the menu, have you? Only you only called an hour ago," said the voice.

"No, I haven't. Who am I talking to, please?" 'Fucking idiot,' she thought, knowing full well it was Raymond. 'I'm the customer and I can call as many times as I want.'

"It's Raymond, Miss MacDowland, the Maître D'."

"Of course it's you, Raymond. I know you will make sure everything is to my satisfaction," Beth hissed down the telephone in her condescending manor.

"I certainly will, Miss MacDowland. Your dinner will arrive promptly at seven o'clock," Raymond replied with absolute politeness in his voice – years of practice!

"Thank you," Beth said, putting the phone down before Raymond had a chance to say anything else. 'It better do, or else,' she thought as she headed for the bedroom to get ready.

Raymond heard the click. 'Charming,' he thought as he removed the phone from his ear. He looked at it for a moment before replacing it in its cradle. 'What a prize bitch.' They knew her all too well at Lou Lou's. She moaned and complained about everything, then hardly ate a mouthful; whereas her chap seemed a decent, down-to-earth bloke, no airs and graces with him. He walked through the restaurant into the kitchen.

"Just double checking the order for Miss MacDowland," he called over to the chef.

"What, again?" The chef rolled his eyes.

"Again," Raymond replied.

"It'll be ready," assured the chef.

Raymond nodded his thanks. Back in the restaurant he cast his eagle eye over the tables: a starched white tablecloth on each, with a vase of flowers placed strategically in the centre screamed freshly picked, and gleaming cutlery.

'Perfect,' he thought. It was like the calm before the storm. Lou Lou's was always fully booked.

Amber grabbed her handbag. "I'd better get going or else I'll be late for my wax," she said to Melanie.

"Have you decided to have it all off?" Melanie asked. "Go on, give Phil a treat."

Amber shook her head at Melanie and tutted. "You don't give up, do you? Have you spoken to Jessica about walking later?"

"Yes, yes, usual time, about 5.30pm. You'll be finished by then, won't you? You're hardly Cousin Itt from the Addams Family," Melanie chirped.

"Very funny. See you later." Amber waved.

"Laters," Melanie said, giving her a wave back.

Amber hurried to her car. 'Hope the traffic's not too heavy,' she thought as she pulled out onto the main road. Luck was on her side. She made it to the salon with nearly 10 minutes to spare. As she walked in a bell tinkled to announce her arrival. She breathed in the scented air, a mixture of all the different products that had been used throughout the day. Before the door had time to close behind her a lady dressed in black trousers with a white tunic appeared, and before she knew it she was being ushered into a treatment room.

"I've got you booked in for a full leg and bikini wax, and a pedicure. Is that right?" asked the beauty therapist.

"That's right," Amber replied.

"We'll start with the bikini wax and work our way down. What would you like? A tidy up or something a little more?" she asked Amber.

'Why not?' Amber thought to herself and before she changed her mind she answered, "Something a little more, I think."

On went the pre-wax lotion. Then the battle began. On with the wax, on with a strip, skin held taught, off with the strip, and so the process repeated itself. The therapist chatted away to Amber as if they were out having a coffee somewhere. Amber did her best to chat back, in between gritting her teeth and trying not to wince every time a strip was pulled off. Why did women put themselves through this? Why hadn't she gone for just the tidy up?

"That's the sides done, now if you bring this leg up to your chest and hold it we can get the underneath done," the therapist said, patting Amber's right leg.

'Oh no,' thought Amber as she did as she was told, 'I'm paying to be tortured. Phil had better appreciate this.'

"All done this side. Other leg now," Gemma said as she guided Amber's leg back down to the beauty couch. "Nearly done here."

'Thank God for that,' thought Amber as she lifted her other leg. It was stinging so much that she hardly felt the other side being done. She would definitely just have a tidy up next time. The therapist made easy work of her legs and was soon slathering on a cooling after-wax lotion.

"All done and looking good," she said, admiring her handiwork. "Now, let's get those feet looking pretty. Would you like something to drink? Tea, coffee or something cold perhaps?"

"Tea would be lovely. I could have done with something stronger to mull the pain before the wax." Amber smiled ruefully.

"Not the most pleasant of experiences, is it? Choose a colour for your toes while I get that cup of tea."

Amber looked at the array of nail varnishes. She picked up a bright pink one, then a red, then a blue, then a brown. 'No, definitely the pink,' she thought, picking up the first one again.

As the therapist worked her magic on her feet Amber sipped her tea. 'Now, this was more like it. This is what beauty treatments were all about, relaxation and enjoyment,' she thought.

Tom Tranter finished the email he was typing and pressed send. He checked his watch. 'Shit, it was nearly five o'clock. Where had the afternoon gone?' he thought. He was going to be late for the letting agent. He buzzed his secretary. She answered immediately.

"Yes, Tom," came her voice.

"Can you do me a favour? Can you call Beth on the flat number and tell her my meeting has run over slightly but I'll be on my way shortly?" asked Tom.

"No problem, I'll do it straight away. What meeting are we talking about?" joked his secretary.

"Very funny," Tom replied, before hitting the off button on the intercom. He logged off then shut down his laptop. He picked up his mobile and closed the windows on his way out. He stopped at his secretary's desk.

"All done." She smiled sweetly up at him. "Don't think Beth sounded too pleased, but I told her the meeting went on without breaking for tea so you didn't get a chance to call earlier."

"You're a star, what would I do without you?" Tom gave her the thumbs up.

"Just make sure that Paul King knows that when he takes over from you," she said.

"He already does. See you Thursday," Tom said, heading for the door.

"See you Thursday." She watched Tom leave, thinking, 'If she were single she wouldn't say no to her boss, that was for sure. She couldn't understand why he was that bothered about being late for Beth, he wasn't going out with the cow anymore. Nobody liked her in the office, the way she paraded in, looking down her nose at everyone.'

Melanie and Vicky started to tidy up the front desk. It was almost 5pm and they wanted to be out the door dead-on. Melanie checked her phone again.

"Anything?" Vicky asked.

"No." Melanie shrugged.

"Never mind, he'll probably get in touch tonight or tomorrow," Vicky said brightly.

"Are you two honeys up to mischief?" Gloria asked, waddling towards them with duster and polish in hand.

"No. We were just talking about the bloke Melanie met at the weekend. She's pretending she isn't bothered whether he calls or not," Vicky told Gloria.

"Is that right, sugar?" she asked Melanie, putting her polish down. She rested her hands on her hips while she waited for a response.

"Okay, okay, if you want the truth I wouldn't mind seeing him again if he does get round to calling me," she answered Gloria, then looked straight at Vicky. "Satisfied now?"

"Absolutely." Vicky smirked.

"I'll be keeping my fingers crossed for you then, honey." Gloria held up her hand with her fingers crossed.

"Thanks, Gloria." Melanie smiled at the cleaner. "You can ask him above to keep his fingers crossed as well, if you have time."

Gloria let out a throaty laugh. "The Lord, he already has his fingers crossed for you, Melanie. Off you two go, so I can get this desk polished." She shooed them away. "God bless."

Outside, Vicky nudged Melanie with her elbow. "Hope you get a call or text later."

Melanie smiled. "Ta. See you tomorrow."

Phil sat in a queue of traffic drumming his fingers on the steering wheel in time to the music playing on the radio. He didn't have to go back to the office, but now he knew the old couple were going to be home all day tomorrow it wouldn't take much time to recall the buyers he'd spoken to earlier and arrange a block viewing, which would no doubt get an offer on the table. 'Piece of cake.' He smiled to himself.

'The traffic always seemed a lot worse when you wanted to get somewhere quickly,' thought Tom. He felt hot and sticky. A cold beer would go down a treat right now. He called the flat on his hands-free. Even though his secretary had already called it was going to take him longer than he thought to get there; every man and his dog were on the road. He hated being late; it always annoyed him if people were late for him and here he was doing exactly what he hated. He waited for Beth to answer, wondering what kind of reception he was going to get. Beth heard the phone ringing. 'That better not be the letting agent saying he's not coming,' she thought as she tottered over, on her enormously high heels and wearing a very tightly fitted dress, to pick it up.

"Hello," she answered.

"Beth, it's me. The traffic's horrendous. Has the letting agent arrived yet?" Tom asked.

Beth took a deep breath. "No, not yet so no need to hurry."

"Okay." Tom ended the call. She seemed to be in a good mood. That would make everything a lot more pleasant. Beth put down the phone. She checked her appearance in the mirror again. There was no way Tom would be able to resist what she had on offer tonight.

CHAPTER 4

As soon as Amber got in she rushed to the bathroom. She gingerly took off her knickers and looked down to survey the narrow strip of hair that the beauty therapist had left. Each side of it bright-red, inflamed skin stared back at her. 'Oh no, she looked like a plucked chicken. There was no way she could go walking tonight,' she decided to herself. Having made up her mind it would benefit her nether region to leave it unclothed she took the rest of her clothes off and slipped into her dressing gown. 'Better call the other two, they would be wondering where she was,' she thought. She walked back through her flat to retrieve her bag, which she had thrown down on her way in. She dug out her mobile and scrolled down until she came to Melanie's number.

Kitted out in her tightly fitted, mid-calf training bottoms, a skimpy vest top, which revealed more cleavage than was necessary to go walking, a cap pulled down so the peak rested on her big wag-like shades, a bottle of water in one hand and mobile in the other Melanie leant against the wall waiting for Jessica and Amber. A van with two workmen in it passed her. While the driver hooted his approval, his workmate leant out of the window and wolf-whistled. She flashed them a smile as she answered her ringing phone.

"Where are you?" she asked, seeing it was Amber.

"At home," Amber whined. "I'm not coming. I've been butchered."

"Did you have it all off then?" laughed Melanie.

"|No, I didn't, but I may as well of. She's hardly left anything." Amber had another quick peep. "It doesn't look pretty."

"Panic not, it'll be fine by the morning. If you had it done on a more regular basis you wouldn't get such a reaction," Melanie almost scolded her.

"Believe you me, I will not be having this much off on a regular basis, that's for sure. Is Jessica there yet?" Amber asked.

"Not yet. Do you want me to ask her to call you?" Melanie offered.

"No, I was just going to say hi, that's all. See you in the morning," Amber said.

"See you in the morning. Oh, and, Amber, don't go flicking your bean tonight, it'll only irritate things more." Melanie shrieked with laughter.

"You are just so disgusting that is not worthy of a reply so I'm going, bye." Amber put down the phone as she burst out laughing.

Melanie was still laughing to herself when she saw Jessica walking up the road. Pushing herself away from her leaning position on the wall, she waved.

"Hi, Mel," Jessica greeted her, with a hug. "Where's Amber?"

Melanie started giggling again. "Come on, I'll tell you as we walk. Shall we do the usual route?"

"If you like," Jessica nodded as they started to walk briskly, pumping their arms backwards and forwards at right angles.

Tom pulled into one of the reserved spaces for the flat. 'Here we go,' he thought as he got out of his car. He hurried inside and up the stairs to find the front door of the flat open.

"Hello," he called out as he entered.

"We're in here," Beth shouted from the direction of the lounge.

As he walked in Tom couldn't help but run his eyes over Beth before turning his attention to the letting agent. "Sorry for keeping you waiting."

"Please don't apologise, I've only just arrived myself," replied the agent as he started to take out some papers from his briefcase.

"Now you're both here can I get either of you a drink?" Beth asked.

"Not for me, thank you," answered the agent.

"Tom?" she asked, flicking her hair back with her hand as she looked at him.

"Yes, please," Tom replied.

Beth smirked to herself as she poured Tom a beer in the kitchen. He liked the dress, she could tell. She had to get a couple of beers down him while the agent was here; that would get his appetite going to ensure he stayed for dinner. 'So far, so good,' she thought. She carried the ice-cold beer back through to the lounge. Smiling sweetly, she handed it to him.

"Cheers," he said as he lifted the glass to his lips and proceeded to drink half of it in one go.

"Right," the agent said. "It's just a formality really. With the more upmarket properties like this one we like to meet with our tenants before they leave to make sure they've been happy with our service and to inspect the property." He looked at Beth, who gave him a charming but slightly vacant smile, then turned to Tom.

Tom nodded, acknowledging that he had been listening, knowing full well that Beth hadn't. He downed the rest of his pint. 'That went down a bit too smoothly,' he thought as he put the glass down onto one of Beth's glass coasters. His fingers had hardly left the glass before Beth was picking it up and heading towards the kitchen again. He would be amazed if the agent found anything wrong, as nothing had time to collect dust in the place, let alone anything else. Then, to his surprise, Beth was back, having refilled the glass she'd just taken.

"You looked like you could do with another one." She smiled. "Had a hard day?"

"So so," he replied, taking the beer. He turned his attention back to the agent. "Where do you want to start?"

The agent looked down at the clipboard he was holding. "Anywhere you like. After you."

Tom led the way with his pint in his hand. Beth made no attempt to go with them. Tom could answer any questions the agent might ask. She had no interest in what was on his clipboard. He would find nothing to quibble about. In fact, the place was cleaner than when they had moved in; she hadn't paid a cleaner to come in twice a week for nothing.

Mike Hunter had hardly lifted his head up from his computer all afternoon. Cheryl had glanced over every now and again, just to check he was still engrossed in whatever he was doing. 'He wasn't a bad looking bloke, probably early fifties,' she thought, 'and in quite good shape, a little reserved for an estate agent maybe.' She wondered what he was like in bed, no doubt a gentleman, unlike Phil who had the potential to be a bit of an animal. Mike Hunter glanced up and caught her looking at him.

"I'm just going to run the post over." She smiled. "Have you got anything that needs going?"

"Just these two, please." He held up two letters.

Cheryl got up from her desk. She took the letters from Mike. Popping them in the red postbag, already nearly full, she zipped it up. "Won't be long."

As she stepped outside she had to squint against the bright sunshine. She dashed across the road as soon as there was a gap in the traffic. Inside the Post Office she waited her turn. It wasn't long before pervert postmaster was licking his lips while he talked to her chest. 'Yes,' she thought, 'you and many more would like to bury your face in my puppies.'

"You were quick," Mike said, looking up as she returned to the office.

"Not much of a queue today," she replied.

"Well, I'm all done. What about you?" he asked.

"Me too," Cheryl answered. The truth was that she had spent most of her time that afternoon placing a huge online Next order, in between answering the phone when it rang.

"In that case, it won't hurt if we close a few minutes early tonight. Can you check everything is off out the back while I put these few things away?" He motioned to the papers on his desk.

"Sure, no problem," Cheryl said, already on her way.

Phil turned onto the high street. He would just about get back to the office before closing. He pulled into the car park just as Cheryl and Mike were walking round the corner. They must have closed up a bit early. He parked up and got out of the car. "What's this then? Half day?" he shouted as they approached.

"You caught us," Mike joked. "We didn't expect you back. Do you want me to come back in with you?"

"No, I'll catch up with you tomorrow." Phil replied. "Everything okay with you, Cheryl?"

"Fine," she said with a wink as she took a step closer to him. Stretching out her hand she patted him on the bottom while Mike momentarily turned his back to open his car door.

"Look, Cheryl," Phil whispered, but before he had time to say anything else Mike turned back to face them.

Moments earlier, as Melanie and Jessica were merrily stepping it out down the High Street, they had both seen Phil driving past them. Unanimously they had raised their hands to wave but he had driven straight past.

"Not very observant, is he?" Melanie remarked.

"Probably concentrating on his driving," Jessica replied.

"Suppose so," Melanie agreed. "Have you made another date for him and Amber to go over to your place yet? One that he won't be working late?"

"Sarcasm is the lowest form of wit, you know. But answering your question, not yet. I was hoping to do it tonight, but seeing as Amber's nursing a sore fanny I'll call her later on in the week," laughed Jessica.

They turned off the High Street. As they passed the entrance to the estate agents' car park Melanie glanced up, just as Cheryl was patting Phil's behind. She grabbed Jessica's arm. Abruptly coming to a standstill, she pointed in the direction to where Phil, Cheryl and Mike stood. "Did you see that?"

"See what?" Jessica asked, looking in the direction Melanie was pointing.

"I just saw that woman who works with Phil put her hand on his ass," she said, still staring.

"Oh, come on, Mel, you must have been mistaken. They're just standing having a chat," Jessica said, starting to walk again.

"I'm telling you, she put her hand on his ass," Melanie said, running a few steps to catch Jessica. "Do you think I should mention it to Amber?"

"Mention what exactly? You thought you saw the woman he works with touch his behind in front of their boss while you were standing some distance away with the sun in your eyes. Are you mad? How's that going to sound?" Jessica said, turning to look at Melanie.

"Ridiculous, if you put it like that, but I know what I saw." Melanie was insistent.

"Okay, okay, I believe you. It was probably just a bit of office fun, nothing more. We both know Amber is absolutely besotted with the bloke. It would just upset her if we went telling tales," Jessica said.

Melanie didn't answer. It hadn't looked like office fun to her.

"Wouldn't it?" Jessica nudged her.

"Alright, I'll keep my mouth shut," Melanie said. "Although I have to say I've never really trusted him."

"Mel, that's enough. Just leave it. Tell me more about the stud monkey you met at the weekend," she said, changing the subject.

"Stud monkey? You need to get out more often." Melanie's voice softened. "I can tell you he's proving to be one hell of a shag."

"Tell me more. Us old married women need some new ideas." Jessica laughed.

Amber took the only two cookery books she owned from the bookcase. 'May as well have a look at some different ways to do chicken breasts seeing as I'm stuck in for the evening,' she thought. She made herself a cup of tea and settled down on the settee. Opening one of the books she ran her finger down the index until she came to poultry. Finding the correct page, she began looking at the recipes. Nothing inspired her. Picking up the other book she did the same. Her wanted inspiration didn't materialise; she would stick with her original plan of chicken stuffed with Stilton – simple but tasty.

As Phil had anticipated it had taken him only a few phone calls to make the block viewings. The sale was definitely in the bag. He picked up the phone again to call Amber, then he put it back down. He would call Cheryl. He picked it back up. No, he wouldn't. He put it back down. He would speak with her later when she came round. 'Christ, will you make your mind up?' he thought. He sat staring at the office wall. 'He'd better order a decent bouquet of flowers for Thursday night if he was going to pop the question. That was, if he was going to pop the question.' He still hadn't quite decided that either. Most of him wanted to but there was still a small part of him that wondered if he was actually ready to settle down. 'Was that the same for most men? Did they ever feel ready?' he questioned to himself. Regardless, he would call in at the florist at the end of the High Street tomorrow, and order something ready for him to pick up just before closing on Thursday. Flowers were always good for brownie points if nothing else!

He got up from his desk, locked up and headed to his car. As he walked he could smell curry from the nearby takeaway. He decided to pick one up. He didn't feel in the mood to cook and he wasn't sure when Cheryl would turn up.

Beth checked her watch again. It was just gone 6.30pm. The prick-of-an-agent was taking far too long for her liking. He'd gone through the checklist. They had both signed the forms. He was just talking bloody rubbish now, as far as she was concerned, although Tom seemed interested enough in what he was saying. She noticed Tom's glass was empty again. One more would make him practically over the limit. She went to pick it up.

"No more for me, I've got to drive," Tom said, stopping her.

Before she had time to say anything the agent cut in. "It's about time I wasn't here. My wife will be moaning about how I'm always late home for dinner."

'What a prat. He really was starting to annoy her. Was that his idea of a joke? Too bloody right, it's about time you weren't here,' she thought. However, she smiled as sweetly as she could. "We wouldn't want to get you in the dog house."

"I'm never out of it." The agent laughed loudly.

'Fucking idiot,' thought Beth as she let out a little tinker of a laugh, hoping it would fool him into thinking she thought he was funny.

Tom stretched his hand out towards the agent. The agent took it and gave it a limp shake.

"I'll see you out," said Beth, ushering him towards the door.

She returned moments later with her sexiest of smiles glued in place. "I've ordered us in something to eat. Thought you'd be hungry coming straight from work."

"Beth, we need to talk," Tom said.

"Great, we can talk over dinner then," said Beth, walking towards the kitchen, not giving him the chance to say anything else. She didn't like the serious tone in his voice.

'This isn't going to be easy,' Tom thought to himself as he watched her go. He would get his last few bits and pieces together first. He shouted after her. "I'm just going to collect the last of my things."

"Ok," came the reply from the kitchen. Opening a cupboard door Beth took out a wine glass. Opening the fridge, she removed the bottle of white wine she had put in there earlier to chill. She poured herself a very large glass.

In the bedroom Tom opened and closed what had been his chest of drawers. It was empty. Opening the wardrobe door he took out the few remaining shirts, a pair of jeans and a dark blue linen jacket his sister had bought him the year before. With it all draped over one arm he went to find Beth in the kitchen.

"Let me get you a bag for that lot," she said, indicating the clothes over Tom's arm.

"No need, I can put them on the back seat of the car." He sighed. "Look, Beth, I've been thinking about us over the last couple of days." This time the doorbell rang, stopping him continuing.

"That will be our Lou Lou's delivery," said Beth as she went to answer it, thankful of the timing.

"Lou Lou's delivery? As in the restaurant?" Tom called after her, puzzled.

"That's right," Beth called back.

"But they don't deliver," Tom said, following her to the door.

"They do tonight," Beth said, smiling at him as she opened the door. Greeting the young man standing before her she accepted the large brown carrier bag he was holding. Tom had to admit that the aroma coming from it was mouthwatering, and he was in no doubt that what was in there would taste delicious. He loved the food at Lou Lou's. It was his favourite restaurant. His stomach started to grumble.

In the kitchen he watched her put the bag on the work surface as he tried to find the right words. "Beth, as I was saying."

Beth took a large gulp of her wine. She had to act quickly. Putting her glass down she closed the gap between them. Reaching up she placed her hands on his shoulders, making gentle massaging movements. She held her body in such a way that her breasts were just touching him through his shirt, tempting him. "You're not going to say you're not hungry, are you?" she purred.

Tom could feel himself stirring at the feel of her against him. Before he could stop himself he had instinctively, with just one of his powerful arms, pulled her to him.

Phil finished his curry. 'Not bad,' he thought as he carried his plate back to the kitchen. He put it in the washing-up bowl along with his breakfast things from that morning. 'He would do that later,' he said to himself. Taking another bottle of lager out of the fridge he wondered where Cheryl was.

As Melanie drove home she still couldn't get it out of her mind. You just don't go round feeling the asses of men you work with; something was going on there, she was sure of it. She would run it by Henry, see what he made of the situation. The only trouble was that Henry could not keep his mouth shut and would probably start blabbing, and if it got back to Amber it would be her that got the blame. 'No, Jessica was right,' she thought, 'she would leave well alone.'

Before she could put her key in the lock the door flew open and Henry was dragging her inside like an over-excited child.

"You've had a delivery, you've had a delivery," he repeated as he pulled her towards the kitchen.

"What are you on about?" she asked, wondering what Henry was so excited about.

"Look," Henry said, pointing to a huge bunch of the most brilliant pink coloured flowers, tied in an equally brilliant pink ribbon.

"Oh my God, they are gorgeous," Melanie said as she picked them up and breathed in their heavenly scent. "When did these arrive? Who are they from?"

"Fanny Ann from next door took delivery of them for you this afternoon. Bet you anything lover boy sent them. Come on, open the card." Henry was almost jumping up and down. "Love is in the air, everywhere you look around," he started singing.

"Shut up." Melanie giggled as she put the flowers down and carefully unpinned the card. She opened the little envelope.

"Well, what does it say? Are they from him?" Henry clasped his hands together.

"Mind your own business," Melanie said, putting the card behind her back.

Henry grabbed her. "Give it, give it." he shouted as he started to tickle her with one hand, grappling for the card with his other. He finally wrestled it away from the screaming Melanie. He read it out loud. "Do you fancy dinner on Thursday night, with me for afters? Gary." He poked her playfully in the stomach. "Well, go on, call him and say yes."

"I'll call him later, I may be busy Thursday," Melanie said with a shrug.

"Busy on Thursday, my ass. Stop pretending you're not interested. You can't spend the rest of your days waltzing in and out of relationships with the I-don't-give-a-damn attitude. I can tell you like him, so what's the problem?" Henry's voice started to rise to an even higher pitch.

"Calm down, cupid, I'll call him. She gave Henry a hug. "I just don't want to seem too keen, that's all. You know it's not my style. Whose turn is it to cook tonight?"

"You know it's your turn, lady, so stop trying to get round me." Henry replied, removing her arms from around him. "But seeing as you're my favourite girlfriend I'll do us a salad while you shower. We can discuss what you should wear on Thursday. Run along, and don't use all the hot water, you know Tuesday night is my beauty night."

In the bathroom Melanie grinned as she surveyed Henry's lotions and potions, all lined up for later that evening. His body brush, body scrub, relaxing face mask and body butter. 'She would have a bit of that after her shower,' she thought. Turning her attention back to Gary she wondered whether to call or text her reply. She mulled it over in the shower, coming to the conclusion she should call seeing as he'd gone to the trouble of sending flowers. She turned off the shower and quickly dried herself. She opened Henry's body butter and massaged some into her legs. In fact, the more she thought of it the more she liked Gary's way of asking her out, it was sweet without being sickly.

Back in her bedroom she called him. 'Stay cool,' she told herself. She waited for him to answer.

Gary's phone vibrated in his back pocket. He took it out and saw it was Melanie. He signalled to one of the bar staff that he had to take a call. 'Stay cool,' he told himself.

"Hi," he answered.

"Hi yourself. Thanks for the flowers, they're beautiful." She paused, waiting for him to say something.

"You're very welcome. Did you read the card?" he asked.

"I did," she replied.

'She's not going to make this overly easy for me,' Gary grinned to himself. "Well?"

"Well, what if I prefer you for a starter instead of afters?" She grinned to herself while asking the question.

"We'd never get round to eating," he answered.

"True. In that case, pudding you are," she said.

"In that case," he mimicked her, "I'll pick you up around 7.45 then. Do you like Italian?"

"Love it," Melanie answered.

"Italian it is then. See you Thursday," Gary said.

Melanie ran down the stairs into the kitchen where she jumped on Henry's back.

"Get off, you mad cow," he shrieked.

Melanie gave him a kiss before slipping down to the floor. "I'm going for an Italian on Thursday."

"Oh, I love Italian, dear heart. Which restaurant is he taking you to?" Henry asked as he put their salads on the table. "Sit, sit," he ordered Melanie.

"He didn't say." Melanie sat down. She stabbed a piece of tomato and put it in her mouth. "And I didn't ask," she continued with her mouth full.

"Dear heart, if you speak with your mouth full like you are now he'll run a mile. Manners maketh man, young lady. Now, what should you wear? Smart-casual, I think, seeing you don't know which restaurant he's booking. Yes, definitely smart-casual." Henry nodded to himself. "Nothing tarty, something that makes you look like you have at least a little bit of class, but there again it's probably a bit late for that, isn't it?

"It's definitely too late for that," Melanie agreed. "But dress-wise smart-casual is a good idea."

Cheryl tottered down the road towards Phil's house. She looked around to see if there was anybody about before she walked up the path. She rang the bell. Phil opened the door to let her in.

"I was beginning to wonder where you'd got to," he said.

"Were you worried about me, sweet?" Cheryl smoothed his face with the palm of her hand as she walked in.

"Well it did cross my mind that you were going to stand me up," Phil joked. As soon as the words had come out of his mouth he could have kicked himself. What a stupid thing to say when he was about to give her the elbow.

"Did it now? Well, seeing as I didn't stand you up you can open me one of those." She pointed to the bottle of lager in his hand. "As it happened I had a message left on my answerphone from an old friend of mine. She's managed to wangle the end of this week off and wants to come down to see me. Would it cause a problem if I had Thursday and Friday off?"

"No, I don't think so. I was looking at the diary before I left tonight, it's really busy tomorrow but there's not much in for the end of the week. Mike and I can cover it." Phil took a bottle of lager out of the fridge. "Do you want a glass?"

"The bottle will be just fine, cheers," she said, taking it from him. "In that case, I'll give her a ring later to give her the good news. If she left straight after work she could be at mine for about eight o'clock but that does mean our little rendezvous for tomorrow night will have to be cancelled. To be honest with you, Phil, the old man's back next week and his next job is going to be local enough for him to come home at night, so I think we're going to have to cool it."

Phil couldn't believe his ears. He didn't have to say a thing now. What a stroke of luck. He stood looking at Cheryl and thinking of the right thing to say, something that didn't make him sound relieved. Cheryl took his silence as disappointment. In an instant she had removed her dress, revealing sexy black underwear. Leaving her high heels on, in two steps she was stood directly in front of him.

"We may as well finish with a bang," Cheryl said as she knelt down. "Have you been a naughty boy today?" she asked in her husky voice as she undid his trousers. She pulled them down gently, then forcefully tugged down his boxers. Glancing up at his face she answered her own question. "By the look of things I would say you have been a very naughty boy today. You need to be punished."

Phil opened his mouth to protest. "Cheryl."

"Shut up. Only speak when I say you can," she ordered.

Phil's legs started to tremble ever so slightly with excitement. He looked up at the ceiling. "This is going to be the last time," he muttered to himself.

"I thought I told you to shut up," Cheryl repeated, hearing him mumble.

"Ok," he gasped. "You're in charge."

Beth pulled down her dress. It wasn't quite the way she had planned things. That should have happened after dinner. 'Never mind, it had stopped him saying whatever it was that he was going to say,' she thought, then asked, "Can you help get dinner out the bag, please? It's probably got a bit cold by now."

"Sure," Tom replied. 'Shit,' he thought, 'why had he let that happen? It was because she looked so hot in that dress. But looking hot didn't change personalities, did it? How could he say he had decided to end things now, two minutes after they had made love? Had sex,' he corrected himself. It had just been sex but he had made it a lot more difficult for himself.

"I think we should help ourselves from here, don't you? said Beth, putting two plates down. "I was going to put everything in serving dishes but we would definitely have to reheat it then."

"Fine by me." Tom nodded, and thought, 'It must have cost Beth a small fortune to have a special delivery made.' He piled his plate high, then plonked himself on one of the bar stools before digging in.

Beth put the usual miniscule amount on her plate before pouring herself another glass of wine. "Do you want another drink?" she asked.

"I'll get myself some water, you sit down. It's good." He indicated to his food as he got up to get his drink.

Beth hoisted herself up onto the other stool. She tasted a forkful. It was good, but to stay the size six she liked to be she could only afford to have a few mouthfuls. She watched Tom clear his plate within minutes, then heap on a second helping.

"Aren't you going to eat yours?" Tom asked, knowing full well she wouldn't. She virtually lived on fresh air. Going out for a meal with her was far from enjoyable. She ordered every course but never ate it; she just moved the food around her plate while watching him eat, which was what she was doing now.

"I had quite a big lunch," she lied.

Tom put his knife and fork down, and looked at her.

"Do you want some more?" Beth asked.

"No, thanks, two helpings was enough."

Beth put her fork down. As she reached for Tom's plate he put his hand on her arm.

"Beth, about us," he said gently. "I really think it would be …" Before he could finish Beth removed her arm, putting up her hand to stop him talking.

"Not now, Tom. I really don't want to talk about us tonight. I haven't had a chance to tell you yet but I've booked a fortnight in Spain with Rebecca. Not that I have to tell you anything now, seeing as we are officially on a trial separation, but there again, who has passionate sex when they're separated?" Beth said to Tom, and to herself. 'A little reminder of what they had just done wouldn't do him any harm.' She then continued to Tom, "I thought if I could just relax at a spa it would give me a chance to think about everything before I start living at Daddy's again." She slipped off the barstool, picked up their plates and turned her back on him to load the dishwasher.

Tom let out a sigh. 'Relax at a spa to think about things. She spent most of every day relaxing in some way or another,' he thought. All of a sudden he felt tired. He didn't have the heart or the energy to pursue the conversation further. She had a fair point. Sensible people did not have sex when they were on a trial separation. He was going to be really busy in the next few weeks, so he would just leave things as they were. He would still be flying up here at least once a week. When Beth got back from Spain they would have this conversation then.

Beth walked back over to him. She put her hand over his. This time it was Tom who removed his hand as he stood up.

"I should be going. I have a really early flight in the morning. I think everything's been covered regarding the flat, but if anything does crop up it's best to call me on my mobile." He stood looking at her.

"Fine." She purposefully put her little-girl-lost pose to good use.

He half smiled at her. "Thanks for dinner."

"I'm glad you enjoyed it. Don't I get a kiss goodbye?" Beth pouted.

Tom kissed her cheek.

As soon as she had shut the door behind him she kicked off her shoes. They had been killing her feet. Things had definitely not gone to plan. They should have been making mad passionate love now, but here she was on her own. 'Damn,' she thought, stomping back into the kitchen. She snatched up her glass of wine. 'Well, the good news was that he had not been able to resist her earlier, that was in her favour, and he did have an awful lot on his mind business-wise. All was not lost,' she decided as she downed what was left in her glass. She poured herself another. 'She would just

95

have to think things through carefully and work out another little plan.'

Phil led Cheryl out of the kitchen. "It's my turn to be in charge now," he said as he pushed her into the lounge. "Bend over that chair, bitch."

Cheryl bent over the chair slowly. As she did so she pushed out her bottom seductively, wiggling it slowly while looking over her shoulder. 'She really was a dirty bitch,' thought Phil as he came up behind her. She liked it rough. He put one hand on the back of her neck, pushing her head down to meet the back of the chair. 'She was going to get it rough as well,' he thought as he slapped her hard on the bottom.

"Oh yes, baby," Cheryl shouted.

Phil slapped her again.

"Oh yes, baby, yes," she shouted louder. "Tell me I've been a bad girl. Tell Cheryl she is going to get another smack."

Tom had no sooner let himself in than Yasmin appeared. "Where have you been?"

"I had to pop over to the flat to meet with the letting agent," he answered.

"Oh, right. I've left you some dinner. Do you want me to put it in the microwave?"

"Sorry, Yas, but I've eaten," he said humbly.

"Not with Beth?" she fired at him.

"Yes, with Beth. She ordered in a meal from Lou Lou's." he replied and thought, 'Here we go,'

"Lou Lou's?" Yasmin almost shouted at him. "They don't do take out. That must have cost the earth. I tell you,

96

Tom, she's up to something. Scheming cow. I thought things were over between you."

"We're on a trial separation," Tom corrected her. The look she gave him was enough to turn him to stone. The difficult people he dealt with on a daily basis were easy compared to one look from his sister. "To be honest, I was going to end things tonight but it was kind of difficult."

"What do you mean, it was kind of difficult? Since when have you found it difficult to be honest?" Yasmin demanded, jabbing a finger at him. "Oh, I get it, you slept with her, didn't you? You idiot, I bet she planned everything and you fell for it. Typical man, weak when it comes to the penis, weak when it's handed to him on a plate."

"Have you finished yet?" Tom mimicked the way his sister had started to hop from foot to foot, the madder she was getting with him. "It's good to know I can always count on your full-support-no-questions-asked policy."

"Well, you know I've never liked her." Yasmin stood still. "She's an evil, self-centred, stuck-up bitch. You've been happier in the last few weeks than you have been in months, Tom, and that's because you haven't been with her."

"Say it as it is." Tom grinned at his sister as he folded his arms. "Any chance of a cuppa?"

Yasmin laughed as she reached for the kettle. "Sorry, Tom, I know it's none of my business but you two are just not suited."

"I love the way you admit it's none of your business then go on to make further comment," Tom said.

"I'm your sister, I can go on and make further comment if I so wish." She grinned.

"You can, indeed, not that I could stop you anyway." He grinned back at her.

"She doesn't make you happy, Tom." Yasmin said, shaking her head slowly, a sad expression replacing her grin.

"I know," Tom agreed solemnly. "You're right, we aren't suited. I should have told her tonight but, hands up, I had a weak moment. I admit, I thought with what's in my boxers instead of my brain. She's off to Spain for a couple of weeks. As soon as she's back I'm going to tell her. Can we leave it now?" Tom put his hand up. "Please."

"We can. Here's your tea," Yasmin said, handing him a steaming mug. "But you're going to have to eat that dinner tomorrow." She smirked.

It was dark as Cheryl walked to her car. She felt tired and, she hated to admit it, a bit stiff. 'Not surprising,' she thought, 'they had been at it like rabbits, wild rabbits. There had been nothing tame about what they had been doing.'

Phil slumped on the sofa. God, he felt knackered. No wonder Cheryl's husband chose to work away a lot, she probably wore the poor bloke out. She hadn't been lying when she said they would finish their fling with a bang – he felt like he'd been exploded. A wave of guilt flooded over him. Amber. He hadn't been able to stop himself when Cheryl had sunk to her knees. He pushed the guilt to one side as he told himself it had been the last time. It was over now, wasn't it? He was no longer being unfaithful.

CHAPTER 5

Amber stretched out to turn off her alarm. She could have another five minutes, seeing as she had made her packed lunch the night before, together with a list of ingredients she needed to pick up. Her five minutes, however, stretched into 15. Throwing back the covers she hopped out of bed. If she quickly made a cup of tea now it would be just the right temperature to drink once she'd finish showering. In the kitchen, as she waited for the kettle to boil, she took a look down her pyjama bottoms to check out her bikini line. 'Thank heaven for that,' she thought, sighing with relief. The redness from the night before had vanished, in fact, she had to admit that it looked rather neat and tidy.

Melanie's bedroom door opened. Henry marched in, carrying two mugs in one hand. He started to sing at the top of his voice.

"Morning has broken, like the first morning, blackbird has spoken, like the first bird."

"Shut the fuck up, Henry." Melanie's voice cut him off from beneath her quilt before he had a chance to sing another word.

"Charming, you old tart, especially as I've brought you up a coffee." He laughed. "Now, move over and let me get in."

Hearing the word coffee Melanie gradually got herself up to a sitting position, shuffling over to make room for him. Passing her the coffees to hold he got in beside her. They sat sipping their drinks.

"Mmm, lovely. Cheers, Henry," Melanie said, mustering her first smile of the day.

"You're welcome, flower." Henry replied. "You're such a miserable bitch first thing."

"I know I am," Melanie agreed. "But you're far too happy first thing."

"Darling, I'm happy all the time," Henry retorted. "Are you in or out tonight?"

"I'm not sure." She shrugged. "I thought I'd offer to give Amber a hand if she needed it, you know, in preparation for her romantic dinner *pour deux* tomorrow night. So it really depends on if she wants help or not."

"What romantic dinner?" Henry asked.

"Henry," Melanie elbowed him, "I've told you already. She's celebrating her first-year anniversary with Phil."

"Oh, yes, that's right. Can't say I'm overly keen on him really, bit too full of himself, if you ask me. Whoops, I mustn't be a bitch." He elbowed Melanie back. "He's alright really. He's probably like he is because he's an estate agent."

"Yeah, well, between you and me I'm not overly keen either, Hennie, but Amber is smitten." For a moment she considered again whether to tell him what she'd seen in the car park the night before. 'No, better not, Jess would kill her if she found out,' she decided and changed the subject. "Aren't you going to be late for work?"

"I've got a late start today and that's why I bought my favourite girlfriend coffee in bed." He gave her a kiss on the cheek.

"You don't want to make your favourite girlfriend another cup while she gets ready, do you?" Melanie asked, giving him a kiss back.

"You do take the piss, but because I love you so much, give us your empty," he said, holding out his hand for her mug.

Melanie plonked the mug in it. "Ta, Hennie. If Amber doesn't need any help after work I promise to cook you a lovely dinner tonight." She beamed at him before jumping out of bed and skipping off to the bathroom.

"It's your bloody turn anyway, you witch," Henry shouted after her.

Tom's flight had left on time. He sat with the papers for the meeting that his secretary had prepared for him on his lap. He would read through them again, just in case he had missed anything. He glanced around the plane. He watched the air hostess serving drinks to the people sitting opposite him. The way she was working he'd be offered a drink next. He wasn't wrong. Turning round she smiled at him politely.

"Would you like a coffee or tea, sir?" she asked him.

"Tea, please." He smiled at her.

"There we go," she said as she handed it to him.

"Thank you." Tom took it from her. Settling back in his seat he started to read.

Amber took Mr L's tea into his office. He was already busy spreading out huge sheets of paper on his desk.

"I'll put your tea over here," she said brightly as she placed the tray on a narrow table just under the window.

"Thank you." Mr L smiled over at her.

"That lot looks interesting," Amber said, pointing at his desk.

"It's just a couple of the many plans for the new site. Come on over, I'll talk you through them."

Amber poured his tea and carried it over. "Wow, it's amazing to think that these drawings will eventually be a reality, isn't it?" she said, looking at the plans.

"Yes, I suppose it is." While drinking his tea he began pointing out different things on the plans, taking time to explain so that she could understand. Amber found herself being carried along with his enthusiasm. It was all so interesting. She asked one question after another.

Following a knock, the office door opened. In came Dorothy. "Good morning, Mr Lockyard. Good morning, Amber."

"Oh my God, is that the time?" Amber put her hand over her mouth. "I'd better get back to the desk. Hope I haven't held you up with all my questions?" She looked at Mr L apologetically.

"Not at all." He liked the way she had seemed genuinely interested. "I think the desk will have survived without you for a while."

Amber made for the door.

"Amber, just a moment." Mr L stopped her leaving. "There will be times when I need someone to drop bits and pieces to the site. How would you feel if I allocated that job to you? It would give you a chance to see things develop."

"That would be brilliant. I'd love the chance to see it at different stages while it's being built. Thank you." She left the office and hurried back to the desk. The others would be in at any minute and she hadn't done a thing yet.

She was just finishing sorting the post as Vicky and Melanie arrived. "Hi, you two," she said brightly. "I'm a bit behind this morning, too busy chatting."

"Chatting? You? There's a surprise," teased Melanie. "What needs doing?"

"I haven't sorted the faxes yet." Amber smiled.

"No problem, I'll do it. Vick, stick the kettle on," Melanie said, throwing down her bag.

"I know my place," laughed Vicky.

"Guess who has a date tomorrow night?" Melanie stood, pointing to herself.

"He called you then," Vicky said excitedly.

"Not exactly. When I got home last night there was a big bunch of flowers waiting for me with a note on it asking if I fancied dinner Thursday night, with him for pudding," Melanie said as she rotated her hips rudely.

The girls burst out laughing.

"Looks like you've met your match with this one. Where are you going?" Amber asked.

"I don't know. I called to thank him for the flowers and accept his kind invitation, like one does," she said, putting on a posh voice. "He asked if I liked Italian, to which I replied 'yes'. So all I know is that it's going to be an Italian."

"It's all happening tomorrow night, isn't it?" Vicky said. "A hot date at an Italian for you and a romantic meal for Amber."

"Talking of which, do you need a hand with anything tonight, Amber?" Melanie asked.

103

"No, I don't think so." Amber shook her head. "I think I have everything under control. All I have to do tonight is make the cheesecake."

"In that case I'll quickly phone Henry to tell him I'm cooking. I owe him, big time. We're meant to take it in turns to cook if we're both in, but he usually ends up doing it. Bless him," Melanie said.

"You have the best housemate in the world with Henry," Amber said. "He spoils you."

"I know," Melanie said as she dialled his number.

"Hello," Henry answered.

"Henry, it's me," Melanie said.

"I know it's you. What's up, flower?" he asked.

"Nothing, just calling to say I'm definitely cooking tonight. Do you fancy steak?" she asked him.

"Steak, yum. Can we have cream and peppercorn sauce to go over it?" he asked.

"Course we can. I'll get one of those sticky toffee puds for afters," Melanie said.

"Oh my God. My waistline is going to take a battering, but, what the hell, I'll just have to do extra crunches at the gym. I'll get us a chick-flick on the way home. We'll have a real girlie night. Can't wait, see you later, sweetness," he said, all excitedly.

As Tom walked through arrivals he checked his watch. He had plenty of time, so he may as well swing by the office. It would give him a chance to say hello to a few people without any fuss, plus it wouldn't do any harm to have a quick catch up with Francis before they had the site meeting. His hire car was all ready for him. 'Let's hope the meeting will be as hassle free as his morning's travelling had been,' he thought. He got into the car and headed towards Bath.

Dorothy sealed the package and then double checked the address before she popped her head round Mr Lockyard's office door.

"I'm going to ask one of the girls to take this to the post office, can I bring you back a cup of coffee?" she asked him.

"Yes, please, Dorothy," Mr Lockyard answered.

Twitching her lips and pushing her glasses back into position on her nose Dorothy walked as if on a mission towards the desk. As she approached she could see the girls. Melanie was on switchboard, Vicky signing in a visitor and Amber busy on the computer. She watched the visitor take a seat.

"Dorothy, what can we do for you?" Vicky smiled.

"I'd like this package to go in the lunchtime post, would one of you take it to the Post Office, please?" Dorothy asked.

"Sure, no problem," Vicky said, taking the package from her.

"Thank you," Dorothy said. She turned to go back to her office, stopping at the coffee machine to get Mr Lockyard his cup of coffee.

"Who fancies a walk then?" Vicky asked the girls.

"I'll go," Amber volunteered. "I need to get a couple of things from the supermarket for tomorrow night. I can nip in and get them on the way back."

"Bring us back some sweets," Melanie said, just before she answered another call.

"Ok," Amber mouthed at her as she picked up the package. 'This was a bit of luck,' she thought as she walked out into the sunshine, 'it would save her stopping on her way home tonight.'

Tom drove into the office car park. Passing the spaces marked 'reserved for management' he parked in the main area. He admired the grounds as he strode towards the main entrance, laptop and briefcase in hand.

Melanie sat waiting for the next call. She caught sight of Tom heading towards the building.

"Vick, quick, take a look at that," she said, nodding towards Tom approaching.

Vicky looked up. "Ooh, not bad, not bad at all. I'll deal with him."

As Tom entered the building he was met by Melanie and Vicky. They were beaming at him like a pair of Cheshire cats.

He beamed back at them. "Morning, ladies," he said as he came to a standstill in front of the desk.

"Good morning," they both replied.

"How can I help you?" Vicky asked.

"I'm Tom Tranter from the Scottish office," Tom introduced himself. "Can you let Francis Lockyard know I'm here, please?"

"Certainly, Mr Tranter. Is he expecting you?" Vicky asked, recognising his name.

"Afraid not. I'm early so I thought I'd drop by to say hello to a few people," he answered.

Vicky dialled Dorothy's number on the internal phone. "Dorothy, it's Vicky. Mr Tranter is in reception for Mr Lockyard."

"Thank you," Dorothy replied. She buzzed Mr Lockyard. "Mr Lockyard, Tom Tranter is in reception."

"Is he? I'll be right out," he replied, thinking as he got up from his desk, 'Typical Tom, turning up unannounced.'

"So, you are Vicky," Tom said as he stretched out his hand towards Vicky once she'd finished speaking to Dorothy.

"Yes." Vicky looked puzzled.

"You said your name on the phone," Tom said, reading her mind. And you are?" he asked, turning towards Melanie.

"I'm Melanie, Mr Tranter," she said, shaking his hand. "I believe you are going to be with us on a permanent basis?"

"That's right, although I'll still be going back up to Scotland regularly. Is it just the two of you on the desk?" he asked them.

"No, there's Amber's as well. She's just popped to the Post Office," Melanie replied.

"So, which one of you ladies do I usually get first thing in the morning when I call?" Tom continued to make conversation.

"That will be Amber, she starts at eight," Vicky answered him.

"Tom." Mr Lockyard's voice made them all look round. "What are you doing here?"

"I was just telling Vicky and Melanie I was early so I thought I'd drop in and introduce myself to a few people," Tom said.

"I see you've started with the most important ones." He indicated towards the girls with his hand and a twinkle in his eye.

"Without doubt," Tom agreed, smiling at the girls. "See you later."

"See you later, Mr Tranter," they both replied.

"Call me Tom," he said as he followed Mr Lockyard.

"Very nice," Vicky whispered as they watched him go.

"Very nice, indeed," Melanie whispered back, nodding her head.

As Mr Lockyard and Tom entered Dorothy's office she looked up. "Good morning, Mr Tranter. I trust you had a good journey down?"

"Not bad at all. How are you?" Tom asked.

"Very well, thank you. Let me get you something to drink," she said, standing up.

"Coffee would be good," he said, following Francis Lockyard into his office.

Amber stood in the Post Office queue. 'I'm going to be here for ages,' she thought, 'better let the girls know.'

"Lockyards, how may I help you?" Melanie's voice answered the phone.

"Mel, it's only me. The queue in the Post Office is horrendous. I'm going to be ages," Amber explained.

"No problem, but you're going to be pig-sick when I tell you Tom Tranter's here and he is bloody lovely," Melanie exclaimed.

"What's he doing there?" Amber asked.

"Called in to say hello before the site meeting. Of course, Vick and I are on first-name terms with him already," she joked. The switch started to beep. "Am, I've got to go, got another call coming in. Don't forget our sweets."

The queue was just not moving. He wouldn't be there long as the site meeting was at 11am. by the time she got back he would have left. 'Never mind,' she thought, 'she would meet him soon enough. She would phone Phil while she waited.'

"Hunter Estate Agents," Cheryl answered the phone.

"Hello, can I speak to Phil, please? It's Amber," she said brightly.

"I'll put you through." Cheryl replied. "Phil, it's your young lady," she said as she transferred the call.

Phil picked up his phone. "Hi, Amber? What's happening?"

"I'm stood in a queue at the Post Office that's refusing to move so I thought I'd call to say hello," she said.

"Aren't you at work?" he asked.

"Yes, I'm on an errand for Dorothy. What did you get up to last night?" she asked him.

"Not a lot. Stayed in. Just watched a bit of television," He replied, justifying his answer to himself, Well, he had stayed in and had watched television after Cheryl had left. He looked over at her. She was listening to everything he said. "Do you want to go out somewhere tonight?"

"No, I'm going to be busy making the dessert for tomorrow," she said.

"I could come and help you," he offered.

"No. I want it to be a surprise for you. Just make sure you have no late appointment tomorrow night, or else." She laughed. "I want you here at 7.30 sharp."

"I'll be there, 7.30 sharp." He put down the phone.

"7.30 sharp." Mike had tuned in on the end of Phil's conversation.

"Order from Amber. We've been together a year tomorrow. She's cooking a special meal to celebrate and I'm not allowed to be late. Flowers, I need to order some flowers," Phil reminded himself.

"Flowers. Definitely a good idea." Mike nodded his head.

"My old man asked me to marry him a year after we met," Cheryl joined in.

"Actually, I asked my wife to marry me after a year, as well," Mike said.

"A proposal's not out of the question. I have been thinking about it. Perhaps it's the year thing," Phil said.

"Well, I'm sure she wouldn't say no to someone as charming and loyal as you." Cheryl smiled demurely.

"Here, here," Mike agreed.

Phil felt himself blush slightly.

"Phil, that's the first time I've seen you remotely embarrassed. It must be love." Mike let out a laugh as he looked at his watch. "It's time I wasn't here. I've got a valuation in 20 minutes." He grabbed his briefcase. "Don't forget to order the flowers or she may say no," he said as he left the office.

Phil looked over at Cheryl. "That remark about me being loyal was a bit below the belt."

"Just a joke. What's happened to your sense of humour?" Cheryl laughed as she got up. She walked over to his desk and perched herself on the edge, close to where he was sitting, her breasts directly in his line of vision. She watched as he ran his eyes over her cleavage, then lifted his head to look at her. "You're being over–sensitive, tiger."

"Yeah, you're probably right. Guilt, I suppose." Phil sighed.

"Course it is. After all, you have been shagging me behind her back. You'll get over the guilt, that is, until the next time." She gave him a look as she got up from his desk. "I'll make us a coffee."

"Very funny. I'm on the straight and narrow from now on. One girl and one girl only." Phil made a face back at her.

"Course you are." She laughed.

"I think we've covered everything," Tom said. "We'd better make tracks."

"Do you want a ride with me?" Mr Lockyard asked.

"No thanks, Francis. I'm viewing some properties before I fly back. I'll follow you down," Tom replied.

"Let's go then," Mr Lockyard said.

They went through to Dorothy's office.

"We're off now, Dorothy," Mr Lockyard said.

Dorothy nodded, her mouth twitching to a smile. "I do hope the site meeting goes well." She turned to Tom. "Mr Tranter, I wasn't sure how well you know the area so I took the liberty of doing an AA route planner so you could find the estate agents without any trouble." She handed it to him. "I wasn't sure if you had satellite navigation in your hire car."

"Thanks, Dorothy. That was very thoughtful," he said, taking it.

"Not at all, Mr Tranter," Dorothy replied. "I'm glad to be of assistance."

They stopped at reception on the way out.

"We're off now, girls. Any problems, let Dorothy know," Mr Lockyard said.

"Okay, Mr Lockyard," Melanie replied.

"Bye, ladies." Tom gave them an impish smile.

"Bye, Tom," they chorused back.

"I'd become a PA if I could work for someone who looked like him," Vicky swooned as soon as they were out of earshot.

"I wonder how big his penis is when it's erect?" Melanie said with a straight face.

"Melanie, you are awful," Vicky said, killing herself laughing.

"What?" Melanie still kept her face poker-straight.

Amber arrived back to find Vicky still laughing. "What's going on?"

Vicky filled her in on what she'd missed while she had been out, finishing off with Melanie's comment about Tom's private anatomy.

"Melanie, you really are a sick individual," Amber said, shaking her head.

Melanie laughed. "Didn't you see him with Mr L in the car park as you came in? They only left a few minutes ago."

"I came through the slip way, must have just missed them," Amber said. "The rumours are right about him being really good-looking then?"

"Not half, even you won't be able to stop your eyes wandering down towards the bulge in his trousers," Melanie hooted.

"Oh, stop it. Have one of these." Amber giggled as she threw a bag of sweets towards Melanie. "They might make you say something sweet and innocent for a change."

Melanie caught the bag. "Jelly babies, my favourite. Cheers, Am, but I bet you anything you won't have innocent thoughts when you meet him," she said, opening the bag and taking out a sweet. She passed the bag to Vicky. "Will she, Vic?"

"I hate to have to agree with Mel when she's being smutty, but he is sexy. Come to think of it, you and him would go well together. He's tall, dark and handsome, and you are tall, dark and pretty," Vicky said, helping herself to a jelly baby.

"Yeah, Vic's right. I have a plan. You play up to him, then once you start shagging him you could get us a pay rise." Melanie clapped her hands together in mock excitement. "What do you think?"

"I think you really must stop reading those magazines," Amber said, giving Melanie a playful push. "Have you both forgotten I'm in a serious relationship and I'm not that kind of girl?"

"As I said, you might change your mind when you see him." Melanie smirked.

"I'd better be on my way," Tom said to Francis Lockyard. "I've got to be at Hunter's Estate Agents at three o'clock."

The two men stood up to shake hands.

"I think we can say the morning has been a success. The site meeting went well, everybody seems happy. I can't see any reason for not getting things under way on time. It will be good to have you down here," Francis said. "Good luck with the viewings. Just let Dorothy know if you need her to arrange anything else for you."

"Will do," Tom said.

He walked through the pub, thanking the bar staff on his way out. In the car he had a look at the map Dorothy had printed off for him. After studying it for a few moments he set off. He added another item to his mental list, a PA. Dorothy had kindly said she'd work for him as well as for Francis for a while, but once Francis reduced his hours she

113

would be doing the same. Still, he had a few months to settle in before he had to sort that out. Hopefully there would be someone internally who would be suitable. He would find out once he got to know everybody.

As he drove he admired his surroundings. Bath really was a beautiful city. He would have the best of both worlds living here but also having to spend time at the Scottish office on a regular basis, which would enable him to see his family and keep in touch with friends. The traffic would take some getting used to. 'It was diabolical,' he thought as he sat waiting for the umpteenth red traffic light to go green. Glancing at his map again told him he was almost at his destination. With the lights changing to green he took the next left. As he drove down the road he spotted Hunter's Estate Agents on the right. After finding a place to park it took him a matter of minutes to walk back.

Entering through the door he was met by Cheryl and her cleavage. 'Christ,' he thought, 'her top's a bit low for the office.'

"Good afternoon, sir. What can I do for you?" Cheryl asked, while thinking she knew what she would like to do for him.

"Hello, my name's Tom Tranter, I have some viewings booked to look at some rental properties," he answered. "I am a little early."

"That's ok, my colleague Phil will be doing the viewings with you. He's just popped to the florist. He'll be back shortly. Can I get you a tea or coffee while you wait?" Cheryl offered, wishing she was the one doing the viewings.

"No, thank you," replied Tom, taking a seat.

Cheryl got up from her desk and went to the filing cabinets. Tom watched as she bent down to open the bottom drawer. Flicking through quickly with her fingers she extracted the details of the three properties he was viewing. Walking over to where Tom was sitting she bent forward slightly to hand him the sheets of paper, making sure he had what she liked to call a bird's-eye view of her puppies.

"Here we go. These are the properties you'll be looking at this afternoon. You're going to find it quite difficult to choose between them," She said, thinking, 'Sell, sell and sell' before continuing, "As you can see they are all quite lovely."

"Thanks," Tom said politely, looking at Cheryl before he looked at the details. He wouldn't want to meet her on a dark night. She looked the type that would eat you alive. She was right about the properties though, they all looked good. He scanned through the details. Yes, they all just about fitted his criteria. Still, he would wait and see. Estate agents had the knack of taking extremely good photographs of properties, making them look as though they were in an ideal spot with panoramic views, while somehow managing to exclude the factory at the end of the garden!

"Do you want to write the card now or take one with you to do later?" the florist asked Phil.

"I'll do it now," Phil said.

"Just choose one from the front here," she said, indicating to where the cards were displayed by the side of the till. "I'm afraid the choice is a bit limited, we're waiting for a delivery."

"I see what you mean," Phil agreed as he looked at the cards. He picked one with flowers on it. 'How original,' he thought to himself. He wrote 'love Phil' on it with three kisses underneath. Pushing it in the envelope he put Amber's name on the front and gave it to the florist.

"They will be ready for you at three o'clock tomorrow afternoon," she said, taking the card.

Phil walked back to the office. As he passed the window he could see a man sat looking at details. He checked his watch, 2.50pm, the man could be his 3pm. He straightened his tie before entering.

Hearing the door open Cheryl looked towards it as Phil entered. "Here we are, Mr Tranter, this is Phil who will be showing you around today."

"Hello, Mr Tranter," Phil greeted him. "I've been told you have limited time, so if you have no objection it would be easier if you came with me. That way I can tell you about each property and answer any questions that you may have about them."

"Sounds good to me," Tom said, quite happy to be driven. It would give him a chance to take in more of the surroundings.

"Great. I've already got the keys out, so if you're ready?" Phil said, putting his arm out, indicating for Tom to go ahead of him. He picked the keys up from his desk.

Tom waited by the door as Phil stopped at his colleague's desk.

"Cheryl, you'll probably be gone by the time I get back so have a good couple of days off and enjoy the weekend. See you Monday," he said.

"Thanks, you too." She moved slightly so Phil was obstructing Tom's view of her from where he was stood. She lowered her voice to a whisper, "I'll think of you while I play with myself tonight." She raised it again and said, all jokily, "Hope the last supper goes well. I mean, the anniversary dinner."

'God, I hope she gets tired of making dirty remarks soon,' thought Phil, 'but what could he say after what they had got up to? Best to just ride it out.' "I'm sure it will," he answered with a smile as he turned towards Tom, who had obviously heard Cheryl's pun regarding dinner as he was smiling.

"My colleague has a very wicked sense of humour," he said to Tom as they left the office. "The girlfriend's cooking tomorrow night. We've been together a year." He felt obliged to explain Cheryl's joke.

"Hence the flowers," Tom said, watching a look of surprise spread over Phil's face. "Your colleague mentioned you were ordering flowers when I arrived earlier."

"Oh, I see. Got to keep the little woman happy." Phil laughed.

'Typical estate agent, full of himself,' thought Tom as they got in the car, but he nodded over at Phil, to be polite.

"I thought I'd show you the cottage in Bathampton first. It ticks all the boxes – village, quick and easy access to the centre of Bath, popular pub by the river, and a cycle track that takes you all the way into Bradford-on-Avon which is also used by walkers and joggers," Phil told Tom enthusiastically.

Gloria walked along the path. Underneath her tabard she wore a tent-style dress, which was the brightest of blue with yellow sunflowers on it. She had a matching turban on her head with Dame-Edna-style dark sunglasses covering her eyes. As she walked in the girls looked up. Melanie let out a wolf whistle.

"Get you, Gloria. You look like a wag," she said playfully.

"I sure ain't no size zero." Gloria said, laughing while waddling up to the desk. "And I ain't never going to be one eating these all the time." She took three barley-sugar sweets from her tabard pocket and placed them on the desk for the girls. "What's been happening?"

"Loads," answered Melanie.

"Well, tell me girl," Gloria said, taking her sunglasses off and waggling them at Melanie.

Melanie told her of Tom Tranter's visit, then of her pending date with Gary.

"My Lord above. Never a dull moment with you girlies, is there? All this excitement." Gloria said, doing a spin in slow motion.

The girls laughed.

"You like my move? I been practising for the office party, hehehe." Gloria put her hands on her hips.

"You are going to knock them dead," Melanie said.

"You'll put my dancing to shame." Amber smiled.

Mike Hunter stood up, putting his briefcase on the desk. He opened it up to check he had everything he needed.

"You off for your five o'clock valuation?" Cheryl asked him.

"Yes. Enjoy your few days off. Doing anything special?" he asked.

"I have an old friend coming down to stay. I've decided to treat her to the Bath Spa tomorrow, then show her the sights on Friday, then maybe a country pub for lunch on Saturday before she heads home," she answered.

"Very nice, enjoy, see you Monday," Mike said as he left.

Cheryl picked up her mobile. She would quickly text Jane to make sure she had packed her swimming costume. After doing that she tidied her desk. Looking at the clock again she was glad to see it was time to close up. She would pop into Sainsbury's on the way home to pick up one of those Dine-for-£10 meals. That would give her plenty of time to make up the spare bed and tidy round.

Having finished showing Tom the third and final property Phil drove back towards the office. "Do you think any of the properties are suitable?" he asked.

"The first one could be of interest. The location is good, it's about halfway between the office and the site I'll be working on," Tom replied.

"Oh, which site is that?" Phil asked.

"Lansdown," Tom replied.

"Oh, the new complex. You must work for Lockyards then. My girlfriend Amber works there on reception," Phil said. "Small world, isn't it?"

"Yes," Tom agreed. 'That's the second time today Amber had been mentioned in conversation,' he thought, 'once by the girls on reception when he had asked who he spoke to early in the morning, and now.' He looked again at the details of the cottage in Bathampton. He'd had enough of Phil and didn't want to get into further conversation with him. He had to admit, he seemed to know everything regarding the properties he was letting, but otherwise he found him to be a bit of a jerk.

Phil turned into the office car park. Seeing as the others had left for the night he didn't bother to reverse back into a space, but just stopped the car diagonally in the centre of the tarmac. The two men got out. Phil walked round the car, stopping in front of Tom.

119

"I appreciate you have other properties to view now, so I'll give you a ring tomorrow. If you want to look at the cottage in Bathampton again, or have any other questions I would be happy to oblige." He extended his hand towards Tom. Tom shook it. "Thank you."

Back in the car Tom checked the map before setting off for his next lot of viewings.

CHAPTER 6

'This place is a bloody nightmare,' thought Melanie as she sat in her car, queuing to get into Sainsbury's car park. She watched people leave the store, wheeling their trolleys, laden with carrier bags full of groceries, towards their cars, and people who had just arrived getting themselves a trolley to start their shopping. It would be her turn soon to fight for a space. 'May as well put a bit of lippie on while I'm waiting,' she thought. She adjusted her rear view mirror so she could see herself in it. Taking her lip pencil out of her makeup bag she expertly drew a line just outside the natural edge of her lips to make her mouth appear fuller. Popping the pencil back she pulled out her lipstick and proceeded to apply it within the lip liner. "Looking good, if I say so myself," she said out loud. Turning her attention back to driving she realised the car in front of her had moved into the car park. 'Thank God for that. I thought I'd be here all night,' she thought as she followed suit.

With eyes like hawks she looked up and down the rows of cars. As soon as one began to move out of a space there was one waiting to go in it. She crawled down the first row, nothing; on she went into the second row. Spotting a couple getting into a car she edged up, and as they pulled out she put her foot down, shooting into the space. Hearing the blare of a horn she looked to see a bald-headed man pointing his finger at her. She got out of her car. He wound down his window and poked his head out.

"Are you blind, young lady? I was sat here waiting for that space," he shouted over at her.

"You should have been a bit quicker then," Melanie shouted back as she began walking towards the store.

"Well, really, how rude you are," he shouted even louder.

Melanie put her hand up without turning round and continued walking. 'Whoops, she hadn't actually noticed him waiting, but, tough, there was no way she was going to get back in her car and give up the space now,' she thought. Entering the store she picked up a basket and headed straight to the meat counter. Pulling a ticket from the machine she waited for her number to be called.

"80," called the butcher.

"That's me." Melanie waved her ticket.

"What can I get you, my lovely?" he asked.

"Two rump steaks, please." Melanie smiled. "Can I have two that haven't got much fat on?"

"Course you can, though you could be doing with a bit of fat on those bones," the butcher joked. "Will these do you?" he asked, holding up two steaks for Melanie to look at.

"They will do just fine, thanks." Melanie nodded.

With the steak in basket she wandered up and down the isles merrily picking up a sticky toffee pudding, peppercorns, frozen chips, peas, cream and finally two bottles of wine. As she waited to pay she couldn't believe it, the man whose car space she had nicked was stood at the next checkout. Turning back quickly she busied herself with unloading her basket.

After paying for her shopping she couldn't help but look over again. The man was staring right at her. "Have a nice evening," she said cheekily, giving him an equally as cheeky smile as she headed for the exit, and leaving him stating out loud that some should have had a good hiding as a child.

Amber switched the vacuum cleaner off and started to attack what little furniture she had with Mr Sheen. She polished until everything shone. She so wanted it all to be perfect tomorrow night and that included the flat looking nice.

She went into the kitchen and checked the recipe that Vicky had given her for the blueberry cheesecake. She weighed out the ingredients and stuck the oven on so it would be the correct temperature by the time she had prepared it. Step one, she read: crush biscuits. 'No problem,' she thought, smiling while getting her rolling pin; step two: melt butter; step three: combine biscuit crumbs with butter and press firmly into loose bottom dish. 'Voila, base done.' The next bit was even simpler. All she had to do was put the remaining ingredients into a bowl, blend well then pour on top of the biscuit base and bake for 35 to 40 minutes. 'Vicky had been right, this recipe was dead easy,' She said to herself, completing the topping. In no time at all it was in the oven.

While the cheesecake was baking she went into her bedroom. Taking out her once-worn black dress she hung it on the outside of her wardrobe to let any creases fall out overnight. Next she hunted through her underwear drawers until she came across the also worn-only-once black push-me-up bra. Holding it out in front of her she pressed the gel-filled moulds with her thumbs. 'Goodness, perhaps she was going a bit over the top,' she thought. But none-the-less she tossed it on her bed and continued to hunt for the matching knickers; eventually she found them. Pushing everything back in she closed the drawer, making a mental note that it was about time she sorted that lot out. She probably still had her old gym knickers from school in there somewhere.

Melanie opened a bottle of wine. 'Screw tops were so much easier than corks,' she thought as she poured herself a glass, then put the bottle on the kitchen table with a wine glass ready for Henry. She looked at the clock. He would be home shortly, she might as well get the show on the road. Around 20 minutes later the chips were in the oven, the peas were in the pan ready to go on, the griddle was ready for the steak, the table was laid and the pudding was awaiting execution in the microwave. She heard Henry come in through the front door.

"I'm home, dear." he shouted as if Melanie was his wife. "Where are you?"

Melanie opened the kitchen door. "I'm in here, you silly sod."

"Always a lovely welcome home," he said, planting a kiss on her forehead as he walked past her into the kitchen.

As he did so Melanie pinched his bottom. "Glass of wine, sweetheart?"

"Ooh, matron," Henry tittered. "That would be divine."

Melanie poured him a large glass, then topped up her own. "I'll start doing the steak now," she said, handing him his drink.

"Goodie, I'm starving. Are we having cream and peppercorn sauce like you promised?" asked Henry.

"Yes, and I got the pudding you wanted." Melanie laughed.

"Oh, I love it when you spoil me," Henry said, giving her a hug. "I got us a chick-flick to make it a proper date night. We can watch it after dinner in our pyjamas."

Amber sneaked a peak at the cheesecake. It looked done to her. She opened the oven door wider, and with her gloved hand gave the baking tin a little shake. It seemed firm, just a little wobbly in the middle. She took it out and put it on the top of the cooker to cool down. According to the recipe the middle should set as it cooled. 'Fingers crossed,' she said to herself. The smell made her feel hungry so she put some bread in the toaster, then switched the kettle on.

The doorbell rang. She went to the intercom in the hall.

"Hello," she said into it.

"Hi, Am, its Jess," came the familiar voice of her friend.

"Hi, come on up. You're just in time for tea and toast," she said, pressing the button to allow her friend entry. She opened the door and waited for Jess to come up the stairs.

"Not gate crashing on anything, am I? Those stairs are a killer," Jess panted as she walked up the last few steps. "I was just passing so thought I'd pop in and say hello, seeing as you didn't manage walking last night."

"Don't remind me. That beauty therapist had no mercy, although I have to say I'm pleased with the results, and, as Mel so kindly put it, I now won't look like I've bought knickers with hair attached." Amber laughed as she ushered her friend inside.

"Something smells nice," Jessica said, sniffing the air.

"Cheesecake for tomorrow night," Amber informed her.

In the kitchen Jessica admired the cooling cheesecake as Amber buttered the toast and told her the planned menu for the following night.

"Sounds wonderful. What are you going to wear to woo him, out of your vast walk-in wardrobe?" Jess asked.

"If only," Amber said, rolling her eyes. "Remember the dress Mel made me buy for your hen night?"

"Only too well, and if I remember it correctly Phil won't be looking at the food on his plate." Jess giggled.

Dragging her friend from the kitchen into the bedroom she picked up the black underwear she'd found earlier. Dangling the bra in one hand and the knickers in the other she held them up. "And on Mel's orders I'm wearing these underneath."

Tom relaxed back in his seat. It had been a long day and he still had quite a drive once the aeroplane landed. He closed his eyes, suddenly feeling weary. Six viewings on the trot were enough to tire anyone out, but it had been worth it. The cottage in Bathampton had definitely ticked all the boxes. He would call tomorrow to sort everything out.

Henry lounged back on the sofa, having changed into his pyjamas, with his slipper-clad feet resting on the coffee table. He had put the DVD in the machine and had the remote-control in his hand ready to press play.

"Have you gone to china for that tea, dear heart?" he shouted to Melanie.

"Piss off," came a swift reply.

"I think I could manage just a teensy-weensy bit more of that pudding, now I have my pjss on." He went on stifling a laugh.

A few seconds later Melanie appeared carrying a tray on which sat two steaming mugs of tea and a bowl containing more pudding for Henry.

"Don't come crying to me in the morning when you've put on two pounds," she said, setting it down then flopping down by the side of him.

"And don't you come crying to me. No doubt, you had a few more spoonfuls while you waited for the kettle to boil." Henry smirked at her as he picked up the bowl.

"I'll work mine off tomorrow night." Melanie winked at him.

"Hussy," Henry said, pressing play.

"Crikey, look at the time," Jess said looking at her watch. "We've been rabbit-ting for hours, John will be wondering where I've got to. I only popped in to say hello."

Amber looked at her clock. It was nearly 11pm. Where had the evening gone? It didn't seem two minutes ago that Jess had arrived.

"Popping in to say hello can take all evening with us." Amber smiled at her friend.

"We're such gas-bags," Jessica said as she stood up. "Hope tomorrow night goes well. Give me a ring on Friday to let me know."

"Ok," Amber said as she saw Jessica to the door.

She watched her disappear down the stairs, then quickly closed the door and locked it before going to the window to watch Jessica walk to her car. As usual her friend looked up to give her a wave before getting in.

As Amber got ready for bed she felt so utterly happy. Absolutely nothing could burst her bubble at the moment. She had no family crisis going on, great friends, work was good, and she tingled with excitement as she thought about the following night. She sent Phil a text reminding him, yet again, not to be late.

Phil heard his phone telling him he had a message. Picking it up he read the message from Amber. He replied straight away, promising he wouldn't be late.

Amber read his reply. 'See,' she thought, 'I've a great boyfriend. What more could a girl want?' She got into bed. 'Maybe just a ring on her finger,' she answered herself as she closed her eyes.

CHAPTER 7

"Dorothy Judith alert." Melanie sniggered as she spotted Dorothy making her way towards the desk.

Amber looked up as Dorothy approached. "Hi, Dorothy, what can we do for you?" she asked.

"I have to go out for a while so I've diverted my phone to the switchboard. Can you note down any messages for me, please? I'll deal with them as soon as I get back." Dorothy twitched.

"Of course we will," Amber answered.

"Are you going anywhere exciting?" Melanie enquired.

"I'm afraid not, nosey parker." Dorothy's lips almost made a smile.

The girls giggled at Dorothy's attempt at being funny.

Dorothy's lips twitched again, this time reaching a smile as she said goodbye.

"Bloody hell. Has she been drinking? A bit of a joke and a smile within a few seconds of each other," Melanie said as soon as Dorothy was out of earshot.

"You're her favourite now you're gardening buddies." Vicky laughed.

"For your information," Melanie pointed at Vicky, "I have actually looked through those books, and, believe it or not, I'm tempted to buy a couple of big pots for the back. Henry's dead keen on the idea."

"Get away," Vicky said with a surprised look on her face.

"Seriously." Melanie nodded. "I'm going to turn all green-fingered outside the house, and into a domestic goddess inside."

"In that case, you won't have time to be a sex goddess," teased Vicky.

"Of course I will. I don't have to try to be one of those," Melanie said, jutting out her chest and shaking her shoulders to make her boobs wobble.

Tom chewed the top of his pen while he waited for Hunter's Estate Agents to answer. It took them three rings.

"Hunter's Estate Agents, Phil speaking," came the reply.

"Phil, it's Tom Tranter. You showed me round some properties yesterday."

"Hello there. You beat me to it, I was just about to call you," Phil said. "I know you were quite interested in the cottage in Bathampton, how did it compare to the properties you viewed through Wicks?"

"It came out on top so I'd like to go ahead, please," Tom replied.

"Great. As you know, the property's empty so you can pretty much have it as soon as the legalities are done." Phil delivered the good news while thinking, 'Another happy landlord and more commission in his pocket.'

Tom looked at his diary. He needed to arrange a flight down a week tomorrow for the office party. He had planned to stay in a hotel that night, so he could pick the keys up the following day. It would give him the weekend to settle in and sort himself out. "Any chance things could be sorted for me to pick up the keys a week Saturday?"

"I don't see why not," Phil replied.

"Good. Now, if you don't mind I'll put you through to my secretary. If you tell her exactly what is needed she will see it's done. Thank you," Tom said. He buzzed his secretary.

She answered immediately. "Yes, Tom?"

"I have Hunter's Estate Agents on the phone. I've found a cottage to rent through them. Can you do the necessary, please?" he asked. "It will save me some time."

"Put them through," she said.

"Thanks and I'm gasping for a coffee." He laughed down the phone.

"Get one for me when you get yours then," she said, cutting him off to take the call.

Tom smiled. He knew he would have a coffee on his desk shortly. 'Now then,' he thought, 'better give Dorothy a call next.' He rang the Bath office.

"Lockyards. how can I help you?" Amber answered the phone.

"Hello. It's Tom Tranter. Can you put me through to Dorothy, please?" he asked.

"I'm afraid Dorothy has had to go out of the office for a while. Can I take a message for you?" she offered.

"No, no, it's ok." Tom thought for a moment. "I'll call her later, thank you. Bye."

"Bye," Amber said, putting down the phone. "That was Tom Tranter for Dorothy."

"Ooh, I wish it was Tom Tranter for me," said Vicky, going all starry-eyed.

Tom put down the phone. He recognised that voice from the times he'd called early in the morning. He began to chew his pen. Seeing as he had met Melanie and Vicky, by process of elimination that had to be Amber, the estate agent's girlfriend, no less.

"A penny for them," his secretary said as she stood in front of him with a coffee in her hand.

Tom looked up. He hadn't even heard her come into his office. "They're worth more than a penny." He smiled at her as he took his coffee. "Thanks."

"Buzz if you want a refill," she said, leaving his office.

"Give me oil in my lamp keep me burning, give me oil in my lamp I pray, give me oil in my lamp keep me burning, keep me burning till the break of day," Gloria sang as she walked along.

"Gloria," Dorothy called. "Gloria."

Gloria looked around to see Dorothy trying to catch her up. "Why, Dorothy, who let you out? Hehehe." She laughed.

"I had a dental appointment," Dorothy said, slightly breathless.

They chatted amicably as they walked into work, stopping at reception.

"Look at these three beautiful honeys." Gloria beamed, reaching into her tabard and pulling out the usual sweet for each of the girls. Have you all been behaving?"

"Of course." Melanie nodded.

"My goodness, that ain't like you, hehehe." Her raucous laugh filled reception.

"Oh, Dorothy, Tom Tranter called for you. He said he'd call you back later," Amber said, crossing his name off the pad of paper kept by the switchboard.

"Ooh, eee, looking forward to meeting that honey," Gloria said, putting her hands on her hips.

"You won't be disappointed," said Melanie, nudging Vicky.

"You two, what are you like?" Amber shook her head. "Anyway, I'll leave you to it. It's four o'clock and I'm off."

"Have a great time tonight. Hope the meal goes well," Vicky said.

"Yeah, enjoy." Melanie nodded as she winked.

"You too." Amber winked back at Melanie.

"All this young love going on, wonderful." Gloria waved.

"Yes," Dorothy agreed, surprising everyone. "I hope you enjoy your evening, Amber. Now, ladies, I need to be getting on. I hope you both enjoy your evening as well, if I don't see you before I go. Are you coming through for a few minutes, Gloria?"

"I surely am." She started to waddle after Dorothy. As she did so she pointed to Melanie. "You have a good date too. I want to know all about it tomorrow and you have a good evening as well, honey," she said to Vicky.

Melanie sighed once they had gone. "Just under an hour to go, then we can get out of here."

"Obviously looking forward to seeing Gary." Vicky chuckled.

"Looking forward to a shag." Melanie grinned.

"Oh, you are so awful." Vicky giggled.

'That's everything,' Amber thought, standing back. The Stilton-stuffed chicken was in a dish ready to go in the oven, the salad was all prepared waiting in the fridge, the new potatoes were scrubbed in a saucepan, and, lastly, the cheesecake was just waiting to be topped with blueberries. She practically skipped into the bathroom. A nice bubbly soak was next on the agenda.

Lying back in the scented bubbles Amber closed her eyes. She hadn't even lay there for 10 seconds before she sat bolt upright. 'Oh no, what if the black dress she was going to wear no longer fitted her?' she panicked. She hadn't worn it since the hen night and it hadn't crossed her mind to try it on. She almost jumped out of the bath. Drying herself quickly with the towel she went into her bedroom, took the dress off the hanger and tried it on. She needn't have worried, it still fitted like a glove, too much like a glove, actually. She smiled to herself, taking it off again. This time, as she lay back in the bubbles and closed her eyes, she was determined to relax, that was until something else popped into her head, of course.

Henry loafed on Melanie's bed, watching her as she sat at her dressing table applying makeup in her underwear.

"Not too much slap, dear heart," he advised. "You're not going clubbing, remember. You're going for a quiet, dignified supper."

"Thank you, personal assistant." Melanie stuck her tongue out at him in the mirror.

"Here to help, dear heart." Henry put his hand up in a grand gesture. "Although in a lot of ways you are beyond it."

"Thanks a fucking million," Melanie retorted.

"We really do have to work on that potty mouth of yours," Henry said, shaking his head.

Amber stood back to look at her reflection in the mirror. 'Good heavens,' she thought, exasperated as she took in her chest; the extra-boost bra was definitely extra boost. She tried to adjust the top of the dress but to no avail, as it just sprang back as soon as she let go. She grinned to herself, remembering Melanie slapping her hands away when she had done that in the changing rooms, telling her it was supposed to be like that and to forget about it. 'Right then, she would do just that,' she said to herself. 'Phil would be here shortly so she may as well put the oven on.'

After double-checking everything was prepared to her satisfaction in the kitchen, she poured herself a glass of wine. Taking it through she put some music on while she waited for Phil to arrive.

Melanie got up from her dressing table. "Well, what do you think?" she asked Henry as she pointed to herself with both hands.

"You look divine," Henry said admiringly. "But I rather think there's something missing."

"What?" Melanie asked, surprised.

"Your clothes, noggin," Henry joked.

"Very funny," Melanie said, going over to her wardrobe. First, she pulled out a floral shift dress. "This?" she asked, holding it up for Henry. "Or this?" she asked, pulling out cream Capri pants together with a black top.

"Oh, choices, choices. Eeny, meeny, miny, moe, catch poor Gary by his toe, if he squeals let him go, eeny, meeny, miny, moe," Henry sang, finishing up pointing to the Capri pants.

Melanie pulled them on, then the black top. Pulling out some black wedges she was just about to put them on when Henry started to shake his head at them. Casting them aside she pulled out some high black strappy sandals to which Henry started to nod. She put them on.

"Happy now?" she asked.

"Very. You look positively scrumptious. If I was straight I'd fight for you, dear heart." He clasped his hands to his chest theatrically.

After buzzing Phil in Amber couldn't help but try to adjust the top of her dress once again, just before she opened her flat door. Phil appeared, carrying the flowers he had picked up that afternoon.

"Wow, take a look at you," he said, giving her the once over, then returning his eyes to her cleavage." He handed her the flowers.

"Thank you, they're gorgeous," she said, taking them.

"Not as gorgeous as you. Where have you been hiding that dress?" he asked, following her inside.

"Just a little number I had in my wardrobe," Amber replied light-heartedly.

In the kitchen Amber poured Phil a glass of wine. He watched as she put the flowers he had given to her in a vase. Picking up her drink she turned to him.

"Well, happy one-year anniversary," she said, raising her glass.

"Happy one-year anniversary," he replied, raising his.

As soon as the doorbell rang Henry leapt off the bed. "I'll go," he said, running out of the bedroom. He thundered down the stairs and opened the door to find Gary standing there.

"Hi. It's Henry, isn't it? We met the other morning in the kitchen?" Gary grinned as he took in Henry's velour tracksuit. "Gary," he said, gesturing to himself.

"Hello, Gary. Do come in. Madam is nearly ready." Henry beamed as he let him in.

"Madam is ready," said Melanie as she came down the stairs, stopping next to Henry.

"Looking good." Gary smiled at her.

"Thank you," said Melanie and Henry at the same time.

Melanie elbowed Henry in the ribs as he stood there smirking. Gary laughed, relieved that Henry had been joking. For a moment he hadn't been sure.

"Have fun, precious," Henry said as he kissed Melanie on the cheek. "So nice to meet you again," he said to Gary.

As they walked to the car Gary cupped the cheek of Melanie's bottom.

"Hey, that's pudding, remember?" she said, turning to look at him.

"Just checking the menu," he said, pinching it gently.

Phil spooned the last of his cheesecake into his mouth. "That was great."

"Another piece?" Amber asked.

"No, thanks, I'm stuffed," he said, leaning back in his chair and patting his stomach. "I let a property to a bloke today who's going to be working at Lockyards."

"Really, who?" Amber asked with interest.

"A Tom Tranter, said he would be working on the new complex," Phil told her.

"Not just working on it. He's going to be overseeing it," Amber exclaimed. "What's he like? Mel and Vicky were drooling over him yesterday when he came in."

"Melanie foams at the mouth over anything in a pair of trousers, doesn't she?" Phil said with a bit too much depth in his voice for Amber's liking.

"Hey, that's one of my best friends, if you don't mind," she said, chastising him.

"Just joking, just joking. Weren't you drooling as well?" he teased.

"I wasn't there when he came in. Anyway, I don't need to drool over anybody else when I have you. You're the only one I want to be with," She said, before thinking, 'That was laying her cards on the table somewhat. Perhaps she shouldn't have drunk that last glass of wine so quickly.'

"Am I?" Phil said, looking at her intently.

"Yes." She smiled almost shyly.

"In that case, perhaps we should make things more official," Phil said.

Amber's heart missed a beat. "What do you mean, more official, like getting engaged?" The words were out before she had time to think.

Phil nodded. Amber squealed with delight. She jumped up out of her chair and ran round the table to where Phil was sitting. Plonking herself on his knee she put her arms round his neck and hugged him tightly.

"Do you really mean it?" she asked.

"Yes," he replied, hugging her back.

Amber jumped up again. "Let's phone everyone," she said, racing to get her phone.

"So, tell me, have there been any major men in your life apart from Henry?" Gary asked Melanie.

"One or two, or so I thought at the time," Melanie answered.

"Were they long-term relationships?" Gary pressed for a little more information.

"Long-term for me," Melanie replied, not giving him any more than that. "What about yourself?"

"Same as you," Gary answered.

"Can I interest you in a dessert?" asked the waitress as she collected their plates.

"We'll look at the menu," Gary answered her politely.

Putting her elbows on the table and resting her chin on her hands she looked at him. "I thought you were dessert," she said sexily.

Gary copied her by putting his elbows on the table and his chin on his hands. "I'm feeling generous, you can have both."

"In that case ..." Melanie picked up the menu and looked at the desserts.

"If I had to choose for you I would definitely pick something naughty," Gary said, watching her.

"Go on then, pick away," Melanie said, not looking up.

"Gooey chocolate fudge cake," Gary said.

"Full marks," Melanie congratulated him. "I'd say cheese and biscuits for you," she said, raising her eyes to look at him.

"You get full marks as well." He clapped his hands.

"I get full marks in a lot of things." Melanie pouted.

"I look forward to marking you later, and if you don't get full marks first time you might have to do it again, and again." He grinned.

"I warn you, I sometimes do things wrong on purpose. I only hope you're able to do it again, and again, and again." She grinned back at him.

"You already know I can do it again and again, but again and again and again, well, I might need some extra tuition myself."

Dessert and a coffee later they realised they were the only people left in the restaurant.

"We're about to be chucked out," Gary said as he summoned for the bill. "Where did everybody go?"

Melanie looked around. "I don't know, the place was full last time I looked," she said truthfully. They had been so busy chatting she hadn't even noticed the people at the next table leave, let alone anyone else.

"Do you fancy coming back to my place?" Gary asked.

"Sure. I'd better let Henry know or else he'll worry. What's your address?" Melanie asked, fishing out her mobile from her bag.

She began to text Henry a message, letting him know she wouldn't be home. As Gary said his address she looked up. "You know that I've told you about my friend Amber? Her boyfriend lives in the same road as you."

"What number?" Gary asked.

"I can't remember, but I know which house it is," she said, finishing the text. "I'll point it out. You might know him."

Amber put her phone down on the table. Taking a sip of her wine, she couldn't stop smiling. "That's the parents and family told. I think I'll text the girls."

"Here we are," Gary said, taking a left.

Melanie looked out of the window as they began to drive up the road. "That's Phil's house," she said, pointing to where Phil lived.

"Oh, I know who you mean," Gary said, looking at the house Melanie was pointing at. "He's always suited and booted."

"Yeah, that's him. You could say a bit slimy with it," Melanie said.

"Not one of your favourite people then?" Gary asked as he parked the car.

"Not really. Oh, he's ok," she corrected herself. "A bit full of himself, that's all. Amber's far too nice for him. Everyone says so."

"I've seen her leave there a few times. She looks a lot older than you," Gary said as they got out of the car.

"She'll be pleased when I tell her that." Melanie laughed.

"I didn't mean to be rude. I have only seen her from across the road. She always seems to park up around the corner somewhere and walk down to his place," Gary said as he opened his front door.

"Oh, I wonder why she does that?" Melanie said, puzzled, but before she could say anything else her phone beeped. Thinking it was Henry replying to her text earlier she had a look. It wasn't Henry, it was Amber. "Talk of the devil, it's Amber. Bloody hell."

"What's up?" Gary asked.

"She's just got engaged to your neighbour," Melanie told him as she started to text back a reply. After slipping her phone back into her bag she looked around. Too busy before to take in her surroundings, she was impressed with what she saw. "Nice place you've got."

"It's even nicer upstairs. Would you like to take a look?" he asked, tongue in cheek.

Melanie nodded. Needing no other encouragement he steered her up the stairs. Leaning around her he opened the first door they came to on the landing.

"This is my bedroom," he said as they stepped inside.

"It's a lovely bedroom, but, oh dear," Melanie exclaimed.

"What?" Gary asked.

"The bed," Melanie said, walking over to it and running her hand over what was obviously fresh linen. "It's going to get ever so creased."

"I'm banking on it, especially if you do it wrong first time." He laughed, already unbuttoning his shirt as he walked over to her.

CHAPTER 8

"Morning," Tom said as he walked into the kitchen.

"Morning." Yasmin replied as she went about packing Luke's lunchbox. "Your phone keeps beeping." She motioned towards his phone on the kitchen table.

"I've been looking for that, must have put it down last night as I came in," he said, picking it up. He read the text from last night. It was from Beth, telling him she was about to board her flight and she would see him when she got back. He wondered whether or not to text her back.

"What is it?" Yasmin asked, taking in the expression on his face.

"Nothing," he replied.

"Liar," Yasmin said, her full attention now on him.

"God, you're nosey." He sighed. "It was just a text from Beth."

"And what did madam want?" she asked.

"If you must know, the text was from last night. She was just letting me know that she was about to board her flight." He smiled half-heartedly.

"You need a few nights out on the town while she's gone. With any luck, you'll meet somebody else, somebody normal." She made a face at him before shouting, "Luke, hurry up, darling, you don't want to be late for school."

Luke appeared in the doorway. "My laces keep coming undone," he said woefully as he looked down at his untied shoes.

"Come over here, sport." Tom beckoned his nephew. "It takes lots and lots of practice before you can do them up tightly, let's do it together."

"Okay, Uncle Tom," Luke said, going over to where Tom stood and plonking himself on the floor.

"Show me how you're doing it," Tom said, kneeling down.

Tom watched as his nephew tied his laces in slow motion. He tried not to smile at the awkwardness of the child.

"See, they're too loose," Luke said once he'd finished.

"They are a bit, but the way you did it was spot on." He gave Luke the thumbs up. "Like I said, it takes lots and lots of goes before anybody can do their laces up tightly. Even now, I have to undo mine sometimes, then do them up again because they aren't tight enough."

"Do you really?" Luke asked, his eyes wide and looking at Tom.

"Really. Daddy does as well, I've seen him." Tom smiled as he tickled his nephew.

Wakey, wakey." Gary called gently to Melanie who lay motionless under the covers. "Wakey, wakey."

"It can't be morning already," came Melanie's reply as she opened her eyes to look at Gary.

"White no sugar, if I remember correctly," he said, holding a mug out to her.

"I'm impressed, thanks," Melanie said as she sat up and took the mug. "What time is it?"

"Just gone six," he told her.

"Bloody hell, that's the middle of the night," Melanie said with a look of horror on her face.

"You did say you wanted to be up early." Gary laughed.

"Early is about seven to me. How long have you been up?" she asked, sipping her coffee.

"About half an hour." He sat on the bed beside her.

"You must be mad," Melanie exclaimed.

"Well, seeing as I have to drop you home, I thought I may as well go on into work. There's always something that needs doing." He smiled at her.

"Voluntarily going into work at the crack of dawn, you are mad." She sighed as she took in his appearance. He was wearing jeans with a pink shirt rolled up at the sleeves, and whatever aftershave he had sprayed on was seriously horny.

"Now I've woken you up too early we have a bit of time to fill before we have to leave," Gary said, moving towards her and kissing her on the lips.

"Yes, we do, but I have to decline," she said, pushing him away gently. "I really do need to get home for a shower and get ready for work."

"In that case, to stop a rejection next time, you'd better bring your overnight bag with you," Gary said, planting another kiss on her lips before taking her mug from her. "Another one?"

"Please," she replied, getting out of bed.

In the bathroom she looked at herself in the mirror. Shit, her make up from last night was smudged under her eyes, and her hair looked like she'd been dragged through a hedge backwards. Still, he was obviously planning on her staying again, what with the comment about the overnight bag,' she thought as she tidied herself up to the best of her ability, then stuck her clothes on from the night before. Back in the bedroom she made the bed for him. 'He really did have a nice place,' she thought, making her way down the stairs and peeking another look at the lounge through the open door. As she neared the kitchen she could smell bacon. Walking in she found Gary, frying pan in hand.

"Your coffee is on the table, this will be ready in a couple of seconds. Take a seat." He nodded towards the table.

Melanie sat down. Taking her mobile from her bag she checked to see if she had any more messages. There was one from Jessica, asking her what she thought of the engagement and asking if they should organise a night out to celebrate.

"Here we go," Gary said, placing a bacon sandwich in front of her.

"My friend Jess," Melanie said, indicating her phone, "asking what I think of the engagement and suggesting we organise a night out."

"Look, I'm working tonight; if you can get hold of whoever it is you want to invite at short notice, why don't you come to the bar? I can put reserved on a couple of tables and I'm sure I can find a few bottles of bubbly that need using up," Gary suggested.

"Sounds good," Melanie replied enthusiastically. "I'll see if I can get hold of everyone this morning. Can I let you know later?"

"Sure," he said, finishing his coffee. "Come on, I'd better get you home, or else you'll be going to work like that."

"Well, at least I've washed last night's make up off now," Melanie joked.

"Have you? I hadn't noticed." Gary laughed.

"Very funny," Melanie said, getting up from the table and picking up her bag. "Come on then, or I'll not only be late but Henry will be sending out a search party."

"I'd hate to imagine what kind of search party that would be," Gary said, picking up his keys.

Amber looked at the list of visitors due for that day, then put it down again. She just couldn't concentrate on anything. She had been floating around on cloud-nine from the moment she had opened her eyes. She felt so happy she could just burst. Looking up she watched Harry pull up outside in his Post Office van. She willed him to hurry up so she could tell him her news. As he entered the building she walked around to the front of the reception desk to greet him.

"Morning, Amber, my dear," he said as he walked through the door.

"Guess what?" Amber said excitedly before he had even reached her.

"What?" he said, matching her excitement.

"I got engaged last night," she told him.

"Oh, my dear, that's lovely. What a lucky fellow he is to be getting you," Harry said, patting Amber's arm.

"Isn't he just?" Amber agreed as she took the post from him.

"I expect you'll be celebrating over the weekend." Harry beamed.

"Already arranged. We're going out with both sets of parents tomorrow night for a meal." Amber could not stop smiling.

"I look forward to hearing all about it on Monday." Harry patted her arm once more. "You enjoy yourself."

Amber walked to the doors with him. As she waved him off Mr Lockyard was walking across the car park. She almost skipped back inside. Going into the back office she flicked on the ready-filled kettle so she could make his tea. By the time he had reached the building he was talking on his mobile. He smiled and mouthed good morning to Amber as he carried on through to his office.

Five minutes later Amber knocked on his door gently as she entered. He was still on his mobile. She set his tea tray down, then poured him out a cup. Grinning from ear to ear she placed it in front of him. As she did so he put up his hand, indicating for her to wait. She stood, listening to him end his call.

"I have a feeling it's going to be one of those days today. Everything alright?" he asked.

"Couldn't be better. I got engaged last night," she blurted out, ignoring that he was actually referring to work.

"Congratulations." Mr L clapped his hands together. "When's the happy day going to be?"

"We haven't got that far down the road yet, but we are going into town tomorrow to look for my ring." Amber couldn't keep the excitement out of her voice.

"I hope he's saved plenty of money," laughed Mr Lockyard.

"So do I," Amber said, holding up both hands with fingers crossed. "I'd better be getting back to the desk, buzz if you need anything."

"Will do," answered Mr L as he watched an extremely happy Amber leave his office. Before he forgot he scribbled 'champagne' on a piece of paper.

Back at the desk Amber tried to busy herself with the usual tasks but she just didn't feel like work. For the hundredth time, she tried to think if there was anyone she'd forgotten to call; there wasn't. Anyway, her mum had been so thrilled that, no doubt, the whole world knew by now, so she knew she needn't be worried about forgetting someone.

"Something's tickled you pink." Dorothy's voice interrupted her thoughts.

Amber nearly jumped out of her skin. "Oh, Dorothy, I didn't see you come in"

"I know you didn't, you were too busy smiling away to yourself." Dorothy twitched.

"More than tickled, I got engaged last night." Amber beamed.

"How wonderful. I am so very happy for you," Dorothy said.

Amber was just about to tell Dorothy all about it when a commotion in the name of Melanie and Vicky coming through the doors stopped her. With squeals of delight, hugs and kisses, the girls' excitement grew louder and louder. Even Dorothy got swept along, but only for a moment before she left the girls discussing it all in depth.

In her office Dorothy switched on her computer before knocking on Mr Lockyard's door. "Good morning," she said as she entered.

"Morning, Dorothy," he answered brightly.

"I have no doubt that Amber has told you her happy news," she said, putting his cup and saucer back on the tray ready for it to be collected.

"She told me first thing, and before I forget …" He handed Dorothy the piece of paper with 'champagne' written on it. "Will you do the honours?"

"Certainly. In actual fact, I'll go now before I get started. I'll get some cakes for everyone as well. I can't see an awful lot of work being done today, I'm afraid."

"They have a good excuse." Mr Lockyard smiled.

"They certainly do." Dorothy nodded. "Can I tempt you with a cake?"

"Why not?" Mr Lockyard nodded. "It is Friday and we are celebrating."

Dorothy walked back through to reception. Two of the secretaries had arrived for work and were being given the news. Dorothy left unnoticed. 'No doubt, as each member of staff arrived for work, the topic of the day would be Amber's engagement, and why not?' thought Dorothy, 'She deserved to be happy, such a nice girl.'

An hour later Dorothy returned. She had the champagne concealed at the bottom of her shopping bag.

"I didn't see you go out," Amber said.

"You were otherwise engaged when I left, if you pardon the pun," Dorothy said as she took a box of cakes out of her bag. "Here we go, I thought we should all have a cake with our morning coffee to celebrate your good news."

Amber took the cakes from her. "Thanks, Dorothy, that's really kind of you."

"Thanks, Dorothy," chorused Melanie and Vicky.

"You're most welcome," said Dorothy as she headed to her office.

A few moments later the girls were in the back office, Amber opening the box of cakes, Melanie making the coffee, and Vicky keeping an eye on the desk from the door.

"So, madam." Melanie pointed at Amber. "Seeing as you are out with both sets of parents to have a very civilised meal tomorrow night, how do you fancy a not–so-civilised drink tonight with a few of your most favourite buddies? I mean, you and Phil, of course."

"That sounds great," Amber squealed. "I'll text Phil. Where do you suggest?"

"It's all arranged. I've already sent a text to the chosen few and everyone is happy to meet at the wine bar. Gary said he would put 'reserved' on a couple of tables for us. I just have to let him know," Melanie said, pleased with herself.

"Thanks, Mel." Amber hugged her friend. "It's very good of him. I didn't know you could reserve tables there."

"I don't think you can. I just happen to be shagging management," Melanie said smugly.

"Well, for once your shagging is to the benefit of others," Vicky said, before taking a bite of her cake. "Can you make sure he puts some decent looking bar staff on as well?"

"Of course, but you do know Henry will fight you for them." Melanie giggled.

"I've got a text back from Phil." Amber waved her phone around. "He says it sounds good to him."

"Fab, I'll give Gary a ring to let him know we want the tables then," Melanie said, already scrolling through her address book to find Gary's name. She pressed call and waited for him to answer.

"Are you hounding me for dirty sex again?" He laughed down the phone.

"I am not that kind of girl," Melanie said as indignantly as she could.

"Yes, you are." Gary laughed again.

"Okay, I am," Melanie agreed. "But don't say you don't like it, and I happen to be working at the moment."

"Shame," Gary said, sounding disappointed.

"Never mind, moving on," Melanie said gaily. "I was actually phoning to take up your offer of a couple of reserved tables for tonight."

"Sure, eight o'clock suit?"

"Perfect, thank you," Melanie replied.

"You can thank me later when I show you the cellar." Gary chuckled.

"My pleasure," Melanie said as she finished the call. "All sorted for eight o'clock," she announced to the girls.

Dorothy knocked before entering Mr Lockyard's office. He looked up as she came in.

"It's nearly three o'clock and you have not had any lunch yet," she said sternly, placing a tray down on his desk with a cup of coffee and a sandwich on it.

Mr Lockyard took off his glasses and rubbed his eyes. "Is it really?" He picked up his coffee and took a sip.

"Yes, and if you don't mind me saying you are looking a little tired. I'm quite up together, is there anything I can do to help you?" Dorothy asked, concern replacing her usual brusque manner.

"No, I'm all but done with this." Mr Lockyard indicated the papers he'd been looking at on his desk. "In fact, you're right, Dorothy, I do feel tired. I don't think these glasses help either, I'm sure they're no longer strong enough."

"I had to have a stronger prescription for mine last time I visited the optician; another sign of getting older, I'm afraid," Dorothy said with a sigh. "Call through if you would like me to refill your coffee, and just to remind you that Amber goes at four o'clock, so you'll be needing to give her the champagne shortly."

"Of course she does. Thanks, Dorothy, and thank you for the lunch," Mr Lockyard said, putting his glasses back on.

Dorothy closed his office door gently behind her. Sitting back down at her desk she put the tape into her audio machine. She was going to do it in the morning, but 'no time like the present,' she thought, putting her earphones on and pressing her foot down on the pedal. Mr Lockyard's voice filled her ears, telling her that this was a report. Her fingers started to fly over the keys.

Before he knew it the clock said 3.45pm. Mr Lockyard stood up. He picked up his briefcase and the bottle of champagne, and went through to Dorothy's office. As soon as he entered she stopped typing. "If it's alright with you, Dorothy, I'm going to slope off a little early. I'll give this to Amber on my way out." He held up the champagne.

"Of course it's all right with me. Enjoy the weekend," Dorothy replied.

"You too. See you Monday," he said as he left.

"Have you finished for the day?" Melanie asked Mr Lockyard as he neared the desk.

"I have. I was hoping to see Amber before I go, do you know where she is?" he asked.

"She's hiding in the back office," Melanie joked.

Mr Lockyard laughed as he came behind the desk. Putting his briefcase on the floor he went through to the back office where he found Amber.

"Mr L." Amber smiled brightly at him.

He smiled back at her as he held out the bottle of champagne. "Just a little something for you and your young man, from Sylvia and myself."

"Oh, how lovely, thank you very much," Amber said as she took it from him.

"Enjoy, and have a lovely weekend. I'll see you on Monday." He went back through to reception. "See you Monday, ladies. Have a good one." He saluted Melanie and Vicky.

"You can count on it," Melanie replied cheekily.

Mr Lockyard smiled to himself as he walked to the car. He didn't doubt for a minute that the girls would have a good time. 'What it was to be young,' he thought as he got into his car.

Amber was ready to leave just before 4pm. She wondered where Gloria was; she so wanted to tell her about her engagement. "I'm just going to say goodbye to Dorothy and thank her for the cakes again," she said. Hurrying to Dorothy's office she tapped the door before entering.

"Hello, Amber, is there something I can do for you?" Dorothy asked as she peered at Amber over the top of her glasses.

"I just wanted to say thank you again for the cakes." Amber smiled.

"You're welcome, my dear. I wish you and Phil every happiness." Dorothy's lips twitched into a genuine smile.

"Thank you, Dorothy. I'm just so excited. Tonight we're celebrating with friends, tomorrow we're going into town so I can choose a ring." She held up her left hand and twiddled her ring finger. "Then we're out with parents in the evening. It's going to be so hectic."

"It is, indeed," Dorothy agreed.

Gloria had arrived while Amber had been in with Dorothy, and it was quite obvious, as she gathered Amber into a strong bear-like embrace, that she had been given the news.

"Oh, my sugar, what happy news," she boomed as she squeezed Amber tightly. "When is you two getting married?"

"We haven't got that far yet," Amber said as Gloria released her.

"Gives me time to save for a fancy new hat then," Gloria said, touching her head with both hands.

"Absolutely." Amber laughed as she checked her watch. "I'd better get going, I said I'd call in to see Mum and Dad on the way home. See you guys about eight o'clock. Bye," she said, practically running out of the doors.

"Just got to get a match for you two honeys now, hehehe." Gloria turned to Melanie and Vicky.

"It's just me, I'm afraid." Vicky pointed to herself. "Mel seems to have found a hunk to keep her occupied for the time being."

"You can say that again." Melanie smirked.

"Good heavens, I hope you been behaving like a lady, Melanie." Gloria looked at Melanie. "You only just met him."

"Of course I have, Gloria," Melanie said innocently.

"And pigs may well fly by right now," Gloria boomed.

"What the bloody hell are you doing in there, Henry?" Melanie banged on the bathroom door. "Hurry up, I need to clean my teeth."

The door opened to reveal Henry showing off his pearly whites. "Dear heart, you're not the only one who needs to keep their breath fresh, you never know where my mouth will end up."

"Perish the thought." Melanie laughed, pushing him out of the way. "No flirting with anybody's boyfriend tonight, especially Phil the fiancé."

"He's not my type. I prefer them a bit more manly, a bit like Gary." He winked.

"Piss off, and check if the taxi has arrived," Melanie said, grabbing her toothbrush.

Henry skipped off to look out of the window. "It's here. I'll go on down. Hurry up, you old tart." he shouted as he thundered down the stairs.

Melanie finished cleaning her teeth, applied her lipstick and thundered down the stairs as loudly as Henry had done. Locking the door behind her she hurried to the waiting taxi. As they set off she sent a text to Vicky, asking her if she was also en-route. Before she had time to put her phone back in her bag she had a message back.

"Everyone is already there except us and the happy couple," Melanie told Henry.

"How many of us are going?" he asked.

"Twelve altogether: you, me, Jessica, John, Vicky, two of our old school friends and their boyfriends, Amber, Phil and Gary," Melanie answered, counting out on her fingers as she said each name.

"How lovely, darling, and have I told you you're looking gorgeous tonight?" he said, playing with Melanie's hair.

"Thanks, Hennie, you're looking pretty damn gorgeous yourself," Melanie returned the compliment.

"I know," Henry said, patting his cheeks with his hands.

The wine bar was already buzzing when they arrived. Spotting everyone at the bar they made their way over. Henry hugged and kissed Vicky, then Jessica, then everyone else, to their horror, as he was introduced to them. Melanie looked behind the bar but couldn't see Gary. Feeling a hand cup her bottom she turned round quickly, only to find him standing behind her.

"Do you do that to all your customers?" she asked.

"Only the ones I'm sleeping with." He winked.

Melanie laughed. "Let me introduce you to everyone." Starting with Jessica, who was stood beside her, she worked her way round until she came to Henry. "You've already met Henry."

"How's it going, Henry?" Gary said, shaking Henry's hand.

"All the better for seeing you," Henry said, unable to stop himself looking Gary up and down.

"In that case, let me get you a drink." Gary laughed.

"Oooh, a medium white wine, please," Henry purred.

"What about you, Melanie?" Gary asked, slipping his hand around her waist.

"I'll have the same as Henry, please," she replied.

Gary gave her a little squeeze before he went behind the bar. Melanie watched him pour two large glasses of white wine, then motion for her to get them. She nudged Henry out of the way.

157

"Thanks," she said, taking the drinks.

Gary leant over the bar towards her. "I need to help out a bit behind here, but as soon as the happy couple arrive I'll come round to crack open the champagne."

"I owe you." Melanie pouted before turning to give Henry his wine. It was nearly eight o'clock. She glanced towards the door, looking out for Amber. She watched as two women came in. Looking more closely she felt sure she recognised one of them. It looked like the woman who worked with Phil. She poked Jessica and motioned towards the door with her eyes.

Jessica turned to look, then turned back again. "What?" she asked, puzzled.

"Those two women who have just come in. Over there." She pointed discreetly. "The red head with the boobs. Isn't that who was talking to Phil in the car park the other day?"

Jessica looked again. "I think you're right. Perhaps Phil's invited the people he works with," she said, lowering her voice slightly as they approached.

"We'll soon find out, here they are," she said, waving madly at Amber as she came through the door, with Phil close behind her.

There were whoops of joy as Amber and Phil joined them. Hearing the noise Gary looked over from where he was serving at the other end of the bar. 'They've obviously arrived,' he thought.

Recognising the red, curly hair and the very big pair of breasts falling out of a very tight top, Phil's smile wavered slightly. 'Shit, what was Cheryl doing here?' he thought. He stepped towards her.

"I didn't expect to see you here," he said.

"Surprise, nice to see you too. Let me introduce you to my friend Jane. We've come to join the party, what's the occasion?" Cheryl's voice was full of sarcasm.

"Hello." Phil greeted Jane then turned back to Cheryl. "Amber and I got engaged last night," he explained, but before he had a chance to say anything else Amber appeared by his side.

"Amber, this is Cheryl from work, who never seems to be in the office when you call in," he said as light-heartedly as he could, while feeling more than a little hot under the collar.

"Hello," Amber said, smiling politely. "It's nice to meet you at last. I've heard a lot about you."

"You too," Cheryl replied. "This is my friend Jane. She's staying with me for the weekend."

Amber was about to say hello but was halted by Melanie calling order. Gary stood by her side, holding two glasses of champagne. The group went quiet.

"Well, we all know why we're here and that is to congratulate Amber and Phil on their engagement, so I think it's only fair to hand them their glass of bubbly, courtesy of Gary who I've yet to formally introduce." Melanie smiled at Gary. "Although it's a small world because he actually lives in the same road as you, Phil."

"I thought you looked familiar." Phil said to Gary.

Gary handed him a glass of champagne. "Congratulations, and I only need a formal introduction to you, Amber," he said, turning towards Cheryl and holding out the other glass of champagne towards her. "Because I've seen you going in and out of Phil's place."

You could, what's commonly known as, hear a pin drop. Amber looked from Cheryl to Phil to Gary, then back at Phil.

Cheryl looked at the champagne and shook her head. Gary looked at Melanie, not quite understanding why she wasn't accepting the drink he was offering. The rest of the group looked on, speechless.

'Shit,' thought Melanie, 'that's why he'd made the comment that Amber looked a lot older than me. Phil was obviously shagging her and Gary had seen her going there.' She looked at Amber who was still staring at Phil. The silence seemed to go on forever.

"That isn't Amber," she said gently to Gary, touching his arm.

He looked at her, his expression changing to one of surprise. "Oh, I …"

"That's Amber," Melanie said, indicating to Amber who was still staring at Phil.

Cheryl looked around the group, who now stood motionless looking in turn from her to Phil to Amber. She turned towards Jane. "I think we should make a move," she said under her breath.

Jane followed her to the door. Once outside the pub she hooked her arm through Cheryl's as they began walking. "Still up to your old tricks then?"

"Afraid so." Cheryl shrugged.

"I'm sorry, my mistake," Gary said, looking extremely embarrassed. He held out the glass of champagne to Amber.

"No, thank you." She put her hand up, refusing the drink. I don't think you've made a mistake," she said, raising her voice slightly as she looked back at Phil. "Why has she been going to your house?"

'Fuck,' Phil thought, 'he couldn't deny it now, could he? Think, think.' After a pause he said, "We had to go through some properties that needed reducing, nothing to get excited about." He tried to sound convincing as he stood there looking horribly guilty.

"I don't believe you. Why has she left then?" Amber's heart was thumping so badly that she felt like it was going to explode, while her stomach felt like it was sinking.

"I don't know." Phil shrugged. "Perhaps she had to be somewhere. Forget about it, we're meant to be celebrating, have your glass of champagne."

"But she didn't even have a drink. You don't go into a pub and not have a drink. You're lying, and seeing as you won't tell me the truth I'm going to get it from her." Turning towards the door she began pushing past people as she hurried to get out.

"Amber, stop," Phil shouted, going after her.

"I bloody told you," Melanie said to Jessica as they, in turn, followed Phil.

"Oh my God. Drama. I need another drink," Henry said, swiping the glass of champagne that was supposed to be for Amber out of Gary's hand, then proceeding to drink it down in one.

"What have I done?" Gary said forlornly.

"Not your fault, mate." Jessica's husband John gave Gary's shoulder a friendly pat.

"No, not your fault." Henry rubbed, more than patted, Gary's other shoulder. "You weren't to know he's been shagging ginger big boobs."

"Like Phil said she could have been going there for work reasons, Henry," said John, not for a minute believing what he was saying. Phil had the look of a guilty man.

"Call it work reason, if you wish, darling," sighed Henry, shaking his head.

"Let's have another drink. We're going to have to stay put until Jess and Mel come back," John said.

"They're on me. It's the least I can do for ruining the party," Gary said.

"In that case I'll have another large white wine, and you may as well fill this up before the fizz goes flat, I hate waste." Henry smiled, handing Gary the empty champagne flute.

Outside the pub Amber looked up and down the road, wondering which way Cheryl had gone. Phil came crashing through the pub doors. They stood staring at each other before Phil spoke, "Amber, there's nothing going on between Cheryl and me."

"Don't take me for an idiot. I've been going out with you long enough to know that you do price reductions in your morning meeting, not at night from home. Couldn't you think of a better excuse than that? After all, you're usually full of flannel. How long has it been going on?"

The pub doors crashed open again. Out spilled Jessica and Melanie, who abruptly came to a standstill just behind Phil.

"How long?" Amber repeated. "If you think anything of me at all, just tell me." Strangely enough, she didn't know whether to laugh or cry. The look on Phil's face was making her feel like she wanted to punch him.

"God, Amber, I'm so sorry." Phil moved towards her. "I haven't really been seeing her, it was just …" he paused, "sex. I swear to you, it's over. It really never started. It didn't mean anything, nothing, it just kind of happened. I'll do anything to make things right." He moved towards her.

"Don't touch me." Amber stepped back, pointing her finger at him. "Just sex, just sex, that's all right then. Silly me for thinking that when you're in a steady relationship you don't go having 'just sex' with anyone else."

"Amber, please, don't make a scene. Let's go back to mine, we can talk about it, I can make it right. I made a stupid mistake." He moved towards her again.

Amber put up her hand to stop him. "Don't make a scene. You're telling me, don't make a scene? Why would I make a scene and make you look like a complete bastard for sleeping with another woman?" she shouted, before lowering her voice to hardly more than a whisper, "How could you? How could you do that to me?"

"I'm so sorry, Am, I'm so sorry. We can sort this out. Come back to mine," Phil pleaded.

"No, no, we can't sort this out." Amber shook her head. "You slept with another woman, we can't sort it out. We're finished." She stepped around him to where Jessica and Melanie stood quietly. "I want to go home," she whispered.

Melanie put her arm around her friend and hugged her close. "Come on."

Phil turned around after Amber. Jessica stood in his way. "Leave it, Phil, I think you've done and said enough for one night. Go home before you make matters worse."

Leaving him staring after Amber, Jessica hurried to catch them up. Gently hooking Amber's arm through her own, as Melanie had done on the other side, they steered their friend towards the nearest taxi rank. Glancing over at Melanie, just a look and it was agreed to say nothing until they had got Amber safely home. There were a number of taxis waiting for passengers. Melanie got Amber into the back seat. She sat there motionless while Melanie put her seat belt on. Jessica got into the front and gave the cabbie Amber's address.

"You girls are going home early," he said in an effort to start a conversation.

"Our friend has a bad migraine," Jessica replied politely.

"Oh dear, best for her to get to bed then," said the taxi driver.

"Yes," said Jessica.

The rest of the journey was made in silence. On reaching Amber's flat Melanie pulled her out of the taxi while Jessica paid. "Keep the change," she said.

"Thanks, hope your friend feels better soon," he said.

"So do I," Jessica replied as she shut the taxi door.

Melanie rooted around in Amber's bag until she found the keys to her flat. "Come on, Am, let's get you inside." She smiled at her friend who stared back with such a sad expression that it made Melanie want to burst into tears. She opened the door, then stood back while Jessica steered Amber inside and towards the stairs. Within minutes they were inside the flat.

While Melanie settled Amber on the settee Jessica hunted out three wine glasses and a bottle of wine from the kitchen. She quickly sent a text to John to let him know they had got Amber home and that she and Mel would probably stay over. Carrying the wine and glasses through she set them down on the coffee table.

"I'll pour," Melanie offered, getting up from beside Amber. As she poured out the wine she looked at Jessica who raised her eyebrows as though to say that this scenario hadn't come as a total shock. "Here we go," Melanie said, handing a glass to Amber.

Amber took it. Taking a sip she looked at her friends. "I think I've just had the world's shortest engagement," she said, before bursting into tears. "I feel such a fool," she sobbed. "I should have guessed. He's been working late such a lot. Anybody else would have sussed it, but not me, not good-old trusting Amber, I'm so stupid."

"You are not stupid," Jessica said, giving her a tissue. "How could you have known? It's not unusual that people want to do viewings in the evening after they've finished work."

"I bet he was with her the other night when we should have come over to your place. I was sat here like a mug while he was in bed with her." Amber sniffed before taking a glug of her wine.

"Jess is right, Am, it's not your fault. No man could wish for a better girlfriend than you." Melanie sat back down beside Amber. She put her arm around her.

"Yes, I'm that good a girlfriend, especially in bed, that he's been sleeping with someone else." She sobbed again into her tissue. "It's quite obvious that he would never have asked me to get engaged if I hadn't practically put the words into his mouth."

"Come on, Amber, there's no way you would have put the words into his mouth. It's just not your style." Jessica tried to soothe her.

"Isn't it? He didn't get down on one knee. He didn't even broach the subject. He was telling me he'd shown Tom Tranter round some properties, to which I commented that Mel and Vicky thought Tom Tranter was good-looking. He asked me if I did as well. Course, stupid me said I didn't need to like anyone else when I had someone like him, and he just said, 'why don't we make it official then', to which I said, 'like getting engaged'. So, you see, it was really me that forced the issue. I feel so embarrassed now, such a fool. I called everyone telling them while he just sat there, more than likely wishing he was in bed with her." She blew her nose loudly.

"Amber, you're just persecuting yourself. It was him that said to make things official, not you. It's him that's been shagging, not you. You have done nothing to deserve this, do you hear me? Nothing," Melanie said, pouring everyone another glass of wine.

"I'm going to be a laughing-stock, a stupid, dim naive laughing-stock. Everyone is going to think of me as desperate." Amber took a large sip of her wine, then sobbed some more into the clean tissue that Jessica had just handed her.

"Of course they won't," Melanie said. "They will think Phil is a stupid bastard who has messed up big time. He'll be the one stuck on his own when you have met a fantastic guy who has swept you off your feet and treats you like the princess you are."

Amber smiled through her tears. "Are you going to tell me I will live happily ever after as well?" she asked.

"Fuck, that was a bit dramatic, wasn't it?" Melanie hugged her friend. "But it's true, Am, you are one of the loveliest people I know. You just wait and see."

"I think I'll give men a miss for the rest of my life," Amber said before starting to cry again.

"I'll go get us another bottle of wine," Jessica said, getting up.

"I'd better call my mum and let her know that her daughter can't keep a fiancé for more than 24 hours," Amber said, standing up as well.

Melanie pulled her back down again. "Wait until the morning, call her then."

Amber started to cry once again. "You're right, she'll only start worrying. If I call her now she'll probably make Dad drive her over." She leant back, staring at the ceiling. "Everyone's going to be whispering behind my back. I'm going to get those looks that say that if I'd been a better girlfriend he wouldn't have gone looking elsewhere."

"Oh, Am, come here," Melanie said, pulling Amber towards her. "The only looks you're going to get are caring ones from people who love you."

"I've brought in two bottles of therapy," Jessica said, holding up a bottle of wine in each hand as she came in from the kitchen. She refilled their glasses.

After the wine therapy they went on to vodka therapy, which ended up with the three of them staggering into Amber's bedroom and collapsing into her bed.

CHAPTER 9

Jessica turned over, bumping straight into Melanie, bringing her from a heavy slumber into semi–consciousness. Unfortunately, there wasn't any bed left to turn on to so she promptly fell out, landing on the carpet in a heap. Opening her eyes she looked up at the ceiling. The room started to spin. 'Oh God, how much had they drunk,' she thought as she pulled herself up the side of the bed. She looked at Amber and Jessica who were still fast asleep, Jessica now taking up the space she had slept in. 'No chance of getting back in there,' she groaned to herself, struggling to her feet. She headed to the kitchen in search of Amber's first aid box. She needed something for her head. No doubt, when the others woke up they would as well.

In the kitchen she surveyed the empty wine bottles and the empty vodka bottle. No wonder she had a pounding head. Finding some tablets she took a couple with a glass of water. Feeling somewhat queasy she made her way to the sofa. She lay down, covering herself with the throw, and dozed off almost instantly.

"Melanie, Mel, wake up," Jessica implored, giving her a gentle shake.

Melanie opened her eyes to bright sunlight coming from the window. "What time is it?" she croaked.

"Nearly 12.30," Jessica answered.

"Is it? Where's Amber?" she asked, sitting up.

"I've pushed her in the shower. She started to cry again as soon as she woke up. She's absolutely devastated," Jessica said sadly.

"I know," Melanie replied. "That bastard, I could kill him, although between you and me she's better off without him."

"You never did like him much, did you?" Jessica sighed.

"In a word, no. Too full of himself," Melanie said. "But Amber thought the sun shone out of his backside. I just hate seeing her so hurt."

"So do I. Let's stick the kettle on and make a cup of tea. Oh, by the way, why were you on the sofa?" Jessica asked.

"Because you turned over and made me fall out the bloody bed," Melanie answered as they wandered into the kitchen.

"Sorry." Jessica giggled.

"It's not bloody funny," Melanie said, giving her a push.

"What's not funny?" Amber asked, appearing in the doorway.

"Jessica made me fall out of bed, so I ended up on the sofa this morning. More importantly, how are you feeling?" Melanie enquired gently.

"Like I've had a terrible nightmare only to realise that it wasn't a nightmare at all. That my fiancé of less than 24 hours has been seeing the woman he works with, correction, been having sex with the woman he works with, obviously because I wasn't enough for him," Amber answered before bursting into tears.

"Oh, sweetie, you're more than enough for any man," Melanie said, putting her arms around her and giving her a hug.

Jessica made some tea, and spying the packet of tablets Melanie had left on the side earlier, popped out enough for two each.

The three of them stood quietly for a moment as they took the tablets and sipped their tea.

"Thanks for staying last night. I don't know what I'd have done without you." Big tears started to roll down Amber's face as she spoke.

"That's what friends are for." Jessica smiled, tearing off a piece of kitchen roll and handing it to Amber. "It's been a while since we all slept in the same bed, hasn't it?"

"And more than a while since we haven't managed to get undressed before we went to bed," Melanie added. "Would you like us to stay tonight as well?"

"I think I'll stay at Mum and Dad's tonight. In fact, I'd better make my way over there soon, otherwise Mum will be phoning about arrangements for later. Phil and I were meant to be going out with both sets of parents to celebrate. I can drop you two home on the way. Do you want to shower or anything before we go?" Amber asked as she dabbed at her tears.

"No, may as well wait until I get home, unless you'd like us to come to your Mum's with you?" Jessica offered.

"It's ok, I'd rather tell them by myself. I'd hate you to see the look of disappointment and pity on their faces." Amber tried to smile.

"Amber, stop that, they won't pity you, they'll just be upset because you're upset. Are you sure you don't want us to come with you?" Melanie asked again.

"I'm sure." She nodded. "But I think I need one more cup of tea before breaking the not-so-good news."

"I'll make it," Jessica volunteered. "How about a bit of breakfast to go with it?"

"You made the last one. I'm still capable of making a cup of tea, you know," Amber said, reaching for the kettle.

"Okay, carry on." Jessica grinned before turning to Melanie. "How's your head?"

"Not too bad. I'd already taken two tablets after falling out of bed, so those last two have done the trick. What about yours?" she asked.

"Bad. I shouldn't have had that vodka," Jessica groaned.

"None of us should have had that vodka," Melanie agreed.

"Have some toast. It might make you feel better," Amber said, putting some bread in the toaster. "Tea's on the side, I'm just going to chuck some pyjamas and a few other things into a bag to take to Mum and Dad's."

"Aren't you having anything to eat?" Jessica asked.

Amber shook her head. "I'm not hungry."

"You should try to eat something," Melanie said.

"No, really, I don't feel like anything," Amber said, disappearing out of the kitchen, leaving Melanie and Jessica looking after her.

When she didn't return they found her sat on her bed, mobile in hand. She held it up. "I've at least a dozen messages from Phil saying he wants to talk, that he loves me, that he's sorry, that he'll make it up to me, that he made a mistake, that it didn't mean anything, that …" She began to sob again before she could get another word out.

Jessica sat down by her side.

"That fucking bastard," Melanie said, plonking herself down as well.

They sat there, all three of them in a line; if they had been a firing squad there would only have been one target.

Eventually, Amber's sobs subsided enough for her to speak, "We'd better make a move I suppose."

The girls tidied round quickly, while Amber splashed some cool water on her face. She looked at herself in the mirror. 'That was a waste of time,' she thought, 'her eyes were just as red and swollen.'

Amber drove to Jessica's house first. She turned to her friend. "Thanks again for staying last night, Jess."

Jessica leant forward from the back seat to give her a kiss. "Are you sure you don't want us to come to your mum's with you?"

"No." Amber shook her head. "Honestly, I'll be fine."

"I'll give you a ring later then," Jessica said, getting out of the car. "Bye, Mel." She stood waving as Amber drove away.

It wasn't long before they pulled up outside Melanie's house. Amber's eyes were brimming with tears as she looked at Melanie.

"God, Amber, I could kill that bastard for you," Melanie said, taking hold of her friend's hand.

"I think I'd like to do it myself," Amber replied, a single tear escaping.

"At least let me help you." Melanie smiled, wiping Amber's tear away with her thumb. "Look, I'll ring you later as well, but if you want me before, just call. I can be over in no time." She gave Amber a kiss. "You will get over him.

Like I said, someone else is waiting for you round the corner."

"He'll be waiting a long time then." Amber sniffed. "I'm giving up on men, they're just a waste of time."

"We'll see." She kissed her friend again before getting out.

Melanie didn't have time to put her key in the lock before the door flew open.

"Dear heart, I saw Amber pull up from the window. How is the poor sweet girl?" asked Henry, dragging Melanie inside.

"Okay one minute, crying the next. She's going to her parents to tell them the engagement's off. Jess and I offered to go with her but she wanted to go by herself," Melanie said sadly.

"I don't blame her. She doesn't want an audience while telling her folks that their no-longer-future son-in-law of two minutes has been shagging some old ginger piece. She was a bit of a dog, wasn't she?" Henry now stood with one hand on his hip.

"Not as much of a dog as Phil turned out to be. I'm going for a shower. I've been in these clothes since last night," Melanie said.

"Yuk." Henry turned up his nose. "Off you pop then. Do you want me to make you anything to eat?"

"No thanks, Hennie. I had some toast not long ago. Wouldn't mind a coffee if you're making." Melanie smiled.

"I'm making, madam. I'll bring it to your boudoir." He touched her face. "Look at you. All down in the dumps because of Amber. Why don't we go out for a while this afternoon? We could buy her a little present to cheer her up."

173

"Good idea," Melanie agreed. "What do you say we go to the garden centre to get a couple of pots and some plants to go in them? They have a nice café there where you can sit outside. We could get Amber some flowers."

"Dear heart, we'll be like Darby and Joan. Hurry along then, up to the shower with you. I'll bring your coffee up in 10 minutes," Henry ordered, motioning for her to go with his hand.

Amber pulled into her parents' drive. Fighting back the tears she got out. 'May as well go around the back,' she thought. A sunny day would find her dad pottering in the greenhouse or amongst his vegetable plot, her mum, no doubt, would be dead-heading her flower border or reading in a deckchair.

She wasn't wrong. As she walked in through the back gate there was her mum kneeling down, mini fork in hand, turning over the earth between her bedding plants.

"Mum," Amber called.

Her mum looked up, her lips breaking into a smile. "My darling bride to be," she said, putting her fork down by her side and getting up. "I've been worrying about you. Phil has phoned so many times this morning, asking us if you were here. I was going to call but your dad told me off for fussing. Everything ok?"

Amber couldn't speak. It was as though there was a large lump stuck in her throat. The tears started to cascade down her cheeks. Seeing her daughter's tears her mother opened her arms as she had done when Amber was a child. Amber flew into them.

"Sweetheart, what on earth's the matter?" she asked as she enveloped Amber in her arms. "Whatever's happened?"

Between her sobs Amber told her mum of the night before.

"Oh, my darling," her mum said, hugging her closer still. "Come and sit down. I'll go and put the kettle on," she said. Leading her over to the garden table and chairs, she sat Amber down.

Amber watched her mum hurry in through the back door. 'Why does everyone think a cup of tea or a glass of wine will make everything ok?' she thought. Looking up the garden she saw her dad heading down the path, waving to her with a huge smile on his face. As he drew closer his smile vanished as he saw her tear-stained face. By the time her mum had returned with the tea Amber had repeated everything once again to her dad. She then listened to her parents' words of compassion, to them telling her in their ultimate wisdom that everything would work out for the best. 'How many times would she hear that old chestnut?' she thought sadly.

"Is it ok if I stay tonight?" Amber asked.

"Of course it is. You don't need to ask," her mum replied.

"I know." Amber smiled weakly. "If you don't mind I think I'll go and lie down."

"What do you want me to do if Phil calls again?" her mum asked as Amber stood up.

"Just tell him I don't want to talk to him," Amber replied.

"You can leave that one with me, my lovely," her dad piped in. "You go and have a nice lie down."

She made her way indoors. Once upstairs she pushed open the door to her old bedroom. Stepping in she instantly felt comforted at the sight of her old bed. As she walked over to it she ran her hand along the top of her old dressing table.

Lying down on top of the duvet she closed her eyes, making two tears roll slowly down her cheeks.

"Over here, dear heart," Henry said as he marched towards an array of garden pots. "Now then, which ones do you fancy? I feel we should have a matching pair, like you and me, a his and hers. What do you think?"

"Sounds good to me. We could put one each side of the kitchen door." Melanie smiled at Henry's enthusiasm. "What about these?" she said, pointing to a group of tall, square stone pots.

"Oh, lovely, just lovely," Henry said. He put two on their trolley. "Now something to go in them. Where does one start with all this to choose from?" he said, waving his arms around frantically.

"Dorothy suggested we plant just one thing that's quite big and flowers a lot." Melanie surprised herself at remembering Dorothy's tip.

"Dotty knows best, bless her. To the shrubs then, wherever the fuck they are." Henry looked around, bewildered at the rows upon rows of plants. "Let's see if there's a pink section," he said, walking off and leaving Melanie to push the trolley. After much debating, and a lot of umming and ahhing, they made their choice: a couple of sacks of all-purpose compost, some plant feed and a set of gardening tools. They were done.

"Now then, dear heart, shall we have a little coffee or get on back so we can sort this lot out?" Henry asked.

"Let's get back. We can have a coffee while we do it," Melanie said, checking her phone. She had a new message from Gary asking if he could call round before he started work. She quickly sent him a text back saying yes.

"Lover boy?" Henry nodded towards her mobile.

"Yep, he's calling round before he starts work. I spoke to him earlier, he feels like shit about last night," Melanie said as they headed towards the cash desks.

"Poor boy, wasn't his fault, how was he to know? Only one man to blame, I'm afraid, and that's Phil for dipping his wick where it didn't belong. Just so unfortunate for sweet Amber having to find out the way she did," Henry said in a very theatrical manner.

"He feels really bad about it." Melanie sighed.

"Well, then we will just have to cheer him up as well as Amber, won't we?" Henry said, patting Melanie's arm. "Now, help me push this, you know how delicate I am. Oh, I say, we'd better have a pair of these," he said, swiping a pair of gardening gloves off a display as they went by. "I do hate to get dirt in my nails, it makes me go all queer."

"You don't say." Melanie chuckled. Henry started to laugh. "Ooh, dear heart," he said, putting his hands up and then down again.

Amber's mum opened the bedroom door as quietly as she could. She tiptoed across to where Amber lay fast asleep on her bed. Looking down upon her daughter she felt a lump in her throat. 'It didn't matter how old your children were, if they got hurt you got hurt,' she thought. She left her sleeping. There was no point in waking her. She closed the door as softly as she had opened it. Walking down the stairs slowly she dabbed at her eyes. Her husband stood waiting for her at the bottom.

"There, there, she'll get over him. She's made of strong stuff," he said, placing his arm round her shoulders gently.

"Yes, I know. I just can't bear seeing her so upset." She sniffled.

"Nor can I. I'd love to box his ears. We just have to tell ourselves that maybe these things happen for the best sometimes." He gave her a gentle squeeze.

"What do you mean by that?" she asked, puzzled as they went into the lounge.

"Well, he could quite often come across as thinking he was a cut above other people. He had a way of looking down his nose at things," he said, picking up the paper.

"You've never said anything before," she said, taking the paper away from him.

"Of course I didn't. Amber was so keen on him and he did have his good points. Anyway, can you imagine the trouble I would have been in if I had said something?" He chuckled. "Can I have the paper back, please?"

She smiled at her husband. He was right about that, he would have been in trouble if he had said anything. "Here you go." She held out the paper.

Henry stood back admiring their handiwork. "If I say so myself, we've done a sterling job. No doubt, we will produce the best blooms for miles around once they get established. Oh, dear heart, listen to me, I sound like Alan Titchmarsh." Melanie giggled as she tidied up the mess they had made.

"I'll get something to put the rubbish in," Henry said, disappearing into the house. A few moments later he reappeared with Gary.

"Hi, I didn't hear the doorbell go." Melanie smiled at him.

"I didn't ring it. Henry saw me through the window and let me in." He gave her a kiss on the lips. "How's Amber?"

"Really upset. She's gone to her mums," Melanie replied sadly.

"Do you think she'll forgive him?" Gary asked.

"Not if I have anything to do with it. She's far too good for him, always has been," Melanie answered.

"Here, here," Henry said, nodding frantically. "It was a good job she found out just what he was like before they got married."

"I only wish that her finding out hadn't had anything to do with me," Gary said woefully.

"She'll thank you for it in a couple of weeks," Melanie said. "Henry, can you pop to the supermarket to get some milk?"

"We don't need any milk, dear heart." Henry replied.

"Yes, we do," Melanie argued with a you-know-what-I-mean' look on her face.

"No, we don't, princess, I got some yesterday." Henry looked at her blankly, shaking his head.

"Yes, we do, Henry," Melanie said, nodding her head.

"Oh yes, we do, don't we? I'll skip off right away," he said, turning, the penny having finally dropped. He turned back again quickly. "Dirty bitch," he mouthed at Melanie before practically sprinting off.

"What was that all about?" Gary asked.

"I thought I'd cheer you up before you head off to work," Melanie said, stepping towards him.

"Oh, did you now?" He grinned. "Then we'd better go upstairs."

"We haven't got time to go upstairs. I'm thinking alfresco," she said, taking off her top.

"What about your neighbours?" Gary asked, already excited at the site of Melanie now standing in front of him in her underwear.

"I don't want them joining in." She laughed at the expression on Gary's face. "I'm joking. Both sets are away on holiday. Just make sure you don't make too much noise, or else the nosey old bag two doors up will come knocking."

CHAPTER 10

Amber sat at reception feeling so miserable. She had made up her mind that it would be much easier just to be honest, to tell everyone she'd found out that her fiancé of two seconds had been seeing another woman and the relationship was over, end of story. She watched as the Post Office van pulled up. Harry got out. She painted what she thought was a smile on her face, ready to greet him.

"Well, how did the celebrations go?" He beamed.

"They didn't, Harry." The smile, which wasn't ever really a smile, disappeared from her face.

"Oh dear." Harry's smile instantly disappeared as well as he took in Amber's sad expression. "I'm sorry to hear that."

'Here goes,' thought Amber. "I found out that my fiancé of five minutes has been seeing someone else."

Harry looked at her. 'Poor lass,' he thought. Leaning over the desk he patted her hand. "Oh dear, indeed. I'm truly sorry to hear that."

"Thanks, Harry." Amber felt touched by the sincerity of his words and very grateful that he was too much of a gentleman to ask any questions.

She was taking a telephone call when Mr L arrived. He mouthed good-morning as he walked past the desk towards his office. Amber finished the call. Going into the back office she picked up the bottle of champagne Mr L had given her on Friday night. She felt she shouldn't keep it now there was nothing to celebrate. She followed him to his office. Tapping the door she entered. Before he had time to say anything she put the bottle of champagne on his desk.

"I thought I'd return this as there is no longer an engagement to celebrate," she said very quickly, followed by tears she just couldn't seem to control.

Mr L hurried round his desk to where Amber was standing. "Come, come now, you sit down," he said, manoeuvring her into a chair. He fished in his pocket for his handkerchief, then handed it to Amber.

Pulling herself together as much as possible Amber suddenly felt embarrassed. "I'm sorry," she said, starting to get up from the chair. "I'll go and get your tea."

"No, you won't. The tea can wait," Mr L said, pushing her back down. "I'm more concerned about you."

"I'm alright, really." Amber attempted a smile.

Mr L patted her shoulder. "Amber, I don't wish to pry into what has happened, but you are obviously not alright."

"You're not prying, you may as well know because I'm sure it's going to be the office gossip for a while. I found out Phil has been seeing a woman he works with," Amber said, trying not to sniff. She wondered how many times she would be patted that day.

"Oh, I see," Mr L said, looking down at Amber. Perhaps he should employ a relationship counsellor. Only last week he had been asking Tom if he could salvage his relationship, now here he was consoling Amber over hers.

"I'm sure you've had more than enough words of wisdom from your friends so I won't add to them, but I will say this: somebody once said to me 'as one door closes another one opens'. I don't know if it's a famous quote or not, but I have found it to be true, although in some cases it has taken me some time to realise it." He patted her shoulder again.

"The trouble is I feel like I've had a door slammed shut in my face," Amber said, blowing her nose.

"I know you do," Mr L said sympathetically.

'Funny, it makes you want to cry more when people are being nice to you,' Amber thought, standing up. "I'm fine now, really, I'll go to get your tea. Sorry if I embarrassed you, crying like that."

"Amber, you didn't embarrass me," Mr L assured her.

After Amber had left his office he sat back in his chair. 'What an idiot that lad must be,' he thought.

At lunch time Amber deleted nine messages from Phil saying that he wanted to talk to her. She then replied to goodness knows how many asking her if she was okay. By the time she had finished she felt quite exhausted. Everyone was being so sweet. She had been patted more times than a pet dog, hugged and squeezed, and told by everyone that she would be fine given time. The afternoon went surprisingly quickly because, before she knew it, Gloria was coming in through the doors. She had the most amazing tent-like dress on with a turban to match. It had every colour imaginable on it.

"Get you, Mrs colourful," Melanie said admiringly.

"You like it, honey?" Gloria beamed before giving Melanie a twirl.

"Love it," Melanie said, pointing her finger at it.

"Thank you, sugar." She turned to Amber. "Did you choose your ring, girlie?"

Amber shook her head. "There isn't going to be a ring."

"No ring? What's happened, sugar?" Gloria asked.

Amber let out a sigh before telling Gloria.

"Come here, child," Gloria said, opening her arms. As Amber stepped into them she breathed in a comforting smell of roses and talc. "You'll be needing some tender care and you got yourself lots of people to give it."

"Yes, she has," said Melanie and Vicky together.

"Thanks," Amber said as Gloria released her from her vice-like grip. "It's time I wasn't here."

"Shall I pop round later?" Melanie offered.

"No, I'll be fine." Amber shook her head. "I could do with an early night."

"Okay, but if you change your mind and want some company, call me," Melanie said, giving her a kiss on the cheek.

After waving Amber out of the door Gloria turned to Melanie and Vicky. "I could shake that boy, shake the living daylights out of him."

"Join the queue," Melanie replied.

Gloria waddled along to Dorothy's office where she found Dorothy talking to Mr Lockyard. They looked up as she entered.

"Am I intruding on company secrets?" she asked with a twinkle in her eye.

"Absolutely, but seeing as it's you, come on in." Mr Lockyard chuckled. "We've just had notification about the annual charity event for local businesses we take part in. It's going to be a two-day hike, camping overnight on Dartmoor.

stairs back down to the foyer, where he handed his room key in to the girl behind reception.

"Have a good evening, sir." She smiled, then turned to her colleague who was staring after Tom. "Wouldn't mind doing room service for him later."

"Me neither," she swooned.

"You girls look like you need a refill," said Mr L, appearing with a bottle. "Having a good time?" he asked, filling up their glasses.

"Yes, but we haven't seen you on the dance floor yet," Melanie said with a cheeky grin.

"No time like the present then. Let's join Vicky; we can show her how it's done." Mr L laughed.

"I'll hold your drink," offered Amber.

"No you won't; if I'm dancing so are you," said Mr L.

They joined the throng on the dance floor. Mr L had surprisingly good rhythm. Amber looked around, the marquee was heaving. She spotted Gloria dancing with the finance director. Even Dorothy was dancing. Already more than tipsy Amber swayed to the music. 'It was so hot,' she thought.

'The party was obviously going well by the sound of things,' thought Tom as he walked towards the marquee. He was stopped by a number of people, some he knew well, others he'd met briefly. Inside the marquee he tried to head towards the bar, not getting very far before he was stopped again. He stood chatting.

"Tom." Mr Lockyard slapped him on the back. "Why haven't you got a drink?"

"Hello, Francis, good to see you," Tom said, extending his hand for Mr L to shake. "I haven't managed to get as far as the bar yet."

"Follow me, I want to introduce you to a few people you haven't met yet. What's your poison?" he asked on the way to the bar.

"Orange juice and lemonade, please. I have a lot to do tomorrow," Tom said.

As he waited for Francis to get the drinks Tom watched people on the dance floor. As his eyes moved around they fell on Amber. He watched as she pushed her long dark hair back from her face and over her shoulders as she moved in time to the music. He ran his eyes down over her body, then further down, taking in the length of her legs. In the distance he thought he heard his voice being called. Pulling his eyes away from her he turned to see Francis standing there with Gloria beaming beside him.

"Francis, sorry, I was miles away," Tom said, taking his drink. "Thank you." He smiled at Gloria. "Are you going to introduce me to this charming lady?"

"Of course, this is Gloria, who I might add is a very important member of staff," Mr L said graciously.

"Gloria, it's a pleasure to meet you," Tom said, smiling.

"My, my, they was right when they said you was a good-looking boy. It's a pleasure to meet you too." Gloria beamed. She was as sure as sure could be that he had been watching Amber.

Tom laughed. He instantly knew he would like Gloria. She had him reeling with laughter as they talked.

"Well, I got to be shaking my bootie to this one, I'll be checking on you later, hehehe," she said, heading to the dance floor.

Tom watched her waddle off. He looked to where Amber had been dancing. She was no longer there. Turning back to Francis he smiled. "That is some lady."

"She certainly is, very popular with everyone, especially the girls on reception. She's also a very close friend of Dorothy," Mr L informed him.

Before Tom had time to say anything they were joined by some of the finance team.

Melanie and Amber pushed their way to the bar.

"What shall we have, some more bubbly?" Melanie asked Amber.

"No, a nice cold G&T, I think," Amber answered.

"Good idea," Melanie agreed. "Two gin and tonics, doubles would be nice." She winked at the barman.

"No problem." He winked back.

It was so hot that Amber had almost drunk hers by the time Vicky joined them.

"Guess who I've just been talking to?" she said.

"Who?" Melanie asked.

"Tom Tranter," Vicky said.

"Where is he?" Melanie asked.

"Over there," Vicky said, trying to point discretely, "with Mr L and the geeks from finance. He tapped my shoulder as I went by and said hello."

Melanie looked over to the group. You couldn't fail to notice Tom, who seemed to be deep in conversation. She nudged Amber. "What do you think then?"

Amber was staring with a glazed expression on her face. She could hardly focus on Melanie and Vicky, let alone somebody in a crowd 20-feet away.

"God, Amber, how many have you had?" Vicky said laughing.

"Too many, but what the hell, I'm drowning my sorrows, I'll have another one of these if you're going to the bar," Amber said, finishing her drink. "Let's dance again," she said, heading to the dance floor.

Melanie and Vicky looked at each other. "You go keep an eye on her, I'll get the drinks," Vicky said.

By the time Melanie got to Amber on the dance floor she had already attracted some admirers who were dancing around her likes bees at a honey pot. They made room for Melanie to join them, then Vicky.

Spotting Amber with Melanie and Vicky on the dance floor again Tom found it hard to concentrate on what was being said to him. 'Something was obviously very funny,' he thought as he watched the three girls erupt into fits of laughter. Nodding in answer to being asked if he wanted to get something to eat he moved outside with the others.

"There's that site worker I was chatting to earlier, right where I put the drinks." Vicky had to practically shout into Melanie's ear above the music.

"Let's go get our drinks then," Melanie said, pushing Vicky in front of her and grabbing Amber by the arm, pulling her behind.

Vicky didn't get a chance to pick her drink up before the stocky site worker accosted her. Melanie handed it to her.

"Bet Vicky gets laid tonight," she said to Amber. "Has anybody caught your eye yet?"

"Will you stop it? I told you I'm off men for good." Amber slapped her arm playfully.

"Until you spot some hunk who takes your fancy," said Melanie.

"That won't happen," Amber said as she drowned the rest of her drink.

"Christ, Am, you drank that quickly, I've hardly started mine. As your therapist I feel I should get some hog roast inside of you, especially as you aren't interested in the other form of pork." Melanie laughed.

Amber went into fits of giggles. Even in her depth of despair Melanie always made her laugh. "I'd rather have another drink," she slurred.

"Okay, we'll get you another one on the way, but you'd better eat before drinking it," instructed Melanie.

With a fresh G&T in her hand Amber was propelled through the crowded marquee. It was almost dark outside. Lanterns had been lit on all the tables. The candles twinkled in the twilight.

"I need the loo," Amber announced.

"I'd better come with you," Melanie said.

"I'll be fine," Amber hiccupped.

"Okay, I'll queue to get us something to eat." She watched as Amber walked away, swaying every now and again from side to side.

Amber hummed along to the music playing as she headed for the toilet, sipping her drink as she went. Once inside the ladies she took what was the last sip of her drink. She looked into the empty glass, wondering where it had gone. 'Oh well,' she thought, placing it down before going into a cubicle. She went to sit down, almost missing the toilet seat. Placing her elbows on her knees, then her chin in her hands, she suddenly felt really tired and her head was

197

starting to spin. 'Pull yourself together,' she told herself. It took her what seemed like ages to wiggle her dress down. Banging out of the cubicle she washed her hands while staring at herself in the mirror, or rather two of herself in the mirror.

Once outside she set her sights on the marquee. 'The grass didn't seem so uneven on the way over,' she thought as she stumbled forward.

"Excuse me, a call of nature," Tom said, leaving the crowd. 'It really was a beautiful evening,' he thought as he headed towards the offices. 'Somebody has had too many,' he grinned to himself as he saw a figure ahead of him fall.

Amber went down like a sack of potatoes. She lay there for a moment before trying to sit up. It was such an effort that she lay back down again. 'Just a little sleep then she'd have another go,' she told herself.

As he neared he watched as she tried to sit up. Recognising the long hair he ran towards where she lay. Sinking to his knees beside her he touched her arm.

"Hey, are you ok?" he asked.

Amber heard his voice. She tried to open her eyes but everything started to spin. "The room's spinning," she mumbled.

He laughed. "I'm sure it is, try to sit up," he said, gently pulling her to a sitting position.

"I don't want to," Amber tried to protest.

Starting to worry about where Amber was Melanie headed towards the offices to look for her. She came across Tom on his knees gently trying to sit Amber up. 'Oh shit,' she thought, 'not good for the new boss to find one of his employees as pissed as a fart.' She knelt down by his side, instantly relieved when he turned to her smiling.

"I see you've met Amber." She grinned.

"Well, not officially but I'll take that as an introduction. I don't think she will be going back to the party, do you?" Tom joked.

"No, I'd better get her home," Melanie said, taking out her phone. "I'll call a taxi. I don't suppose you'll believe me if I say Amber never gets like this?"

Tom laughed. "I believe you. Look, I can take her home if you show me where she lives," Tom offered.

"Really? That would be great but what about the party? Won't they wonder where you are?" Melanie asked.

"You're not going to tell me she lives miles away, are you?" Tom said as he stood up, still managing to keep Amber sat up.

"No," Melanie said, standing up as well.

"Good," he said, pulling Amber – a dead weight –to her feet. He bent slightly before tipping her over his shoulder into a fireman's lift. "Come on, the truck's in the car park."

"The room's still spinning," Amber mumbled from her upside-down position.

Melanie giggled. "Amber, you're outside."

Between them they managed to get Amber lying across the back seat of the truck. As they drove Melanie directed Tom to Amber's flat, in between chatting and turning to check Amber was alright. When they arrived Tom looked out of the window.

"I suppose you're going to tell me it's not the ground floor flat now." He grinned.

"You're right, it's not. Let me get the key out a minute," Melanie said, opening Amber's bag.

As Tom manoeuvred Amber in order for him to get her out she opened her eyes. "Am I falling out of my dress again?" she asked before closing her eyes again.

Tom looked down. She certainly was. "You'd better do something about that." He smiled at Melanie standing back.

"Will you believe me when I say she didn't want to wear this dress either?" Melanie said as she made Amber look a little more decent.

"I believe you," Tom said again as he got Amber out of the car and over his shoulder once more.

Once inside the flat Tom followed Melanie into the bedroom. He deposited Amber on the bed. She let out a sigh as he did so. Standing back he looked down on her. 'Even though she looked more than a little dishevelled she was so beautiful,' he thought.

"I'd better get back to the party, will you be able to manage alright?" he asked Melanie.

"Sure, thanks for the lift," Melanie said.

"No problem. I'll let myself out, see you Monday," Tom said as he left.

"See you Monday," Melanie said.

After he'd gone Melanie turned her attention to Amber who was sleeping peacefully. "I'm sure there are a lot of girls who would love to be thrown over his shoulder. Trust you to miss it, and you've lost a sandal," she said, taking the remaining one off. She pulled the duvet over the still-clothed Amber. She locked the flat door, sent Vicky and Henry a text letting them know the state of play before crawling into bed next to Amber. "Fuck me, I've slept with you more times than Gary this week."

CHAPTER 12

Amber ran down to where her car was parked. She hated being late. As soon as she turned the key in the ignition the petrol light lit up, reminding her she had driven home with practically an empty tank on Friday night. She had intended to fill up on Saturday but having spent most of the day in bed nursing the hangover from hell, and not feeling much better on Sunday, it had completely slipped her mind. Now she had no option but to fill up on the way to work, which was going to make her even later. 'Great way to start the week,' she thought as she pulled off. 'Why was everything going so wrong for her lately?' She thought about Phil. She constantly found herself going over their relationship, analysing it, trying to work out if she had missed a warning signal that he had been cheating on her, if it had been her that had driven him towards another woman, torturing herself that it was somehow her fault.

Tom pulled into the petrol station. Jumping out of the wagon he whistled to himself as he pushed the nozzle of the petrol pump into the tank. Glancing around he gave a rather plump middle-aged woman who caught his eye a cheery smile. On his way in to pay he picked up a paper.

As Amber arrived at the petrol station she was wondering if perhaps she should have been more adventurous in the bedroom; maybe her underwear was a bit on the boring side, well, she had to admit, very on the boring side if you compared it to Melanie's bedroom attire. She turned in and stopped. 'Why did it have to be so busy when she was so late?' she said to herself. She sat there gazing out of the window, waiting for a pump to become free. Hearing a car horn honking she looked over. Was that man making those signs at her? 'Surely not,' she thought as she heard another honk of a horn. Turning in that direction there was a woman waving her hands frantically. 'What was going on?' Now a man walking to his car started pointing at something behind her. She turned to look, the penny finally dropping. 'Oh God,' she thought, 'she had driven in the exit and was now blocking everybody trying to get out.'

After paying for his petrol, paper in hand, Tom wondered what all the commotion was about as he stepped outside. 'Whoops,' he thought as he spotted the car blocking the exit, 'somebody's having a bad morning.' As he walked to the wagon he looked more closely, then began to chuckle as he recognised the long dark hair framing a somewhat harassed looking Amber. He headed towards her car.

'Shit,' thought Amber, 'shit, shit, shit. Whatever had possessed her to drive in through the exit? She had been using this petrol station for years.' Noticing the man walking towards her car, laughing, her heart sank. 'Now she was going to get some sanctimonious bloke telling her she should have been blonde, no doubt,' She said to herself as she wound down her window. 'Well, she would be ready for him.'

"I'm well aware of what I've done. I'm just about to move, so you really don't need to say anything," Amber spouted defensively to Tom as he bent slightly so he could look in at her.

"I was going to offer to see you back." Tom tried to keep a straight face.

"I don't need any help, thank you. Believe it or not, I'm quite capable of reversing." Amber's cheeks coloured slightly as she put her car into reverse.

"I'm sure you are." Tom smiled before stepping back as Amber began to reverse.

'How embarrassing,' Amber thought as she edged backwards then forwards, goodness knows how many times, before she was in the right position to get out. She wished she was invisible as she then drove a few hundred feet up the road and into the entrance.

Out of politeness Tom knocked on Francis Lockyard's door as he entered.

"Morning, Francis."

"Tom, good morning. Sit yourself down. I'm not sure what's happened to Amber this morning, so I'm afraid we're going to have to wait for tea." He motioned towards one of the high-back leather chairs on the other side of his desk.

"I might be able to help you there." Tom grinned to himself as he sat down. "I've just seen her. You could say she was a bit stuck at the petrol station, the one just along the road."

"Oh, there we are then, mystery solved. It's so unlike her to be late. Take a look at this." He handed Tom a folder.

Amber rushed in, grabbing the post that Harry must have left. She quickly stuck the kettle on. After preparing Mr L's tray she stood willing it to boil, 'Why did things take so long when you were in a hurry?' Finally, tea brewing contentedly in the teapot, she hurried to Mr L's office. Outside his door she balanced the tray on her left arm before knocking, then she entered.

"So sorry I'm late." She smiled apologetically at Mr L as she headed to the little table to put down the tray. "I overslept, forgot I had no petrol in the car, then, to make matters worse, I drove in through the exit of the garage, which didn't make me very popular, I can tell you. I'll stay late to make up the time," she gabbled, turning with the teapot in her hand, only to realise they weren't alone. She stopped talking and stood staring at Tom, who sat looking at her with more than a little amusement. 'Oh no, it was the bloke from the garage. What was he doing here?'

"Are you alright, Amber?" Mr L asked as he watched her standing there staring at Tom, her mouth wide open.

Amber turned to look at him, trying to regain her composure. "I, um, yes, I'm fine."

"Tom said he'd seen you at the garage," Mr L went on.

"Oh," was all Amber managed to get out as she looked back at Tom. 'This morning was going from bad to worse. This must be Tom Tranter who was taking over from Mr L and she had only gone and snapped at him before almost reversing over his toes in the garage earlier. But how did he know who she was?' All this was going through her mind as she stood there.

"Is there enough tea in that pot for me?" Tom asked, still smiling at Amber from where he sat.

Amber blushed as she realised she was still staring at him. "I'll get another cup and saucer." She started to walk towards the door.

"I'd prefer a mug," Tom said, standing up and stepping in front of her before she got to the door. "You can leave the teapot. I promise not to use Francis' cup."

Amber looked down at the teapot in her hands, then back at him without saying anything. He might be her new boss but he was still a man obviously used to women laughing every time he thought he said something funny. 'Well, she wouldn't,' she thought defensively. She turned around quickly and half marched to the tray to put the teapot down. "A mug it is then," she said, side-stepping Tom to get out.

The phone was practically ringing off the hook as she neared the desk. 'He can wait for the mug,' she thought, hurrying around to take the call. By the time she had finished Melanie and Vicky were waltzing in.

"Am I glad to see you two." Amber sighed.

"Still suffering?" Vicky laughed.

"Feeling much better today." Amber rolled her eyes. "Just worried I embarrassed myself Friday night, although I should be used to feeling stupid by now."

"Stop that," Melanie chastised. "You didn't embarrass yourself any more than anyone else, but I do need to tell you how we got home."

"What do you mean? How we got home?" Amber looked puzzled. "We got a taxi, didn't we?"

"Well, not quite. I was going to tell you Saturday morning, but when I woke up you were still away with the fairies so I left you sleeping. Then when I called you later you practically put the phone down on me because you felt so dreadful …"

"Sorry about that." Amber put her hand on her forehead. "Why did I drink so much?"

"Morning, ladies," Tom interrupted as he strode towards the desk.

"Good morning," said Melanie. "What can we do for you?"

"I've come searching for a mug," Tom said with a glint in his eye as he looked at Amber.

"You should have just buzzed," Vicky said. "One of us would have brought one through to you."

"Amber was going to get me one, but seeing as I had to return this to her I thought I'd save her a job." Tom moved his arm from behind his back where he had been keeping Amber's sandal out of sight. He held it out to her. "You left it in my truck Friday night."

'Goodness. Don't tell me he had given them a lift home,' Amber panicked, then looked at Melanie who stood with an I-was-just-about-to-tell-you look on her face.

"Don't you want it back?" he asked, waving the sandal at her.

"Yes." Amber took the sandal from him. "Thank you, and I'd better thank you for taking me home on Friday night. I hope you didn't have to go too far out of your way."

"Don't mention it." He bowed slightly. "I'm sure you'll be able to return the favour in some way. Now, if one of you would be so kind as to point me in the direction of the mugs, I'd better get back to Francis before he comes looking for me."

"I'll show you where they are," Vicky offered quickly. "Come with me."

"I'll make you a fresh brew," Melanie said, smiling at Tom as he followed Vicky. Turning back to Amber she grinned again. "That's what I was about to tell you. It was Tom Tranter who took us back to your flat."

Amber held up her sandal. "I didn't even know I'd lost it. I didn't get round to doing anything over the weekend. My bedroom looks like a bomb has hit it. I'm surprised I didn't hurt my feet walking barefoot."

"Well, that's another thing. You didn't walk, Tom carried you." Melanie made a face.

"What? What do you mean? He carried me?" Amber gasped. "Why didn't you tell me?"

"I'm telling you now and I did try to tell you. It's not my fault you haven't been in a fit state to listen." Melanie laughed. "But seeing as you're listening now, where shall I start? Oh yes, I found you lying on the grass with Mr gorgeous trying to sit you up, or was he lying on top of you?"

"Be serious," Amber pleaded.

"I am." Melanie laughed again. "No, just joking. Look, Am, you'd fallen down. He was trying to get you up when I came looking for you. You were in such a state that he very kindly offered to take you home. He did have to give you a fireman's lift to his truck though and another one up to your flat."

"He's been in my flat?" Amber went white.

"Afraid so, and in your bedroom. When he put you on the bed he gave you more than the once over, probably because you were flashing all you've got at him." Melanie cupped her own breasts and jiggled them up and down.

"Stop," Amber said, holding up her hand. "I'll never forgive you for making me buy that dress. And it only gets worse." She told Melanie what happened in the garage earlier, then finding Tom in with Mr L.

"I've never known you to make such an impression on anyone. Perhaps you should take this fresh brew in and try to make amends?" Melanie suggested.

"No way." Amber shook her head. "You take it. I'm keeping out of his way. He obviously thinks I'm an airhead. Not that I care what he thinks. I can't say I like him. He obviously thinks he's something special. I'll get on with opening the post."

"Amber, you're rambling." Melanie touched her friends arm. "Everybody gets pissed now and then, don't worry about it. He's a really nice bloke, not the kind to hold it against you."

"No bloke is nice when it comes down to it." Amber sighed, picking up a letter.

"That shithead has something to answer for, he really has," Melanie said, referring to Phil as she picked up the tray. "I'll make us a coffee when I've taken this in." She smiled at Vicky who had just got back. "Get Am to tell you what happened this morning."

Beth shut her suitcase. She checked her appearance in the full-length mirror. 'Yes,' she thought, 'I look fantastic.' The past two weeks of sun had left her with the deepest of tans, with only the tiniest white triangle where her thong bikini bottoms had been. She smirked at herself, and thought, 'Tom was sure to have missed her.' All work and no play makes for a very dull existence. Looking like she did she felt sure she could seduce him again. As soon as she got home she would arrange a flight down to Bristol, surprise him at the Bath office, make him see what he was missing. 'Oh, what an entrance she was going to make.'

She checked her watch. Rebecca would be waiting in reception and she still had to settle her bill before the taxi arrived to take them back to the airport. As she stepped out of the lift into the hotel foyer she saw Rebecca talking to the two gym instructors that they had been more than friendly with. 'Surely they weren't so stupid as to think they were going to swap email addresses to keep in touch, were they?' Beth said to herself. As she neared she saw the keen expression on the face of ... what was his name? It had slipped her mind already, probably because they hadn't done a lot of talking.

"Beth, I've been waiting for you. I have my email address here so we can keep in touch, you know, after having such a good time together, if you know what I mean." He held out a neatly folded piece of paper.

Beth looked at the piece of paper then at him. "I don't really do email," she said, with more than a hint of sarcasm and a sickly-sweet smile on her face, before walking away.

As she waited at the desk to settle her bill Rebecca joined her. "You could have taken it, poor bloke."

"I could have." Beth shrugged. "But let's face it, he'll be shagging someone else next week, won't he?"

"More than likely." Rebecca laughed.

Gloria hummed as she waddled in.

"Time for me to go, thank goodness." Amber sighed as Gloria reached the desk.

"Amber, honey, you been having a bad day?" Gloria asked as she pulled out the usual sweets from her tabard pocket.

"It hasn't been one of my best, but then I don't seem to be having many good ones lately, do I?" Amber said sadly.

"Now, you listen to old Gloria. She say things will be looking up in no time, you just see if they don't."

"That's exactly what we've been saying," Vicky added.

"They're looking up already. I've just had a text from Henry. He's cooking you tea tonight. He's not taking no for an answer as he's already bought the ingredients. He also said, 'don't worry, it will be an alcohol-free night'." Melanie giggled. "You have to be at ours by seven o'clock. No bringing a bottle in your handbag."

"Very funny. I was going to tidy my room tonight, you know, find my other sandal, or could that be somewhere else and you haven't got round to telling me yet?" She said raising her eyebrows at Melanie.

"See you later," Melanie said, pushing her out from behind the desk.

"You coming for tea at mine this week as well. Remember, honey, something Caribbean to thank you for babysitting," Gloria said, catching Amber as Melanie pushed her out.

"I haven't forgotten. I'm looking forward to it, I love your cooking." Amber gave Gloria a kiss.

"You sure is a good girlie," Gloria said, kissing her back. "Mr right is waiting for you round the corner, you just see if he ain't."

Amber left with a wave of her hand. She walked to her car slowly. 'When was she going to start feeling happy again?' she asked herself.

Tom sauntered towards the desk, smiling broadly at Melanie, Vicky and Gloria, who had all clocked his approach.

"My oh my, he sure is a good-looking boy," Gloria said to the girls.

"He sure is," Vicky agreed.

"Gloria," Tom addressed her first. "I'm liking the dress," he said, taking in the multi-coloured fabric.

"Why, thank you, sugar." Gloria gave him a twirl. "You leaving now?"

"Yes." He grinned at Vicky and Melanie, then quickly glanced over their shoulders. "Just you two at this time, is it?" he asked casually.

"Just us. Amber's just gone. She finishes at four," Vicky told him. "We both finish at five."

"And I was meant to start at four so I'd better get myself going," Gloria said.

"Me too, bye ladies, have a good evening," Tom said, heading for the door.

"That boy was fishing to find out where Amber was," Gloria mumbled to herself as she waddled off.

"What did Gloria just say?" Vicky asked Melanie.

"Don't know, didn't catch it," Melanie answered.

As Tom walked through the car park Amber was just reversing out of her space. She checked how far she was from the car next to her and saw Tom. He couldn't resist it. "Do you want me to see you back?" he mouthed wickedly. "Very funny," she mouthed back at him before continuing to reverse out. She didn't look back again. He watched her drive off for the second time that day. 'What was it about her?' he said to himself, 'It wasn't just how incredibly beautiful she was, it was, Christ, he didn't know what it was, only that he had found himself thinking about her since Friday night.'

Melanie walked into the kitchen to find Henry chopping onions in his floral apron, singing at the top of his voice. She turned the CD player down so all you could hear was a very out-of-tune Henry belting out 'I'm saving all my love for you ....'.

He turned round to find Melanie laughing. "Don't you just adore Whitney?" he said, before cracking up.

"Hennie, I know she's one of your favourites but I don't think Whitney songs are going to do much to cheer Amber up," she said, turning it off and removing it.

"Ooh, you're so right, I'm such a noggin. There's the door bell. You turned it off just in the nick of time," Henry said, wiping his hand over his brow theatrically.

Melanie returned moments later with Amber.

"Dear girl." Henry kissed, first one of Amber's cheeks, and then the other.

"Love the apron." Amber stroked it.

"Cath Kidston don't you know," Henry said, flipping his hands. "Spag bol for din dins. Sit yourself down. Now you're here I'll get it going."

"Lovely," Amber said, sitting down at the table opposite Melanie who had already plonked herself on a chair.

Henry put the onions and mince into a big pan. "You're looking a bit thin, sweet pea. Have you lost weight?" he asked Amber over his shoulder.

"A little bit," Amber answered.

"More than a little bit," Henry said in his concerned– about-you voice. "Melanie, dear heart, will you get the garlic bread out the freezer, please? The oven's hot enough for it now, oh, and lay the table."

"I'll lay the table," Amber offered.

"Stick a CD on as well," Henry said, giving a crafty wink to Melanie. He carried on keeping the girls amused while he cooked. Before long they were sat down twirling spaghetti around their forks.

"Who wants the last piece of garlic bread?" Melanie asked.

"Me," Henry answered quickly. "Manner, manners. Me, if nobody else wants it."

"You have it, Henry, I'm full," Amber said, surveying her empty plate.

Henry swiped the bread.

"What about me?" Melanie squawked.

"You are not a guest." Henry laughed as he bit into the garlic bread, but then gave the remainder to Melanie who shoved it into her mouth quickly.

"Just popping up to the loo," Amber said, standing up.

"Try my new hand cream. It's in the window," Henry called after her.

"Hennie, that was bloody lovely." Melanie sat patting her tummy.

"Why, thank you, dear heart, and we have choc pots for dessert." He beamed. "Low fat ones, of course."

Amber's mobile phone started to ring in her bag.

"I'll get that for her," Melanie said, getting the phone from Amber's bag. "It's Phil." She made a face at Henry as she answered it. "Hello, Amber's phone."

"Melanie, is that you? It's Phil, um, tell Amber I'll call back." The phone then went dead.

"What did he want?" Henry asked.

"How the hell do I know? The bastard rang off," Melanie said, waving the phone about.

"I'll get the choc pots, you look like you could do with something sweet. Scowling does make you look ugly, dear heart, and it will give you wrinkles," Henry said, getting up from the table.

"What's she scowling at?" Amber asked, returning from the loo.

"Nothing." Henry smiled, not too convincingly.

"Am, your phone was ringing so I answered it. It was Phil. Is he still harassing you?" Melanie asked, giving Amber her phone.

Amber put it straight back in her bag. "Um, well, you know," she mumbled.

"No, I don't know." Melanie looked at her questionably.

Amber slumped down in her chair, avoiding Melanie's eyes. Henry hovered by the table, holding the choc pots he had taken from the fridge.

"Amber," Melanie's voice rose, "don't tell me you're going to have him back?"

"Oh my God. Let me sit down before I drop these," Henry said, his eyes fully fixed on Amber's face.

"No." Amber shook her head. "But I have arranged to meet him."

"What do you mean, meet him?" Melanie asked.

"Yes, what do you mean, meet him?" Henry repeated.

"Well, the thing is, as you know, he keeps turning up at the flat begging me to talk to him." She put her hands up to stop them interrupting. "I have just shut the door in his face. He keeps phoning, but I cut him off." She put her hands up again. "And he keeps texting saying he will do anything to put things right."

This time, Henry did manage to interrupt, "Sweet pea, he shagged some ginger piece behind your back. How can he put that right?"

"He can't, but you see, I keep torturing myself that it was somehow a failure on my part that sent him elsewhere. I just want to hear what he has to say. Then when he's convinced me that it was him not me, it will just prove the point that men really are bastards. I'm meeting him about six o'clock at The George on Friday." She looked at Melanie, then Henry, bracing herself for the onslaught. Which to her surprise didn't come. Instead, Melanie reached over and squeezed her hand. Henry did exactly the same to the other one.

"Am, why are you doing this to yourself? It was nothing you did," she said gently. "But if you really need to, fair enough. But why didn't you tell me?"

"I was going to, but afterwards. I thought you might try to put me off," Amber said ruefully.

"I can see there's no point putting you off. I know how hurt you are and if you really feel you need to hear the gory details to be able to move on then that's what you have to do," Melanie said.

"You will tell us all the gory details, won't you, sweetness? Then when we arrange to have a contract out on him we'll know how much to make him suffer before he's finished off." Henry grinned.

"Oh, Henry, you're so sweet. When I say I hate men, I don't mean you. I love you to bits." Amber rubbed his arm affectionately.

"I know you do. Everybody does." He held his hands to his heart.

Melanie slapped him. "Shut up blowing your own trumpet and put the kettle on."

Henry stuck his tongue out at her before jumping up.

"Am, you will like men again, I guarantee it. Just give yourself time." Melanie smiled at her friend.

"I don't think so." Amber shook her head.

215

"That's ok, you two just sit there, I'll see who's at the door," Henry said, flouncing out of the kitchen, exaggerating the movement.

"Didn't hear the bell," Melanie called after him.

"Nor did I," Amber called.

Gary appeared at the kitchen door, closely followed by Henry.

"Hey, Henry didn't say you had company," he said rather awkwardly, seeing Amber sat at the table.

"She's not company, she's part of the family," Henry corrected him.

"Hi," Amber said, seeing how uncomfortable Gary looked.

"Hi," Gary answered. "Please let me apologise for opening my big mouth. I feel just awful about the whole situation."

"It wasn't your fault, no need to apologise," Amber said sincerely.

"Now that's over with, who's for tea, who's for coffee?" Henry stood, hands on hips.

"Coffee," Amber and Melanie replied together.

"Not for me, thanks, Henry. I've interrupted your evening enough," he said turning to Melanie. "I'll call you later." "Stay," Amber encouraged. "You'll make me feel bad if you go."

"In that case, I'd better have a coffee," he said, joining the girls at the table.

"Coming right up," Henry said, reaching for another mug.

They sat listening to Gary relaying funny stories of happenings in the bar. Amber noticed how Melanie was looking at him. It was quite obvious she was more than keen, maybe, just maybe, he was the one that was going to win her heart. 'Only to probably break it.' She immediately scolded herself for that thought; not everyone was as unlucky as she was.

"More coffee, anyone?" Henry asked.

"Is that the time?" Amber said, surprised. It was nearly 11pm. "Not for me, thanks. I'd better be going. I don't want to be late again tomorrow."

"At least you have a full tank of petrol now." Melanie laughed.

"Have I missed something?" Henry asked, puzzled.

"No," Amber said quickly, giving him a kiss. "Thanks for a lovely evening. Bye, Gary."

"Bye, Amber." Gary raised his hand.

Melanie went to the door with her. "See you tomorrow," she said, hugging her close.

"See you tomorrow. Gary seems really nice, you two are suited," Amber said, hugging her back.

Melanie stood giving Amber a wave as she drove off. Walking back into the kitchen Henry was just taking his apron off after washing up the mugs.

"I'm off to bed." He pointed at Melanie, then Gary. "Make sure you two keep the noise down when you come up."

Gary closed the door behind Henry. "In that case, we'd better make the noise down here because something has definitely come up in my trousers."

CHAPTER 13

"Come and look at this, you two," Melanie called from the back office.

"What?" Vicky asked as she appeared in the doorway.

"Hang on," Amber called back before she picked up an incoming call.

Vicky read the email over Melanie's shoulder.

SOMETHING TO THINK ABOUT OVER THE WEEKEND

The annual charity event we take part in is on us again. It is going to be the second weekend in October. This year we are looking for a man/woman team for a 20-mile two-day hike on Dartmoor. (Hopefully a reasonably fit man/woman team.) I'm sure you will be pleased to hear what was going to be just an overnight camp has now been extended to an extra night (Sunday). This means that once the hike is over everyone can nurse their tired feet by the fire while enjoying a hot dog. (Of course, the Monday will be given as a courtesy day's holiday.)

Email your entry to Dorothy by Thursday. We are expecting at least one entry from each department (no pressure) please. The lucky participants will be picked on Friday.

Francis Lockyard

"Oh dear, you'll have to count me out, my cousin's getting married the second weekend in October," Vicky said with a smirk. "Didn't you two do the Ten Tors there when you were at school?"

"Yes. It was a bloody nightmare," Melanie said.

"What was a bloody nightmare?" Amber asked, joining them.

"The Ten Tors on Dartmoor as part of our D of E," Melanie said.

Amber nodded. "Yes, it was. Never again."

"Well, actually, again, but only 20 miles. Read this." Melanie motioned towards the computer screen.

Amber read the email. "We can probably get away with the at-least-one-entry seeing as there are only the three of us."

"Only the two of us. Madam has fortunately got a wedding that weekend, so that counts her out." Melanie gave Vicky a playful slap.

"Sorry." Vicky laughed.

"No, you're not." Melanie slapped her again before turning towards Amber. "At least whoever ends up doing it gets the Monday off."

"Shall we flip a coin for it? Loser has to enter," Amber suggested.

"Good idea. I'll do the flipping," Vicky said. "I'll just get a coin."

"Heads or tails?" Amber asked Melanie.

"Tails," Melanie said, crossing her fingers.

"Ready?" Vicky asked.

"Ready," they both replied.

Vicky tossed the coin. Catching it, she put it on the back of her other hand. "Heads it is, you'd better check your walking boots are in good order, Mel."

"Hard luck," Amber commiserated.

"Thanks a bloody bunch. I can think of nothing I'd like better than a two-day hike on Dartmoor," she said as she closed the email.

"Where's your drive and enthusiasm?" Vicky laughed, jumping back before Melanie could take another swipe at her.

"Funny, but I just can't seem to find it to go hiking for charity." Melanie stood up. "Now, if it was for something a little more interesting, I'm your girl." She started to gyrate her hips.

"What are you girlies up to back there?" Gloria's voice interrupted them from the front desk.

"Only Melanie being Melanie," Amber said, still giggling as she led the way out of the back office.

"Is you being naughty?" Gloria asked Melanie, waggling her finger.

"Of course not," Melanie said, giving a little shimmy.

"You is always naughty girl," Gloria boomed.

"I know. I just can't help it," Melanie said, running round the front of the desk to hug Gloria.

Amber quickly got her bag. Slinging it over her shoulder she tried to edge past Melanie and Gloria, hoping to make a swift exit, but Melanie was too quick for her.

"Hang on a minute, lady." Melanie grabbed her arm. "Before you go I want the promise of a phone call after you've met prick-stick so I know you're ok."

"I'll be fine, stop fussing." Amber smiled weakly.

"A phone call or else I might just turn up." Melanie looked threateningly at Amber.

"Okay, okay, I'll call you." Amber gave her a kiss on the cheek.

"Good girl," Melanie said, kissing her back. "Are you sure you're doing the right thing?"

"I'm sure. Stop worrying. Bye, all," Amber said, making her escape.

"Dear Lord, please don't let that scoundrel talk her into giving him a second chance," Gloria said, looking up to heaven.

"I'll second that prayer," Melanie said as they watched Amber walk towards the car park.

"And I'll third it," Vicky added.

"Hey, take a look at the tangoed Barbie getting out of that taxi." Melanie motioned towards the taxi that had just pulled up outside.

Gloria and Vicky turned their attention from Amber to the taxi that Beth was just getting out of. Instructing the driver to wait she sashayed in through the doors, draped head to foot in designer clothes with the hugest pair of black Dior sunglasses on. Her sandals were a good five inches, her false nails gleaming bright pink.

"My oh my, is any part of the girlie real?" Gloria asked, a bit too loudly.

"I actually think the tan is, but that's about it," Vicky whispered as Beth approached the desk.

Beth was aware she was being discussed. 'Not unusual,' she thought, 'they probably don't get to see women like herself that often.' She put on her most gracious smile as she stopped, placing her Mulberry bag down on the desk.

"Good afternoon, will you let Tom Tranter know he has a visitor, please?" she purred.

"Certainly," Melanie replied. "Can I take your name, please?"

"I'm what you might call a little surprise," she said, too sweetly.

Melanie pressed Tom's extension.

"Hello," came his reply.

"Tom, it's Melanie on the desk," she said.

"Hello, Melanie on the desk, what can I do for you?" he asked, leaning back in his chair.

"Can you come out? I need your help, um, you could say, rather urgently. It's a bit personal." Melanie smiled at Beth politely, even though she was tapping her nails rather annoyingly on the desk.

"Okay," Tom said, replacing the phone. 'It was a shame it wasn't Amber who needed his help,' he thought. 'He had tried in vain to engage her, but to no avail. She somehow managed to end a conversation before it had begun, and when she was with the other girls on the desk she always let them do the talking while she disappeared into that bloody back office.'

"Ha, ha," Phil replied. "Are we ready to lock up? I've got to get going."

"Oh, do you now? Smelling like that it has to be a woman." Cheryl winked.

"Actually, I'm meeting Amber. I'm hoping to convince her that you and me were, well, you know ..." Phil tried to find the right words.

"A mistake, a fumble in the dark. Good luck, darling," Cheryl said good-naturedly.

"Thanks. Keep your fingers crossed." Phil held up crossed fingers.

As Phil drove to meet Amber he thought about Cheryl. She had sent him a text on the Saturday morning to say sorry Amber had found out about them. Then on the Monday at work she'd behaved as if nothing had ever happened between them. He couldn't really blame her for the mess he was in. She had offered herself to him on a plate. He had taken it, and a lot more than once. He still felt awkward at work, even though Cheryl obviously didn't; no doubt, that was because she was used to the scenario they were in. If only she hadn't been in the wine bar that Friday night he and Amber would be happily engaged now. He pulled into the car park. Looking around he couldn't see Amber's car. He turned off the engine and opened the car door in the hope of getting a breeze. It had suddenly become very humid.

Amber saw Phil as she pulled in. She decided not to park beside him, even though there were plenty of spaces.

"Hi, you look pretty," he said as they walked towards one another.

"Hello, Phil," Amber replied, choosing to ignore his compliment.

"Shall we sit outside?" he suggested.

"Okay." Amber nodded.

After getting their drinks they found a table. They sat down and looked at one another for a few moments, before Phil placed his hand on Amber's arm as she twiddled with her wine glass.

"Amber, I've missed you so much." He sighed. "I'll do anything to put things right."

Amber pulled her arm away and looked him straight in the eye. "Why did you do it?"

"I don't know." He shook his head. "I honestly don't know. It just kind of happened."

"I want to know everything." Amber sat very still as she spoke.

"Where should I start?" Phil shrugged his shoulders in despair.

"The beginning would be good," Amber said sarcastically.

Phil took a deep breath. "It was just Cheryl and me in the office one afternoon. We were having a joke, a laugh, like you do, you know, the usual office banter. We ended up flipping a coin to see who was going to make a coffee, and I lost. While I was waiting for the kettle to boil Cheryl came up behind me. We, well, we ended up ..." He shrugged his shoulders again.

"Having sex? Is that what you're trying to say? You ended up having sex in the office kitchen?" Amber tried not to raise her voice.

"Yes." Phil looked down at his lap. He'd left out the bit about Cheryl rubbing herself against him whilst whispering in his ear that she had locked the office door. He looked up again. "I felt so guilty after it had happened."

"Did you? So guilty that you did it again and again, and God knows how many times. Is she married?" Amber asked.

"Yes, she is. They have an understanding," Phil said quietly.

"How nice for them. The thing is, we didn't have an understanding, did we? Not one that I knew about anyway." As she stared at Phil she wondered what she ever saw in him. How had he ever made her heart skip a beat? He looked almost pathetic now. He honestly thought he could win her back with a bit of an explanation, a sorrowful expression and promises that it would never happen again.

"Amber, it's you I love, it's you I want to be with, nobody else. I never wanted to hurt you, please forgive me. We can put this behind us. Lots of people go through this kind of thing and are stronger for it." Phil put his hand over Amber's arm again.

Tom opened the back door. He could hear music coming from upstairs. He guessed Beth was probably hanging a vast amount of clothes in his wardrobe. He put his laptop and briefcase down. As he mounted the stairs the smell of perfume got stronger. As he passed the bathroom it was obvious Beth had been in the bath. Pushing open his bedroom door he found her fast asleep on the bed, wearing his dressing gown. The music was coming from the radio on the bedside cabinet. He decided not to disturb her. He would go for a run. It would give him more time to think. He quietly got changed. In the kitchen he wrote her a note and left it on the table where it would be easily spotted.

He looked at his watch. He would run for half an hour, then turn back. He headed for the towpath. It was so humid. He looked up at the sky. It was starting to cloud up. They were in for rain.

"Did you ever go out as a couple?" Amber asked, moving her arm away again.

"No, we never went out." Phil shook his head.

"It was just sex at home then? In your bed, the bed you had sex with me in. Did you change the sheets in between?" Amber watched him squirm.

"Amber, please, it sounds so sordid when you put it like that," Phil said uncomfortably.

"Doesn't it just," Amber said vehemently. "Was she good in bed? I guess she must have been or else you wouldn't have gone there again. I suppose you slept with her, then came round and slept with me. Oh, and then scored us both out of 10. No wonder you always seemed so tired. Silly me thought it was because you were so busy selling houses."

"It wasn't like that. Really, it wasn't like that," Phil said desperately.

"It was exactly like that. You just got found out, that's all," Amber said sadly.

"I would do anything to turn back the clock, and I'll do anything you want me to do to make things right between us, anything, just say what." Phil smiled pitifully at her.

"You can't turn back the clock, or put things right. You know, I just haven't been able to shake the idea that somehow it was something lacking in me that drove you to have an affair, sorry, sex with another woman, but just sitting here listening to you has made it quite clear that it was something lacking in you, not me. There is not a single chance that I will ever forgive you." Amber stood up. "Goodbye, Phil." She turned and walked away, her heart beating like a drum.

As she walked she heard Phil call after her. She didn't turn round but kept walking. She hadn't quite made it to her car when he caught up with her.

"Please, give me another chance," he begged as he walked beside her. "Please, Amber." He grabbed hold of her.

"No," she said, pulling away from him and walking on. Reaching her car she got the keys out of her bag. She turned to Phil who had followed her again. "Just go, Phil. Nothing you can say will change my mind. It's over." She got into the car just as there was an almighty clap of thunder. Phil stood looking at her momentarily, before touching the window with his hand. He then turned and walked away. She watched him get into his car and drive out of the car park. She leaned back in her seat and closed her eyes. She felt utterly exhausted. Another clap of thunder made her jump. She looked at the sky; it was as black as ink. 'Better get home,' she thought, starting the car.

As Phil had turned left out of the car park she decided to turn right and go through the village. She passed people still sat outside enjoying their drinks. No doubt, they would soon be moving inside. The table where she had sat with Phil had not been taken by anyone else. She pulled in to wait for an oncoming car. As the driver drew level with her he wound down his window. "You've got a flat, love. Do you want a hand changing it?"

"Have I? It's okay, thanks, I'll call the AA." She smiled at the man. It was nice of him to offer but he had a baby in the back of the car and a dog that had started to bark.

"It's no problem, it won't take me long," he offered again.

"No, it's fine, let them earn their fee." She put her hand up as she drove off slowly up the road until she found a safe place to pull in.

She got out and had a look. She wondered if she had driven to the pub with it like that. More than likely with the way things were at the moment. More thunder boomed overhead. 'Oh, deep joy,' she thought, 'all the great weather they had been having and her car decided to have a flat tyre just in time for the storm of the century. She'd better call the AA.' Having sensibly put the number in her phone she rang it. As soon as she did so it came up as call-ended. She tried again. Up came call-ended. 'Great. No signal. She would have to walk back to the pub. If she couldn't get a signal there hopefully they would let her use their phone,' she said to herself. She locked her car – not that anyone would want to steal it with a flat tyre – and hurried towards the pub. As she got to the bridge the heavens opened. The rain absolutely lashed down; she was drenched within seconds. It was so hard that she could hardly see in front of her own face. She put her head down and started to run, her feet slipping all over the place in her flip-flops.

Tom approached the bridge, slowing slightly to check for traffic. As he crossed the road he speeded up again. The rain against his face forced him to look down at the pavement. It was too late to avoid the collision with what he thought was another runner.

"Aaaaaa ..." Amber shrieked on her way down to meet the ground.

"I'm very sorry. Are you alright?" Tom shouted to be heard above the rain as he bent down.

"I am, but I think my flip-flop has had it," Amber shouted back as she retrieved the now broken flip-flop that had come off as she had fallen. "Anyway, it was my fault too," she added as she looked to see who had knocked her off her feet.

Tom just couldn't believe it when his eyes met Amber's. He pulled her to her feet, but didn't let her go. "Are you sure you're ok?" he asked again. "What are you doing running around in this?"

'Oh my God,' thought Amber, 'of all the people.' "Yes, I'm fine." Suddenly aware he still had hold of her she stepped back slowly. As she did so he let her go. "My car has a flat tyre. I can't get a signal on my mobile so I was going to the pub to see if I could use their phone, and it just started to tip down."

"I only live just down there." Tom pointed in the direction she had just come from. "Come back with me, I'll change your tyre for you."

"No, it's alright. I have AA cover, but thank you anyway," Amber half stammered.

Tom took hold of her arm and held it up. "At least come back to mine to use my phone, you can't walk to the pub then back to your car with nothing on your feet."

Amber surveyed the broken flip-flop she still had in her hand. He had a point.

"Come on, we can't stand in the rain all night while you make up your mind. I'll give you a piggy-back," he said cheekily.

Amber looked horrified.

Tom burst out laughing. "A fireman's lift then."

"I'll manage without either, thank you," Amber said indignantly.

"Have it your way. Shall we go?" Tom said, already starting to walk back in the direction of her car. Amber began to walk beside him. They hadn't got 10 feet before she stood on a sharp stone. Screeching out in pain she started to hop around. "Get on," Tom ordered, turning his back to her and holding out his arms.

Amber stood on one leg, looking at his back. 'If only the ground would swallow her up. She couldn't see the pavement properly in the pouring rain. He was right, she'd end up cutting her feet to shreds,' she thought. Burning with embarrassment she hobbled over to him and put her hands on his shoulders before launching herself off the ground on to his back. As she did so she felt Tom's hands on her bottom, lifting her up. As soon as she was in place he moved them down around her thighs until she was sitting on his forearms.

"Comfy?" he shouted over his shoulder as he strode off, making Amber put her arms around his neck to hold on. She just couldn't answer. Here she was in the pouring rain on her boss's back on their way to his house. At least last time he had carried her she hadn't known anything about it.

"There's my car," Amber said, finding her voice as she pointed to it.

"Right opposite my place," Tom said, turning into his drive.

He had to grapple to open the back door. They somehow almost fell through it, which sent Amber into fits of giggles, more out of nerves than it being funny.

"Well, hello," said a voice.

Still on Tom's back Amber looked to see a lady dressed somewhat provocatively sitting at a large farmhouse table. She instantly stopped laughing and wriggled slightly, indicating she wanted Tom to let her off his back. He did so and she slipped to the floor.

"Beth, this is Amber; she mans reception at work. Amber, this is Beth." Tom made the introduction. "We've literally bumped into each other. She has a flat tyre and needs to use the phone," he explained.

"Hello, nice to meet you," Amber said politely, feeling very uncomfortable stood before Beth who was immaculately made up, in what was obviously a designer dress with a designer cleavage to match, while she looked like a drowned rat, wet hair stuck to her head, wearing the very latest from H&M. As Beth was looking at the broken flip-flop she still had in her hand Amber held it up. "Broken flip-flop, hence the piggy-back ride." She smiled awkwardly.

"I'll pay for a new pair," Tom said. "If I hadn't knocked you over you wouldn't have broken it."

"No need, I was as much to blame. I wasn't looking where I was going," Amber said.

"I insist." Tom smiled.

"No, really, they weren't expensive, thank you anyway," Amber argued.

"Tom, darling, just give her some money." Beth smiled, oh so sweetly, at Tom, then looked at Amber. "You'll be able to treat yourself to a decent pair," she said, a little too condescendingly, even though she had a smile on her face.

Amber dropped her arm to her side. 'Why hadn't she just struggled on to the pub? She may have cut her foot open but at least she wouldn't have been made to feel bargain basement,' she thought. "If I could just use your phone?" she asked Tom, blushing furiously.

"Just behind you." He pointed. "But let me change the tyre for you, it won't take a minute."

"No, thank you, I have AA cover." Amber turned. She quickly found the number from her phone. Her hand shook slightly as she dialled.

Tom looked at Beth who was still sat at the table. She hadn't even offered to get a towel for them. He left the kitchen, returning rubbing his hair with a towel and carrying a fresh one for Amber. He handed it to her once she'd finished on the phone. She took it from him.

"I can lend you a dry shirt," he offered.

"It's ok, the AA said they would be here in a few minutes so I'd better get to the car," she replied as she dabbed herself with the towel, then handed it back to Tom. "Thanks for the use of your phone." She looked at Beth. As much as she did not want to speak to her after the rude remark she'd made she was too polite not to. "Nice to meet you," she said again.

Tom followed her outside, pulling the door behind him. "Amber, your feet, at least let me …"

She put her hand up to stop him talking. "I can manage. It's stopped raining so I can see where I'm walking now. Enjoy your evening." She turned and gingerly headed up the drive. Tom watched her until she disappeared.

He stepped back into the kitchen, slamming the door behind him. "How rude could you be?" he shouted at Beth.

"What do you mean?" She shrugged.

"You didn't offer to get Amber a towel, a coffee? The only words that came out of your mouth were cutting." He glared at her.

"I thought I was being nice," Beth said, standing up.

"Being nice is not making one of my work colleagues embarrassed about where she buys her footwear," he said angrily.

"Oh, for God's sake, you're overreacting," Beth said as she sashayed towards him. She put her arms around his neck and started to kiss him. "Calm down, forget about it. She's only a receptionist, no one important."

Tom removed her arms from around his neck. Standing back he looked at her. "You just don't get it, do you?"

"Get what? I can't believe you're making so much fuss over nothing," Beth said as she put her hand, this time, on Tom's chest, gently caressing him as she began to move it downwards. "Anyway, I'm sure we could be doing something much more interesting than talking."

"No," Tom said, removing her hand. "No, Beth."

"Okay, I'm sorry if you think I upset your work colleague. What more do you want me to say?" Beth glared at him.

Tom shook his head. "Beth, you and me, we're not right for each other, we're so different in the things we like, in the things we enjoy doing."

"What are you saying?" Beth looked up at him.

"Beth, please don't make this more difficult than it is. I'm saying I thinks it's for the best if we go our separate ways."

"I suppose you've met somebody else since you've been down here? Well, that didn't take you long, did it?" Beth spat.

"There is no one else. I was going to tell you next week up in Scotland, but …"

"But I turned up, to surprise you, to tell you I think we're good together, to tell you I've decided to move down here to be with you. I suppose that nasty sister of yours was feeding you poison while I was away. She's never liked me."

"Stop it, Beth," Tom interrupted her. "Stop blaming other people. Neither of us have been happy for some time, and you know it."

"You were happy enough to have sex in the kitchen the day before you flew down here," Beth threw at him.

"We both know you planned that little seduction, and we both know how good you are at it. It's over, Beth. You don't want me any more than I want you, if you are completely honest with yourself." Tom sat down, still in his wet running gear.

Beth looked at him. He was right. They were so different. They didn't make each other happy. He was the faithful type, wanting a house in the country with kids, dogs, walks in the park. Whereas she wanted no screeching kids, no stinking dogs, only to walk as far as the next boutique; she wanted to see and be seen at all the best places, and being faithful was out of the question. Daddy wouldn't be pleased but she would get round him, she always did. "You're right." She surprised herself saying it. "I'll book into a hotel; my flight home isn't until Sunday."

"There's no need for you to do that, there's plenty of room here," Tom said.

"Fine, as long as you'll drop me into the centre tomorrow. I hear there are some fantastic boutiques in Bath." She half laughed.

"No problem." Tom smiled at her, shaking his head.

She shrugged at him.

Amber unlocked her front door. She dropped her flip-flops into the bin. Turning on the shower she peeled off her wet clothes. 'What an evening and it was only nine o'clock,' she thought. She shivered slightly. Having been in wet clothes for so long she felt quite cold. It felt like heaven as the warm water cascaded over her. As she shampooed her hair she thought about Beth. 'She had to be Tom's girlfriend. She was awfully pretty under all that make-up, not that he would have an ugly girlfriend. Although she didn't think much of her personality, that was ugly; still, he obviously did. After she had dried herself she saw no point in getting dressed again so she put her pyjamas on. Pushing her feet into her slippers she suddenly felt really tired. Opting for a cup of tea instead of a glass of wine she put the kettle on. Better call Melanie or else she'd be in trouble.

Melanie answered the phone. "At last, Henry and I were about to send out a search party."

"Sorry, but it's been quite an evening," Amber said.

"Go on," Melanie urged. "I'm putting you on speaker so big-ears can listen as well."

"I'll do the same. Hello, Henry," Amber said.

"Dear heart, we're ripping our hair out. What happened?" Henry asked. Amber gave a detailed description of her evening, leaving nothing out.

"Oh my, oh my, that man is like your knight in shining armour." Henry gasped, once Amber had finished.

"I don't think I would go that far," Amber said. "It was all very embarrassing getting on his back."

"Yes, but I bet he wished he had been climbing aboard you instead of the other way round, sweet pea," Henry hooted.

"I don't think so. If I ever decide I want a man again, which I doubt I will, I can quite confidently say I would not be his type. His girlfriend must spend hours on herself to look like she does," Amber said.

"She came into the office after you left. She's a right stuck-up cow, thinks she's something special. We all thought Tom didn't seem that pleased she'd turned up," Melanie said.

"Why don't I come over and get you? You can stay the night with us, dear heart," Henry suggested. "Then we can have a right old girlie bitch."

"Thanks, Henry, but I'm ready for bed," Amber replied.

"Are you sure?" Melanie asked, concern in her voice.

"Do you know, I feel better than I have in weeks. When I saw Phil tonight I thought I'd break down but I didn't. I ended up looking at him thinking how pathetic he was. I'm just going to put my life back together and move forward," Amber said.

"Such a positive attitude, dear heart. Welcome back, Amber. Another week and I feel a manhunt coming on." Henry laughed.

"I'm back, but I definitely don't want another man," Amber said. "I'll catch up with you two tomorrow, night-night."

"Night-night," Melanie and Henry said together.

CHAPTER 14

"Not much post for a Monday morning," Harry said, handing a couple of letters to Amber. "I don't know where the weekends go."

Amber took the post. "Nor do I, they just seem to fly by."

"How are you getting along?" Harry asked.

Amber smiled. 'He was so sweet,' she thought. 'He'd asked her the same question every couple of days since she'd split up from Phil, as if he was checking she hadn't been alone over the weekend or too much during the week.' "Good, I've picked myself up, brushed myself off; saw friends Saturday night, so onwards and upwards." She tried to sound positive.

"That's the spirit, see you tomorrow then." He left, blowing her the usual kiss. "Morning," he greeted Tom on his way out.

"Morning," Tom replied, then grinned at Amber as he walked casually up to the desk, coming to a standstill in front of her.

Amber hadn't seen him come in. She blushed slightly at the thought of Friday night.

"Good morning," she said. "Thanks for the use of your phone Friday night." She thought she'd mention it before he did.

"You're welcome, but aren't you going to thank me for the piggyback ride as well?" he asked, still grinning.

Amber blushed again. 'He obviously found her a joke,' she said to herself, 'drunk at the party, going into the garage the wrong way, and now the episode in the rain.' "Thank you," she said as graciously as she could muster.

"Amber, I was just joking. Look, let me give you some money to replace your flip-flops. It was my fault they got broken." He took out his wallet.

"I said no and I mean no. It was my fault as much as yours. As your girlfriend pointed out they weren't expensive so I can quite afford to replace them myself, thank you," Amber said, quite indignantly.

"I apologise for Beth, she doesn't realise how she comes across sometimes, and for your information she is …"

Before Tom had time to finished he was interrupted by a good morning from Francis Lockyard.

"Good morning. I'll bring your tea through right now." Amber smiled at him, grateful that he had arrived, then without looking at Tom she turned and scurried into the back office.

Tom watched her go, finishing under his breath, "… not my girlfriend."

"Haven't interrupted anything, have I?" Francis Lockyard asked as he looked at Tom who was now just staring at the door Amber had gone through.

"No, no." Tom turned to Francis. "How was your weekend?" he asked as they walked to their offices.

"Good, very relaxing. How did Beth enjoy Bath?" Francis asked.

"Well," Tom paused, "in a nutshell, as of Friday night our relationship is no more. The funny thing was, after that we had quite a pleasant weekend. Did a few sights, Beth did some shopping, yesterday we had lunch at the pub before I took her to the airport, it was all very civil, which is not her way at all. Wonders will never cease.

Amber appeared with the tea tray. She avoided looking at Tom; instead she focused on Mr L. "It needs to brew for a few minutes," she said as she put the tray down.

"Thanks, Amber. How was your weekend?" he asked.

Amber quickly glanced at Tom, who had been watching her since she'd come to the office, then back to Mr L. "Very nice, thank you. I'd better get back to the desk," she replied, already making for the door.

'Strange,' thought Mr L, 'Amber was usually so chatty. Still getting over her boyfriend, no doubt.'

"Tom …" Began Mr L.

"Excuse me a moment." Tom put his hand up to stop Francis continuing and followed Amber out of the office, leaving Mr L wondering, again, if he had interrupted something earlier.

"Amber," Tom called after her.

She stopped and turned round. "Yes."

"Look, about Friday, I just want to say …"

"I'm not interested in what you have to say," Amber cut him off. "I'm well aware you think I'm some kind of charity case, a joke, but I'd just like to inform you that I'm not. You've just happen to have been present on a couple of unfortunate occasions, that's all, so can we just leave it at that." Before Tom had time to say anything she hurried back to the desk.

'God, she was beautiful,' Tom thought as he watched her scurry away. He just couldn't stop thinking about her; he felt a bit like a schoolboy with a crush. For the first time in his life he fancied the hell out of someone but didn't know what to do about it. The only times when he'd gotten to talk to her he had ended up annoying her, then standing like an idiot watching her walk away from him, or drive, as the case may be. He stepped back into Francis' office.

"I want to have sex on the beach, come on move your body ..." Melanie sung along to the radio as she took a bra out of her underwear drawer.

Gary came up behind her, and before she had a chance to put it on he slid his hands around her, cupping her breasts and caressing them gently.

"How about having sex on the beach in Menorca?" he asked, kissing her ear.

"What do you mean?" she asked, whizzing round.

"Well, seeing as you sing that song so nicely, I have to go to Menorca the second week in October. If you came with me and sung it again," he said as he put his hand on Melanie's neck, sliding it downwards, "I could indulge you."

"Ooh, I'd love to, and go to Menorca." She grinned, easing her hand down his boxers. "But seeing as I've found something quite stiff I think we should have a quick practice.

"So do I," Gary agreed as he began to kiss her.

"You've made me late for work now," Melanie said, still panting slightly.

"I could make you later still," Gary said, kissing her again.

"One knee-trembler is enough before work," Melanie said, laughing.

"Okay, but don't say later I didn't offer. I'll leave you to get ready. Book a week off. It doesn't matter which day we go as long as we're there for the second weekend in October," Gary said.

"Why that weekend?" Melanie asked.

"We'll be staying with my brother and his wife. It's his birthday," Gary told her.

"I didn't know your brother lived in Spain," Melanie said.

"You do now." Gary smiled. "I think it's time you met the rest of the family as well. I've told them about you, but if they don't meet you soon they will probably think you're a figment of my imagination."

"Will I pass their inspection?" Melanie put her hands on her hips.

"You will if you put some clothes on." Gary chuckled.

"In that case, you'd better meet mine," Melanie said.

"Just say when." Gary kissed her on the cheek. "Text me later about the dates."

Melanie had another quick shower, threw on some clothes, pulled back the duvet on her bed to let it air, then hurried downstairs. Henry was in the kitchen.

"Bloody hell, sweetness. Was heaven and earth being moved up there a minute ago? One needed some ear plugs, you know." He grinned.

"Sorry, Henry, got a bit carried away. Guess what?" Melanie beamed.

"You've broken a piece of furniture and you want me to mend it, or you'd already pulled the curtains and now you want me to apologise to fanny across the road because she saw everything and nearly had a heart attack?" Henry put his hand on his mouth as though he was still thinking.

"No, the curtains were not open. Mind you, it might have given fanny a heart attack, but her old man would have enjoyed it. He probably hasn't bent her over since their honeymoon. I've been invited to Menorca to stay at Gary's brother's, and to meet the rest of his family."

"Dear heart, that's wonderful. It means its serious, you're in a serious relationship, yippee. Do you think he has any male gay members in his family that are single and as dishy as he is?" Henry asked, grabbing her and swinging her around.

"I'll find out for you, but I must go, I'm late." Melanie gave him a kiss on the cheek.

"We could have a double wedding," Henry called after her.

"Not bloody likely. I couldn't have you looking a better bride than me," Melanie called back as she left the house.

Tom and Mr Lockyard were pouring over plans when Dorothy popped her head round the door.

"A very good morning to you both," she said. "Can I get either of you another tea or coffee?"

"Tea for me, Dorothy," Mr Lockyard answered.

"A coffee would be great, Dorothy." Tom smiled.

"Coming right up," Dorothy said, picking up the tea tray. She looked around. "Where is your cup?" she asked Tom.

"I haven't got one," he answered.

"Did Amber not make you one earlier?" Dorothy asked.

"I didn't want one earlier," Tom replied. "We're just about finished here, do you mind bringing the coffee to my office?"

"Certainly," Dorothy said before bustling out.

Melanie came skipping through the door as Dorothy appeared with the tray. "Good afternoon, Melanie," she said, glancing at the clock.

"Sorry I'm late, Dorothy, but I forgot to water my pots yesterday so I thought I'd better do it first thing. I'm so pleased with them, I don't want them to die," Melanie said innocently.

"I always do mine when the sun goes down; that gives them a chance to have a good drink overnight," Dorothy said, her mind completely taken off Melanie being late.

"Full marks for that one," Vicky said after Dorothy had gone.

"I've got news, I've got news," Melanie sang, dancing about.

"Tell us then," Amber urged.

"I've only been invited to meet the family, and go to Menorca in October to stay with Gary's brother. What do you think of that then?" she asked, all smiles.

"Bloody hell, Melanie, I've never known you pleased to meet a bloke's family. When in October?" Vicky asked.

"Well," Melanie said, grabbing the calendar. "Any day as long as we're there for the second Saturday because it's his brother's birthday. I've just got to call him with the dates."

"You've forgotten something," Vicky said.

"What?" Melanie asked, taking her eyes off the calendar and looking at Vicky.

"That's the weekend of the charity hike," she reminded her.

"Shit, shit, shit, I'd forgotten all about that. Mind you, what's the likelihood of my name being drawn?" Melanie said, shrugging her shoulders.

"The same as anyone else, but don't worry I'll enter instead of you," Amber offered.

"Am, thanks a million," Melanie said, hugging Amber so tightly she could hardly breathe.

"And I can manage on my own on the Monday, so you can go whichever day you want," Vicky said.

"You two are brilliant," Melanie said, giving Vicky an equally as emotional hug. "I feel a coffee coming on.

Amber and Vicky smiled at each other as Melanie went into the back office.

Moments later she returned with the coffees. "Have you updated Vicky about Friday night?" she asked Amber.

"Yes, and this morning," Amber grimaced.

"What happened this morning?" Melanie asked, putting the coffees down.

"He offered to pay for my flip-flops again. I told him I'm not a charity case and I could afford to replace them myself," Amber told her.

"He was only trying to be nice," Melanie said. Vicky nodding in agreement.

"It amazes me how he seems to have trapped all the women, and men, come to think of it, into his web of so-called niceness." Amber sighed.

"Maybe because he's a genuinely nice bloke," Vicky replied.

"If he's that nice why has he got such a nasty girlfriend?" Amber said, making a face.

"We don't know that she is his girlfriend. We all thought he was single," Vicky said.

"Perhaps we all had it wrong. Let's face it, the way she threw herself at him and the fact she was staying with him would state otherwise." Melanie shrugged.

"He didn't look over the moon when she turned up," Vicky said.

"That's true," Melanie agreed. "Even Gloria said he didn't seem pleased to see her, but that doesn't mean she isn't his girlfriend, the false cow."

Tom waited for his sister to answer her phone, but it just rang. He'd try her again later. He sat back in his chair, chewing the end of his pen. 'Amber,' he thought, 'Amber, Amber, Amber. What was he going to do about Amber? He had to speak to her, but how was he going to engineer it? He was on site for the next couple of days, then flying up to Scotland for a couple of weeks. It would have to be when he got back.'

"Everything alright?" Dorothy asked, standing in the doorway with his coffee.

"Yes, deep in thought, that's all," Tom answered.

"Here's your coffee. Just buzz when you want another one." She placed it on his desk.

"Thanks." His mobile started to ring. Seeing Yasmin's name he picked it up quickly. He put his hand up to Dorothy, signalling another thank you, as she left his office. "Yasmin."

"Hi, sorry I missed your call, what's up?" she asked.

"Nothing, just wanted to let you know I will be needing a bed for a couple of weeks, if that's ok?" he said.

"You know it is, so what is it really?" she asked.

'She knows me too well,' he thought, smiling. "Just thought I'd let you know that I had a surprise visitor this weekend," he said, knowing that putting it that way would wind her up.

"Beth," Yasmin spat her name.

"Correct." Tom wanted to laugh. He could almost picture Yasmin's face.

"Now you're going to tell me you've had a little chat and are back together. That scheming bitch, she would have said anything to keep her claws in you. You're mad. I can't believe it. She makes you miserable. You hate all her stuck-up ways. You hate all those false friends of hers who look down their noses at everyone. I just can't believe it," she said again, crossly.

"Actually, I was going to tell you that we have ended our relationship," Tom said in a calm manner.

"You bastard," Yasmin said with relief.

"Why, thank you." Tom laughed.

"You're welcome. Thank God for that. Did she attack you? Beg you to reconsider?" Yasmin asked.

"It was really weird. She started to get a bit aggressive, then just suddenly stopped and agreed. It was as simple as that. She actually stayed the rest of the weekend. What was even weirder was that we had a good time together," Tom said.

"That is weird, but I am so glad you've split up. Now you can find someone who is normal in every sense of the word." Yasmin laughed.

"I'm working on it," Tom said.

"Really? You like someone? Tell me more," Yasmin urged.

"I might when I see you at the end of the week," Tom teased.

"Tell me now," Yasmin whined.

"Can't, have to get on with my work, see you Friday," Tom said, ending the call with a laugh. She would be beside herself, wanting information, by Friday.

Yasmin smiled as she switched off her phone. He had always been able to wind her up. There was no use calling him back. He would make her wait until she saw him.

Tom finished his coffee. Deciding to get a refill he left his office, cup in hand. As he neared Dorothy's desk she saw the cup.

"Why didn't you buzz? Give me a moment to enter these names and I will get you another coffee," she said.

"It's okay, Dorothy, I'll get it. I'm already causing you more work than you can cope with. I promise when I get back from Scotland I'll sort myself a PA. What are you entering names for?" he asked, peering at her computer screen.

"The charity walk in October," Dorothy replied.

"Of course," Tom said as he noticed Amber's name on the screen. "Add my name to that list, it will save me sending you an email."

"Certainly, Mr Tranter." Dorothy smiled at him. 'Such a nice young man,' she thought as he left, 'so popular with everyone. She could see why Mr Lockyard wanted him to run his business. He reminded her of Mr Lockyard when he was younger, full of enthusiasm, willing to join in, not for a minute thinking he was above others.'

CHAPTER 15

Amber knocked before entering Mr L's office with his tea. "Here we are, do you want me to pour?" she asked.

"Yes please," he answered.

She poured his tea and handed it to him. Taking it from her he smiled. "How are you?" he asked.

"I'm fine, you know." She shrugged. "Looking forward to a lie-in tomorrow morning."

"That's you and me both. It seems to have been a long week." Shrewd enough to realise Amber didn't want to discuss her private affairs he changed the subject. "I was looking over the entrants for the charity walk with Dorothy last night, I see your name is on it."

"Yes, the entrants are being picked today, aren't they?" Amber replied.

"I think Dorothy was going to do it first thing, but don't quote me on that or else I may be in trouble." He laughed.

"I won't." Amber laughed as well.

"Have I missed something funny?" Tom asked as he entered the office.

"I'd better get back to the desk," Amber said, making her escape quickly.

'Odd,' thought Francis Lockyard as he watched Amber literally scurry out of his office. He made a mental note to have a word with Dorothy, just to double check on her welfare; it was probably nothing more than just getting over her young man. "Just chatting about the charity walk," he said, answering Tom who he noticed was still staring at the door that Amber had closed behind her.

"Impressive amount of entries. Couldn't be anything to do with the 'no pressure' bit on the email, could it?" Tom said, turning to face him.

"I don't know what you mean," Francis Lockyard answered innocently.

"Of course you don't." Tom grinned.

"What are you doing here anyway? I thought you were flying up to Scotland today?" Francis asked, sipping his tea.

"I am. I'm not staying, just dropping this off and picking a couple of things up on the way to the airport," Tom said, placing a folder on Francis Lockyard's desk.

"More light reading," he said, looking at the bulging folder. "Got time for a coffee?"

"No, I must get going," Tom replied, holding up his hand. "Catch up with you Monday before the conference-call."

"Right you are." Francis Lockyard nodded. "Regards to Yasmin and her family."

"Thanks," Tom said as he left. Within seconds he had collected what he needed from his office and was heading for reception. As he neared he could see Amber, head down, so engrossed in whatever she was doing that she hadn't noticed him approaching. 'Good,' he thought. He glanced at his watch. 'Great. Now that he had an unexpected chance to talk to her, he didn't have time.'

Amber nearly jumped out of her skin when she looked up to see him standing there.

"Sorry, didn't mean to startle you," Tom said as their eyes locked together for just a moment too long.

"You didn't," Amber said, blushing because she was lying. "Do you need me to do something for you?"

"Not right now," Tom said, resting his arm on the desk. "Just thought I'd say goodbye. I'm in Scotland for the next two weeks, but when I get back would … "

"Good morning, Mr Tranter. Good morning, Amber," Dorothy's voice came from behind Tom.

Amber watched as Tom gently thumped his fist on the desk before turning round to greet Dorothy. He had done it good-naturedly, but she could tell he hadn't wanted to be interrupted. 'What on earth was he going to say? Had she over-stepped the mark with him? Was he going to have her in his office to put her in her place? After all, he was her boss,' she thought.

"Good morning, Dorothy. How are you?" he asked politely.

"Very well indeed. Shouldn't you be on your way to Bristol International?" she asked.

"Yes," Tom said, looking at his watch. "In actual fact, I'd better make tracks, I'm pushing it as it is." He looked at Amber. This time he just patted the desk a couple of times before removing his arm. "See you both in a couple of weeks."

"Safe journey," Dorothy said as Tom left. She turned her attention to Amber who was still wondering what Tom had been about to say before Dorothy had arrived. "Amber, you look miles away."

"Sorry, Dorothy," Amber apologised.

"Don't apologise, it wasn't a criticism, just an observation," Dorothy said, her lips twitching into a Dorothy-smile as she began to walk away.

"Dorothy," Amber called after her.

Dorothy stopped and turned around. "Yes?"

"Dorothy," Amber repeated. "My work, um, it has been up to standard in the last couple of weeks, hasn't it?"

Dorothy walked back to the desk. "It most certainly has, why do you ask?"

"Just checking my personal life isn't affecting my work." Amber smiled ruefully.

"Amber, dear, your work remains of the highest standard. Nobody expects you to be jumping for joy at the moment. You've been hurt very badly. However, I must say, I have noticed a little of the Amber we know reappearing, and it is lovely to see."

"Thanks, Dorothy." Amber felt quite touched.

"My office door is open at any time if you need some reassurance." Dorothy patted Amber's arm before heading for her office.

Amber remained standing. Staring out of the glass doors she watched the branches of the trees move ever so slightly in the morning breeze. 'If my work is ok, it must be personal then. He obviously doesn't want what he considers a joke working for him,' she said to herself. She was still standing on the same spot 10 minutes later when Vicky and Melanie arrived.

"What are you doing? Guarding the crown jewels?" Melanie teased.

"I wish." Amber sighed.

"What's up?" Melanie asked, realising Amber wasn't joking.

"I think Tom Tranter is going to try to sack me," she said glumly.

"Don't talk crap. Why would he do that?"

"He stopped on his way out this morning to say he was going to be in Scotland for the next couple of weeks, and when he got back would ..., then Dorothy arrived and he stopped. I think he was going to say would I make an appointment to see him when he gets back."

"Amber, don't be daft. It sounds more like he just wanted to talk to you. Anyway, you haven't done anything wrong so how can he sack you?" Vicky said.

"Yeah, Vicky's right. Come to think of it, he's always trying to get you to talk to him," Melanie said.

"No, he isn't," Amber protested.

"He is," Melanie argued. "He quite often makes a point of coming out here to chat."

"Only when he has something he wants doing, and you two fall over yourselves to offer. Anyway, whose side are you on?" Amber said as she plonked herself down on a chair.

"Yours, noggin," Melanie said, putting her arms around Amber. "But you've got him wrong, he's a really nice bloke."

"He could easily get Dorothy to do the things he asks us to do. I think he asks us because it gives him an excuse to come out here," Vicky said.

"Or to catch me doing something stupid to give him ammunition," Amber said.

"Amber, he thinks it's funny that you were drunk at the office party, funny about the petrol station, funny about the other night in the rain. Even you said you burst out laughing when he almost fell through the door, remember?" Melanie said, giving her a squeeze. "You're just not thinking straight at the moment."

"What was he going to say then?" Amber whined.

"He was probably going to offer to pay for your flip-flops again," Vicky suggested.

"Very funny." Amber thought for a moment. "Maybe you're right, perhaps I'm just being over sensitive, but I've been made a fool of by Phil and since then I seem to do nothing but make a fool out of myself."

"Am, you're still upset over the git. It's only been a few weeks so stop being so hard on yourself. Give yourself a bit of time, get a new bloke, Bob's your uncle." She squeezed her again.

Here, here," Vicky agreed.

"No, thank you." Amber shook her head. "I've decided spinster of this parish is the best protection from being cheated on again."

Dorothy tapped on Francis Lockyard's door as she entered. He looked up. "Aah, Dorothy, who are the lucky two?"

"Amber and Mark Gibson," Dorothy answered.

"Mmmm." Francis Lockyard nodded, rubbing his chin.

"Mark, I know is a very keen cyclist and Amber power walks, so they should do very well, don't you think?" Dorothy peered at him over the top of her glasses.

"Yes." Mr Lockyard nodded. "Talking of Amber, am I missing something? It just seems that if Tom, oh, I don't know, I was talking to her this morning and when Tom arrived she practically ran out of the door. Oh, and then there was the other morning when I came in, I can't be sure, but I think they were having words."

"I think she feels a little embarrassed in front of him, that's all," Dorothy answered tactfully.

"Why on earth would anyone feel embarrassed in front of Tom?" Mr L asked, looking puzzled.

"Well, you see, it's like this. The night of the office party Amber had, how can I put it, a glass too many, which resulted in ..." Dorothy paused.

"Which resulted in?" Mr L prompted.

"Which resulted in Tom having to give her a fireman's lift to his car and take her home, I'm afraid. Apparently when he returned her sandal that was somehow left in his car Melanie hadn't told her exactly how she had got home. Then there was the incident at the petrol station when he witnessed her cause mayhem after she entered through the exit. Then there was the other night when he had to give her a ride on his back in the rain."

"On his back, in the rain? I obviously have been missing something." Mr L chuckled.

"Yes, Amber had a flat tyre, got caught in the rain near Tom's house, her flip flop got broken, so the story goes, and Tom gave her a piggy-back ride to his house to use the phone. So, you see, it is quite understandable that she feels a little embarrassed in front of him," Dorothy said, taking her glasses off.

"Indeed. When I asked I didn't expect a catalogue of events in reply. Poor Amber, she's not having a good time of it, is she?" Mr Lockyard said sincerely.

"No, it's such a shame. Things will look up for her soon, I'm sure. I only said to her earlier that in the last couple of days she seems brighter. On a lighter note, can I fetch you another tea or coffee?" Dorothy asked, noticing his empty cup.

"I think I need one after that." Mr Lockyard smiled. "Am I the only person who isn't in the know?"

"It is rather like a soap opera." Dorothy shook her head slowly. "Gloria is keeping me informed."

"I see, and, of course, in true soap opera fashion I would be interested in any other happenings," Mr Lockyard carried on with a sparkle in his eye.

"Tut-tut, Mr Lockyard," Dorothy said, chastising him as her lips twitched into a smile. "In that case, there is just one more thing, strictly between Gloria, myself and now you, of course."

"I'm all ears?" Mr Lockyard said, intrigued.

"Gloria thinks our Mr Tranter has an eye for Amber, and I have to say I think so too." With that she turned and left.

'Well, well, interesting,' Mr Lockyard thought, sitting back in his chair.

"Melanie, your phone keeps beeping, you must have a new message," Amber called from the back office.

"Cheers, Am," Melanie said, appearing. After checking her phone she started to sing and dance, "Oh, this year I'm off to sunny Spain, *y viva espania*, I'm taking the Costa Brava plane, *y viva espania* ..."

"I take it he's booked then," Amber said, laughing at Melanie who was now playing non-existent maracas.

"He most certainly bloody has. I'd better text him back to find out how much I owe him. I can stop at the bank on the way home." No sooner had she got back to the front desk than Amber was calling her again.

"A reply already," Melanie said, hunting her phone out once more. She read the reply from Gary. "He's bloody paying. All I have to do is buy some extremely sexy undies so he can be extremely dirty with me. I think I can manage that. I feel a little outfit from Ann Summers coming on. He's quite partial to my little maid number."

"Mel, you haven't introduced him to your dressing-up box already, have you?" Amber couldn't help giggling.

"Of course, variety is the spice of life. A bit of dressing up now and again is good for the soul," Melanie said, giving a little shimmy.

"Oh no, guess what?" Amber squealed. "Look at this email. I've been drawn to do the charity walk."

"Oh, Am, I feel really guilty now, it should have been my name there," Melanie said, making a face. "Who are you doing it with?"

"No, you don't, and I'm doing it with Mark Gibson." Amber smiled.

"Oh, he's nice. He's got twin girls, hasn't he?"

"Yes, they're so sweet. I'll go down to see him later. Better pop into Mum's on the way home as well, to dig out my old walking boots. I want you to think about me when you're walking along the beach in the warm sunshine," Amber said, giving Melanie a playful swipe.

"Of course I will, but I tell you it must be fate that your name got drawn. Only the other night Jess and I were saying we were going to have to drag you out walking, you haven't been once since you broke up with Phil. Come to think of it, you haven't been out at all. Now you have no excuse, you need to train," Melanie said, pointing at her.

"Yes, yes, you're right. I do need to start making an effort again. Don't suppose it's doing me much good sitting at home every night, and I don't want to turn into a blob," Amber said, puffing out her cheeks.

"Exactly, but I can't imagine you ever becoming a blob," Melanie said.

"Thanks, but in my defence, I have been out a few times, just not walking," Amber pointed out.

"Only because you were forced," Melanie reminded her.

"True." Amber nodded. "So I blame you for my drunken state at the office party then."

"That was the start of your rehabilitation, you were allowed to get as pissed as a fart." Melanie laughed.

"So drunk I had to be taken home by our new boss?" Amber retorted.

"Yes, noggin, just think how lucky you were. There are plenty working here that wouldn't mind his hands on their ass," Melanie said, turning and shaking her bottom at Amber.

Amber turned back towards the computer, shaking her head. She wished she was more like Melanie.

Gloria waddled along the path, singing to herself. She caught sight of Amber on her way to the car park. "Is I late, child? or is you skipping off early?" she called after her.

Hearing Gloria's voice Amber turned around. Waving she walked back to where Gloria stood. "I'm skipping off a little early. You look nice in that pink dress."

"Thank you, sugar." Gloria put her hand on Amber's arm. "Old Gloria is in all day tomorrow, got the grandbabies, promised to do some baking with them. If you ain't busy come over. You look like you need some of my cake to put some meat on those skinny bones."

"If your cake is on offer I can't refuse. About three o'clock?" Amber suggested.

"About three, see you tomorrow," Gloria said as she waddled off.

Amber thought about Gloria as she drove to her parents. It amazed her how she seemed to have so much time for everyone. She was always jolly and so caring. She would pick her up some flowers on her way over tomorrow, she certainly deserved them. Amber found her parents sitting in the garden.

"Hello, darling, what a lovely surprise. We didn't expect to see you," her mum said as she appeared.

"I'm on a mission," Amber said as she joined them at the garden table.

"Really, what kind of mission?" asked her mum.

"To dig out my walking boots," Amber said. "You haven't thrown them out, have you?"

"No, they're in the garage, more than likely covered in cobwebs. Going walking then?" asked her mum.

"As a matter of fact, I am. My name was drawn at work to do the charity walk in October," Amber told them.

"Where's this taking place then?" asked her dad.

"Dartmoor," Amber answered.

"Good heavens above, can you remember the state you were in when you finished the Ten Tors?" laughed her dad.

"Yes, thank you very much, how kind of you to remember. Fortunately this is only 20 miles, split over two days." Amber poked her tongue out at him.

Chuckling, her dad got up from his chair. "I'll get them for you."

"What have you been doing today?" Amber asked her mum.

"Not very much. I spent about two hours chatting to Aunty Lucy on the phone this morning and pottered in the garden this afternoon. That's about it, I'm afraid."

"That's funny, I was thinking about Aunty Lucy earlier. I might ring her to see if she'd put me up. I've got a fortnight off in two weeks. Phil and I had planned to get a last minute deal, but …"

Amber's mum didn't give her time to finish. "What a good idea, she'd love to have you, sweetheart. The sea air will do you good, put some colour back in those cheeks. Plenty of coastal paths to get you used to those walking boots again. It would be just perfect, give you a chance to recharge your batteries."

"Okay, calm down," Amber said with a laugh. "You've definitely talked me into it."

"Sorry, love, it's just that we've been so worried about you. Dad and I hate seeing you so down in the dumps." She placed her hand over Amber's.

"Mum, you don't need to worry, I'm fine, really I am." Amber smiled weakly.

"You're not, but you will be." She squeezed Amber's hand gently.

"Here we are then, good as new." Amber's dad appeared with her walking boots and a glass of squash.

"Thanks, Dad." Amber took a sip of the drink before placing it on the table.

"Mummy, Mummy, Uncle Tom's here," Luke shouted as he scrabbled down from the chair where he had been staring out of the window. He raced to the front door. "Hurry up," he urged his mother as she walked up the hall, wiping her hands on a tea towel.

She smiled at him. "I told you he'd be here in a minute, didn't I?" she said, opening the door for him.

Luke flew out. "Uncle Tom, Uncle Tom."

Tom was lifting his case out of the boot. Hearing his nephew he looked up to see him running towards him. He quickly set his case on the ground, freeing his arms ready to catch Luke. He lifted him high into the air where he swung him round and round. Luke squealed with delight. Setting him down on the ground he pretended to be dizzy, which set Luke off in a fit of the giggles.

Coming to a standstill in front of his nephew he ruffled his hair. "How good have you been?" he asked.

"Very good," Luke said, nodding his head eagerly.

"Is that right, Mummy?" he asked Yasmin, who had joined them by the car.

"That's right," his sister said, smiling at Luke.

"In that case, this is for you," Tom said, taking a brand new scooter out of the boot.

"Oooh," Luke said, his eyes wide with excitement. "Thank you, thank you, thank you." He was soon scooting up and down the drive. "Can we go round the block?"

"Of course. Let me just take my case indoors." Tom smiled.

"Honestly, you spoil him rotten," Yasmin said to Tom.

"That's what uncles are for." He gave his sister a kiss on the cheek.

Yasmin was in the kitchen when they got back. "Did you have fun?" she asked Luke.

"Yes, I love my scooter. I can go really fast on it, can't I, Uncle Tom?" Luke looked up at Tom.

"You certainly can. I think we should go round the block again tomorrow," Tom said.

"Goodie." Luke grinned.

"You can watch a few cartoons while I finish dinner," Yasmin said, hardly finishing before Luke disappeared. She then turned her attention to Tom. "You aren't going anywhere until you tell me about this girl you've met."

"I wondered how long it would take you to enquire." Tom smiled at her. "There's nothing to tell really."

"There must be something, come on," Yasmin prompted.

"She works on reception. Her name is Amber. The first time I kind of met her was at the office summer party," Tom said.

"Kind of met her, what does that mean?" Yasmin asked.

"I met her, but she didn't remember meeting me. She was paralytic. I helped take her home. Then on Monday I stopped at the local garage on my way to work, and who should enter through the exit but her; she caused a right jam. Being the gentleman I am I was going to offer to help see her back but she refused." He started laughing as he remembered it.

"I'm not surprised if you were laughing like that." Yasmin flicked him with the tea towel.

"I couldn't help it. It gets better or worse, as the case may be. When she arrived late I was in with Francis. She was honest with him and told him about the garage before realizing I was in the room. When he told her I'd already told him she was stuck there, literally." He laughed again. "I could see how puzzled she was. I tried my best to lighten the situation by asking for some tea, but that didn't go down too well as I didn't get one, so I went to find one myself, returning her sandal that had fallen off in the back of the truck in the proceeds. And to cap it all it materialised her colleagues hadn't told her I'd taken her home."

"Bloody hell, I need a glass of wine," Yasmin said, reaching into the fridge. "Beer for you?"

Tom nodded. "That's not all." He took the can of beer.

"Go on," Yasmin said as she poured a large glass of wine.

"The night Beth arrived I bumped into her, just along from the cottage I'm renting. When I say, 'bumped into her', we literally collided; I knocked her off her feet. It was pouring down. Somehow her flip-flop got broken so I ended up giving her a piggy-back ride. When we got back to mine Beth was sitting at the kitchen table. I kind of introduced them, offered to pay for a new pair of flip-flops, which Amber declined I hasten to add, to which Beth made a snide comment; something along the lines of me just giving her some money so she could treat herself to a decent pair."

"Why doesn't that surprise me? What a bitch," Yasmin said.

"Yes. Once Amber had left I said something about it. One thing led to another and that was it, end of relationship. It turned out she didn't want me anymore than I wanted her. Bizarrely we ended up having quite a good weekend." Tom took a sip of his beer.

"Oh God, you didn't, did you?" Yasmin's voice raised an octave.

"If you're asking if I slept with her, the answer is no. She stayed the weekend as a friend. I took her to catch her flight on Sunday night," Tom said.

"So now you're footloose and fancy free, why haven't you asked Amber out?" Yasmin asked.

"I don't think she likes me. I also have the feeling she thinks I don't like her." He sighed. "I have tried to talk to her, but she takes what I say all the wrong way or we get interrupted. I just can't stop thinking about her. It's driving me mad."

"Good grief, it sounds like a rom-com. I've never known you not impress the ladies. Are you sure you're telling me everything?" Yasmin asked.

"I do know she found out her fiancé of one day had been shagging the woman he works with, and they both just so happen to work for the estate agents that I rent the cottage from. He showed me round actually, typical estate agent, can't see they seemed suited."

"Says he who stayed with queen bitch for so long," Yasmin butted in.

"Fair comment." Tom shrugged.

"Tom, she probably hates all men at the moment after finding out she was being cheated on. Keep working your magic. Your budding charm and personality will win her over," Yasmin said encouragingly.

"Thanks for the vote of confidence."

"That's what sisters are for," Yasmin said in the same tone Tom had used earlier when referring to himself as an uncle.

"Henry, you old dog, where are you?" Melanie shouted as she shut the front door behind her.

"In here, you old tart," came Henry's voice from the kitchen.

Melanie bounded through. Slinging her bag down she leapt on to Henry, wrapping her legs around his back.

"Christ, dear heart, have you got ants in your pants?" Henry laughed as he hugged her.

"No, but I'm looking forward to getting sand in them. It's all booked. We're off in October, and guess what? Gary is paying." Melanie grinned as she slipped to the floor.

"Oh goodness, now listen, you'll need to impress. We have a couple of months to work on your wardrobe. As for toning those wobbly bits, um," Henry said, taking a step back as he looked Melanie up and down.

"Wobbly bits? What fucking wobbly bits?" Melanie shrieked, looking down at herself.

"Just joking, dear heart, don't be so paranoid. However we do need to work on what comes out of that mouth, sweetness. You have got a tendency to swear like a trooper." Henry placed his hands on his hips.

CHAPTER 16

"*Val da ree valda ra*, my knapsack on my back," Melanie sang as she pranced around pretending to have a rucksack on her back.

"Thank you, Melanie. As much as your singing and acting are of the highest standards I think they would be better suited to an amateur dramatics society, rather than a front desk," Dorothy's voice cut in to Melanie's singing.

"Whoops, Dorothy, didn't see you there," Melanie said, trying to keep a straight face as she came to a standstill.

"Obviously not," Dorothy said, raising her eyebrows. "Can you please try to behave yourself?"

"Yes, Dorothy, I'll try," Melanie answered sweetly. "I was just trying to get Amber into the swing of things before she goes away."

"I'm sure." Dorothy raised her eyebrows again. "I'm just double-checking that you and Vicky have the hours covered between you while Amber is away?"

"All covered," Melanie said, standing to attention and saluting Dorothy. "We are going to take it in turns to start at eight o'clock."

"Heaven help us." She turned to Amber. "I do hope you have a lovely time in Cornwall, a perfect place to do a bit of training for the charity walk, all those lovely cliff paths, fresh sea air, wonderful."

"Thanks, Dorothy, I'll bring you back some clotted cream." Amber smiled.

"How lovely, I shall look forward to that." Dorothy twitched before heading to her office.

"Do you think she will put it on certain parts of her anatomy, then order her old man to lick it off?" Melanie giggled.

"Now let me think about that. No, I feel certain it will be part of a cream tea, and on that note it's four o'clock and I'm off," Amber said, standing up.

"Are you coming out for a drink tonight? Henry said I wasn't allowed home until you promised." Melanie said. "Come on, no excuses, you're not going down to your aunt's until Sunday," she added, seeing Amber was about to protest.

"Mel's right, no excuses. It will be fun to have a girlie night. Oh, and Henry, of course," Vicky said, having returned from collecting the post.

"Okay, okay." Amber put her hand up. "I'll call Jessica to see if John will mind picking me up on their way."

"All done. Be ready at eight o'clock. Now, off you go," Melanie said, pushing Amber out from behind the desk.

"Are those two girlies bullying you again?" Gloria asked, witnessing the scene as she arrived.

"Of course we are. She's coming out tonight, no excuses." Melanie beamed.

"Hehehe, that's alright then." She put her arm around Amber, squeezing her tight. "You go, sweetie, let that pretty hair down. Have a good holiday too. I want to hear all about it when you get back."

"Hurry up, you old queen, what the hell are you doing in there?" Melanie banged on the bathroom door.

Henry opened it, toothbrush in hand. "Just checking perfection in the mirror, dear heart. One feels lucky tonight."

"Does one, indeed. In that case, I'll get my ear plugs ready. I don't want to be listening to you panting like a dog while I'm trying to get to sleep." She darted past him. Grabbing her toothbrush she squeezed some toothpaste on it and started to clean her teeth.

"It will make a change from me having to put up with the racket you make when lover-boy is here. See this?" Henry held up his toothbrush. "I was about to clean my pearly whites, you know."

Melanie smiled as him while she continued to clean her teeth, then rinse her mouth with mouthwash. Drying her toothbrush she put it back in the holder. "Finished, just some lippy and I'm ready to rock. See you downstairs."

"Is it ok if I clean my teeth now?" Henry asked, waving his toothbrush around.

"Be my guest," Melanie said, passing him the toothpaste.

"So kind," Henry said, taking it from her.

With a towel wrapped around his waist Tom walked back into his bedroom. Throwing open the wardrobe doors he pulled out a pair of trousers and a shirt. He was looking forward to dinner with Pete and Becky. He had met Pete whilst studying at university. They had been good friends since, seeing each other regularly but not often enough due to work pressure and distance. Now that he was living in Bath he would get to see a lot more of him. He dressed quickly, picked up his watch and made his way downstairs.

The taxi would be here in a minute. 'May as well lock up and walk up the drive to the road,' he thought.

Walking into the restaurant he was greeted by the Maître D', who escorted him to join Pete and Becky. They stood up to greet him.

"Looking gorgeous, as always," he said, giving Becky a kiss. "It's good to see you."

"Why, thank you." She beamed. "Good to see you too."

"Pete." Tom extended his hand towards his friend who shook it rigorously. "Looking good, but not as good as Becky."

"How's it going, buddy?" Pete asked as they sat down. "It's great to have you in Bath."

"It feels good to be here." Tom smiled at his friends.

"Two beers, one gin and tonic," the waitress said, appearing at their table.

"I took the liberty," Pete said, raising his pint to Tom. "Cheers."

Melanie and Henry entered the wine bar. As soon as Gary finished serving a couple some drinks, he leant over the bar to Melanie. "Hi, babe," he said, giving her a kiss on the lips. He turned to Henry. "Hi, Henry."

Hi, Gary." Henry gave him a little wave.

"What are you drinking?" he asked them.

"White wine, I think." Melanie looked at Henry.

"Why the devil not." Henry nodded.

Gary got a couple of bottles from the huge wine fridge and put them on the bar. "On me. How many glasses do you need?"

"Six, and thank you." Melanie smiled at him.

"You're welcome." Gary smiled back as he put six glasses on the bar. "Henry, can I leave you in charge of pouring?"

"It will be a pleasure," Henry said, lifting a bottle. "Cheers."

"Here they are," Melanie said, waving out so Amber could see her.

Henry passed everyone a glass. "Here we go, courtesy of Gary, and we have another bottle once we've finished these." He raised his glass. "Now then, you pretty bunch, because there are six of us we have to visit six pubs and everyone has to choose one. Down the hatch."

By 11pm they were heading down the steps to a cocktail bar. Henry gathered the girls around. "Now then, ladies, seeing as this is my choice the cocktails are on me. A Between the Sheets for you, dear heart?" he asked Melanie. The girls screamed with laughter.

After agonising over the blackboard the cocktails were ordered. Amber stood sipping hers, glad she had been pressurised into coming out as she was having a ball. They had not stopped laughing.

"Hey, take a look at Henry, he's being chatted up," Melanie said to the girls. "Over there."

They all looked over to where Henry had been stopped on his way back from the loo. He was chattering away, nodding his head and flipping his hands around. He glanced over to where the girls were standing. They all instantly turned away, pretending they hadn't been looking. A couple of minutes later, beaming from ear to ear, Henry rejoined them.

"I saw you all looking. Isn't he beautiful? Can we make it seven pubs, I've just been invited round the corner for another one. Of course, I said I would only go if I could bring my girlfriends. Please don't be mean." Henry put his hands up, pretending to beg.

"Of course. Who are we to stand in your way of a shag? Good job you're wearing clean boxers," Melanie said, making everyone roar with laughter again.

"Goodie." Henry turned, putting his thumb up to the man he had been talking to. He gave Melanie a poke in the ribs. "He's coming over, behave yourself. If he knows I live with you he'll run a mile."

Tom, Pete and Becky left the restaurant.

"I really enjoyed that" Becky said as she put one arm through Pete's and the other through Tom's, and they began to walk along the road. "I think you two should take me for a nightcap. There's a bar just along here that usually stays open quite late."

"I think that is one very good idea," Pete replied as they crossed the road. They walked up the steps on the other side when he suddenly stopped. "My glasses," he said.

"I put them in my bag, didn't I?" Becky opened her handbag. Sticking her hand in she felt around. "Or perhaps not, I thought I did."

"You did, but I asked for them back to read the dessert menu. I'll dash back," Pete said.

"I'm going to have to buy you a chain for those," Becky shouted after him. Turning back to Tom she stuck her arm back through his. "Tom, I have to say this. You seem a lot happier, more relaxed than you have for quite a while. Nothing to do with being footloose and fancy free, is it?"

"Becky, you sound like Yasmin." Tom laughed.

"Us girls notice these things," she said, squeezing his arm.

"Beth had her good points." He smiled.

"Always the gentleman," Becky said.

Another cocktail later the girls, Henry, plus his conquest attempted to make their very noisy way up the steps to the pavement. Melanie was first. As soon as she reached the top she saw Tom directly in front of her with Becky. As Vicky appeared she pointed to him. Before they had a chance to say anything Henry's voice boomed from behind Amber on the steps.

"Amber, sweetness, I can see your knickers. Does your mother know you wear skirts that short?"

Amber burst into fits of giggles, knowing full well Henry could not see her knickers. As she did so she caught her heel on the last step.

Hearing the name 'Amber', Tom looked over, just in time to see Amber being caught by her friends. As she regained her balance she was still laughing, until she looked up to see Tom only a few feet away.

"Having a good time, ladies?" Tom grinned at them.

"Sweet cheeks, you really must try harder to stay on your feet," Henry said, killing himself laughing as he came up behind Amber and put his arms around her.

Tom laughed as he held Amber's eye. "Becky, let me introduce you to some of my work colleagues. This is Amber, Melanie and Vicky. Ladies, this is Becky. I'm sorry, I don't know your friends' names." He looked back at Amber once they had exchanged hellos with Becky. She now had no option but to do the introductions. She did so, finishing with Henry.

"How lovely to meet you," Henry said as he shook Tom's hand energetically.

"Well, we've taken up enough of your time, enjoy the rest of your evening," Amber said, smiling politely to Becky, whilst tapping Henry on the arm to encourage him to let go of Tom's hand which he was quite enjoying shaking.

"You mind your step," Tom said to Amber, not letting her get away without looking at him again.

Everyone laughed.

"We'll keep an eye on the old girl," Henry boomed.

Seeing as everyone else was laughing at Tom's comment Amber forced a laugh. It didn't sound very convincing, which made her blush, which in turn made her want to kick herself. Here she was making herself look like a fool again.

As they walked away Tom's eyes were fixed on Amber's legs. They seemed to go on forever in that skirt. 'Nice, very nice,' he thought as he smiled to himself.

"She's very pretty," Becky said, giving him a nudge.

"Who is?" Pete asked, having returned from the restaurant waving his glasses.

"One of the girls Tom works with. You've just missed her," Becky informed him.

"Oh, I see." Pete grinned.

"We've just bumped into some of my work colleagues. They are all very nice." Tom nudged Becky back as he exaggerated the 'all'.

"Of course they were." She grinned at him. "Are we going to get that nightcap?"

CHAPTER 17

Amber sat in the early morning traffic. There was no sea air, nor walking barefoot along the sand watching the waves gently lap against the shore this morning. It was back to work, back to the daily grind of life, instead of the solitary walks she had taken daily, enjoying the peace and tranquillity of the sea. 'It was always hard on your first day back to work after being away,' she thought as she parked her car.

She walked into the office. Nothing had changed. 'Why would it in two weeks?' she thought and smiled to herself. She put the clotted cream she had bought for Gloria and Dorothy in the fridge, leaving the rock and sweets for the girls in the bag. Popping the kettle on she got Mr L's tray ready.

Harry was the first to welcome her back as he delivered the post, with Mr L arriving not long after.

"Amber, good to have you back. We've missed you," he said cheerily as he stopped at the desk. "Did you enjoy your holiday?"

"Yes, thank you, I had a lovely time. It was really good to spend some time with my aunt, and the weather stayed kind which was an added bonus," she answered.

"I can see that from the suntan. Did you manage a swim in the sea or was the water too cold?" he asked.

"I certainly did, every day, and the water was very cold," she said, making a face.

After taking Mr L's tray in Amber busied herself behind reception. Glancing at the clock she hoped the girls would be in before Tom. As much as she had tried to keep him out of her mind she had found herself thinking about him. She was still worried that he was going to have her in his office for a dressing down. It hadn't helped her paranoia that he just so happened to be standing a few feet from the steps where she had missed her footing before she had gone away. She still wasn't quite sure how she had done it. She had blamed Henry for distracting her. He, in return, had blamed the last cocktail she had drunk.

"Look at you, Miss fit and healthy," Melanie almost shrieked as she hurried in to give Amber a hug. "So glad you're back. Where's my rock?"

"Oh no, I knew there was something I'd forget." Amber laughed.

"Liar, give or else I won't tell you all the gossip," Melanie said, holding out her hand.

"I know all the gossip, you phoned me every day," Amber said as she presented Melanie with a carrier bag of goodies. "For you and Vicky."

"Ta, my favourite," Melanie said, pulling out a stick of pink rock. "I had to call you every day to check you weren't going to throw yourself off some cliff into the sea."

"I would never do that without a life jacket." Amber grinned.

"Thank fuck for that." Melanie giggled.

"Your language hasn't improved much while I've been away." Amber pointed her finger at Melanie like a school mistress. "But I'll let you off if you make the coffee and fill me in on anything you did forget to tell me."

"Fair do's." Melanie nodded before slipping into the back office. She put the kettle on, then began banging the stick of rock she had in her hand on the desk.

"What are you doing?" Amber shouted on hearing the noise Melanie was making.

"Trying to break this rock so I can have some. I love to be rough with something so hard." The rock began to break into pieces as she repeatedly knocked it on the desk. "Ah, here we go."

Amber appeared at the door. "Will you behave? It's not even nine o'clock yet."

"Sorry." Melanie laughed as she put a piece of rock into her mouth seductively, making Amber wince.

Vicky arrived squealing her delight at having Amber back. It wasn't long before the three of them were seated behind reception, a mug of coffee each, discreetly placed where the public couldn't see it.

"Well, come on, there has to be something I don't know. No Mr Tranter today. Is he in Scotland again?" Amber asked.

"Funny that your first question is about him," Melanie said, raising her eyebrows.

"Just an observation. He usually gets in early, that's all." Amber shrugged her shoulders a little too defensively.

"He's on site this week," Vicky said, smiling at Amber. "The first Monday you were out I did the early. As soon as he came in he asked where you were. He said he didn't realise you were on holiday for two weeks."

"Why would he? It's really none of his concern," Amber said a little aggressively.

"Amber, don't be like that, he was being nice. He asked where you had gone and who with. He seemed quite interested actually. He even asked if you'd got home safely on the Friday." Vicky laughed. "He has a wicked sense of humour."

"I'm sure that was more sarcasm than humour. At least you guys caught me before I hit the deck in front of him and another one of his girlfriends."

"It wasn't his girlfriend, it was his friend's wife," Melanie corrected Amber.

"Why doesn't that surprise me?" said Amber, rolling her eyes.

"Am, you have it all wrong. That's why they were stood there, they were waiting for him. They had all been out for a meal; her husband had left his glasses at the restaurant and gone back for them," Vicky explained.

"Okay, okay," Amber said, holding up her hands. "My mistake. I shouldn't have jumped to conclusions."

"No, madam, you shouldn't. I'm telling you straight, you have it all wrong about him. Nobody has a bad word to say about him. Talking of which, Carol from the Business Office is now his PA. When she heard he was looking for one she went to see him; 10 minutes later she came out with the job. So they're now looking for a replacement for her. She started last week," Melanie said.

"Really, you didn't tell me that when I was away. Come to think of it, Carol didn't say anything when she came in this morning," Amber said.

"That's because you've got it fixed in that nut of yours that he has it in for you, where as we think he has a bit of a thing for you, don't we Vic?" Melanie looked at Vicky.

"We certainly do." Vicky nodded in agreement. "Carol didn't say anything because she probably thought you already knew."

"Have you two been taking drugs while I've been away? Whatever gives you that idea?" Amber asked, surprised.

"It's just a feeling." Melanie burst into song, swaying her shoulders from side to side.

"In that case, both of you need your nuts examined," Amber said, before answering the phone that had just started to ring, leaving Melanie giving Vicky a wink behind her back.

Mr Lockyard put his mobile back on the desk. He looked at the clock. It was just before 3pm. As he sat there watching the second hand move around there was an efficient tap at his door. He looked up as it opened, knowing it would be Dorothy.

"Cup of tea?" she asked.

"Um …" He paused. "Yes, I think so, please. I was considering going. Tom needs some papers dropping off at the site, but I think I'll get Amber to do it. That way I can finish a few things off here."

"I see," Dorothy said, looking over her glasses at Mr Lockyard.

"Dorothy, don't look at me like that." He grinned. "Amber has shown considerable interest in the complex. I think it's a very good opportunity for her to see the site being prepared."

Dorothy carried on looking over her glasses at him. "I'll buzz her to come over. A biscuit with your tea?" she asked, pushing her glasses back up her nose as her lips twitched into a smile.

"That would be lovely," Mr Lockyard answered.

As Amber dried her hands she looked at her reflection in the mirror. 'Well,' she thought, 'that's my first day back nearly over.' She wandered back to reception, adjusting the clasp on her necklace that had worked its way round to the front.

"While you were in the bog, Dorothy Judith has requested your presence," Melanie said, leaning over the desk towards Amber.

"You mean, powder room," Amber corrected her with a plum in her mouth as she carried on past the desk towards Dorothy's office. As she entered, Dorothy looked up. "Melanie said you wanted to see me."

"Yes, Mr Lockyard has some papers that need to go up to the site. He'd like you to deliver them," Dorothy told here.

"Oh, okay," Amber replied.

"Well, in you go then, he has them all ready." Dorothy motioned towards the door.

Amber knocked on the door before entering.

"Ah, Amber," Mr L said, standing up. "I have some papers that need be taken up to the site. After our conversation a while back I thought it would be a chance for you to see the site being prepared."

"Great, thank you," Amber said, taking the briefcase that Mr L was holding out to her.

"I've called Tom, he's going to keep an eye out for you," Mr L said with a smile.

"Tom." Amber paused. "Oh, right." Another pause. "Lovely." Another pause. "See you tomorrow then."

"See you tomorrow then." Mr Lockyard grinned at her.

"See you tomorrow then," Amber repeated.

She said goodbye to Dorothy on her way past. 'No, oh no,' she groaned to herself as she walked back to the desk. 'Tom was the last person she wanted to see. Why hadn't she kept her mouth shut about being interested in the site?' As she grabbed her bag she explained to Melanie and Vicky where she was going.

"Lucky you, wish I was the one going, all those dishy builders in hard hats," Vicky said, pretending to wipe her brow.

"When they see you at least one of them will have a hard thing in his trousers as well." Melanie smirked.

"You are just so gross," Amber said.

"Only telling the truth," she said, waving goodbye to Amber who stood shaking her head from side to side. "Run along, Am."

Amber pulled into the site entrance. She undid her window as the security man on the gate began to walk towards her car. "Hello, I have some papers for Tom Tranter," she said, pointing to the briefcase on the seat next to her.

"The boss said you were coming. Just park over there, where it says visitors. I'll bring you over a hard hat." He walked back to open the barrier before waving her through.

Amber parked her car. She sat there for a moment, listening to her heart thump against her chest. Taking a deep breath she got out. She smiled to the security man who was on his way over.

"Here we go, try this on for size," he said, handing her a hard hat. "Regulations, I'm afraid."

Amber put the hat on.

"Suits you." The security man smiled. "Just walk straight over there."

Briefcase in hand she began to walk in the direction the security man had indicated. Why did she feel so nervous? 'There was no way Tom Tranter could say anything to her, not here, she would simply hand over the briefcase and that would be that. Wow, it looked huge,' she thought as she left the area where all the cars and vans were parked. There were mountains of earth everywhere, massive diggers and an army of workmen milling about. She carried on until she came to where the ground sloped away. Looking down she saw Tom Tranter talking to another man. She stood there for a moment wondering whether to shout out that she was there. 'No, she would just carry on until he noticed her. It didn't look too steep; she would just walk straight down, instead of around to where there was a sort of makeshift access. It would be quicker,' she said to herself.

Tom looked up just as Amber started down the slope. "Amber, no," he shouted, but he was too late. As Amber looked at him it felt like the earth was moving under her feet. Down she went. As she slipped down the bank she tried her best to keep her skirt from riding up, but without success. It was as though she was sat on one of those mats at a theme park as the moving earth took her down to where she landed, skirt practically up around her waist, legs akimbo. She was desperately trying to yank her skirt down when she felt a pair of strong hands grip her under the arms, lifting her to her feet.

"Are you hurt?" Tom asked, turning her to him but not letting her go.

She could hardly bring herself to look at him. "Just my pride, but I'm used to that. I seem to be one shoe down."

"Now, that is something you should be getting used to," Tom said, smiling at her. "It's over there." He nodded over to where it lay about half way down the bank. The workman he had been talking to was already on his way to rescue it. "I was going to say not to take the shortcut as it wasn't safe, especially if you happen to be wearing that kind of footwear."

"Yes, well," she stuttered slightly, suddenly aware of how close they were to each other; his hands still holding her arms made her feel strangely secure. 'Oh God,' she thought suddenly, taking a step back, 'what am I thinking?' Picking up the briefcase that had travelled down with her she handed it to him. "Yes, well," she said again. "I would have worn something more appropriate had I known I would be delivering this."

"Amber, I was ..." Tom began.

"Here we go, lass," the workman said, returning with her shoe. "You ok?"

"… was only joking," Tom finished under his breath as Amber turned towards the workman.

"Yes, yes, I'm fine, thank you, and thank you for getting my shoe," Amber said, taking it from him.

"Let me steady you while you put it on," the workman said, offering her his hand.

"That might be a good idea." She made a face at him as she took his hand, grateful that he was there so she would not be alone with Tom.

"My pleasure, lass." The workman touched his hard hat.

'Ah, how sweet,' thought Amber as she gave him a smile that lit up her face.

"Right then, I'll walk you back to your car," Tom said once Amber had her shoe on.

"No," Amber almost shouted at him. "No," she said again a little more quietly. "That's not necessary, thank you." She began to walk towards the makeshift exit.

"I think it is," Tom said, following her.

"No, it isn't," Amber said, speeding up. She practically marched over to where she had to start making her way up to the top with Tom at her heels. The workman stood holding the briefcase Tom had flung at him as he started after Amber. 'Oh yes, it is necessary,' he chuckled to himself as he watched.

No sooner had Amber started to walk up the slope than her feet were slipping all over the place. Where she had fallen the earth had been loose. Here it had been so compacted down that her shoes, that had absolutely no grip on them, seemed to be out of control. Yet again she felt Tom's hands on her as he almost propelled her up the slope. At the top he released her. She stood there for a moment, not wanting to turn around, but she did to find Tom laughing.

"Hilarious, isn't it," she said sarcastically. "Just don't say I told you so."

"I wouldn't dare," he replied.

"In actual fact, don't say anything." Amber put up her hand.

"Boss, can we have a word?" Two workmen joined them.

"Head down to Bert, I'll be down in a minute," Tom replied, pointing to the man who had rescued her shoe. He was watching them. 'No doubt, he had witnessed her being pushed up the slope.' She felt the colour rush to her cheeks. 'Why couldn't the earth just swallow her up?'

"I can see how busy you are, I really will be fine from here, it's only over there," Amber said quickly. She smiled briefly at the two workmen before hotfooting it towards her car.

Tom sighed slowly as he shook his head.

"Sorry, boss, didn't mean to interrupt," one of the workmen said as he watched Tom watching Amber.

Tom turned to the workman. "Come on, Bert has the answer to what you're going to ask in that briefcase." He glanced again at Amber who was now almost back to where her car was parked. 'No point going after her now, she would more than likely tell him where to go, again,' he thought. They headed back down the slope.

By the time Amber got back to her car she was sweating. She would have liked to have said perspiring, because that's what ladies were meant to do, but she was sweating streams. It was so hot. She was so embarrassed. She was so going to have a bruise on her backside by tomorrow. She suddenly felt so exhausted.

CHAPTER 18

"Shit, I'm going to be late again," Melanie moaned.

"I keep telling you to leave some of your things at my place," Gary replied as he stopped the car. "Then you could go straight to work."

"I know, I know, I'm just so bloody disorganised," Melanie said, leaning over to give him a kiss. "Bye."

"Bye." He watched her run up the path. 'Disorganised, yes,' he smiled to himself, 'but there hadn't been a dull moment since he'd first met her.' She turned to wave before disappearing inside.

"Good morning, dear heart." Henry appeared on hearing the front door. "Been shagging the night away again, you dirty bitch?"

"Of course. Can't stop to chat, I'm late," Melanie said as she ran up the stairs.

"If you kept some things at his place you wouldn't keep being late," Henry shouted after her.

"Don't you bloody start, Henry, Gary's just said that," she shouted back.

Ten minutes later Melanie came thundering down the stairs.

"That was a quick flick with the flannel. Here, I've thrown together a sandwich for your lunch," Henry said, holding it out, all neatly wrapped in cling film.

"Cheers, Hen, you're a star." Melanie smiled, taking it from him. "I did have a shower at Gary's house this morning, I'm not that much of a dog, you know."

"Who would suggest such a thing? But we both know that you are," Henry hooted.

"I know." Melanie nodded. "Gary just loves it." She opened the front door. "Catch you later."

"Don't forget we're having a girlie night in tonight," Henry yelled after her.

"Now, would I? You're one of my favourite girls," Melanie yelled back.

"Here she is," Vicky said as Melanie came hurtling through the doors.

"Good afternoon, nice of you to join us." Amber grinned. "I was just about to call you. We were starting to get worried."

"Sorry, I should have called. Stayed at Gary's last night," Melanie said as she gyrated her hips.

"Liking the dance move, Melanie." Mark Gibson's voice made the girls turn around to find him standing there with his arms folded as though he had been there for ages.

"Why, thank you, Mark. I'm always practising," Melanie replied cheekily. "What can we do for you?"

"I've come to see Amber actually," he said, smiling at Amber. "I was wondering if we should start doing a bit of training for the charity walk. It's only a month away now. I was going to speak to you this morning but you were busy."

"It might be a good idea. What did you have in mind?" Amber asked.

"Well, neither of us are unfit, so I was thinking if we do a few hours next weekend, and the following two, then that will leave the weekend before the walk to rest, leaving us as fresh as daisies."

"Sounds good to me." Amber grinned at him.

"Great. Oh, before I forget, do you need a tent? I have a spare one you can borrow," he offered.

"No, it's okay, I have one that will do, but thanks anyway," Amber replied.

"Keep dancing," he said to Melanie as he left.

"Ah, he's really sweet," Vicky said after he'd gone. "You'll have a good time on that walk."

"Yes, if I can keep up with him." Amber sighed.

"You'll be fine," Melanie said.

"Says the girl who will no doubt be sat on a sunny beach while I'm trekking over rough terrain." Amber put her hands on her hips.

"I know. I can't wait. I can almost taste the sangria, but coffee will have to do for now. Fancy one?" Amber and Vicky both nodded. "Coming right up. Oh, by the way, you're not thinking of using the tent you used when we were at school, are you, Am?"

"As a matter of fact, I am." Amber nodded. "Why?"

"Bloody hell, it was falling apart then," Melanie exclaimed. "Why don't you borrow the one Mark was offering? His is probably some high-tech, super-duper model."

"Mine will be perfectly sufficient, thank you very much. It saw me through Guides and the Ten Tors. I feel more than confident it will see me through another couple of nights in the wild. Weren't you supposed to be making coffee?" Amber said, pointing at Melanie.

"Just a suggestion, my lovely." Melanie smiled, holding up her hands.

"All things bright and beautiful, all creatures great and small," Gloria sang as she waddled along.

"All things wise and wonderful, the Lord God made them all," a voice finished off.

Gloria turned round to find Tom just about to catch her up. She stopped to wait for him. "My, my, that sure is a fine voice. We got room for another honey in the choir, hehehe," she laughed.

"The only choir I'd be good for is the cats' choir," Tom joked. "How are you, Gloria? You're looking very pretty today."

"Hehehe," Gloria chortled, "not as pretty as you," she said, starting to walk again, now that Tom had caught her up.

"Your boss is on his way in," Vicky said to Carol, Tom's secretary, who was at the desk. "And I don't mind saying he looks good enough to eat."

They all turned to look at Tom, still dressed in his jeans and work boots, looking quite dishevelled after a hard day on site. He was obviously having some kind of joke with Gloria, as they could hear her cackling with laughter.

"He is good enough to eat," Carol replied.

"We have a welcoming committee," Tom said to Gloria as they walked in to find Carol, Vicky, Melanie and Amber watching them.

"We do, and they is all as sweet as honey," Gloria said.

"Just the person I need," Carol said to Tom. "I have some letters that need signing."

"In exchange for a coffee?" He smiled at Carol.

"Of course, it will be on your desk in a minute," she said, greeting Gloria before heading off towards the coffee machine.

"I think that was a subtle way of telling me to hurry up," he said, turning to the girls. In the time he had spoken to Carol, Amber had managed to slip into the back office. He quickly glanced at the clock. It was four o'clock. 'If he had been a bit later he would have come across her in the car park. He could never seem to get the timing right,' he thought. As he chatted to Melanie and Vicky he kept glancing towards the back office door. As soon as Amber reappeared with her bag their eyes met.

"Amber, how are you? I haven't seen you since ..." Tom stopped there. 'He could hardly say – since you landed at my feet with your skirt up round your waist, displaying the most amazing pair of legs and some rather fetching pink knickers, could he,' he said to himself.

"Fine, thanks," Amber answered before he had time to finish his sentence. Blushing, she adjusted the bag on her shoulder for something to do.

"Apart from a behind that's black and blue," Melanie chipped in.

Amber shot her a look.

"Sorry." Melanie grinned.

"Painful," Tom said sympathetically.

"I'll live," Amber replied as she came out from behind the desk.

"You been rubbing that arnica cream in I gave you, honey?" Gloria put her hand on Amber's arm.

"Yes, it really helped." Amber gave Gloria's hand a squeeze. "See you all tomorrow," she said quickly, and before anyone had a chance to say anything else she hurried towards the doors. 'Great, just great,' she thought as she headed to her car, 'she could murder Mel sometimes. Now he knew she was suffering from a bruised bum, something else to make him laugh at her.'

"Well, I's going to say hello to Dorothy before doing my chores," Gloria said, looking at Tom who was still gazing after a disappearing Amber.

"I'd better sign those letters," Tom said, turning to look at her.

Gloria nodded her head at him. "See you girlies in a minute," she said to Melanie and Vicky as she headed towards Dorothy's office. Tom saluted the girls before joining Gloria. They walked for a few moments in silence. "Amber sure is a sweet flower," Gloria said.

Tom smiled at Gloria. "Yes," he replied simply, thinking, 'No point saying anything else. Nothing seemed to escape Gloria.'

"Mmmm." She smiled back at him.

CHAPTER 19

"Have I mentioned that this time tomorrow I'll be on my way to Spain?" Melanie asked as she flicked back her hair. "Oh, and have I mentioned I'll be staying with my boyfriend's brother in his villa with a private pool, also a stone's throw from the beach?"

"Now, let me see, have you mentioned any of that already …" Amber drummed her fingers on the desk.

"Only about 100 times and it's only 9.30am.," Vicky said, throwing a paperclip at Melanie before answering the phone. "Certainly, Dorothy." She looked at Amber, making a face as she spoke. She replaced the receiver. "You've been summoned by Dorothy Judith."

"Have I? I wonder why? I don't think I've done anything wrong." She tried to think. "Oh no, please don't say I have to take anything up to the site."

"As long as you have clean knickers on you won't have to worry about slipping down and showing them off, although I'm sure Tom would welcome another flash." Melanie pushed Amber in the direction of Dorothy's office. "Now, off you go. I want to know why Dorothy Judith wants to see you."

"Did I mention that Melanie will be on her way to Spain tomorrow? Won't it be nice not to have any abuse for a week?" Amber wrinkled up her nose at Vicky as Melanie continued to push her out from behind the desk.

As she entered Dorothy's office she found her talking to Mr Lockyard. They looked up as she entered.

"You wanted to see me?" She smiled.

"Yes, but with not very good news, I'm afraid." Mr Lockyard shook his head. "Dorothy has just taken a call from Mark Gibson. He's in A&E waiting for his ankle to be put into plaster."

"Oh no, what's happened?" Amber asked.

"He got knocked off his bike on the way to work this morning. Apparently a car pulled out of a side street straight into him," Mr Lockyard explained.

"Oh dear, poor Mark. Has he got any other injuries?" Amber asked, concerned.

"A few cuts and bruises but nothing serious, luckily. He did say to tell you he didn't do it on purpose to get out of the charity walk." Mr Lockyard laughed.

"Really? I'll believe him, thousands wouldn't. But what are we going to do about the walk? It's on Saturday?" Amber exclaimed.

"It's up to you. I quite understand if you want to call it a day, or we can send out an email. There might be someone who has no plans for the weekend that will step in," Mr Lockyard suggested.

"It would be a shame to pull out, especially seeing as it's for charity. I'd also feel I would be letting Mark down if we didn't try to get someone to take his place. He's been so enthusiastic about it all." Amber sighed.

"Good for you," Dorothy said, her lips twitching into a Dorothy-smile.

"I'll second that." Mr Lockyard beamed at Amber. "You're a good sport."

Mr Lockyard's words made Amber feel as though she was going to cry. 'Don't be stupid,' she told herself. "I'd better get back to reception," she said, turning to leave. She walked slowly back to the desk. 'You are an emotional wreck, pull yourself together,' she repeated to herself as she walked.

"Dorothy, can I leave this in your capable hands?" Mr Lockyard smiled at Dorothy.

"You can, indeed," she replied as she started to type. "It will be done by the time you sit at your desk."

"Thank you," Mr Lockyard said as he started to walk towards his office door. He stopped. "Dorothy?"

"Coffee?" Dorothy said as she looked at him over her glasses.

"You're a mind reader." He grinned before entering his office.

"I know," she said to herself as she pressed the send button.

"Well, what did Dorothy Judith.com want?" Melanie asked before Amber even had a chance to get behind the desk.

"Mark's been knocked off his bike, he has to have his ankle plastered," Amber told her.

"Shit, poor bloke, but looking on the bright side it does get you out of the charity walk," Melanie said.

"No, it doesn't," Vicky interrupted. "I've just opened an email from Dorothy asking if anyone is up to filling Mark's boots at short notice. It goes on to say if they are, to email her back by 4pm today."

"You didn't volunteer to carry on with it, did you?" Melanie asked, shaking her head at Amber.

Amber nodded. "I couldn't let Mr L down, plus it will do me good. So if anyone is daft enough to put their name forward I will be fighting the elements while you are fighting off another sangria."

"So theatrical," Melanie said, pretending to wipe her brow.

"Talking of theatrical, I nearly started to cry in front of Mr L and Dorothy because they were so sweet," Amber admitted. "I've turned into a fruit loop."

"What do you mean turned into, you've always been one," Melanie said, giving Amber a hug. "Just joking, you're still a bit up and down, that's all."

"Maybe you're right." Amber shrugged.

"I'm always right," Melanie said, giving her friend another squeeze.

Tom sang along to Plan B as he parked the truck. 'The day had been good so far.' He checked his watch after pulling on the handbrake. He would just have time to give Carol a few things that needed doing before the meeting started. He continued to sing to himself as he hurried across the car park. 'Things were getting even better,' he thought as he walked in to find Amber on her own behind the desk.

"Hi, all alone?" He smiled at her.

"No, no," Amber repeated. "Melanie and Vicky are around."

He stopped at the desk, resting some papers he had in his arms on top. As he did so Amber automatically took a step back, her heart beginning to beat faster. 'Why did he make her feel so threatened?' she wondered.

"How are you?" he asked.

"If you're referring to my minor injuries they're all better, thank you," Amber answered quite defensively.

"I wasn't, but seeing as you've mentioned them I'm glad they're better." He grinned.

Amber blushed. 'Here he was, laughing at her again.' She couldn't think of anything to say. They stood looking at one another. 'Why doesn't the phone ring when you want it to?' she thought, pulling her eyes away from his to look at it.

"Expecting a call?" Tom asked, raising his eyebrows.

"No," Amber said, shaking her head as she looked back at him. "Not that I know of," she added.

"Hi, Tom," Melanie's voice purred his name as she slipped behind the desk.

"Hi, Mel, how's it going?" Tom replied.

"Good, thanks. It will be even better tomorrow, because as you know I'll be in Spain. Is Amber looking after you?" she asked with a wicked look in her eye as she stood next to her.

"Are you looking after me?" Tom asked Amber in turn.

Amber could have swung for Melanie. Instead, she mustered a laugh from somewhere, which sounded so utterly false. "Mr Tranter hasn't let me know what he wants yet." She cringed, 'Oh God, she hadn't meant to say that.'

Tom's eyes lit up. He looked at Melanie who was making a shocked faced, then proceeded to laugh. "Have fun in Spain."

"I will." She beamed.

He looked back at Amber laughing along with Melanie as he picked up the papers he'd put on the desk, before walking away.

As he left Amber nudged Melanie with her elbow. "Thanks a bunch for that."

"Am, lighten up, it was just a bit of fun," Melanie said, still giggling.

"Why aren't I laughing then? And when did he start calling you Mel?" Amber asked, being a little too prickly.

"Jealous?" Melanie questioned, tongue in cheek.

"Oh yeah." Amber made a face.

"What were you two talking about before I came back?" Melanie enquired.

"Nothing. I try my best not to have any sort of conversation with him; in actual fact, I go out of my way to avoid him. He thinks I'm an idiot. I'm still waiting to be called in to see him," Amber almost snapped.

"Shame, because he tries so hard to have one with you," Melanie said sweetly.

"Don't be ridiculous, didn't you just hear what I said?" Amber said, busying herself tidying the desk.

"Yes, but I chose to ignore it because it's crap. I'm telling you, he fancies the pants off you, literally." Melanie smirked.

"That remark is not even worthy of a reply. This conversation is over," Amber said, giving Melanie's hair a playful pull. "I'm going to get my bag. It's nearly time I wasn't here."

Melanie followed her into the back office. "See you tonight then. Henry's going to order the takeaway for about seven o'clock, then after you can both help me pack."

"Okay, I'm just going to have a word with Dorothy on my way out. See you later."

"Are you sure you're not going to Tom's office to find out what he wants?" Melanie called after her.

Amber replied with a two-fingered salute, which sent Melanie into fits of laughter.

"Sorry to disturb you, Dorothy. I was just wondering how we were doing with replies to the email?" Amber asked as she entered Dorothy's office.

"It is truly amazing how people rally when the need be. I have more names to pick out of my hat than I did initially," Dorothy stated.

"Wow." Amber was amazed.

"Are you staying to find out who will be the lucky chap?" Dorothy asked. "I'm just about to sort the draw out for Mr Lockyard to pick a name before he goes into the meeting."

"No, I think I can wait until the morning." Amber smiled.

Tom walked into Carol's office. She didn't give him time to say anything. "Tom, I've been trying to call you. You said you would be back by three o'clock. There's an email from Dorothy that needs answering by four o'clock. Mark Gibson's been knocked off his bike so can no longer take part in the charity walk. A replacement is needed at short notice. Anybody interested needs to put their name forward."

"I must have left my phone in the site office," Tom said, feeling in his pockets. "Put my name forward, please, and can you try to locate my phone and organise for it to get back to me by the end of the meeting? And apologies for being late."

"You're forgiven. I was just about to email Dorothy to put your name forward, as you volunteered last time so would I have done the right thing?" Carol asked.

"You would, and that is exactly why I wouldn't want anyone else to be my PA. Oh, and also because you do a lovely coffee, and because you'll know what to do with that lot too." Tom indicated to the papers he'd just put on her desk as he went into his office.

Carol laughed. "I'll bring your coffee through."

Dorothy opened the new message from Carol just after Amber had left. Exactly as she had expected, Tom's name had been put forward. Sitting back in her chair she sat looking at it. Tom was such a nice young man and Amber was such a nice young lady.

"Everything alright, Dorothy?" Mr Lockyard asked. It was so unusual to find Dorothy just sat.

"Oh goodness, I didn't hear you come in." Dorothy almost jumped. "I was deep in thought. I'm just about to prepare the draw for the walk, shall I call you when it's ready?"

"I have a few calls to make. Would you mind doing the honours on my behalf?" Mr Lockyard asked.

"Not at all," Dorothy replied.

Gloria appeared in the doorway, a vision of colour. Even her tabard was the brightest green imaginable.

"Good afternoon, Gloria, you are looking wonderful today." Mr Lockyard smiled.

"Ooh, eee, you sweet talking me, hehehe." Gloria let out her hearty laugh.

"Of course." Mr Lockyard nodded.

"I just popping my head round, but I can see you two is busy. I come back later, Dorothy," Gloria said.

"No need, we're all done here," Mr Lockyard said. "I'll leave you ladies to it. If you could just let me know who you pick out, Dorothy."

"Of course," Dorothy replied.

"You had a good day, Dorothy?" Gloria asked after Mr Lockyard had left.

She was answered with the saga of Mark Gibson's accident, finishing with the email she had in front of her from Carol putting Tom forward. The two women looked at each other, a twinkle in both of their eyes.

"I would put my hand on the Lord's book, I'm so sure that our Mr Tom is sweet on Amber." Gloria put her hands on her more than ample hips.

"I have to say, I agree with you." Dorothy nodded.

"They surely would make a good-looking couple." Gloria nodded in unison with Dorothy.

"Yes, they would. The problem is dear Amber. She was so upset finding out what that rat had been up to that she told me, I think her words were 'off men for good'," Dorothy said.

"What's needed is the Lord's helping hand," Gloria said, nodding again slowly.

"As we both know he does move in mysterious ways." Dorothy twitched as she gave Gloria a look over her glasses; it said 'I think we are both thinking along the same lines.'

"Would you be kind enough to assist me with the draw?" Dorothy asked.

Gloria beamed from ear to ear. "I surely would."

CHAPTER 20

"Good morning, Amber." Dorothy's lips twitched. "Before you ask, I can tell you we have a very fit young man to take Mark's place. Tom Tranter."

Amber was speechless. She stood, her mouth open. 'Please no, please no, say I didn't hear right,' she thought.

Taking her silence completely the wrong way Dorothy carried on. "I knew you'd be pleased. The both of you are very active people. When I told Mr Lockyard he said straight away that we have an excellent chance of doing well. Any calls for him this morning put straight through to me, he won't be in until lunchtime." Dorothy twitched a smile at the still open-mouthed Amber before heading to her office.

Amber almost started to shake. 'What was she going to do? There was no way on this earth she could do it with Tom Tranter, anyone else but not him,' she told herself. She sat down, putting her head in her hands. 'She would have to pretend to be ill. No, that was too obvious. She could throw herself down the stairs, a broken leg would be better than spending two days walking with him, but then again, knowing her luck she would probably give herself brain damage. Melanie, yes Melanie would know what to do.' She looked at the time. She would be at the airport now. Picking up the phone she rang her mobile.

"Hello," Melanie's voice answered.

"Hi, it's me." Amber tried not to cry. "Sorry to call ..."

"I know it's you. What's up?" Melanie asked, not giving Amber time to finish.

"Tom Tranter is what's up. He's been picked to do the charity walk with me," Amber half wailed down the phone. "I need a good excuse not to do it. You're the only one I know that may be able to think of one, and please don't say I should have said I didn't want to carry on and do it while I had the chance."

Melanie almost jumped for joy, but made her voice sound sombre. "I won't, but even I can't think of anything to get you out of this one. You're just going to have to do it. We keep telling you that Tom is a really nice guy; now's your chance to find out."

"I don't want to find out," Amber whined.

"Listen, young lady, you get your ass in gear, stick your chin out, and your tits, of course. You can do it. I want a full report when I get back," Melanie said sternly.

"Are you sure you can't think of a get-me-out-of-jail card?" Amber pleaded.

"No, sweet pea, I can't." Melanie softened her voice. "Amber, you'll be fine, you said yourself it will do you good."

"But not with Tom Tranter. I'll be like a lamb to the slaughter." Amber let out a big sigh.

"Now you're sounding like Henry." Melanie let out a little laugh.

"I am, aren't I? You have a great holiday," Amber said, trying to sound more cheerful.

"I will. See you when I get back. Good luck for the weekend. Bye," Melanie said.

"What are you smiling about?" Gary asked Melanie as he slipped his hand around her waist.

"Tom Tranter has only gone and been picked to partner Amber at the weekend. I'm telling you, it has to be fate," Melanie said, giving him a kiss on the cheek.

"But you told me Amber doesn't like him," Gary said.

"She just thinks she doesn't, but he more than likes her." Melanie beamed.

"God, you're hard to understand." Gary laughed. "The way you tell it makes it sound like it always ends in disaster when they have anything to do with each other."

"Well, it kind of does. Well, more with Amber being embarrassed in some way or another. I can't wait to find out how it goes," Melanie said excitedly.

"You are wicked. I may have to punish you later," Gary said, squeezing her bottom.

"I'm not being wicked, it will do Amber the world of good, but I can definitely be wicked about something else so that you have to punish me," she answered him.

"You really have got the most incredibly dirty mind," Gary whispered in her ear.

"I know, and you love it," she whispered back.

Tom sat in the site office having coffee with the workmen. They had just finished a briefing on what he wanted accomplished that day. The men began to leave in dribs and drabs after finishing their drinks. After switching on his laptop he saw there was an email from Dorothy. Opening it up he read the short message telling him that he had been picked from the draw to partner Amber on the charity walk. He laughed to himself. He could just imagine the look on her face when she had found out that she would be doing it with him.

A quick call to Pete set him up with a tent, a double blow-up camping bed and what Pete described as a box of tricks that would be ready for him to pick up after work. It was also the incentive he needed to organise for the rest of his stuff to come out of storage. Luckily, he hadn't stored his walking boots; they were down here. He couldn't resist making a final call.

"Hello, Lockyards, how can I help you?" Amber answered the phone.

"Amber, it's Tom Tranter. I've just found out I'm the lucky person who's been picked to do the walk with you. I'll try not to let you down," he joked.

'Was that sarcasm in his voice?' Amber wondered. 'Probably,' she prickled. "I'm sure it will be the other way round."

"We'll need to get our heads together regarding arrangements," Tom went on, ignoring her comment.

"No need. I can tell you now," Amber said quickly. She didn't want to spend any more time with him than she absolutely had to. "The walk starts at midday but we have to be ready by 11.30am. They advise people to arrive early enough to put their tents up first."

"Fine. I'll pick you up at 7.30am," Tom said.

"No need," she said again. "I don't want to put you out. I can make my own way down."

"Amber, you won't be putting me out. It makes sense for us to go together. I'll see you Saturday at 7.30am. I know where you live. Bye for now." Tom finished the call before she had time to object.

"Well, you were assertive, as usual, weren't you?" Amber said out loud to herself as she put down the phone. 'She was now going to have to endure the journey down and back with him,' she thought.

The day dragged by. Vicky did her best to cheer Amber up, without success. 'The only good thing about the day was that by the time she had left, Tom Tranter hadn't arrived. At least she didn't have to see him. Hopefully the same would happen tomorrow, but after that it would be Saturday. Oh God,' Amber said to herself.

CHAPTER 21

Picking up her rucksack Amber locked her front door. She made her way slowly down the stairs. At the bottom she opened the door onto the street. It was all dewy outside. She plonked her rucksack on the pavement, then turned to pick up the tent she had already brought down, placing it down beside it. She pulled the door closed behind her. She gave it a nudge with her elbow just to check it was secure.

She mentally went through what she had packed, although she had checked and double-checked at least 10 times. She rubbed her hands together; it was going to be a beautiful day, but it was a bit chilly. She looked at her watch. He'd be here in a minute. 'Well, at least he couldn't say she was late,' she thought. Her heart started to beat a little faster. 'Deep breaths,' she told herself as she tried to control her breathing in a vain attempt to get a grip. She closed her eyes. 'In through the nose, out through the mouth, in through the nose, out through the mouth,' she repeated over and over again.

She was concentrating so much that when she heard Tom's truck pull up it made her jump. He smiled at her before getting out. 'Here we go, no turning back now,' she thought as she hauled her rucksack over one shoulder, then bent to pick up the tent.

"Were you saying your prayers?" Tom asked with a big grin on his face as he walked round the front of his truck.

"Do I need to?" Amber answered the question with her own question.

"Maybe. Give me those," he said, indicating her rucksack and tent.

"I can manage, thank you. Shall I put them in the back?" she asked, turning away from him as she walked towards the back of the truck.

In a stride he was behind her lifting the rucksack from her shoulder. She looked at him; he was still grinning. She let him take the rucksack. 'No point in starting things with her being petty,' she thought. He lifted it over the side of the truck. She passed him the tent.

"Thanks," she said, looking at all the stuff in the back.

"That's what you get when you borrow a tent from a mate. His wife insist I have this, that and the other. It was much easier just to say thank you. In actual fact, I was with them the night you had that argument with some steps." He laughed.

"Very funny. But if I remember correctly, you were just with the wife," Amber said accusingly.

"You're right. We were waiting for the husband, he'd left his glasses in the restaurant," Tom said, choosing to ignore her tone. "Sure you've got everything?"

'Why had she said that? Melanie had told her he had been with both of them. You were trying to catch him out, that's why,' she thought, answering her own question. She could hear Melanie's words, 'Lighten up.' "Yes, I think so." She nodded.

"Let's go then," he said, making his way round to the driver's side.

'Well done, Amber, good start. In the space of two minutes you've managed to be rude and accusing, making yourself look like a total nutter, not that he needed convincing otherwise.' She got into the truck and fastened her seat belt. Feeling his eyes on her she looked at him, but he just smiled before turning his attention to the road as they set off.

They drove in silence for a while, both deep in thought regarding the other. Tom was happy he was alone at last with Amber, but now that he was he wasn't exactly sure how to handle things, which annoyed him; he wasn't used to not knowing what to say or do. 'Small talk,' he decided, 'that's where to start.' Amber, on the other hand, was desperately trying to tell herself to just be herself. 'But, what was herself? She didn't seem to have a problem speaking to anyone else like she did him. Small talk, that's where to start.'

They both went to speak at the same time.

"After you." Tom glanced at her briefly.

"I was only going to ask what kind of music you liked?" Amber said tentatively.

"That's funny because I was going to ask you exactly the same thing," Tom replied. "I like all sorts. My iPod is in there." He pointed to the glovebox compartment. "What about you?"

"I like all sorts too. Can I?" she asked.

"Be my guest." His eyes twinkled. "But no laughing when you see what's on there."

Amber rummaged around in the glovebox department until she found his iPod. She scrolled through it. As she did they chatted about the different types of music that he'd put on there. She was quite impressed with the selection. He wasn't lying when he said he liked all sorts. Deciding on some Motown she plugged it in. They chatted, keeping the topic of their conversation general, both careful not to ask the other anything that was too personal.

They stopped at the services for some breakfast. In the ladies Amber looked at her reflection in the mirror. 'Hardly the glamour puss,' she thought as she ran her fingers through her hair, 'unlike the woman sat at Tom's kitchen table that night.' She leaned in to look at herself more closely. 'Perhaps she should have put a bit of mascara on.' Horrified at what she'd just thought she stood back. 'Why on earth was she comparing herself to his girlfriend?' "You're mad," she mouthed at herself. She found Tom waiting outside.

They walked over to the food area to see what was on offer. "Fancy egg and bacon?" he asked.

"Mmm, yes." Amber nodded.

They picked up a tray each, selected what they wanted from the hot counter, then proceeded to get some tea to go with it.

"Two all-day breakfasts, two pots of tea." The girl on the till pouted at Tom.

"No, we're paying separately," Amber interrupted.

"It's together." Tom grinned at the girl.

With that, she completely ignored Amber's protests, taking the money from Tom. As soon as they sat down she got her purse out. She put some money in front of him on the table. "That's for mine," she said.

He pushed the money back at her. "It's on me."

"I'd rather pay for my own," she said, pushing it back.

He pushed it back at her again. "I insist."

"So do I," she said, pushing it back towards him. "I can afford to pay for my own breakfast."

"Are we having our first row?" He laughed as he stabbed at one of the sausages on his plate.

Amber couldn't help but laugh at his comment. "Not if you take what I owe you."

"If it makes you happy," Tom said, leaving the money where it was. "I'd forgotten you have issues when it comes to paying for things."

"I do not," Amber protested. "What's that supposed to mean?"

"When I tried to pay for your flip-flops you refused." Tom gazed at her.

"Only because it was as much my fault as it was yours that they got broken, and you can tell your girlfriend I did replace them with a decent pair." Amber shot back, then as she put some bacon into her mouth she thought, 'Oh dear, why had she put that sarcastic comment on the end?'

"Unfortunately, I can't, because she's no longer my girlfriend, but seeing as you think it was both our faults your flip-flops got broken, won't you put that money towards buying the left one? then I won't feel so bad about it." He pointed to the money on the table with his knife.

'Why can't I keep my snide comments to myself?' Amber thought as her face fell. To try and make amends she pulled the money towards her. "Fair enough, thank you. I'm sorry about your girlfriend, by the way."

"Don't be." Tom took in Amber's expression and had a sudden urge to touch her face. He took a bite of his toast to give himself a moment. "We weren't a match made in heaven. We'd agreed to a trial separation just before I started down here. I'd moved out and was staying with my sister. The night we ran into each other, Beth had turned up earlier at the office to surprise me. I did make an attempt to apologise for her rudeness, but if my memory serves me correctly you didn't give me the chance. Anyway, to cut a long story short, by mutual agreement our relationship ended that evening."

"Oh, I see. How long had you been together?" Amber asked while thinking she might well have formed a wrong opinion of him.

"We lived together for about six months, we were seeing each other for …" He shrugged, "probably about the same length of time before we moved in together. Have you finished your tea?"

'Oh dear, he probably thinks I'm being nosey now,' Amber thought. "Yes, I'm ready when you are."

"I'm ready," Tom said, standing up.

They walked to the truck in silence. After getting in they caught one another's eye as they went to fasten their seat belts. Amber felt her cheeks flush. 'Why did he always make her blush?'

"I wasn't prying back there, you know, when I asked you how long your relationship had lasted."

"I think you were prying," Tom said, looking at her intently.

"I was not." Amber's voice rose with indignation. "I was just trying to make conversation, that's all."

"Amber, I'm joking." Tom laughed as he started the truck.

"Forgive me if I don't get your jokes then." Amber made a face at him as she felt herself relax a little.

It didn't seem to take any time at all to finish their journey. Being such a big event it was well signposted. They pulled in to join a small queue. When they reached the front Tom wound down his window. A man in a reflective jacket greeted them. He quickly ticked them off his list, issuing them with an information pack, a parking permit and their entry numbers. He wished them good luck before pointing to another man wearing an identical jacket to the one he was wearing who was obviously in charge of parking. Tom's truck made easy work of the bumpy field as they headed over.

After several trips back and forth to the truck they were ready to put up their tents.

"I'll put yours up first," Tom offered.

"No, you won't. Believe it or not, I can do it myself." Amber made a face at him.

"Here we go again. I've no doubt in my mind that you can, but it won't take me a minute," Tom replied, smiling.

"It won't take me a minute either," Amber said. Kneeling down on the ground she started to unpack her tent. She looked up, giving him a steely glare.

"Okay, okay." Tom laughed as he put up his hands. "But don't come crying to me when you get stuck."

"Your jokes just get funnier and funnier, don't they?" Amber said sarcastically, but with a smile. 'I'll show you,' she thought as she began to unroll her tent. 'I'll prove that I'm an intelligent individual, not the hapless woman I've portrayed myself to be.'

Concentrating as though her life depended on it she began to erect her tent. She could hear Tom whistling to the side of her, but refused to look round. As she worked on the tent she realised how ropey it was. Some of the pegs were missing and it seemed to be a little out of shape for some reason, but she couldn't see why. 'Oh well, she only had to sleep in it for two nights.' She battled on until it was up. Standing back, pleased she'd actually got it up but somewhat apprehensive about its durability, she looked at Tom who was hitting a peg into the ground with a hammer. She cringed, 'His looked like a palace compared to hers.'

He walked over to join her, taking in her tent as he did so.

"Keep your comments to yourself," Amber said before he had time to say anything.

"I was only going to offer you the use of my pump if you needed it." He grinned.

"Oh," Amber said, not convinced. "I don't, thank you. I brought a roll-up camping mattress to put my sleeping bag on."

"Much more organised than myself. I pulled the duvet and pillows off my bed," Tom said as he began to pump up the double airbed he'd borrowed.

Walking boots on, they checked in. They were given a map with five checkpoints on it, plus a packed lunch. An official made a note of their set-off time as they started.

They chatted as they walked. Tom couldn't resist teasing Amber about the state of her tent, she retaliating to the best of her ability. Without realising it they bickered their way to the first checkpoint. They continued on to the second. On arriving at the third Tom looked at the map.

"This next bit doesn't look too bad. How do you feel about speeding up a tad?" he asked Amber.

"Set the pace, I'm sure I'll be able to keep up," she joked. She had to admit that she was starting to enjoy his company. They had quite a bit of banter going on between them. Now she was getting to know him she could see why everyone liked him.

"Ready then?" Tom smiled.

'Oh God, have I been stood here staring at him?' she thought as she blushed. "Ready," she squeaked. 'God, that sounded so pathetic. Pull yourself together,' she told herself as they set off. She retreated inside herself. Tom took her silence as a sign he had set too fast a pace.

"Do you need to slow down?" he asked, snapping Amber back into reality.

"What gives you that idea? I can more than keep up with you," she answered defensively.

"You haven't said a single word for nearly half an hour. I was wondering if you were conserving your energy."

"I don't need to. What about you?" She made a face at him.

"I'm just about managing." He grinned at her.

Amber was relieved to reach the fourth checkpoint. That meant just one more to go. They continued at the faster pace. On reaching the last one she was even more relieved that they could see the base camp from it. Now, not against the clock, they ambled back to be met by mugs of steaming tea. They chatted amicably to other walkers. After comparing times they realised they had done very well.

"Well done, partner." Tom laughed as he put his arm round Amber's shoulders to give her a hug.

"Well done to you too." She laughed.

They went back to the tents to pick up their things for the showers. It was getting quite nippy. As they walked to the facilities, in the form of big trailers, Amber hoped she would be warm enough in her sleeping bag.

She took her time under the hot, steamy shower. After rubbing herself dry, as always, even when camping, she rubbed in her body lotion before putting on her fleecy pyjamas. She made her way over to one of the free little compartments, where she sat down. She dabbed her face with toner, then massaged in her night cream. Surprised at how powerful the hair dryer was she blasted her hair.

Her tummy rumbled as she put on a thick pair of Jack Wills tracksuit bottoms over her pyjamas, followed by a hooded fleece. Then came a fluffy pair of bed socks before she pulled on her Ugg boots. She made her way back to the tent to find Tom waiting for her.

"Do you want the good news or the good news?" he asked.

"Both," she answered.

"While I've been waiting for you a fish-and-chip van has arrived, and they've lit a fire," he said, pointing to where a huge bonfire was starting to burn.

"Good, I'm starving," Amber said, pulling on her walking jacket. I thought it was tomorrow night they were lighting a fire."

"Looks like both. Good job because it's got quite cold," Tom said, rubbing his hands together.

They walked over to the fire, instantly feeling the warmth, the smell of fish and chips beginning to fill the air.

"Can you be trusted with alcohol?" Tom smirked at Amber after spotting a makeshift bar.

Amber's face fell. "I know what you must think of me, but those times ..."

"Amber, I'm kidding, lighten up. Red or white?" Tom interrupted, putting his hands up. 'Bad joke again,' he told himself as he took in Amber's expression.

"I don't mind." She shrugged, turning away from him as some of the walkers they had been talking to earlier joined them. That meant she didn't have time to dwell on Tom's comment.

By the time Tom got back with the drinks she was in fits of laughter from one of the men who was proving to be quite a comedian. He only had time to pass Amber her drink before he was monopolised by one of the women in the group. After a while Amber glanced over at Tom. He was still talking to the same woman; well, it was more like he was still listening to her. Amber watched the woman keep touching Tom's arm as she talked; it was so obvious she fancied him and it certainly didn't look like he minded.

"Another one?" the comedian asked, nudging Amber.

"Oh yes, lovely, thanks." Amber smiled. "I was miles away then." She sneaked another look at Tom, then instantly wished she hadn't as he caught her eye.

"Don't worry, I'm taking care of her," the comedian said, seeing Tom looking at Amber. He held up her empty cup and waved it around.

Amber noticed Tom still had almost half of his drink left. 'Oh great, he probably thinks I knocked that back in one,' she thought, looking at the ground. People were coming away from the van, eating their fish and chips with little wooden forks. The smell was making Amber feel hungrier than ever. She managed to drink her second drink in what she considered a reasonable amount of time, then made her excuses that she could wait no longer to eat. She walked over, joining the end of the queue.

"I thought we were meant to be a team. Why didn't you rescue me?" Tom whispered in her ear.

Amber nearly jumped out of her skin. She turned around so quickly that Tom caught her in his arms. They stood for a couple of seconds looking at each other before he let her go.

"It's a nasty habit, creeping up on people," Amber said, regaining her composure. "You didn't look like you needed rescuing to me, In fact, quite the reverse."

"I was being polite," Tom replied.

"If you say so," Amber said, a lot more sarcastically than she meant. It almost sounded like she was jealous.

"I do. Did you hear her laugh? It was enough to give anyone nightmares. God, I hope she doesn't know where I pitched my tent. We're next, I'm starving," he nudged Amber on.

The evening wore on with the same woman monopolising Tom; every time he tried to talk to someone else she would wheedle herself in. She constantly shrieked with laughter, which now amused Amber as Tom would somehow catch her eye.

"I'm sure it's raining," somebody said.

As Amber looked up at the sky she felt a drop on her cheek. "It is. I think I'm going to turn in now, get myself sorted in case it decides to pour down."

"Good idea," Tom chipped in.

Everyone seemed to have the same idea. People were drifting off towards their tents. Tom and Amber walked over to the facilities together. It was cold away from the fire. As Amber cleaned her teeth she wondered again if she would be

320

warm enough. She decided it might be an idea to leave her tracksuit bottoms on. When they got back to their tents Tom turned towards her.

"Are you going to be ok in this thing?" he asked, looking doubtful as he gave one of the ropes a little tug, which made the tent wobble.

"Thanks for your concern, but I'll be fine. Goodnight," she said, crawling into her tent with her torch switched on.

Tom had just zipped his tent up when the heavens opened. He switched on the camping lamp. With his head torch on he took out the book he'd brought with him.

Amber lay in her sleeping bag. Every couple of seconds a large drop of water would land on her head. She put on her torch. Shining it above herself she tried to work out where the leak was coming from, only to have another drop land in her eye. She shifted to her left slightly, which made no difference, then to her right, and still no difference. 'Just great,' she thought crossly, 'what a night she was going to have with the wind battering against the canvas making the sides billow in and out. A leak, but she didn't know where. Why had she said she would carry on with this when she'd had the chance to pull out?' Sitting up she began to wriggle round so she could lean against her rucksack. As she did so her tent started to collapse around her, making her scream out for help.

Hearing her, Tom was outside in a flash. Within seconds he was hauling her out while killing himself laughing.

"That's right, you laugh. It's just hilarious, isn't it." Amber squawked.

"Yes." He carried on laughing in between thanking others who had rushed out of their tents to help, and telling them that everything was fine. He plonked Amber in his tent, returning a couple of seconds later with her rucksack and boots.

"Thought I'd better salvage these. Your sleeping bag, I'm afraid to say, is somewhat wet, so I left it. Apologies for laughing, but on a serious note, you are alright, aren't you?"

"Yes," she said, slumping into the camping chair that Tom had been reading in. She put her head in her hands. "I can see why you find it all so hilarious, but please don't say I told you so about the tent."

"I wouldn't dream of it," Tom said, feeling sorry for her now.

"Would it be ok if I slept in your truck?" Amber asked, looking up at him.

"Don't be ridiculous, you'll freeze to death. For a start, you need to get those damp things off, and it's still howling a gale outside so you'd be soaked again by the time you got to it. Need I go on? You'll have to sleep with me. Luckily, there's plenty of room," he said, indicating the double blow-up mattress made up with sheet, pillows and duvet thrown over the top.

"I can't sleep with you," Amber said, jumping up.

"You don't have a lot of choice unless you want to sit in that chair all night," Tom said, pointing to the chair before proceeding to pull off the wet fleece he was wearing to reveal a t-shirt.

"But …" Amber protested.

"But nothing." Tom interrupted. "Get those wet things off. Have you got anything else to wear in your bag?"

Amber felt herself blush. "I've got pyjamas on under here and they're still dry."

"They won't be in a minute if you continue to stand in those wet joggers." Tom was now unfastening his jeans.

She watched as he took them off. 'Oh my God, why hadn't she checked that bloody tent properly?' she said to herself. Her heart started to thump against her chest with nerves. She dragged her eyes back upwards, past his fitted boxers, meeting his. 'Oh my God,' she thought again.

"Your turn." He grinned.

Amber stood, routed to the spot, all too aware that she didn't have a lot of choice. He was right about getting to the truck, she would be soaked and freeze once she was there as her sleeping bag was wet. The chair wasn't appealing and he was obviously not going to give up his bed. She couldn't seem to get any words out. She stood staring at him, suddenly feeling very cold.

"Hurry up, or are you going to stand there all night?" Tom asked as he got underneath the duvet.

"I just can't get undressed in front of you like this. You'll have to turn the lamp off," she managed to whisper.

"If you insist," Tom whispered back before turning off the camping lamp.

"Don't forget your head torch," she said, pointing to it.

"Number one, you won't be getting undressed, because you just told me you have your pyjamas on under there; and number two, what with your little misdemeanour at the office party, if you were getting undressed you need not worry because you've already revealed all you have in that dress you were wearing." Tom laughed softly as he turned his head torch off.

Taking the bait he'd dangled, Amber bit back. "You're enjoying this, aren't you? I wondered how long it would take you to bring that up." She stumbled around, taking off her damp things in the pitch black. "Anything else you want to mention while you're at it?" she snapped as she felt around for the bed. As she did she tripped over one of the boots she'd just kicked off, which sent her flying onto the bed, landing on Tom.

"I would just like to mention that there's no need to throw yourself at me." Tom laughed after catching his breath.

"Don't flatter yourself, we're not all like Miss laugh-a-minute earlier on," Amber snapped as she found her way under the covers. She positioned herself right at the very edge of the blow-up mattress. "Goodnight."

"Goodnight," Tom replied, smiling broadly in the dark. It was laughable. Here he was in bed with who he wanted to be in bed with by complete accident. 'Well what do you know?' What he did know was that having her so close was making him hard. 'Shit,' he thought.

Amber lay there. Even though she wasn't touching Tom she could feel his warmth. 'Weird,' she thought, 'she found it comforting.' Replaying the events of the day she lingered on the times he had put a casual arm around her, given her a playful nudge, and held her in his arms after catching her in the queue. 'Stop it,' she told herself, 'you're only thinking these things because you're lying next to him.' She cringed, thinking of how she had just fallen on him. 'What must he think? He must think I'm a right one,' she thought, drifting off as tiredness engulfed her.

CHAPTER 22

Amber opened her eyes. She found herself held in Tom's arms, her body spooned against his. 'Oh my God, how on earth had they ended up like this?' She lay perfectly still, wondering what to do. 'He must still be asleep. If she lifted his arm gently she might be able to ease herself out before he woke up. That way it would save any embarrassment, and she didn't want him to see her in her pyjamas,' she thought. She placed her hand on his arm and began to lift it slowly.

"Ah, you're awake. I was just contemplating giving you a nudge, but you were snoring so soundly I thought I'd give you another five minutes," Tom spoke into the back of her head.

Amber threw off his arm. Sitting up quickly she turned to him. "I do not snore."

"Oh yes, you do." He nodded with a grin on his face. "Nice pyjamas, by the way."

Amber looked down at her brightly coloured, striped brush-cotton pyjamas. 'He was probably used to slinky see-through negligees,' she thought. Looking back at him she pointed to where she had been lying.

"I don't know." He shrugged. "But when I woke up that's how we were."

"Oh." Amber didn't quite know what to say. They must have somehow snuggled up in their sleep. She pushed her hair back.

Tom watched, aching to have her back in his arms. When he'd woken earlier he couldn't believe his luck finding her there. He sat up. The movement of the airbed made Amber topple towards him. He caught her, laughing as he did so. "You find it quite hard to keep your balance, don't you?"

"That was your fault, you made the bed dip sitting up, and I don't snore." Their faces were only inches apart. Amber could feel the warmth of his body. She felt her heart miss a beat as she looked into his eyes. Her feelings frightening her, she gave him a playful push before scrambling in a not-so-ladylike fashion off the airbed. Hurrying over to her rucksack she started to get her clothes out. 'What's happening?' she thought, 'Two days ago you didn't like him; yesterday you thought maybe you had him wrong and he was okay; and now you're staring into his eyes wanting him to kiss you.' Almost panic-stricken, she rammed the things she didn't need back in.

Tom followed her off the bed, pulling on the jeans he'd worn last night. He watched her bend over her rucksack. 'You idiot,' he scolded himself, 'you had a chance to kiss her then. Why the fuck didn't you?' Shaking his head to himself he unzipped the tent to reveal a clear blue sky, not a rain cloud in sight. Picking up his stuff for the shower he looked at Amber again. 'What a strange scenario this was,' he thought. 'In fact, there was always something about the times they were together.' As he watched her shove things back into her rucksack he remembered the first time he'd seen her at the office party, first on the dance floor, then later on the grass, so worse for wear that she couldn't sit up on her own. The petrol station had proved amusing, and so had the night they had run into each other, literally, in the rain. So also had been the way she had tripped up the steps, and how she had slipped down the bank at the site that day. Even the way she had landed on top of him getting into bed last night had been amusing. He smiled ruefully as he remembered how long it had taken him to get to sleep, having her lying next to him, but how wonderful it was to wake up with her in his arms, even if he didn't know how she'd ended up there. "Hurry up."

"You don't have to wait, you know," she replied tartly.

"I don't trust you to go on your own. God only knows where you'll land next." He chuckled.

Amber stuck out her tongue as she marched past him. The awkwardness she felt only moments ago had vanished. Outside she looked at the sodden piece of canvas that was once her tent. "My sleeping bag is in there somewhere."

"Don't worry about it now. Let's get showered and have some breakfast. I could murder a cup of tea."

Over breakfast, as she had anticipated, she took some stick about her tent collapsing. She was taking it all with good humour until Miss laugh-a-minute kept on about her making it happen on purpose so she could get her wicked way with Tom. Eventually Tom came to her rescue, joking that it was he who'd sabotaged Amber's tent after seeing her sexy pyjamas.

On the way to the starting point Miss laugh-a-minute caught hold of Tom's arm. "Maybe she could have my tent tonight. Better still, leave her in yours and come to mine," she purred into his ear. Amber couldn't believe what she was hearing. 'Talk about giving yourself on a plate,' she said to herself. She strained to hear Tom's reply, but couldn't.

At the start Amber joined Tom. "Ready?" he asked. Amber nodded. They set off at a reasonable pace. The sun was shining but the wind made it chilly. 'Thank goodness we had the rain last night and not today, or else it would have been awful,' thought Amber. They fell into the relaxed chatty banter of yesterday.

By mid-afternoon they only had two checkpoints left. As they were making their way over a stream Tom shouted over his shoulder, "Mind your footing, these stones are really unstable."

It was too late. As she put her weight on the edge of an uneven stone it tipped, causing her foot to go into the water and get lodged. "My foot, I can't get my foot out," she shouted, frantically wriggling it.

"Hang on," Tom said, making his way back to her. Pushing up his sleeves he bent down, plunging his hands into the icy water. Within seconds he had freed her boot. "I always seem to be rescuing or breaking your footwear," he joked as they made their way over to the other side.

"My hero," Amber joked back as she followed him.

On reaching the other side he turned, holding out his hand to her. She took it as she jumped onto the bank.

"Is your foot ok?" he asked.

"Yes, it's fine, but my sock's soaking wet." She grimaced.

"Lucky I have a spare pair then." He smiled.

"But the inside of my boot is wet as well," Amber almost whined.

"Trust me, come on, take it off," he said, pointing to the boot Amber had got stuck in the water.

She did as she was told, glad to get the wet sock off as it was making her foot very cold. She put on the sock Tom handed her. "Thanks, but as soon as I put my boot back on it's going to get wet."

Grinning, he handed her the plastic bag that his socks had been in. "Put that over the sock. Hopefully it will keep your foot dry."

"Thanks, it's horrible being stuck in wet things." She smiled.

"Bit like last night," he joked.

"Don't," she groaned, tying her lace. "What am I going to do about my tent?"

"Bin it," Tom answered.

"I'm serious," Amber said as Tom hauled her to her feet.

"So am I. Bin it," he repeated.

"Ha, ha," Amber said, giving him a look.

"We'll sort something out later. Worst case scenario you'll have to sleep with me again, and I'll just have to borrow some ear plugs." He put his hands over his ears.

Amber pushed him playfully.

Smiling, he pointed to her foot. "How does it feel?"

"Okay, I think," Amber said, twirling her foot around.

"Good, we'd better get going then. We need to make up for lost time."

As they walked Amber couldn't help herself. "Talking about tonight, I heard you having an invite."

"Did you now? Hasn't anyone told you it's bad manners to eavesdrop on other people's conversations?"

"It was hardly eavesdropping. She didn't exactly whisper, did she? She's been all over you like a bee at a honey pot. Well?" Amber prompted.

Tom thought for a moment. "Thank you for your keen interest in my love life but what about yours? Some would say Mr funny guy is all over you like a bee at a honey pot, and you seem to find him extremely funny. Well?" he mimicked her.

"He is not, and you know damn well everybody finds him funny." Amber's voice rose with indignation.

Tom just looked at her, saying nothing.

"They do," she reiterated.

"If you say so," Tom said, teasing her.

"Oh, shut up. And for your information I'm off men." Amber could have kicked herself that that had slipped out because she'd let him wind her up.

"Why's that then?" he asked.

"I don't want to talk about it," Amber answered, looking ahead.

"Fair enough, but you did start the conversation," Tom reminded her.

They carried on in silence. Amber sped up without realising it. She felt guilty about snapping at Tom, seeing as he was right: it was her that had started the conversation, joking about Miss laugh-a-minute inviting herself to sleep with him, then not liking it when he had turned the table on her. They reached the checkpoint and a big sign greeted them saying 'ONLY ONE TO GO'."

Tom checked the map. They set off again. Amber took a deep breath. "I'm sorry for back there. You were right, it was me that started the conversation."

"I'm sorry too. I've obviously upset you," he replied.

"Men are a bit of a sore subject, that's all," she said. 'May as well be honest,' she thought. "The truth is I was out celebrating my engagement, the whole 24 hours of it, only to find out my fiancé had been sleeping with a woman he works with. So you can blame him for the state I was in at the office party. I didn't even want to go; the girls made me and it was Melanie that made me wear that dress because I got lipstick on the one I was going to wear while we were getting ready."

"I know, she told me," Tom answered.

"Told you?" Amber turned to look at him.

"Told me everything while we drove you home. I thought you looked nice in that dress, by the way," he said, smiling at her.

"You don't have to be nice. I'm not going to break down in tears, if that's what you're worried about." She tried to sound a little more light-hearted.

"I'm not being nice. You did look good in it, especially when you were horizontal." He gave her a nudge with his arm.

"Ha, ha." She gave him a nudge back. As they continued to walk Amber found herself wondering if he had meant it about the dress or was just being nice. The afternoon drifted on with the light beginning to fade slightly.

"Look, the final checkpoint," Tom said, pointing to what was little more than a spec in the distance.

Amber squinted as she focused in the direction he was pointing. "I'm not sorry to see that, my feet are really starting to ache."

"Are you up to marching out the last little bit?" Tom asked.

"Absolutely." Amber nodded while trying not to think of what felt like a blister on her heel.

As they neared the finish they saw two other walkers coming from a different direction. Speeding up even more they just got to the checkpoint before them. They handed the official their card. He wrote in their arrival time before putting it on a pile in front of him.

"Well done," he said. "Help yourselves to tea and cake. BBQ starts at 7.30pm, results at 8.30pm.

"I'm going to have to get these boots off. I think I've rubbed a blister," Amber said.

"You go on, I'll get the tea. Do you want cake?" Tom asked.

"Yes, please." Amber nodded.

Tom arrived back at the tent to find Amber sat in the chair, her boots and socks off. He passed her a cup of tea before placing a plate of cake next to her. Reaching into his back pocket he pulled out two little bags. "Blister packs. I visited the Red Cross tent on my way to get the tea."

"I'm definitely in need," Amber said, pointing to her ankle.

Tom sat on the floor in front of her. He lifted her foot gently. "That looks painful. More than likely a combination of my sock, which was too big for you hence the padding wasn't protecting the correct places, the plastic bag and the wet boot. Why didn't you say anything?"

"I didn't think it was as bad as that," Amber said, sipping her tea. "How do you think we did?"

Resting the sole of Amber's foot on his leg Tom kept his hand around her toes whilst gently massaging them. It felt so soothing that Amber sat back, closing her eyes. "As well as we could, considering you cost us valuable time getting this foot stuck."

Amber's eyes flew open as she sat bolt upright before leaning towards him. "Do you think it did?"

Tom leaned towards her, catching hold of her arm with his other hand. "Loosen up, I'm joking. The only way we could have gone any faster would have been if we ran."

She could feel the warmth of his breath on her face. Her heart suddenly started to have its own rhythm; panic engulfed her. "I'm quite loose, thank you," she almost stammered.

"Really?" Tom's eyes twinkled.

'Oh God, what on earth had made her say that? Of all the things to say she had to say something with dual meaning,' she thought in horror, stammering again, "I mean, I didn't mean …"

"I know what you meant," Tom interrupted her.

Embarrassed, she let out a laugh, sitting back almost as quickly as she had sat up and making Tom release her arm. 'God, that laugh sounded so stupid,' she thought, finishing her tea because she didn't know what else to do. 'He must think I'm so unsophisticated, not that I care, or do I? I don't seem to know what I think any more.' She sighed out loud.

"That's a big sigh." Tom jolted her back to reality.

"I was just thinking about having to hobble over to the showers." Saying the first thing that came to mind she looked down at her foot where Tom still had his hand around her toes.

"There's not a lot of point dressing it yet if you're about to have a shower. I'll help you over, then come back for my things."

Outside it was already getting dark. "You're right about that." Amber nodded at her collapsed tent. "I'll bin it before we leave tomorrow morning."

After drying her hair Amber studied her reflection in the mirror. 'A healthy, you've been out in the fresh air complexion looked back at her,' she thought. She rubbed in some lip cream, contemplating whether or not to put any make-up on. Deciding against it she turned her attention to her ankle. Opening one of the blister kits Tom had given her she dressed it. Socks and boots on, she headed back to Tom's tent, only to find an empty space next to it.

"My tent, it's gone," she said to Tom.

"After dropping you off at the showers I thought I'd do the honours. I've slung your sleeping bag in the back of the truck, it's soaked through," he said.

"Thanks. Look, about tonight's, um, arrangements. I'll be quite comfortable on the back seat of the truck if I can borrow a blanket." She smiled at him.

"Well, you have slept on there before, but I'd be no gentleman if I let you do it again. You have the bed, I'll take the truck."

"Very funny. How good of you to remind me. It's your bed. You have it. I'll take the truck," she said, pointing from the bed to Tom, then in the direction of the car park.

They headed to the BBQ, still bickering.

"Can you stop arguing with me for a minute while I get us something to drink?" Tom laughed. "What do you want?"

"I'm not arguing with you, you're arguing with me, and I'll have a glass of red please," Amber said before laughing as well.

Tom smiled to himself as he got the drinks. 'I don't want this weekend to end,' he thought. He felt like he'd known Amber for years: the easy way they chatted, the easy way they bickered, the easy way she had somehow ended up in his arms last night. He wandered back with the drinks, acknowledging people as he did so. Amber took her drink.

"Thanks. I've been thinking," she said, taking a sip of her wine.

"Is that a good thing?" Tom chuckled.

"Your just so hilarious, aren't you?" she said, screwing up her nose at him. "I've come up with a solution. We'll toss a coin for it. Loser gets the truck. What do you think?"

"Whatever makes you happy," he said, putting his arm around her and giving her a playful hug.

"Not interrupting anything, are we?" Miss laugh-a-minute cackled, arriving with Mr comedian and the others they had been with last night.

"Not at all. Amber's just come up with the idea of tossing a coin to see who gets the truck," Tom said.

"Nothing like a good toss to sort something out, is there?" Miss laugh-a-minute said before practically cutting off her own air supply as she snorted with laughter. Which in turn led to a not-so-clean round of jokes by individuals of the group while the beer and wine flowed freely.

It came as no surprise to Amber that Miss laugh-a-minute was trying to monopolise Tom as she had done the previous night. What did, however, come as a surprise was when she suggested to Amber that they go to get some food together.

As Amber spooned some onions on top of her hotdog, Miss laugh-a-minute snorted, "Not worried about bad breath then?"

Amber looked at her questioningly.

"You know, later on. We all know the tossing of the coin was rubbish."

"It wasn't," Amber said, shocked at the bluntness of the woman.

"In that case, every woman for herself." She snorted again before scurrying off, leaving Amber staring after her.

'Well, I never,' thought Amber as she squeezed mustard from one end of her hotdog to the other. It was quite obvious that the only reason she had suggested getting something to eat was to find out if Tom was available. She wandered back to the group to find Miss laugh–a–minute all over Tom like a rash. She bit into her hotdog as she watched, saying to herself, 'Talk about desperate and, oh, so obvious.' She took another bite of her hotdog. Tom looked over catching her eye. He raised his hand to her. She raised her hotdog back. A few moments later he was at her side as she was wiping her mouth with a napkin.

"You look like you need another one of those." He smiled.

"I'm okay for the moment, thanks," Amber replied.

"No, you're not, you look extremely hungry to me," Tom said, taking her arm and propelling her towards the BBQ again. "That woman is evil and you are going to save me."

Amber laughed as he frog-marched her through the crowd.

"Seeing as you forced me over here I may as well have another hotdog," Amber said, helping herself. She piled on the onions again before giggling to herself.

"What's so funny?" Tom asked, adding onions onto his burger too.

She explained What Miss laugh-a-minute had said earlier. With that Tom put an extra spoonful on his burger.

"Might stop her getting so close. She does spit a bit when she snorts." He laughed.

As they ate Tom kept her amused at some of the things Miss laugh-a-minute had been saying to him. They grabbed another drink before making their way back to the crowd where, straightaway, she glued herself to the other side of Tom.

"Where have you been?" she snorted, stroking his arm.

Tom put his arm around Amber. "Seeing to my partner's needs," he joked.

"Really?" She raised her eyebrows at Amber suggestively, making the group hoot with laughter.

"Can I have your attention please?" a man on a makeshift platform said into a microphone. "Time for the all-important results."

The crowd quietened as they turned their attention to him. They listened as he gave a speech. Amber was more aware of Tom's arm still around her than to what he was saying. He began reading out the results, starting with third place, then second, then to her utter amazement he read out their names as the winners, calling them to go up. With that Tom moved his arm. Grabbing Amber's hand he raised it into the air before pulling her along behind him through the crowd as everyone clapped.

They each had a medal on a long ribbon placed around their necks.

"Well done, partner." Tom turned to Amber, smiling broadly.

"Well done to you too." She beamed back at him.

With that, he put his hand on her shoulder. Almost in slow motion he leant towards her; she went to turn her head but somehow their lips met; as they kissed her stomach did a somersault. She could hear the crowd whoop and cheer as they clapped. Laughing, they shook the official's hand once again before they made their way back through the crowd to another round-of-applause. As she smiled all Amber could think about was the way Tom's lips on hers had made her feel.

The evening wore on. It was so atmospheric in the night air with the fire burning. Miss laugh-a-minute, once again, did her best to monopolise Tom, but somehow he managed to keep the topic of conversation general, involving everyone. The crowd started to thin out, most people a little worse-for-wear as they almost shouted their goodnights. Amber finished her wine. She stepped over towards Tom.

"Sorry to interrupt." She smiled.

Tom smiled back. "Ready to turn in?"

Amber nodded.

"Poor Tom hasn't finished his drink yet." Miss laugh-a-minute gave Amber a why-don't-you-get-lost look.

"I have now," Tom said, downing the rest of his drink. "Come on, partner, we have some business to attend to." He grabbed Amber by the arm. "Goodnight, everyone."

"Goodnight," they chorused back.

As he marched a merry Amber away, the look on Miss laugh-a-minute's face was a picture. Inside the tent they fell about laughing.

"I think I've upset your friend." Amber made a silly face. "Just give me the keys to the truck and you can go back and make amends."

"I think you did." Tom took a step towards her. "But if I remember correctly we have to toss for it." He pulled a coin from his pocket, then held it up in front of her face, grinning. "I'll toss, you call." He threw the coin into the air, caught it, then placed it on the back of his other hand, keeping it firmly covered.

"Tails," Amber shouted.

Tom peeked at the coin. "Sorry, but it's heads." He shook his head.

"You're lying." Amber tried to move his hand so she could look at the coin. "Come on, let me see."

They tussled as Amber tried her best to move his hand off the coin. They stumbled around the tent, laughing hysterically.

"Okay, I give up, you win," Tom said, showing Amber the coin.

She took it off his hand and waved it around. With that last glass of wine giving her a little Dutch courage she held up the coin to him. "Seeing as you're being most hospitable, and I kind of have a confession, we'll do best out of three."

"Confession? That sounds interesting," he said, moving closer to her. "I do like a good confession. What have you done?"

"Nothing," she said. "I just want you to know that I misjudged you, that's all."

"I like an apology even more, please go on." Tom smirked.

"I'm not apologising. It was your fault." Amber's voice rose as she smacked him on the arm.

"My fault." Tom laughed. "You just said it was you who made the misjudgement."

"Yes, but only because you made me. After those few unfortunate incidents, the way you were, I got the wrong end of the stick, that's all, and I ended up misjudging you."

Tom carried on laughing as he nodded his head.

"See, look at you, making fun of me. Perhaps I didn't get it wrong after all. Maybe we won't do best out of three."

Tom moved quickly. He grabbed the wrist of the hand she had the coin in, pulling her to him as he looked into her eyes. "You promised best out of three."

"People do go back on their word, you know." Her voice was barely more than a whisper. She ran her tongue over her lips as she held his gaze.

"I don't think you do, and just to confirm, you definitely did get the wrong end of the stick," he said as his lips met hers.

He kissed her gently, slowly and sensuously; as his lips explored hers Amber heard herself gasp. He drew away from her, his hand still holding the back of her neck. "You don't know how long I've been wanting to do that," he said before pulling her to him again. This time when he kissed her it was with the passion that had been growing inside of him since the first time he'd seen her. He unzipped her coat, slipping it from her shoulders. She, in turn, helped him as he shrugged off his jacket. As they undressed one another the cold air hit their bodies. He took her by the hand.

340

"Come on," he said gently as he pulled her towards the bed. "We don't want to freeze to death." He pulled back the duvet for her to get in, following quickly. As soon as he touched her Amber felt her body come alive. As he kissed and caressed her she ached for him, wanting him as much as he wanted her.

"Christ, Melanie, you're such a noisy bitch." Gary laughed.

"You know how I like it from behind." Melanie giggled.

"Baby, you like it any way," he said, kissing her.

"You're damn right I do. Good job your brother's guest room is at the opposite end of the house, isn't it?"

Gary nodded in agreement. "I was thinking …"

"Thinking that we should do it again, I hope," Melanie interrupted as she shook her boobs at him.

Tom held Amber in his arms. "I can't believe the way that made me feel," he said, kissing the top of her head.

"I can't believe the way that made me feel either," she replied sleepily.

He squeezed her gently.

"I'm still thinking," Gary said as Melanie walked to the bathroom. She stopped at the en-suite door, turning round to look at him.

"Again? What have you taken, some kind of Viagra?" She laughed. "I'm game."

Gary put his hands behind his head as he looked at her. "I was thinking, seeing as you take a lot of, how can I say it, satisfying," he grinned, "you might consider moving in with me when we get back."

"I might consider it." She smiled before turning and entering the bathroom. As she stepped into the shower she couldn't believe she'd just said that. 'Consider moving in, shit, commitment, but it felt right.'

Gary stretched, before getting out of bed. He followed Melanie into the en-suite. Poking his head into the shower he grinned at her before stepping in. "I know we haven't known each other that long, but it just feels right, you and me, we're just right."

CHAPTER 23

Tom looked down at Amber. She was still fast asleep, snuggled under the duvet. He put down the tea he had in his hand. Leaning over he kissed her gently on the cheek. "Wakey-wakey," he whispered in her ear before sitting on the airbed.

She opened her eyes to see him smiling at her. "I've got you a cup of tea," he said, reaching to pick it up. As he did, Amber clocked her clothes strewn around the tent. "Here you go," he said, holding it out to her. "You might find it easier to drink if you sit up."

"Um, yes, thank you, I know, but ..." She looked around the tent at her clothes again. Following her eyes Tom raised his eyebrows as he stood up. He began picking them up. Amber cringed as he bent down to pick her knickers off the ground. She felt herself blush as she remembered how eagerly they had pulled each other's clothes off, casting them aside. 'How he had led her to bed and then, and then, oh my God, and then how he had touched her, kissed her, how he had made her writhe with excitement, their bodies shuddering together as they...'

"I think this is all of them," Tom said, turning to face her. He couldn't help but smile. Amber was now sat up, the

343

duvet pulled up under her chin, her cheeks flushed, her long, dark and somewhat dishevelled hair tumbling around her.

'Oh no, he knows what I've been thinking,' Amber thought as she took in his amusement. She took the clothes from him. Pulling the t-shirt from the pile she put her arms in, then tried to get it over her head while holding the duvet up with her knees.

"Bit late for false modesty." Tom grinned as he leant towards her, pulling it down at the back. Her skin tingled at his touch. She looked at him, blushing once more. "Ready for your tea now?" he asked, still grinning as he bent to pick up her tea once more.

"I think so," she said, taking it from him. "What time is it?"

"Nearly 9am. They want the site cleared by 11am," he answered as he sipped his tea.

"I'd better get to the showers then," Amber said.

"We've plenty of time, drink your tea." Tom smiled.

Amber took a sip. "That's nice." She smiled.

"Can't beat a cuppa, can you?" Tom agreed.

"No," Amber replied.

As they chatted all Amber could think about was how she was going to get dressed with him still in the tent, although he was right, it was a bit late for false modesty, but it was still the morning after the night before. Luck was on her side as Tom took her empty mug, saying he'd take them back to the catering tent. As soon as he'd left the tent she leapt out of bed, pulling on the rest of last night's clothes as quickly as she could. Grabbing her wash bag, towel and some clean clothes she rushed to the showers.

As she stood under the hot water she mulled over the previous night's happenings. 'Now then,' she told herself, 'it's all very simple, we both had a bit too much to drink, had sex, said things we didn't mean, of course he said all the right things because that's what men do, then they end up doing the dirty on you, they end up sleeping with someone else behind your back, playing you for a fool.' Turning the shower off she felt all the hurt of a few months ago sweep over her. 'Be strong, come on, pull yourself together,' she told herself as she grabbed the towel. 'Play them at their own game. Before he has a chance to thank you for a good time get in there first. But what shall I say?' she half wailed to herself as she dried.

She walked back to find Tom had already taken the tent down. He was talking to one of the walkers as he folded it up.

"We have company on the way home, Martin is coming back with us," Tom said.

"You don't mind, do you?" Martin asked.

"Of course not." Amber smiled at him. It would give her more time to think about what she was going to say to Tom.

With the help of Martin they loaded everything onto the truck, then went for brunch where Amber successfully managed to talk to everyone except Tom. It seemed to take forever to say goodbye to everyone, with hugs, kisses and promises of seeing them all again next year. Back at the truck, as soon as Tom unlocked it, Amber hopped in the back, shutting the door only for Martin to open it again.

"I'll sit in the back," he said.

"No, I'm fine here." Amber smiled at him. "You get in the front."

"Really, I insist. If you're relegated to the back seat you'll make me feel guilty for having a lift," Martin joked.

"Don't be silly, I'm more than happy here." Amber laughed, pulling the door shut again.

As they set off towards the gate Tom glanced at Amber in the mirror. Their eyes met briefly. Unable to hold his gaze Amber turned away. 'Is it my imagination or am I getting the cold shoulder?' Tom thought as he manoeuvred the truck slowly over the bumpy field. 'Now they had Martin with them he couldn't even ask what the hell was going on. Last night things had just fallen into place, resulting in them making love. He had to face it, albeit on a blow-up bed, it had been pretty sensational. This morning, yes, Amber had seemed a little bashful, but since coming back from the showers she had done her best to avoid him. Now, here they were on the way home and he couldn't even ask why.'

Martin chatted away, oblivious to what had happened between them. Amber sat in the back, so grateful he had asked for a lift. She gazed out of the window. 'Right, time for a bit of therapy. Here we go again. Last night was what is commonly known as a one-night stand, the only difference being it was with your boss. Oh my God, my boss!' She almost started to hyperventilate. 'Breathe, slowly,' she told herself.

"Everything okay in the back?" Tom asked. "You're making some funny noises."

"Pardon," Amber said, only half taking in what Tom had said.

"I said, everything okay in the back? You're making some funny noises," Tom repeated.

"Oh gosh, am I? Sorry. Everything is fine," Amber answered, trying her best to sound normal, whatever normal was. 'I'm mad,' she thought. Was I thinking out loud and I didn't even know?'

Most of the journey she spent in a trance-like state, reliving the night before, going over what to say to Tom and trying to anticipate his reply. As they entered the outskirts of Bath she grew increasingly nervous. Tom followed Martin's directions to his house. As they pulled up he invited them both in. Tom looked at Amber.

"It's very kind of you but I really should get home, lots of sorting out to do before work tomorrow." She smiled.

"No problem, I understand. I've exchanged mobile numbers with Tom so it would be nice to arrange to meet up for a drink." He smiled back at Amber.

Tom helped him get his stuff off the back of the truck. He opened the door where Amber was sitting. "Are you going to get in the front?" he asked.

Amber got out. She kissed Martin goodbye before climbing into the front. She watched as Tom shook his hand. Climbing into the driving seat beside her Tom fastened his seat belt. As they pulled off they both waved to Martin.

"What's going on?" Tom's voice sliced through the silence. "First thing this morning you were fine. Then, since coming back from the showers you've done everything you can to avoid talking to me. In fact, you're finding it almost impossible just to look at me. What have I done?" He felt his hands tighten on the steering wheel.

"Nothing, you've done nothing, you know, it can be kind of awkward after a, a one-night stand, that's all," Amber answered, looking straight ahead.

"So that's how you view last night, is it? A one-night stand, that's all?" Tom mimicked her.

"Of course. We had a bit too much to drink and got carried away. It happens. The last thing I'm looking for is anything more, and let's face it we both know I don't fit the bill of your usual type." She turned to look at him at exactly the same time as he looked at her. She hadn't meant to add the last comment. It had just popped out.

"And what is my usual type?" Tom asked with an edge to his voice.

'Oh dear,' thought Amber, 'this isn't going well.' "The woman I met at your cottage." Her answer sounded more like a question.

They turned into her road. Tom pulled up sharply outside her flat. Yanking on the handbrake he turned to look at her.

"Forgive me for having completely misread the situation, and you, for that matter. You're obviously nothing like I thought you were. Quite the little actress really, a few drinks then a shag; how about one for the road?"

Without saying a word Amber got out. Tom banged his hand down on the steering wheel. 'What on earth had made him say that? It was so unlike him? Rejection,' he answered his own question. Opening the driver's door he was out and at the back of the truck within seconds to find Amber reaching over for her stuff. He leaned over her, picking it up with ease.

"Amber I'm sorry, I didn't mean that." He stood with her rucksack in his hand. "It was a horrible thing to say. Last night, it ..."

Amber grabbed her rucksack. "It should never have happened, I wish it never had."

She turned her back on him. Hurrying to her front door she fumbled with the key. He followed her over, putting his foot in the door to stop her closing it on him.

"Is that really the way you feel?" he asked, looking at her intently.

"Absolutely." She held his gaze. "If you don't mind," she said, dropping her eyes to look at his foot.

He removed it. She closed the door. They both stood either side of it for a moment before she rather shakily made her way up to the flat, him swearing to himself as he walked back to the truck.

Amber slumped down on the settee. 'What a disastrous end to the weekend,' she thought miserably. For the rest of the afternoon she tried to occupy herself by tidying the flat, but all she could think about was Tom and the way it had felt making love to him.

Tom switched off his laptop. 'It was no good, he couldn't concentrate on work, all he could think about was Amber. Should he go back round to her flat? No, his spiteful comment had so obviously upset her, she would more than likely slam the door in his face. He would speak to her tomorrow He decided to go for a run, hoping to clear his head. Then he would call Yasmin for some sisterly advice, no doubt to be told he was a complete dickhead for the way he'd handled things,' he thought.

'Tuesday morning, back at work, normal enough,' thought Amber, 'except for the fact she had slept with her boss, left him on bad terms and practically slammed the door in his face. If she didn't think he wanted to sack her before, then he sure as hell would find some way to do it now.'

Morning, Amber." Harry smiled as he brought in the post. "How did you get on then? Have you got sore feet?"

"We won," Amber answered, raising a smile that didn't meet her eyes.

"Good for you." Placing the post on the desk he wondered why she didn't seem that happy about it. He guessed she was tired. "See you tomorrow then."

"Yes, thanks, Harry, have a good day." She gave him a wave.

Within minutes of him going Mr Lockyard arrived. "Result," he said, raising his hand in the air. "Well done. Dorothy had the official times sent through yesterday afternoon, you both did so well."

"Thank you." Amber smiled. "I'll get your tea ready," she said, pointing in the direction of the back office.

"Lovely." It was unusual for Amber not to want to chat for a while, especially after something like coming first in the walk. 'Oh well, more than likely a bit tired,' he assumed.

Everyone congratulated her as they arrived for work, but there was only one member of staff she wanted to catch on the way in: Carol, Tom's secretary. At last she arrived.

"Good morning, congratulations." She grinned at Amber.

"Thanks, Carol. Busy day ahead?" Amber fished.

"Oh yes." Carol nodded. "Tom's on site most of the day but it won't stop him emailing me with a list as long as your arm. See you later."

"See you later." Answered Amber as she thought, 'Good, when he's on site he doesn't usually get here until after I'm gone or as I'm leaving. Hopefully we'll miss each other.'

As soon as Vicky arrived Amber swore her to secrecy before telling her everything. By the time she had finished Vicky stood gawping at her.

"Say something," Amber urged.

"What can I say to that? Vicky raised her hands. "Most of the women working here would like to bed him. You have, then for some bizarre reason you start spouting about one-night stands. Why? That's not you."

"Weren't you listening? I've had enough of men getting one over on me, so I got in first. I'm glad I did, especially after his how-about-one-for-the-road comment," Amber exclaimed.

"You're only kidding yourself, Amber. You've fallen for him but you're in denial. You are trying to protect yourself from getting hurt again. Which is understandable, hence your reaction, which in turn triggered his. You see?" Vicky raised her hands in the air again. "I should have been a psychotherapist."

Before the conversation could go any further the phone started to ring, in conjunction with umpteen visitors arriving. They were rushed off their feet for the rest of the morning. Before she knew it, Amber was grabbing her bag; if she hurried she could fit all the errands she had to do in to her lunch hour. She whizzed round town as though her life depended on it. Pleased that she'd gotten everything done she drove back to work, trying her best not to think about Tom but not being able to think about anything else. As she pulled into the car park she spotted his truck. 'Why did she even think she wouldn't see him today?' she thought.

"You don't need to tell me. I saw his truck," Amber said to Vicky as she came round the desk.

"He asked where you were. He seemed quite annoyed when I told you you were at lunch; he drummed his fingers on the desk, mumbled something then went to his office. Just before you came back I had to send some visitors through to him so I guess he's having some kind of meeting. I'll have my lunch in the back office if you want me to," Vicky offered.

"No, off you go. I have to see him sooner or later; I was just hoping it might be later," Amber said woefully.

"Why the long face?" Dorothy made them both jump.

"Oh, Dorothy, oh, um, no reason. I was just saying goodbye to Vicky; she's going to lunch." Amber smiled.

"She'll only be gone for an hour, my dear." Dorothy twitched. "But I'm glad I've caught you both," she said.

"Right, Amber, can you come to Conference Room One at 3.45pm? Vicky, you as well, but if you wouldn't mind standing at the door to keep an eye on reception it would be appreciated."

"What's going on?" Amber asked.

"Wait and see; 3.45pm sharp." Dorothy nodded her head before turning and marching towards her office.

The girls looked at each other before shrugging their shoulders at exactly the same time.

"Someone's got promoted, no doubt," Vicky said. "See you later."

All afternoon Amber kept one eye on the direction of Tom's office. Tea, coffee and cakes had been taken in but nobody had yet come out. Looking at the clock it was nearly 3.30pm. Another half an hour and she would escape seeing Tom.

"Is you clock-watching, my girl?" Gloria's voice boomed.

"Gloria, you're early." Amber beamed at Gloria as she waddled towards the desk.

"I have to admit I am. How are you?"

"Not as well as you sugar, hehehe." She reached into her tabard pocket to get out the usual sweets. She put them on the desk, then rested her elbow on it. "I just know'd you'd win that walk, I just know'd it."

"You don't know the lottery numbers for this week as well, do you?" Amber laughed.

"He hehe. If I get a sign from him above I'll let you know. See you girlies in a minute." She waddled off to see Dorothy.

"Goodness, is that the time already?" Dorothy smiled at her friend as she entered her office.

"It surely is." Gloria nodded.

"I'm glad you could come in early." Dorothy smiled as she stood up. She buzzed Mr Lockyard. "Mr Lockyard, you have about 10 minutes."

"Thank you, Dorothy," came Mr Lockyard's reply.

"Shall we wander over now?" Dorothy asked Gloria.

"Good idea. These old bones will get a seat, that way," Gloria joked.

Amber and Vicky watched people as they passed the desk.

"Come on, Amber, it's nearly 3.45pm," Vicky said.

The girls walked along to the conference room.

"I'll stay at the door with you. We can both watch the desk then. Apart from anything else there's hardly any room left in there." Amber leant against the door frame; mirroring her Vicky leant against the other as they chatted.

"Don't look now but Mr Lockyard and Tom are on their way," Vicky said, standing up straight.

Amber's eyes seemed to grow in size as she too stood up straight without turning round. Her heart started to thump as she focused on Vicky. 'Calm down, calm down. He won't say anything in front of this lot,' she told herself.

"Ladies," Mr Lockyard said as he approached.

Having no choice now Amber turned, only to look straight into Tom's eyes. She could feel herself blush but could do nothing to stop it. They stood looking at one another. Mr Lockyard and Vicky stood looking at them, then looked at each other. Vicky kind of smiled and shrugged at the same time. 'Bloody hell, even though she knew what had happened between them you didn't have to be a genius to work out something was going on, she thought.

"After you, Amber," Mr Lockyard said, interrupting the silence.

Amber pulled her eyes away from Tom to look at Mr Lockyard. "No, it's okay, thanks. We're not going in, we're watching the desk."

"Vicky is, you aren't. I need you in here." He motioned with his arm for Amber to go in. "Come along." He ushered her in before she had a chance to ask why. He chivvied her to the front of the room. "Lovely, if you just stand there." He smiled at her. Tom came to stand next to her.

"Ladies and gentlemen." The room quietened. "Thank you for all coming along to join with me in congratulating Amber and Tom for coming first in the charity event." A round of applause followed. Dorothy joined Mr Lockyard, holding a big bunch of flowers in her hands. Mr Lockyard thanked her as he took them. "Amber, these are from me to say a big thank you for doing so well." He held them out to her.

'Oh no, how embarrassing,' thought Amber as she took the flowers, accepting Mr L's kiss on her cheek. "These are beautiful, thank you."

"Tom, you get a handshake." Mr Lockyard held out his hand. Tom shook it as everyone laughed. Mr Lockyard turned to the audience once more. "I won't bore you all with a speech. Tom has provided Dorothy with a few photographs, which I'm sure you'll find a lot more interesting."

Dorothy got up and started to fiddle with the laptop. "Ready when you are, Mr Tranter," she said, almost standing to attention as her lips twitched into her Dorothy-smile.

"Thanks, Dorothy." He gave her a nod, which obviously indicated for her to start the slideshow.

'Oh my God,' thought Amber, 'the first shot was of her tent.' She turned to look at Tom who was grinning from ear to ear. The look on her face must have been a picture because everyone started to laugh. Tom put his arm around her casually, hugging her to him, which made everyone laugh again.

"Well, everyone, this is how it started," he addressed the room.

Amber had no option but to pin a smile on her face. He had set her up, but she could hardly run out the door. He carried on telling everyone about her tent with the next shot showing his. As the picture slide continued he pointed out Miss laugh–a–minute, joking about her in a good-hearted manner, telling everyone to look out for her in the pictures to come. On it went to a shot of them both at the starting point. More of the day continued, then on to the evening, with Tom keeping everyone amused with funny stories about individuals and how the day had gone. Reliving the weekend along with the slideshow Amber knew only too well what was coming next, the collapse of her tent. Sure enough, she wasn't disappointed. Tom delighted in the fact that his tent had been big enough to accommodate "her bunking up with him." Everyone oohed loudly at that. 'Where had he got all of these pictures from?' she wondered.

He went on – "Day two …" – telling them about her slipping and getting her foot stuck in the water. She remembered him taking photographs of her taking her boot off and putting the bag on her foot, and them arriving at the finishing line. 'It was, she had to admit, funny the amount of times Miss laugh-a-minute appeared,' she thought. Each time, Tom pointed her out, making some comment or telling a little story that had everyone in stitches. Then there they were up on the platform, both smiling broadly. The next one was of Amber having the medal placed round her neck, then there was one of Tom having his put on. "And finally," Tom said again, hugging her to him casually as the last photograph appeared, the one of them kissing. A cheer went up from the room. Amber didn't know where to look while Tom simply grinned from ear to ear. He said nothing more regarding the photograph but thanked everyone in the room for their time and support. The room erupted into a round of applause.

Tom squeezed Amber again as he whispered in her ear, "We have to talk." He then dropped his arm from her shoulder. They were bombarded with questions, some of which were a little too personal for Amber's liking, but she was relieved that Tom gave nothing away regarding their sleeping arrangements or anything else. He managed to answer everything with ease but seemed to purposefully leave what everyone wanted to know unanswered. The room began to thin out. 'Time to escape,' thought Amber, her eyes on the door.

"Dorothy, Gloria, leave that." Tom's voice made them turn round from the chairs that they were starting to tidy. "Amber and I will put everything back in its place."

The two ladies exchanged a rather knowing look with each other before looking back at Tom. "Right you are, Mr Tranter." Dorothy twitched. Gloria just nodded her head with a smile as broad as could be. They started to move towards the door, ushering the remaining few out with them. Amber stood watching, her plan for escape not even having had time to begin. She turned to look at Tom.

"Shall we?" he said, indicating the chairs.

"I don't seem to have a choice, do I?" Amber answered, grabbing a chair.

"It seemed the only way of getting to talk to you before you made a bolt for the door," Tom said, taking a step towards her.

"I wasn't going to bolt for the door." Amber reddened as she lied. "Anyway, I can't think there is anything left to say." She placed the chair she had hold of between them. "I think we've both made our feelings perfectly clear."

"Have we?" Tom said, moving the chair out of the way. "I know I haven't, you didn't give me a chance and I'm confused over yours. You see, the ones you showed on Sunday night were completely different to the ones you displayed on Monday morning after returning from the showers."

They stood looking at each other. He was so close. Her body felt like it was screaming at him to touch her. She opened her mouth to speak but nothing came out.

"Amber, you seem to have been thrown into my path in the most bizarre ways, time and time again. Every one of those times has triggered something inside of me, but every one of those times you somehow managed to get the wrong end of the stick, for whatever reason. When you confessed to that on Sunday night, then the way we made love, I took it we would just carry on from there, but then you completely blow me out. I just don't get it and, believe me I hate not to get things. It made me, I have to admit, angry, hence the nasty remark, for which I'm truly sorry. I didn't mean it. It was the absolute last thing I meant. I just need to know if you meant what you said?" he asked, his eyes not leaving hers.

Amber shook her head slowly. "No, I didn't."

'She hadn't meant it, any of it. What was happening to her? She felt like she was in a whirlwind. The way she felt, the way she couldn't get him out of her mind, the way she wanted to feel his hands on her body, to feel him making love to her. She never felt about Phil the way she was feeling now about Tom, it was crazy. Vicky was right, she was in denial,' she said to herself.

Tom pushed her hair back from her face. "I know how badly you've been hurt and how hard it must be for you to trust anyone so soon. The last thing I want is for you to feel pressurised. I'm flying to Scotland tonight. I'll be back at the weekend. Can I call you when I get back?"

Amber nodded. As she did so Tom moved towards her. Their lips were about to meet when the door suddenly opened, making them both jump away from each other. Carol, Tom's secretary, aware she had interrupted something, stood there.

"Sorry to interrupt," she apologised. "I have the Scottish office holding for you," she said to Tom, almost apologising again.

"I was just leaving." Amber smiled at her before looking at Tom.

"I'll call you as soon as I'm back," he said quietly as he touched her arm briefly. He watched her smile at Carol as she left the room.

More aware than ever that she had interrupted something Carol hesitated for a moment. "I'm sorry, Tom," she said.

Tom smiled. "For what?"

'Poor Carol, she looked so uncomfortable,' he thought. "Can you tell them I'll call them back in a minute?"

"Of course." She turned to go.

"Oh, Carol." Tom stopped her. As she turned to face him he grinned at her. "If I promise not to leave too much work for you while I'm away, any chance of a coffee?"

"Every chance." She smiled before hurrying back to her office.

Alone, Tom began to restore order to the room. He worked quickly. In no time he was just about to push the last chair under a table when, instead, he sat down on it. 'Of all the luck for Carol to walk in at the moment he was about to kiss Amber,' he thought. He sighed out loud just as the door opened again. Looking round this time he saw Gloria. She stepped into the room, scrutinising him as she did so.

"You caught me having a rest," he said, almost woefully.

"I caught the tail-end of that sigh. Sounds to old Gloria like you got something heavy on your mind." She waggled her duster at him. "I just seen Amber leaving."

"Have you now?" Tom said, standing up, smiling as he did so.

"Mmm." Gloria nodded her head. "I was just saying to Dorothy that those pictures of yours tell a story, yes, they tell a story."

"Were you now?" Tom said as he walked over to her.

"Mmm." Gloria grinned as she nodded her head again.

"Keep your fingers crossed the story has a happy ending," Tom said, stopping in front of her.

"Ol' Gloria says it will," she said, patting his arm.

He smiled at her before leaving the room. Gloria set about her dusting. Satisfied everything was just how she liked it she waddled back to see Dorothy. Hands on hips she told her of the conversation she had had with Tom. Dorothy's lips twitched into a smile as she did so.

"The Lord certainly does work in mysterious ways," she said.

"He sure is trying," Gloria agreed.

"What's going on?" Mr Lockyard's voice made both Gloria and Dorothy jump. The ladies looked at each other, then back at Mr Lockyard.

"Goodness, I didn't hear you come in, Mr Lockyard," Dorothy said.

"Dorothy, I don't think you have ever not heard me come in, so I know something's happening. Spill the beans?" He looked at Dorothy who looked at Gloria. "Gloria?" Gloria looked at him, then back at Dorothy. "Dorothy, I do believe you're hiding something."

"Goodness." Never having told a lie in her life, at least as far back as she could remember, Dorothy took a deep breath. "I have to admit, there is something, something I did, which was, I'm afraid, somewhat underhand. You see, it was like this: when Tom was picked to accompany Amber on the walk it was with a little bit of help from myself."

"From both of us," Gloria added.

"Oh!" Intrigued, Mr Lockyard made a gesture with his hand for them to continue.

Dorothy went on to tell him how they thought Tom and Amber would be so well suited, that when she was picking the male candidate to accompany Amber on the walk she had decided to give things a bit of a helping hand. Gloria again interrupted to say they both did it.

"Dorothy Judith Brown, are you telling me you fiddled it?" Mr Lockyard asked, trying not to laugh.

"I'm afraid, I did," Dorothy said. "And obviously I am prepared to take the consequences for it. I quite understand that what I have done will warrant a disciplinary. I just want to reiterate that Gloria was present but it was me that did the deed, as one might say."

"We's both guilty," Gloria almost boomed.

"Ladies, all I can say is well done. On occasions it is not called fiddling but an executive decision on what is best for the company and the welfare of staff members, which I firmly believe was taken into consideration when doing the draw. The court is closed. You're both innocent." He smiled broadly as he turned to go into his office.

The two women looked at each other, and, believe it or not, did a high-five.

As the week wore on the only thing on Amber's mind was Tom. She analysed every time they had met and every conversation they had had, well, except for when she'd had one too many at the office party, but she couldn't analyse that because she'd been three sheets to the wind. Looking back, she realised how often she had thought about him, about the way he made her feel – annoyed, angry, uncomfortable – when he stood close to her; about how he made her blush so easily; then latterly, when they were walking, how he'd made her laugh, how easily they had chatted, the banter and squabbling good-heartedly, and how they had made love. 'Did it all mean she'd fancied him all along but just didn't realise it? She had felt so hurt and humiliated by what Phil had done to her, could it be she hadn't seen what was staring her in the face?' she asked herself.

"Uncle Tom, you're not listening to me." Luke sighed.

"Sorry, soldier, I was miles away," Tom apologised, fluffing his nephew's hair. Well, it was almost the truth. His mind was miles away at least. Amber. God, he could not get her out of his mind.

CHAPTER 24

Gary lifted Melanie's case out of the boot and placed it down on the pavement. Melanie pulled up the handle.

"I'll carry that in for you," he said.

Melanie stepped off the pavement. She put her hands around his neck and rubbed her breasts against his chest suggestively as she kissed him on the lips. "It's on wheels, I can pull it. I know you're itching to get to the bar."

"If you keep rubbing yourself against me like that you'll have to relieve me before I go," he said, clasping her bottom with both hands and giving it more than a gentle squeeze.

"You'll have to wait until tomorrow, big boy," she said, kissing him again on the lips. She hopped back onto the pavement, giving him a little wiggle as she took hold of her case. "Bye."

Gary laughed as he got back into the car, giving her a beep as he drove off.

"Is that you, dear heart?" Henry shouted, hearing the door open.

"Who do you bloody think it is, King Kong?" Melanie shouted back.

"I wouldn't mind a bit of a King Kong, if you know what I mean." Henry shrieked with laughter as he ran down the stairs. He swept Melanie offer her feet. "I've missed you, sweetness."

"I've missed you, Hennie." Melanie giggled as he swung her round.

He put her down. Holding her at arm's length he looked at her. "Bit of a tan there. Does it go all over?"

"Not quite, I have a few white bits." Melanie winked.

"Oh, I say! Come on, come on, I want to hear all about it, especially the dirty bits." Henry pulled her towards the kitchen.

"You've been busy." Melanie surveyed the kitchen.

"I have, indeed. Took the day off to welcome you home. Been sweeping and buffing all morning, prepared dinner, the lot. These hands are seriously in need of a manicure now." Henry sighed as he looked at his hands.

"I'll give you one later." Melanie grinned.

"Goodness, a manicure, I hope. You know I'm not your kind for anything else." He chuckled as he picked up the kettle. "Tea or coffee, sweetness?"

"Tea, please." Melanie smiled at him as she sat down. He was so adorable. She loved him to bits. It was going to be hard telling him she was moving out. 'Commitment was a big step for her,' she thought. 'She had amazed herself the way she had been so honest with Gary about it, then so pleased to find out he felt the same way. So, together they had decided she would stay over a few nights a week to begin with, gradually increasing it when she felt comfortable. She really had met her soulmate in every way.'

"Here we go, glum nuts," Henry said, putting a mug of tea in front of her. "It's a bugger being home, isn't it?"

She looked at Henry, giving him a rueful smile. "Yeah."

He sat down opposite her. "Well then, start from the beginning, I'm all ears."

"Well, there is quite a bit to tell." Melanie rubbed her hands together.

"Stop acting off. Start with the bit where you were on the beach, he took you in his arms, then ..."

"Henry, you have to stop reading Mills & Boon." Melanie laughed. "I'd like to think it was more like Confessions of a Pole Dancer."

"That's just it, knowing you, my love, it probably was." Henry curled his lip. "Will the DVD be out in a couple of months?"

"Joking aside, it was a bit Mills & Boonish, I'll have you know." Melanie sighed.

"Really? Good God above, tell me." Henry sat forward, putting his elbows on the table and resting his chin on his hands.

Melanie told him all about the holiday including how lovely Gary's brother and his family were, and the naughty bits that made him hoot with laughter. Getting serious, she put her hand on Henry's arm. "There is one more thing, Hennie."

"Dear heart, what on earth is it? You're not preggers, are you?" he half gasped.

"No, I'm bloody not," Melanie answered.

"Thank God for that, I'm not ready to be an uncle. What is it then?" he urged.

"Gary has asked me to move in with him and I've said yes, but I feel awful about you." She sat back in her chair, waiting for his reaction. When nothing came she sat forward again "Say something, Hennie."

"I was just working out how much better off I'm going to be. No more going to do my weekly face-pack only to find out you've used the last of it. My No7 Protect and Perfect night cream, oh, and day cream, left where I left it, not where you left it. Then there will be the food bill, taxi fares, your pocket money …"

Melanie slapped him playfully on the arm. "I thought you'd be upset."

"Dear heart, I am upset, but not surprised." Henry put the most serious expression on his face he could muster. "Right from the beginning there was something about him. I saw it the first time I met him. In fact, it was staring me in the face from beneath his boxer shorts that very morning in the kitchen."

They both screamed with laughter as Melanie slapped him again.

"No, seriously, dear heart, you are a match made in heaven; just so right for each other. It was meant to be, just meant to be." Henry threw his arms around theatrically.

"Thanks, Hennie. I was really worried about telling you. I'm not moving out straight away, more in stages, just to be sure it's the right thing." Melanie gave him a kiss on the cheek.

"Sweetness, it will be wedding bells next, you mark my words." He looked at the clock. "Nearly wine o'clock, we may as well crack open a bottle to celebrate your good news."

"There is something else, just a little bit of info," Melanie baited him.

"Tell, tell." Henry got all excited.

"Calm down, it's nothing really, it's just that Gary told me he doesn't just run the wine bar but owns it with his brother, and the bar in Spain. He runs this one and his brother runs the Spanish one." Melanie's eyes widened.

"I want to be bridesmaid and godmother, which will entitle me to free drinks for the rest of my days." Henry clapped his hands in delight.

"Silly sod, open that bottle." Melanie laughed.

"Okay, back for just a minute and bossing me around like no one's business. Where's Amber? She said she'd be here by 6pm and it's six now." Just as he pulled out the cork the doorbell rang. "Speak of the devil."

Melanie went to get the door. She hauled Amber in, embracing her as she did so. The girls screeched their hello as though they hadn't seen each other for years, not a week.

"Will you two get your backsides in here?" Henry shouted from the kitchen door. The girls did as he asked, with Amber giving him a hug and a kiss. "You smell delicious," Henry said, referring to Amber's perfume. "Right, girls, wine is open on the table ready to pour. I have to get the dinner on." He grabbed his apron.

While he cooked dinner Melanie told Amber her news, with Henry interrupting every other minute. The three of them discussed the whole situation. They laughed and joked as they analysed almost all of Melanie's previous relationships, only to determine that this was it, the real thing.

Henry placed dinner on the table. Sitting down with the girls he raised his glass. "To Melanie."

"To Melanie," Amber repeated, raising her glass.

"To me," Melanie said, raising her glass too.

They all sipped their drinks. Henry raised his glass again. "Now we have you all sorted, dear heart, we have to turn our attention to sweet cheeks here." He nodded towards Amber. "Off you go, no leaving anything out."

"I'll drink to that. To Amber. Definitely leave nothing out, we need all the facts." Melanie held up her glass.

"To me," Amber said, before taking a sip. "Where do I start?"

"I always say the beginning would be good, sweetness." Henry smiled at her.

"Glad we have all night," she joked before telling them the whole saga of the charity walk, leaving nothing out except for a few really intimate details, even though Henry and Melanie tried their best to get them out of her. She finished up telling them about the way Tom had put together the picture show, intimating to the whole of the firm that there was something going on between them, but on the other hand giving nothing away, and of their conversation before Carol had interrupted them. "And that's it, you're both up to date." She shrugged and let out a big sigh.

"Blood hell. Are you mad? Why the hell have you left him dangling on a bit of string? Men like him don't get off the train that often," Henry almost shrieked. "One minute you're telling him you didn't mean the things you said, your chance to throw yourself into his arms, I hasten to add. The next you're running for cover." Henry covered his eyes, shaking his head from side to side. In just as an over-the-top manner he then grabbed hold of her arm. "But I know why." He squeezed her arm.

"For fuck's sake, calm down, Hennie," Melanie said, making a face at him.

"I can't, I have an idea, listen. It is more than obvious that you are besotted with the bloke. The facts. Number one, you have admitted you can't get him out of that pretty little

368

head. Number two, after spending the weekend together, getting to know him in more ways than one has frightened you, which is normal after what dickhead Phil did to you. Number three, your head is not listening to your heart. Well, it is a bit but not enough to take the plunge. Number four, he is obviously a very clever bloke the way he engineered that picture show. I like that. He is in hot pursuit of you, my dear, in a, how can I put it, mature, respectful, non-pushy, almost fun kind of way." Henry looked up at the ceiling as he nodded his head in agreement with himself.

"Henry, shut up with the crap. Just tell us your idea." Melanie flicked his ear with her fingers to pull him out of Henry zone.

"Oh, oh yes, where was I?" He looked at the girls, smiling, knowing full well where he was but loving the attention.

"Your idea." Amber played the game.

"Of course. Plan of action. Instead of waiting for him to call you, why don't we drop you off at his place tonight? Take him by surprise. His reaction will give you the answer you're looking for. If he's ecstatic to see you and sweeps you off your feet, then you can be sure to let your head listen to the rest of your heart and give the poor bloke a chance. If not …" Henry paused for effect. "He's a bastard, and you can simply walk away to wait for the real prince charming. Mel and I will wait in the car, hidden out of view; just a precautionary measure because I know deep in my heart that you won't be coming back with us tonight." Henry beamed at the girls. "What do you think?" he asked, throwing his arm up in the air.

Amber looked horrified. "I can't do that."

"Why not?" Melanie asked. "I have to admit, I think it's quite a good idea. Did you get it from one of your Mills & Boon books, Hennie?"

"Of course, and it had such a happy ending it almost made me shed a tear." Henry went all gooey-eyed.

"But this is not a Mills & Boon. It's real life. Mine, in case you've forgotten." Amber put her head in her hands.

"Now who's being theatrical?" Henry prodded her. "Think about it. It makes sense. If he's going to call you anyway, the next step would be to meet up. All we're doing is bringing that forward."

"I don't know. It's not really me to do anything like that." Amber looked at them both.

"Amber, do you want a relationship with Tom or not?" Melanie asked.

Amber sat back in her chair. "Yes, yes I do." She nodded. "But …"

"But nothing. Get upstairs and tidy yourself up," Melanie ordered.

"But we've been drinking too much to drive," Amber said as she took another sip of her wine.

"I'm fine to drive, haven't even finished my first glass yet. Off you go, can't use that as an excuse." Henry pointed towards the door.

"He might be staying in Scotland another night." Amber looked at her friends with pleading eyes, to which they both now pointed to the door.

Upstairs in the bathroom Amber looked at herself in the mirror. She really didn't think this was a good idea. 'What on earth would Tom think, her just turning up unannounced? What would she say? "Hi Tom, I was just passing. Thought

370

I'd knock on your door to say I've decided I do want a relationship and couldn't wait for you to call me. Oh dear, you weren't going to call me, I can see that by the look on your face." Well, at least all would be clear, one way or another. Henry was right about that,' she said to herself. She ran a brush through her hair, swished some mouthwash to freshen her breath and reapplied her lip gloss before returning to the kitchen.

"Here she is, pretty as a picture. I'll get my car keys." Henry winked.

Amber looked at Melanie. "I really don't think this is a good idea."

Melanie put up her hand. "Stop, it is a good idea. He wants you, you want him, end of story."

"You've changed your tune. What's happened to love them and leave them, use and abuse them?" Amber smiled.

"I'm a changed woman since I've found the one for me." Melanie grinned as she propelled Amber through the kitchen door. "Let's go before you have a meltdown."

"I'm not going to have a meltdown," Amber protested.

"Glad to hear it, dear heart," Henry said as he opened the front door for them. "Although a bit of drama never goes amiss."

As they drove, Henry, in an over-excited voice, gave Amber tips on what she should say, how she should say it and how she should hold herself. Amber, not listening, made noises in what she hoped was the right places while asking herself how she had got talked into this. Before she knew it, she was telling them which cottage Tom lived in. Henry pulled up and turned the engine off. He and Melanie turned to look at Amber in the back seat.

"Okay, sweet cheeks, are you ready to go in? We'll remain in the car for backup," Henry said.

"Henry, it's not a fucking police raid." Melanie hit him.

Amber couldn't help but giggle, even though her heart had started to beat wildly in her chest. "Not really."

"Of course you are, off you go. Kiss before you go," he said, pointing to his cheek.

Amber leant forward. She gave Henry his kiss, then Melanie hers.

"Go, girl," Melanie said, giving her a kiss back.

Amber got out of the car. She walked a couple of steps before stopping at the top of Tom's drive and turning round. She smiled at her two friends in the car. Melanie started to make hand signals, ushering her on. Henry put both his thumbs up in encouragement. They were both grinning like Cheshire cats. She gave them a somewhat feeble wave before turning back round. Taking a deep breath she began to walk down the drive. It seemed to take forever to get to the front door. She knocked straight away, so as not to give herself any more time to think. 'She would just act relaxed, go with the flow, if only her trembling body would let her,' she said to herself. She could hear someone coming to the door. It opened to reveal a very attractive woman in a bathrobe, obviously belonging to Tom, with a towel wrapped around her head. She smiled a perfect smile at Amber who didn't give her a chance to say anything.

"So sorry, I have the wrong house," she said, stumbling away.

"Wait, you must be …"

"Amber," Tom said her name, appearing in the hall after hearing Amber's voice. He was out the front door, striding after her within seconds.

"Amber, stop," he shouted.

On hearing Tom she increased her speed, only to leave one of her pumps behind. She carried on, one shoe on, one shoe off. Tom picked it up on his way to catch her up. He caught hold of her arm.

"Isn't it a bit rude to call on someone then run off before they have time to get to the door?" he asked.

Amber pulled away from him. "Haven't you humiliated me enough? Did you have to follow me up the drive to gloat? Give me my shoe." She went to grab it but Tom moved his hand so she missed. In an instant he bent, grabbed her legs and lifted her over his shoulder in a fireman's lift. He turned and started to march back down the drive.

Henry and Melanie, who had been listening with the car window down, were now out of the car so they didn't miss anything.

"Put me down," Amber shouted. "You're just like all the rest, a bastard, making women think they are special when all the time they're sleeping with other women."

"What is it with you and footwear? You're forever leaving shoes lying around for me to return to you – to stand on and break, pick up for you, free for you while your foot is still inside. I think you do it on purpose," Tom said in a completely normal voice, as though he hadn't heard any of what she was screaming at him.

"How dare you." She thumped him on his back. "That is just typical of someone with an oversized ego. Have you ever considered that all those times were accidents? that you just happen to be there?"

"Yes," Tom said as he put her down at his front door. "And I'm glad I was."

"Oh." Amber looked at him, then at the woman who was still standing in the doorway, then back at him again.

"Let me introduce you to my twin sister. Yasmin this is Amber. Amber this is Yasmin."

"Ah." Amber's cheeks went scarlet as she grimaced.

Yasmin smiled the same perfect smile that she had earlier. As she did so it was quite obvious they were brother and sister, they were so similar. "Lovely to meet you at last, I've heard so much about you."

Amber smiled back. "It's lovely to meet you too. Um, did he happen to mention I'm completely off my rocker?"

"Didn't need to. I think you're quite self-explanatory." Tom laughed, taking her in his arms.